PASSION'S BOUNTY

"Creed . . ."

She spoke his name! Relief flooded through him. "You're all right now," he whispered, dropping his face into the curve of her neck. "I should never have let you . . ."

"You saved my life," she said. "You could have drowned, too." Her arms wound around his back and neck. Through his soaked shirt he could feel the fullness of her breasts. His lips stole over her cool temple and down her cheek; he gathered her protectively to him, and felt her arms tighten. Her eyes, like pinwheels of gold, searched his face, and her lips trembled as she spoke his name again. "Creed . . ."

Powerless to stop himself, he crushed his lips to hers in a hungry kiss—claiming, possessing her as she arched up to him, meeting his urgency with her own. Splaying his fingers against the cold fabric of her shift, he drew her even closer until heat leapt from every point of contact and surged through his veins.

Her fingers twined in the hair at the nape of his neck, pulling him closer still. He breathed her name against her mouth and felt her lips part in welcome as the kiss deepened . . .

Barbara Ankrum
Renegade Bride

ZEBRA BOOKS
KENSINGTON PUBLISHING CORP.

To my mother-in-law, Joan Ankrum, for her support and for teaching me about risk. To David, as always, for everything. To Barbara, Karen, and Patty for their enduring patience. To Dick Pace, Virginia City historian, and Bob Clark of the Montana Historical Society for keeping the light of Old Montana burning. And to Melanie—she knows why.

ZEBRA BOOKS

are published by

Kensington Publishing Corp.
475 Park Avenue South
New York, NY 10016

First printing: July, 1992

Printed in the United States of America

TO BE WISE AND LOVE
EXCEEDS A MAN'S MIGHT.

—William Shakespeare—

Chapter One

Montana Territory
June 1864

Creed Devereaux wasn't a man to ignore a feeling. Anyone in his line of work who did, more than likely ended up dead.

Leaning against the green wood wall of Nielsen's Feed and Grain, his gaze scoured the crowded Fort Benton levee for the hundredth time in two hours, searching for the cause of his uneasiness. Instinctively, he sensed it had nothing to do with the overdue steamer — travel on the Missouri in spring was notoriously unpredictable. Nor did he believe it was about the woman he'd been sent here to meet. Despite his misgivings about her, she was Seth's problem, not his.

No, this unpleasantly familiar feeling had his gut churning like a hot spring. He slid one long finger beneath the edge of the bone and bead choker circling his throat. He knew about intuition, just as he knew other things some men never would.

Out of habit, his fingertips brushed over the walnut-handled army Colt seated securely in his cross-draw holster and he turned his gaze once more to the milling crowd nearby. Most were soldiers, miners, or tradesmen, here today — he gathered from snatches of conversations he'd overheard — to meet the women they'd left behind.

In sharp contrast to Creed's fringed buckskin, the clothing of most of the men on the levee marked them as outsiders to this Montana frontier—homespun, patched chambray and denim, crisp blue wool uniforms. Yet, strangely, it was Creed who felt like an outsider. The others seemed content to exclude him from their cliques of commiseration.

That suited him just fine.

A faint sound upriver turned the head of every anxious miner and soldier waiting on the levee. It was like wind singing through a stand of pine, though no breeze stirred the air and no needled spires broke the rolling sweep of prairie in the distance. Creed straightened, his gaze joining the rest. On the horizon curled a telling black plume of smoke.

"There she is!" shouted a fellow peering through his collapsible spyglass from atop a pile of wooden crates.

As one, seventy men broke from their clustered ranks and crowded to the levee's steep banks, straining to catch a glimpse of the boat.

"Can you see, John?" another shouted. "Is it her?" The sidewheel-steamer rounded the bend just then, chugging toward the levee.

"It is! It's painted right under the sidewheel, clear as day—*Luella*."

A cheer broke from the crowd and the men pressed closer together, slapping each other on the back with good cheer. Aboard the ship, the helmsman in the wheelhouse yanked the chain on the sidewheeler's horn again. The four-note chorus, like the blast of a Scottish pipe, carried across the tumbling current of the Missouri, bringing sighs of relief from the crowd.

The happy shouts and waves of the men ashore were greeted with a flurry of fluttering white hankies from the ship, whose white-wooden rails were jammed with passengers.

Creed tipped his black felt hat back from his eyes and

pushed away from the wall of the feed store. Despite the muddy, uneven streets, his walk held the measured gracefulness of a cat. His considerable height gave him an unobstructed view of the docking steamer.

"Pardieu," he muttered, drawing closer. Despite the dozens of would-be miners cramming its rails, Creed's conservative guess put the number of arriving females at close to forty. Some stood beside children. More did not.

Creed lifted his hat and ran an uneasy hand through his black hair. Even with the description Seth had given him, how would he know which one she was?

The crowd surged forward as the burly helmsman dropped the gangway to the new wooden dock with a bang. "Foo-rrt Benton!" he sang out in a seasoned voice. "All ash-ooore!"

From his place in the wheelhouse, a red-bearded captain greeted several of the men on the dock with a hearty wave.

"What kept you, Cap'n Ainsworth?" called a man from the shore who, except for the neat string tie at his throat, was dressed in the raggedy homespun clothing of a miner.

"Snagged us a helluva piece of deadwood," Ainsworth shouted back, climbing down from the wheelhouse. "Forty miles back, near 'Eye of the Needle.' Had the devil's own time getting free of it."

"You won't be catchin' any deadwood here in town tonight," the man joked in return, pushing his way closer to the gangway filled with women. "I aim to make darn certain of that, myself!"

The din grew louder as one by one, the men caught sight of their loved ones. Two and three abreast, the passengers hurried down the narrow walkway. Women ran into the arms of their husbands. Flat-capped émigrés from Eastern cities stood on Montana soil for the first time, some spinning around in wonder, taking in their first solid glimpse of their new home.

9

Creed pulled a tired hand down his face, where his touch encountered a three-day growth of beard. *Damn.* After seventy-two hours of hell-bent riding to get here from Virginia City, he'd had neither the energy nor the inclination to find a bath house. Not to mention a proper bed. Still, he supposed he should have at least made an attempt to look presentable. Seth had told him Mariah Parsons was a lady.

He frowned. Ladies rarely survived long on the Montana frontier. They were either fragile as tended lilies or plain outraged by the day-to-day brutality of it all. What the hell. It wasn't his job to make her like it here, only to bring her home to Seth in one piece.

Creed scanned the deck of the *Luella* for the lady in question and searched his brain for the sketchy description Seth had given him: golden eyes, unruly brown hair, on the skinny side. No, Creed remembered, *scrawny* was the word Seth had used.

The raucous laughter of three young women sidling down the gangway caught his attention immediately. Garishly dressed in low-cut satin gowns and ostrich-plumed hats, the trio was being sniffed after like rabbits in fox season by several would-be miners. Indeed, the potent scent of ambergris with which they'd liberally anointed themselves filled Creed's nostrils as they indelicately hiked their hems out of the mud and sashayed past him.

A vague smile curved his lips. Aside from the fact that they looked older and infinitely harder up close than they had from a distance, he knew Fort Benton could stand an infusion of fresh female blood. Men outnumbered white women three hundred to one in Montana Territory. He doubted anyone would mind the fading beauty of these three. In fact, if he weren't so tired—

"Jamie O'Hurlehy! Whooo-oo! Jamie, me darlin'—"

At the sound of the woman's voice, Creed's gaze flicked up to the deck of the steamer. He spotted two

10

more women sandwiched between the rail and the crush of men. The redhead, her plump arm pumping like a Fourth of July flag at her Jamie, was definitely not the one Creed sought. She was too old, too large, and obviously taken.

It was, however, the young woman standing beside her who made Creed's breath catch in his throat and caused his body to go tight all over. She stood out from the crowd like a white-petaled daisy in a field of sweetgrass. Her skin was the delicate color of new ivory, her features, befitting a sculpted Grecian goddess.

His gaze traveled down the length of her sage green, black-trimmed traveling gown which hugged her tiny waist then blossomed from her hips like an opening flower. Wisps of cinnamon-colored hair escaped beneath the brim of her black-frilled morning bonnet. And, Creed noted with amusement, she clung to the tapestry grip she was carrying as if it might sprout legs and escape.

He was too far away to see the color of her eyes as she anxiously scanned the crowd below in search of someone as she was pulled with the tide of passengers down the gangway. Unwillingly, Creed tore his gaze from her to try to determine who was meeting her.

Incredibly, no one seemed to claim her.

Yet, even as he dismissed the idea that this breathtaking girl and Seth's scrawny Mariah Parsons could be one and the same, her gaze met his. It lasted only seconds — long enough for Creed's fingers to find the brim of his hat in acknowledgement and for her lovely face to flush pink as a sunrise.

"Maeve, me girl!" called a blue-coated sergeant who waved as he shouldered his way toward the gangplank. "You're a sight for sore eyes, darlin'."

"Jamie!" the older woman cried again, hauling the green-clad beauty by the arm through the press of bodies. "Saints preserve us! Come lend us a hand before

11

Mariah and me are squashed like bugs on this gang-way!"

Mariah. Creed's throat tightened and he took a step forward. So, it *was* her. It seemed Seth's ugly duckling had turned into a swan. He didn't relish seeing disappointment in those lovely eyes when he told her why *he'd* come to fetch her instead of Seth.

Creed pushed closer. Mariah was nearly to the levee when he halted abruptly. His blood turned to ice as he stared at the tall, dark-skinned man not twenty feet away. The bitter taste of bile rose in Creed's throat.

He should have known.

It was Étienne LaRousse.

Fury pumped his heart, pounded through his veins. The choker that circled his throat seemed to tighten, while the memory of his father's tortured eyes flitted through Creed's mind like a brief glint of light.

The sight of the half-breed, LaRousse, laid open an old festering wound that had poisoned Creed's life for the last four years. Cursing the timing of finding him now, his mind emptied of everything but his need to get LaRousse.

The woman could wait.

Experience coached caution. The unsuspecting crowd demanded it. Slowly, Creed shouldered his way closer, fixing his gaze on the trademark streak of white that punctuated Étienne's cropped black hair at the temple.

As Creed drew nearer, he eased his gun from its holster. That action — or perhaps the fierce expression that had settled over his features — had wary men in his path scuttling out of the way. Murmurs of alarm arose from the crowd, but he paid them little heed. He kept coming.

Étienne LaRousse leaned to whisper something in his companion's ear, but the collective movement of the crowd behind him and the resolute sound of approaching footsteps compelled him to turn around. His black eyes went wide at the sight of Creed—not because he recognized him, but because it was eminently clear Creed meant to kill him.

Stumbling backward in the slippery mud, Étienne pushed aside several bystanders, clearing a path of escape. The man he'd been standing with melted into the throngs.

"LaRousse!" The name was more growl than shout. Creed's gun was raised, but there were too many people between them.

Étienne didn't spare Creed a glance over his shoulder, but a low snarl tore from the half-breed's throat. One hand groped for his revolver, the other swept a frantic arc in front of him, knocking people out of his way.

Too late, Creed realized Mariah Parsons stood directly in Étienne's path.

"Mariah—!" The warning scraped against his suddenly dry throat. Her eyes, the golden color of fine whiskey, flashed to his at the sound of her name. *"Get out of the—"*

Étienne's steely arm swung sideways, catching her hard across her shoulder and jaw. In a flash of green skirts and white crinolines, Creed saw Seth's fiancée careen backward into the thick mud. The screams of the woman beside her drowned out Creed's own thudding heartbeat, but he didn't have time to stop. LaRousse was slipping away.

A bullet whizzed by Creed's ear. He ducked and tried to get a clear shot at LaRousse's legs. Creed wanted the bastard dead, but not before he learned what he needed to know.

A few steps past Mariah, Étienne crashed into a giant of a man, bounced off his chest and sprawled to the ground. He rolled instantly to his knees, gun in hand, but the crowd had scattered for cover, leaving him completely vulnerable.

13

"Drop it, LaRousse." Legs splayed, feet planted unequivocally in the mire, Creed had his Colt aimed directly at the man's face.

"Qui es-tu? LaRousse demanded. Spittle flecked the corners of his mouth. His hands were raised slightly, but he did not drop his revolver.

"Tu sais pas? You don't know me?" Creed smiled a smile that didn't reach his eyes. His finger tightened on the trigger and the spring made an ominous creaking sound. "Take a closer look, LaRousse. Perhaps you remember my face after all."

The half-breed's eyes narrowed and he blinked rapidly, obviously at a loss. His dark face was as angular and hard as the edge of a finely honed blade. His breath came raggedly. "No."

"Pity," Creed replied, but there was no compassion in his voice. "Where is he, Étienne?"

Étienne glanced around at the gaping crowd. "Who?"

"Your brother. Pierre."

Again, LaRousse shifted his fingers around the grip of his gun while his eyes sought escape. Seeing none, he worked his mouth and flung a wad of spit at Creed's feet.

"Drop the damned gun," Creed snarled through clenched teeth. "It would give me great pleasure to blow you in half."

LaRousse laughed nervously and glanced at the revolver still in his hand. "Ah, but you are not fast enough to kill me before I kill you. Eef you know of me, zen you know I speak ze truth."

"The truth? Cowards like you have only one truth," Creed retorted. "Their lack of nerve. No, you're much better at back-shooting, LaRousse. Or hanging an innocent man slowly, until the breath is squeezed out of him."

The half-breed's eye twitched and the first flicker of recognition registered on his face. Before he could reply, however, another man's voice broke the heavy silence

14

that had fallen between them.

"Étienne!" the stranger called. "Yew nigger redskin sumvabitch, Ah got yew now!"

As if it were happening in slow motion, Creed watched LaRousse wrench sideways, leveling his gun toward the sound of the voice. The half-breed's pistol exploded only a fraction of a second before the other man's bullet tore into his shoulder, flinging him two feet backward. Another bullet followed closely behind, plowing into the dirt beside him. LaRousse managed another shot that went wild into the crowd. It hit not his attacker — whom Creed now recognized as a bounty hunter named Lydell Kraylor — but a bystander only partially hidden behind a hogshead of nails.

Swearing loudly, Creed wondered how the situation had slipped out of his control. He was distracted only long enough to miss the swing of LaRousse's gunbarrel in his direction. Creed dove to the ground as he heard the gun's retort.

Reflexively, he raised his own gun and fired. A neat crimson hole appeared between LaRousse's surprised eyes and the man fell limply back to the ground, staring sightlessly into the midday June sun.

"Haw, haw! Yew sumvabitch! Ah tol' yew Ah'd git yew someday," Kraylor laughed, swaggering toward the fallen man, his smoking army Colt dangling from his left hand. The filthy bounty-hunter looked at Creed, still stretched out in the mud. "He's half mine, Devereaux. Half, fair 'n square. He done shot fust, an' Ah got witnesses."

Creed slowly got to his feet, glaring at Kraylor. He raised his pistol again and the confident tobacco-stained grin slipped from the man's face as he took a step back.

"Now . . . now y'all just wait —" Kraylor licked his lips and ran a hand over a four-year growth of graying beard. "Y-yew ain't got no call to —"

"You stupid bastard, Kraylor." Creed advanced with

15

murder in his eyes. "I had him."

"Heah, now—" Kraylor flung his hands up between them. "Ah been trackin' that slippery little half-breed for two months, just like yew. A man's gotta earn a livin'. Yew ain't got no right to keep 'im all fer yer—"

Creed's fist interrupted Kraylor's little speech, catching him sharply under the jaw and sending him flying backward into the mud. Kraylor landed hard, clutching his bleeding mouth. "Ohhh-hnn . . . sumva—"

"All right now, none o' that," came a voice from behind Creed as someone grabbed his arm. He whirled to find himself nose-to-nose with Jamie O'Hurlehy, the blue-coated sergeant who just moments ago had been headed to meet his Maeve aboard the ship.

"What in the devil's name is goin' on here?" O'Hurlehy demanded. "Speak up, before I arrest the two of ye an' throw ye in the stockade for murder."

"Nobody's lockin' me up fer shootin' that piece of scum," Kraylor protested, a thin trickle of blood dripping down into his beard. "Ah got me legal papers sayin' *dead or alive*. Dead suits me jist fine." He got to his feet, still rubbing his jaw, and pulled a rumpled WANTED dodger from his dirty shirt pocket. "He's half mine. Yew remember that." He shot Creed a meaningful look.

Creed barely controlled his impulse to strangle the bastard. Around them, the crowd pressed in and Creed felt like a caged animal in a traveling side-show. For the first time since the gunfight, his eyes were drawn to the girl he'd been sent here to meet.

Mariah Parsons—pale-faced and trembling—was being helped up out of the mud by her lady-friend. But Mariah's horror-stricken gaze was fixed on Creed. Her amber eyes accused him without a word, causing his anger to shift into something more closely resembling regret.

He glanced down at his arm, noticing for the first time the bloodstain spreading across his sleeve.

16

LaRousse's bullet had torn a furrow across the muscle in his upper arm. Suddenly it burned like hell.

Creed winced and covered it with his hand. Around him, the levee came back to life. People crawled from behind hastily assumed hiding spots and gathered around LaRousse's lifeless body.

"And what have you got to say for yerself?" O'Hurlehy demanded of Creed. "Are you a bounty hunter, as well?"

"Oui," he muttered.

"What?"

"Yes," Creed repeated louder. "I am a bounty hunter. This man was wanted for murder in the township of Bannack."

O'Hurlehy frowned at the piece of paper Kraylor had handed him. "You sure this was your man?"

"I'm sure," Creed answered, glancing back at the inert form of Étienne LaRousse.

O'Hurlehy nodded. "Well then, best be seein' to that arm after we get the particulars sorted through here."

Creed shrugged, sliding his gaze toward Mariah Parsons who had turned her back on him.

"Who should we see about the pay?" Kraylor demanded.

"Pay?" O'Hurlehy repeated icily.

"For the hide. Who pays for the hide?"

Creed smoothed a hand irritably over his disheveled hair and fitted his hat back on. "Shut up, Kraylor."

"Well, if them soldiers ain't gonna settle up," Kraylor went on, "Ah ain't haulin' the redskin back to Bannack with me." He fingered the old Green River knife at his belt. "That red nigger's scalp alone oughta be proof enough."

"Colonel Paullen will be able to take care of this whole affair back at the fort," O'Hurlehy replied grimly. Creed turned away, anxious to leave this business behind him.

"Wait a minute, Devereaux—" Kraylor called to him. "Where're yew goin'? Hey, don't yew want a piece o'

17

this?"

"No," he muttered, then changed his mind seeing the eager disbelief on Kraylor's face. "Yes. O'Hurlehy, send my share to an Eleanor Wilcox in Bannack. LaRousse made her a widow. It's the least he can do for her now."

"Aye, that I will," the sergeant answered.

Creed nodded, then headed resolutely toward Seth Travers's woman.

At the edge of the levee, some twenty feet away, Mariah Parsons rubbed her aching cheek with the back of her muddy, shaking hand. She'd watched the men with growing revulsion. Bounty hunters. That's what they were. Hunters of men. Mercenaries of the worst ilk. And to think, only moments before, one of them actually tipped his hat to her. Her already shaky stomach had twisted another notch when she'd glanced back at him and found him staring directly at her. The nerve of the man! she thought, her cheeks hot with indignation. If Seth were only here, a man like that wouldn't dare look at her twice in such a way.

Yanking at the black satin ribbon beneath her chin, she tore off her hopelessly damaged hat. Her legs were trembling, forcing her to lock them in place consciously to keep from falling back in the mire.

Beside her, Maeve O'Hurlehy brushed at the mud on Mariah's ruined gown. They had met in Chicago through an ad Maeve had placed in the *Daily Tribune* for a traveling companion. Both were headed toward the same place and both were alone. Though Maeve was older by a good fifteen years, she had become a good friend whom Mariah would sorely miss after she left with Seth for Virginia City.

"I'm afraid it's no use, Maeve. It's ruined," Mariah murmured, trying to hide her disappointment. "What will Seth think when he sees me this way?" She'd spent extra time dressing this morning so that Seth would see her at her best after four long years. Now, she looked like something that had been dragged through a rain gutter.

"Arrah," Maeve replied with a shake of her head and a gentle touch to Mariah's cheek. " 'Tis not this poor gown that's important. Nothing's broken and for that we can be grateful. Why, that awful brute might have killed ye."

Mariah gingerly massaged her shoulder, recalling with a shiver the awful face of the man who'd collided with her. Another memory came rushing back as well: a male voice crying out her name just before she'd been knocked to the ground. The thought creased her brow. She could have sworn it was that dreadful man. That . . . that bounty hunter.

Mariah, he'd called, as if he knew her. But that was impossible. She knew no one here but Seth.

"Where could he be, Maeve?" Mariah's worried gaze swept the sea of men on the levee.

Maeve glanced up at her. "You mean Seth?"

"You read his letter, promising to meet me here. He couldn't have forgotten or gotten the dates confused, could he?"

"Don't ye be worryin'. He'll be along. At any rate, ye'll come along with me an' Jamie and get yerself cleaned up a bit. Why, by the time your Seth see's ye—" Maeve halted abruptly and her eyes widened.

"Miss Parsons?"

Mariah gave a start at the sound of a man's deep voice behind her. When she turned, the tall bounty hunter was standing close, not two feet away. His black felt hat was pulled low over his eyes, without the slightest deference to social politeness. The man's gaze traveled rudely down the muddy length of her then back to the swelling bruise on her cheek. "Are you hurt?"

She felt her world tilt ever so slightly on its axis as he towered over her. His voice was as rough as the growth of beard that darkened his angular jaw. His accent was undeniably French, and despite the fact that she'd just watched him gun down a man in cold blood, it was the most sensual male voice she'd ever heard. Shocked by her own observation and embarrassed by his scrutiny, she averted her gaze.

"I've had better days, if that's what you mean." There was cool dismissal in her voice as she tugged at the ruined cuffs on her sleeves. She hoped her answer would make him leave, but he didn't move.

"I'm sorry you were caught in the middle of all that."

Was that sincere regret in his voice, Mariah wondered. It surprised her that a man like this would worry about such things.

"Perhaps," he went on, finally lifting his hat, "we should have the fort doctor look at that cheek."

We? With a sickening start, it occurred to her he'd called her by name again. Against her will, she forced her gaze to meet his. "That won't be neces—sary . . ." The rest died on her lips and she found herself staring.

His eyes captured her attention first. Not exactly green nor truly blue, they were the depthless hue of the ocean just before a storm—stirred up and infinitely dangerous. The thick fringe of lashes fencing those unfathomable eyes were the same ebony as the long hair curling intractably at his neck and the shadow on his jaw.

An odd-looking choker circled his throat, made of what appeared to be finely-carved bone with blue and red trade beads. It was beautiful, unique, and obviously Indian. A shudder raced through her. It shouldn't have come as a surprise that a man as dangerous-looking as he would consort with savages, but the thought horrified her.

"Miss?"

Mariah blinked, unable to summon the courage to respond. She imagined her face looked as chalky as her stomach felt.

"Are you all right?" he asked in a surprisingly gentle voice. "Perhaps you should sit—"

Retreating from his hand as he reached toward her, she answered, "No, I'm fine. I'm waiting for my—" It was then she noticed the blood streaking his shirt sleeve.

"Merciful heavens, your arm . . ."

Creed followed her glance, then shrugged. "It's just a graze."

Why she even cared, Mariah couldn't imagine. After all, the man had just snuffed out another man's life as if it were nothing. She turned away taking Maeve's arm. "I appreciate your concern," she said firmly, "but if you'll excuse us now—"

"Miss Parsons—wait."

Setting her teeth on edge, she whirled back to face him. "Mister—?"

"Devereaux. Creed Devereaux."

"If I'm not mistaken, Mr. Devereaux, that's the third time you've called me by my name. We haven't been introduced, have we? And since you have a most memorable way of introducing yourself, I'm certain I would have remembered."

Something akin to a smile played across his lips and he fitted his hat back on his head slowly. "Seth sent me to bring you home."

Chapter Two

Mariah felt the blood drain from her face. "I—I beg your pardon?"

"Your fiancé? Seth Travers?" Devereaux repeated slowly, as if she were dimwitted. "He sent me to escort you back to Virginia City on the stage."

He might as well have told her he was from the moon. "Seth . . . sent *you?*" She glanced imploringly at Maeve, but the woman looked equally confused. "Why, that's impossible," Mariah argued. "Seth would never . . . I mean, you're a . . ."

All traces of humor disappeared from his eyes. "Bounty hunter?" he supplied tightly. "That's true. I'm also a friend of Seth's."

Mariah swallowed hard and stiffened her spine. "There must be some mistake."

His jaw grew tight. "I'm afraid not. Seth was taken ill suddenly and couldn't come himself. That's why he sent me to fetch you."

"Seth—ill?" she echoed in a small voice. *Dear Lord . . . not Seth . . . not now . . .*

Creed shifted uncomfortably. "He came down with camp fever the day before he was supposed to come here. Quite a few of the miners in Virginia City are down with it."

Numbness crept into her voice. "Camp fever. Is it . . . serious?"

He glanced at the ground, unable to meet her eyes.

22

"Serious enough to keep him from coming here for you. He would have tried, too, if I hadn't threatened to tie him to the bed."

It was worse than he was telling her. She knew that from his evasive glance. She blinked at the tears that burned the backs of her eyes. *Seth. Oh, Seth.*

"I . . . I don't even know you," she managed at last. "How do I even know you're telling me the truth?"

Devereaux pulled what looked suspiciously like her last letter to Seth from his pocket along with a small heart-shaped pin she'd given him four years ago when he'd left for the West.

"He gave me these so you wouldn't doubt my word."

Mariah took both in her trembling hands, unable to deny they were hers. Her gaze returned to the bounty hunter. What could Seth have been thinking, sending a vicious killer like Creed Devereaux to protect her? It must have been the fever. He *couldn't* have been in his right mind.

"I . . . I suppose you're who you say you are." She blinked rapidly, determined not to cry. "He . . . Seth could have just sent word to me. You needn't have gone to all the trouble of riding up here to fetch me, Mr. Devereaux. After all, there *is* a stage that runs between here and Virginia City, isn't there? I would be perfectly safe—"

"No," Devereaux interrupted. "No, you wouldn't."

"He's right," put in Jamie O'Hurlehy who had walked up beside his wife. "Not a soul's safe on the road 'tween here and Virginia City, miss. It's bein' used as a kind of toll road for a gang of highwaymen callin' themselves 'The Innocents.' Even though they hanged the gang's leaders this past winter, a fair number of 'em are robbin' stages every week for the gold shipments, or the miners traveling with their dust."

"Well, why doesn't the law do something about it?" Mariah demanded.

23

"You're not in Chicago now," Creed reminded her. "I'm afraid there's not much law out in these parts yet."

"Except for men like you."

A muscle twitched in his cheek. "That's right."

"I suppose the Montana Territory hasn't caught up with the American concept of 'innocent until proven guilty' either, has it?" she pressed on recklessly. "Do you always shoot men down in cold blood, Mr. Devereaux, or only the ones you have personally convicted and sentenced?"

"I've never killed a man who didn't need killing, Miss Parsons. Nor have I ever felt the need to answer to anyone but myself."

"Not even to God, Mr. Devereaux?"

Something in his eyes—perhaps the flicker of pain that seemed to vanish as soon as it appeared—made her wish she'd kept quiet. He was, after all, Seth's friend. Or so he claimed. But for the life of her, she'd never understand how her gentle Seth could have fallen in with a man as ruthless as Devereaux.

His eyes narrowed with his scowl and it took him a moment to answer. "That's between Him and me, isn't it? Look, Miss Parsons, you're not obliged to like me, but I promised Seth I'd bring you to him, safe and sound. I intend to do just that. I suggest, however, if we're to be traveling together, you keep your opinions of me to yourself and I'll do my best to do the same. Do we understand each other?"

Never, she thought, hitching up her chin defiantly. "Perfectly."

"Good. Now, if you want to change out of those things before we take off, I suggest you hurry," he continued, cracking open an incongruous-looking gold pocket watch he'd withdrawn from a pocket in his fringed buckskin pants. "The only stage for Virginia City leaves in about forty-five minutes."

Creed placed his hand over hers on the handle of her

24

bag intending to relieve her of it, but a peculiar shock traveled up his arm at the contact. For a moment, he felt as if the wind had been knocked out of him. He sucked in a breath and with an effort, blinked the sensation away. He wondered if she'd felt it, too, as he took her bag from her.

Mariah, seemingly unfazed by his strange reaction, cast a forlorn glance at her filthy attire. "W-we're leaving now? So soon?"

Creed forced a casual shrug, belying the tension in his jaw. "Or, you can wait until tomorrow, as you wish."

Maeve patted her arm. "Mari, dear, why don't ye wait a day or so? Get yer bearings straight. Ye've had quite a scare." She shot a cold glance at Creed, then returned her attention to Mariah. "Yer welcome to stay with us."

"Aye," agreed Jamie. "There's room at the fort, lass."

Mariah shook her head. Her throat was knotted with emotion. "I haven't seen Seth in over four years, Maeve. Now he's sick and he needs me. He . . . he could be dying, for all I know. The sooner I go, the sooner I'll be with him.

"I'll need my things," she told Devereaux curtly. She snatched back the tapestry grip, then turned to Maeve. "If you can find a suitable place where I can change, I'll be ready whenever Mr. Devereaux is."

The bounty hunter glanced at the steamer. "You have more luggage, I assume."

"Only a small trunk. It has yet to be off-loaded."

"I'll see to it. Meet me at the stage depot at the end of the street in thirty minutes. I'll have your ticket." He turned his back on her without waiting for a reply and stalked up the gangplank.

Mariah scowled after him, giving a mock salute to his back. "Yes, *sir*." If he heard her, he didn't turn around. Mariah paced, twisting her hands around the the leather handles on her valise.

25

"Imagine," she fumed to Maeve, "Seth sending a man like that to protect me! Why, I think I'd be safer in that randy crowd of miners we just rode in with than with that . . . that barbarian."

"Faith . . ." Maeve shook her head sympathetically. " 'Tis sure ye are that goin's the right thing, lass?"

"What else can I do? But I can tell you, Seth will have a piece of my mind for this." Her anger faltered. "When he . . . when he gets well, that is."

"And he will, Mari. Don't you be worryin' yerself sick over it. Yer man'll be fine. You'll see." She patted Mariah's arm. "Come along now. Jamie will find us a place close by where ye can change out of these things."

Mariah cast one last, disparaging glance at the tall man aboard the *Luella*. She wondered exactly how long it would take to travel the almost two hundred miles between here and Virginia City. Four days? Five? How would she stand being near him for that long?

One thing was certain: however long it took, she'd be counting the minutes until Creed Devereaux would be out of her life and she'd be safely back with Seth.

The hand-lettered wooden sign above the A. J. Oliver Stagecoach Depot swung in the rising breeze and nudged the still-green wood frame building with a steady, annoying thud. Creed leaned one shoulder against the storefront wall, keeping time with the toe of his boot against the wooden walkway.

Tossing his cheroot down, he ground it to ashes beneath his heel and yanked his watch out of his pocket for a third time. Thirty minutes, he'd told her. It had been nearly forty and the driver was stowing the last of the luggage into the canvas-covered boot of the mudcoach. Creed's agitated gaze swept the crowded street. *Where is she?*

"Pow, pow!"

Two young boys careened by him in the muddy street, shooting imaginary guns at each other.

"You're dead, Jeremy!" cried the older of the two, a boy whose worn britches were held up by a piece of twine.

"Ain't neither!" retorted the smaller one, balling his fists on his hips. His small face clouded like a thunderhead.

"Are so! I got ya 'tween the eyes, outlaw!"

Turning to make good his escape, the younger boy raced up the steps and collided with Creed's knees with a whoof of breath.

"Whoa, there," Creed said with a gruff smile as he caught the boy by the shoulders before he could fall to the planked flooring. He steadied him while the towheaded child, wide-eyed and open-mouthed, scanned Creed's extraordinary height.

"Sorry, mister," Jeremy mumbled. "I didn't mean to—"

"It's all right, boy. You didn't do much damage," Creed answered with a grin, brushing a smear of dirt from the boy's shoulder.

"Jeremy! Michael!" came a woman's shrill voice from the walkway behind Creed. Hot on the boys' heels, she gathered Jeremy up under her wings like a prairie hen, then cast a wary look up at Creed. It was a look he'd seen a hundred times before. He'd grown used to it, in fact.

"Come along boys," the woman went on. "It's time to go home."

"Oh, Ma . . ." the older boy complained. "We was just—"

"Not now, Michael. I swan," she muttered, looking pointedly at Creed, "decent people aren't safe on this street anymore."

Creed's body tensed like an overwound spring as he watched the woman hurry her boys by him—the same

27

way he'd seen mothers hurry their children by tattered beggars in the streets of St. Louis years ago with his father. Creed folded his arms tightly across his chest and tried to ignore the stares he'd drawn from the group of male stage passengers waiting nearby.

"You buyin' a ticket for yourself, too, mister?" asked the balding clerk behind the barred window. He peered above his spectacles and pointed toward Creed's gelding. "The horse won't cost ya no extra to tow."

"No," Creed snapped, imagining three days of close confinement with a woman who'd made it clear she despised him. "I'm not buying a ticket."

With a knowing shrug, the clerk glanced up at the gathering clouds. "Looks like rain. Eh-yup."

Creed's eyes flicked up toward the darkening sky, then back to the road that led to the fort. He wasn't in the mood for small talk or weather predictions. He wasn't in the mood for much of anything but a good, stiff drink.

"You're *him,* ain't you?"

Creed's glance slid to the clerk. "What?"

"You're that fellow who gunned down that half-breed up on the levee." A knowing smile brightened the clerk's face. "The whole town's talkin' about it. They say you hit that injun square between the eyes. That true?"

"Forget it," Creed recommended, turning his attention back to the street.

"Forget it?" The man chuckled. "Hell, we ain't had so much excitement since they hung Red Yager and George Brown here last January."

"I said leave it alone."

"Not that I have anything against gettin' rid of them redskins," the man prattled on. "Mangy bunch of heathens. But just between you an' me, what'd that feller do to get you so riled?"

Creed shook his head, then leaned closer to the window and gave the clerk a menacing look. He kept his

28

voice low and conspiratorial. "You really want to know?"

Wide-eyed, the balding man nodded.

Creed's lips were almost touching the iron bars on the clerk's cage. "I killed him 'cause he was too damned nosey."

The clerk's Adam's apple bobbed in his throat and his spectacles slipped to the tip of his nose. He pushed them back in place with one shaking finger and forced his attention back to the sheaf of papers on his desk.

"Mister Devereaux?"

Creed turned to find Mariah standing beside him on the boardwalk, mud-free and dressed in a fresh, pale blue gown with a white lace collar and cuffs. A delicate white shawl circled her shoulders and fell softly over her shapely breasts, contrasting sharply with her flushed cheeks. One slender eyebrow was arched in annoyance.

She looked like a schoolmarm or a minister's daughter, he mused darkly. Just Seth's type. Behind her like the rear guard stood Maeve and Jamie O'Hurlehy— arms linked.

Creed pushed away from the wall. "It's about time."

Mariah's whiskey-eyes flashed and her lips parted as if she were about to retort. Instead she snapped her teeth together and glared at him. A sudden breeze tugged at a strand of her hair, whipping it across her face.

Creed nodded toward the stage. "They're nearly loaded."

"I changed as quickly as I could," Mariah told him, noting that he, too, had changed out of his muddy clothes. He'd traded his bloody buckskin for a clean maroon wool shirt with two ties lacing the deep slash at the neck. It made his eyes look suddenly greener, she thought warily, and his face seem less—

"Give me your bag," he demanded gruffly, erasing any gentle quality she'd been about to ascribe to him.

Mariah tightened her grip. Inside was not only the meat and cheese she'd brought to nibble on, but her needlework. Tatting was a skill she'd acquired during long days and nights spent sitting beside her dying grandmother. A sharp pang of nostalgia passed through her. Now, the needlework merely occupied her empty hands and kept her mind distracted from thoughts of Seth. What would she do if she lost him, too, she wondered miserably.

"I'll keep the bag with me."

"Not with nine passengers and express packages crammed inside that mud-wagon, you won't. There'll be barely enough room for you." This time he didn't touch her, but waited for her to hand over the small bag.

Stubbornly, she refused. "But my needlework—"

Devereaux's eyes met hers with a hard look. "You've a long ride ahead, Miss Parsons. Enjoy the scenery, but if you're expecting a Sunday social, you're bound to be disappointed. By the time you reach Virginia City, you'll never want to see the inside of one of A.J. Oliver's stagecoaches again."

She released the tapestry bag in a huff, and angrily tipped her chin up. "I was hardly expecting a social, Mister Devereaux. I'm well aware of the rigors of travel, having just completed a considerable journey from Chicago, if you'll recall. You needn't try to frighten me."

"You won't need me for that, Miss Parsons," he replied ominously. "Best get your goodbyes said." Without another word, he turned and stepped off the walkway to hand her bag to the driver, who was lashing the leather covering of the boot together.

Traffic filled the street beyond the stage, with horses and vehicles negotiating the mud gingerly. A freight wagon, pulled by mules, rolled by and the driver shouted obscenities while slapping the traces against the teams' backs.

Mariah breathed in a lungful of calming air, then turned to Maeve and her husband. The older woman's eyes were misty and her smile stiff. "Goodbye, Maeve," Mariah whispered, giving the woman a hug, already missing her. "Thank you for everything."

Maeve shushed her with one hand. "If there's ever anything ye need — anything at all, just ask."

"That goes for me as well, Miss Parsons," Jamie put in. " 'Tis glad I was to know my Maeve didn't have to face that trip alone. It's been a pleasure meetin' ye, as brief as it was." He cast a sidelong glance at Creed Devereaux then looked back. "You're sure we can't change yer mind about goin'?"

Mariah shook her head. "Don't worry about me," she told them, kissing each on the cheek. "Either of you. After all, I'll be traveling with a whole stage full of passengers. What could possibly happen?"

She wondered at the worried look Maeve and Jamie exchanged, then hugged them goodbye. "Now, I've kept you two long enough," she said, forcing a smile. "I'm sure you have plenty of catching up to do. Go on, both of you, and God bless."

"I'll write, Mari," Maeve called over her shoulder as Jamie led her back toward the fort.

"Me, too!" Mariah returned in a tone that was brighter than her mood. She watched them go, a hollow emptiness settling in the pit of her stomach as she turned back toward the stage. She was alone now. Truly alone.

"All aboard! I got a schedule to keep!" called the grizzled driver as he climbed to his perch at the front of the coach. Beside him an armed guard sat at the ready with a large bore coachgun.

The male passengers plowed through the fifteen feet of mud separating the stage from the walkway and began boarding. Mariah looked for Devereaux, but he wasn't among them. She found him adjusting the cinch on his roan horse nearby. With his back partly to her, she took the opportunity to appraise the man.

Behind that rough shadow of beard and the deep lines of fatigue written on his face, she guessed he was younger than she'd thought at first—perhaps only six or seven years older than her own twenty. His body was long, lean, and graceful, without a spare ounce of flesh. The maroon fabric of his shirt pulled against the ridges of muscles along his spine and broad shoulders. His buckskin pants hugged the muscular contours of his legs and were neatly tucked into an expensive-looking pair of brown leather boots. No doubt purchased with blood money, she mused.

"You'll not be riding in the coach, Mr. Devereaux?" she called out hopefully.

He glanced back at her and shook his head. "I'll be following along behind."

Relief swept through her. At least she wouldn't be forced to endure his constant presence on the trip. She'd only have to see him at the swing stations.

She cast a disgusted look at the quagmire beneath the walkway. Her only pair of boots were already soaked, but she didn't relish the prospect of sitting for hours in a wet, muddy gown. Nevertheless, she started down the steps.

It wasn't until he was almost in front of her that she heard him approach. She looked up just in time to see Devereaux reach for her and scoop her up into his arms. Fear and mortification rifled through her as he lifted her off the step, wrapping his arms intimately about her.

"Oh! *Mister* Devereaux!" Through the fabric of her dress she felt his hand tighten around her thighs as he negotiated a two-inch-deep puddle of water. His face was only a whisper from hers, near enough to catch the starchy scent of lye soap, close enough to be sure he could feel the pounding of her heart against the wall of his chest. It flustered her beyond reason. "Please — I — "

"Please what?"

"Put me — "

In three more steps, he'd deposited her on the retractable step of the red A.J. Oliver Stage. His large hands circled her waist, steadying her for a moment until she'd caught her balance on the canvas cover.

"You're welcome," came his sarcastic reply.

"Th-thank you," she managed stiffly, but he was already slogging back through the mud puddle for his horse and she wasn't sure if he'd even heard her. Mariah took a shaky breath and pressed a hand to still her thudding heart.

The stuffy interior was crammed with men along the three benched seats. Eight pairs of curious eyes turned toward her as she ducked into the opening. She had the urge to deny knowing the man who had just carried her to the threshold as if he owned her. But she kept quiet, deciding denial could only compound her embarrassment.

Two tufted leather benches lined the front and back walls of the wagon. The third straddled the middle with only leather straps to hold onto for support. The only position open was one of these. She smiled uncomfortably at the men and started for the seat.

"Allow me, miss." A slender, rather sickly-looking man in his late twenties jumped up, offering his position by the window. "You'll be more comfortable here, where you can lean back." He swept a gallant arm in that direction and maneuvered over the canvas express bags on the floor at their feet.

"Why, thank you, Mr. — "

"Lindsey," he said, tipping his bowler. "Albert Lindsey." With his index finger, he pushed at his glasses, shoving them back into place on his narrow nose. "My pleasure, ma'am."

"Thank you, Mr. Lindsey. That's very generous of you." At least there were a few gentlemen in this godforsaken wilderness, she mused, wedging herself into the fifteen inches of space between the window and the large fellow taking up the center seat. With chagrin, she realized that Devereaux had been right. Needlework would have been difficult if not impossible in such a cramped space.

The man beside her shifted, glancing down at her with a gray-toothed grin. "How do, ma'am." He tipped off his short-billed cap to reveal a nearly bald head.

It was then that his rank odor assaulted her. It must have been weeks since the man had been on friendly terms with a tub of water. His unwashed body stank to high heaven, and it occurred to her that Mr. Lindsey might not have been so gallant after all to have offered her this seat.

As genteelly as possible, she withdrew a lily-of-the-valley-scented lace hanky from inside her sleeve and pressed it against her nose. At least she'd have the breeze once the coach got moving.

With that thought came the sound of the driver's loud "H-yaw!" The vehicle lurched violently, whipping her head backward against the stiff, tufted leather wall so hard her teeth clacked together.

The men in the middle fought for balance, too, clinging to the leather straps suspended from the ceiling.

"He rather means it when he says he has schedules to keep, doesn't he?" Albert Lindsey commented dryly, hanging on to his tether for dear life. The others laughed with good humor, breaking the tension that had kept them all strangers.

"Are you going far, miss?" Lindsey queried, looking directly at her.

"Virginia City," she replied, dropping her hanky long enough to be polite.

"You don't say. That's my destination as well."

Several others concurred. The young man on the opposite side of the coach, David Conner, and his red-headed cousin, Jeb, were going only as far as Bannack to try their luck at mining. Another man, a well-dressed dandy named Powell, said he was headed for Salt Lake City.

As the town disappeared behind them, the coach's wheels rattled over the rutted road. The heavily-slung leather thoroughbraces kept the discomfort to a minimum as the vehicle assumed the rocking rhythm of a ship.

"I daresay, mining gold isn't your goal, is it, Miss — ?"

"Parsons," she supplied, foregoing the formality of introduction. "No, Mr. Lindsey. I'm going to meet my fiancé, Seth Travers. He runs a thriving mercantile in Virginia City. Perhaps you've heard of him?"

"I know Travers," put in a rangy-limbed man seated on the opposite side of the coach. He slipped his cap off and a smile softened the weathered lines on his face. "Name's Nate Cullen, ma'am. Honest as a lookin' glass, Seth is. Sold me my first outfit — on credit, too." With a wink of pride, he added, "Paid him back every cent."

Her heart tripped in her chest to hear someone who knew Seth speak of him. "Oh . . . I hope that means you've had luck in the goldfields, Mr. Cullen."

He tugged at the colorful scarf around his neck. "I ain't complainin' and that's a fact. Some say the mother lode is right in the gulch, ripe for the takin'."

That comment started a spirited discussion on the prospects in the Alder Gulch. Most of those aboard, she learned, were headed for the placer camps of Ram's Horn, Deer Lodge, and Virginia City. All of these settlements fell within a half-mile of each other along Alder Creek, and each claimed its own merits as to the richness of its little strip of creek bed.

Nate Cullen had been there the longest — one year in

all. Of the others, two had done some mining in Bannack and farther west. The rest were green first timers, like her.

A shiver of apprehension traveled down her spine. Mariah repositioned her hanky and gazed out the window at the passing scenery, turning her thoughts to Seth. Four years was a long time, she mused. Worries that had plagued her since she'd received his final letter last month resurfaced. What if things weren't the same between them? After all, she was not the same young girl he'd left behind in Chicago. She'd grown up.

Seth, like her late father and grandmother, was always overprotective of her—much like a big brother. Five years older than she, he'd fought her battles for her, from Bobby Barnes snatching apples from her lunch-pail in school to making sure she and her grandmother never wanted for anything while Seth established himself in the West. His love was dependable—something she'd always taken for granted, like the sun coming up or the seasons changing.

Seth had never felt the need to propose to her. Not down on one knee at any rate, the way she'd always dreamed about. No, their plans for a future together just seemed to happen. She was comfortable with Seth in a way she'd never been with another man. And she loved him. She'd not questioned that then, nor did she now. Seth was her life, and she'd kept herself only for him.

The countryside passed by in a blur and the thought came again—four years *is* a long time. What if his feelings for her had changed? Suppose he no longer really wanted her, but had agreed to let her come out of some misguided sense of duty? After all, he'd known many women, she supposed. Most, undoubtedly, prettier than she. Some, Mariah thought with a pang of jealousy, perhaps even in the biblical sense. The thought sent a flush of heat to her cheeks and she brushed at a loose tendril of cinnamon hair that had escaped her chignon.

It was then that she caught sight of the bounty hunter riding his blue roan at an easy lope some thirty feet away from the stage. Something sharp and unexpected turned in her stomach at the sight of him. He was actually handsome in a dangerous sort of way, she realized, with strong, undeniably masculine features. And despite his obvious human failings, he rode as if he were born to it: back straight, yet relaxed, and those long, muscular legs molded around the saddle—

Beneath the brim of his hat, the bounty hunter glanced up to catch her watching him. He didn't smile, but something in the shift of his posture seemed to mock her.

Mariah shrunk back in her seat and slammed her eyes shut. She was mortified at the direction her thoughts had taken only moments before. What in the world was wrong with her, looking at him that way? Why, her heart raced as if she'd been running a foot race, for heaven's sake!

Thankfully, no one seemed to notice the flush that had made her cheeks grow hot. The men in the coach had broken out decks of cards and started games of whist and poker. Mariah pulled the fabric of her gown from her damp skin. Black clouds gathered in the distance—the atmosphere was thick and muggy with the impending storm. The stifling air inside the coach was relieved only by the soothing fragrance of sage that wafted through the open window.

Turning her cheek against the leather-padded wall, Mariah tried to forced her wayward thoughts from the mysterious Creed Devereaux. It baffled her that Seth could have befriended such a man. Perhaps he had changed more than his letters revealed.

The stage rocked back and forth like a cradle and

slowly, her eyes drifted shut. Exhaustion from the long trip took hold of her. But try as she might to picture Seth's dear face as she fell asleep, it was the dark image of the bounty hunter that plagued Mariah's thoughts like an ill wind.

One fat droplet of rain slapped against the brim of Creed's hat, then another. With a curse, he pulled the collar of his rain slicker up around his ears. There was something unappealingly familiar about it. How many storms, he wondered idly, had he ridden through in the last few years, heedless of the weather and the fact that he was alone? Too many. He was anxious to be home, anxious to be done with the responsibilities that weighed him down.

He kicked his gelding into a lope after the stage rumbling down the road toward Bannack. Soon the heavens opened in a torrent of driving rain cutting visibility in half, soaking the greening land. Just ahead, a stand of hemlock and mountain ash hemmed in two sides of a slope-walled canyon. Sprays of coral root and red columbine swayed beneath the deluge and clung to the muddy soil.

The stage had stopped at the first swing station two hours ago — just long enough for a new driver to take over and to replace the six-horse hitch with fresh teams. Creed had watched Mariah dismount from the cab to stretch her legs, all the while pointedly avoiding meeting his gaze.

He'd told himself it didn't matter as he watched her allow a puny-looking tinhorn to help her back onto the coach without batting an eye. Yet, Creed remembered how his touch had made her draw back in fear.

Her attitude galled him, but what did he expect? He'd dragged her smack dab into the middle of a gunfight and nearly gotten her killed at the hands of one of the most ruthless men in Montana Territory.

He pondered that for a moment with a frown. Ruthless? As far as Mariah was concerned, *he* was the one who fit that description.

Creed shoved his hat down lower over his eyes, fending off the sheeting rain. It had been a long time since he'd given a damn what people thought of him. And certainly not some prissy schoolmarm type like Mariah. She was the chain around Seth's neck, not his.

Two hundred yards up the road, Creed's heart constricted at the sight of a slender fallen tree lying halfway across the road. Panic crept up the back of his neck. He'd been so busy thinking about her, he hadn't seen it. He kicked his horse forward to catch up with the stage.

The driver, Tom Stembridge, hauled back on the traces. "Whoa!"

"Stembridge! Go around!" Creed shouted, pulling up almost even with the driver.

"Say what?" Stembridge yelled, cupping one hand around his bearded mouth.

"Keep moving—" Creed returned, trying to make himself heard over the thundering rain. He yanked his Henry rifle from the boot at his knee.

"Storm's got a tree down ahead," the armed guard told him, leaning forward and clutching his coachgun.

Creed opened his mouth to tell him it was a trap, but the explosion of a gunshot cut his words short. The impact launched the guard backward against the tarp-covered baggage and rolled him off the cab to the ground.

Then Creed saw them. Like ghostly apparitions in the sheeting rain, five masked riders clad in pale dusters exploded from the cover of trees just beyond the roadblock, armed to the teeth and heading directly for the stage!

Chapter Three

"Sheee-it!" cursed Stembridge, ducking as low as he could in the driver's seat. With a violent slap he urged the teams of horses toward the open shoulder of the road. "H'yaw, h'yaw-w!"

Shouldering his rifle, Creed fired. One of the bandits flew off his horse and somersaulted hard in the mud. Creed caught the scent of gunpowder as a bullet whizzed past his ear. He took aim and fired again. A second duster-clad man doubled over in his saddle and veered away into the stand of trees. The remaining three took aim at Creed.

He hauled back on the reins of his gelding and dropped back behind the cover of the stage. Creed heard Stembridge grunt as a bullet tore into him, knocking him sideways on the seat. The traces slipped unnoticed from his fingers, the unleashed team jerking forward in terror, heading directly for the fallen tree.

Panic rose in Mariah's throat as the gunshots erupted outside. The careening stage threw her forward and her shoulder collided painfully with the wooden door frame beside her. Albert Lindsey caught her before she could sprawl into his lap. He pushed her back to her seat.

"Hellfire!" Nate Cullen roared, yanking his holstered handgun from beneath his seat, "We're bein' robbed!" He threw open the leather shade in time to see the guard's body fall past the window.

"Damn!" Jeb Conner cried, leaping to his feet in the cramped space. "That weren't no warnin' shot! They're killin' them!" The crackle of more gunfire erupted outside.

"Get the hell down and hold on!" Cullen shouted to Jeb. But the younger man had already lost his balance, falling across the middle seat. The other men ducked to the floor, piling one on top of the other in a tangle of limbs.

"Good Lord—" Mariah's voice was barely heard amidst the confusion. Her first frantic thought was for Creed Devereaux. What if they killed him, too? Her fingers numbed by fear, she tore aside the shade. The landscape flew by in a blur. Cold, needle-like rain pelted her face.

She took a sharp, quick breath when she spotted Devereaux not ten feet away—shouldering his rifle. Fire exploded from the barrel. He ducked low on the neck of his gelding, the thunder of gunfire ceaseless. For a split second, their eyes met—hers wide with fear, his dark with some emotion impossible to read.

"Devereaux—"

"Get down, you little idiot!" Hauling back on the reins of his horse, he disappeared behind the stage.

Albert Lindsey yanked her down to the floor just as a bullet pierced the swinging leather shade and thudded into the back of her seat. A scream caught in her throat.

"They'll kill him," she cried, struggling to be free. "Somebody has to help him!" She felt Lindsey tremble as he pulled her against him and covered her with one arm.

Nate Cullen took aim with his pistol and fired twice out the window, drowning out the shrill screams of the panicked horses. "Thunder!" he crowed. "They're turnin' tail and—"

The coach jerked violently, flinging Nate and several

41

others up against the low ceiling. Then, with an ominous splintering of wood, the stage collided against an obstacle, then lifted off the ground, airborne.

Mariah slammed toward the back wall like a rag doll and felt the breath-stealing impact of a body striking hers just before her world tilted into utter blackness.

"She's coming around."

"Thank God."

Silence. Cool nothingness floated around Mariah as she fought the bothersome light behind her eyelids.

"Mariah?"

Like sound filtered through a thick ball of cotton, Mariah heard the deep voice, felt the gentle sift of fingers through her hair and the pressure of something cool against the ache in her head.

Her eyes fluttered open. A man's face loomed close to hers and it took a moment to focus on it. "Seth?" Relief warred with humor in the man's expression.

"No such luck," Devereaux said, pulling a wet cloth away from her head. "Welcome back." His eyes searched her face with concern and something else she couldn't identify. Rain-slick wisps of dark hair lay plastered to his face and rivulets of water trailed down his overcoat. From behind his shoulder, Albert Lindsey, Nate Cullen, and several of the others stared at her, mouths agape with worry.

Mariah blinked, disoriented. Outside, the rain beat a hard tattoo against the roof of the coach. "I don't . . . what happened?"

"You took quite a hit in the accident," Devereaux told her. "How do you feel?"

She blinked her eyes to clear her thoughts. *Accident?* With a rush of memory, the robbery came back to her: the gunshots, Devereaux chasing the outlaws off like some single-handed calvary brigade . . .

42

"They . . . they didn't kill you," she whispered before she could stop the words.

His full lips twitched with a grin. "Disappointed?" Her answering silence evoked a broader smile. "It would seem you fared worse than I, mademoiselle."

Gingerly, she explored the swelling on her forehead with the pads of her fingertips. It struck her then that it had been Devereaux's gentle hand in her hair only moments before, encouraging her to wake up. That thought, unlike his touch, gave her little comfort.

"I'm . . . fine," she replied, regaining her wits. "Really I am." She tried to sit up and promptly regretted it. "Ohhh-hh," she moaned, squeezing her eyes shut.

"Take it easy," Devereaux warned, pushing her back down on the leather seat. "You're not going anywhere for a few minutes. In fact, none of us is until we get that hitch fixed. The team jumped the tree those bast—" he stopped himself, glancing at Mariah, "—road agents left to stop us. If this mud-wagon weren't built like a rock, you'd be sitting in a pile of splinters right now."

She rolled her eyes. "That makes me feel ever so much better, Mr. Devereaux. What of the thieves?"

"Gone," he answered, swiping at the moisture trickling down his stubbled cheek. "All but two were wounded or killed."

"Them fellas is off licking their wounds somewhere," Nate expounded. "They won't be robbin' any more honest folks for a while. You're one hell of a shot, Devereaux, in case I forgot to mention it. I'm obliged for what you done. I had me a fair stake at risk in the driver's treasure box."

Creed's eyes flashed to Nate's. "You have gold aboard?"

He nodded. "Dust I've been keeping at Fort Benton."

"Who else knew about it?"

Nate scratched his thinning hair. "The driver . . . the feller in the stage office. A few men back in Virginia

43

City knew I was comin' back for it. I'm partnerin' up to invest in a hotel in town. I needed my capital. That's why I come here."

From the other side of the stage came a low moan. Mariah jerked her gaze to the wounded man sprawled on the narrow seat. It was the driver, Stembridge, with Nate Cullen's colorful scarf, now soaked with blood, wrapped around his shoulder. The dandy, Mr. Powell, was sitting beside him. She shot a questioning look at Devereaux.

"Stembridge was lucky," he told her. "The armed guard was killed instantly."

A sick feeling rose in her throat, remembering the sight of the guard flying past the window. Good Lord! What had she gotten herself into, coming out here to this godforsaken land full of murderers and criminals? Not a thing had gone right since she'd stepped off the boat.

Of course, that's when she'd met Creed Devereaux.

"He's in a bad way," Powell said. He reached up and loosened the silk tie at the driver's throat. "The bullet passed right through his shoulder. I ain't much on doctorin', but this looks like it's gonna keep on bleedin'."

"Anybody here have doctoring skills?" Creed asked. When no one volunteered, he turned back to Mariah. "Your father was a doctor back in Chicago, wasn't he?"

For a moment, she could only stare at him, shocked that he would know such personal information about her. Then she realized Seth must have told him. What else did he know about her, she wondered.

"Yes, my father practiced medicine. Occasionally, he even let me help him with patients, but I — I've never dug a bullet out."

"This one went clean through. Do you swoon easily, Miss Parsons?"

Affronted, she narrowed her eyes. "Swoon? I'll have you know I've never *swooned* in my life!"

44

Surprise edged his smile. "That's good. Because Stembridge will take what he can get at this point." His expression softened and he added, "If you're up to it."

Devereaux couldn't know how often she'd wished her own father had trusted her not to faint at the first sight of blood. But, of course, he never had. That was in her past, she reminded herself. It seemed a lifetime ago. Before the war, before she'd witnessed the realities of life and death.

While Chicago had seen no actual battle within its limits, the war still raged back East, pouring thousands of wounded men into the gates of the city. She had spent many days in the makeshift military hospital in Chicago sitting beside wounded men. She'd seen enough gunshot wounds to last a lifetime. She'd transcribed their letters, guided soup spoons to their mouths, held their hands when they suffered. It had made her feel . . . useful, alive. It was something she'd never written to Seth about, for she felt sure he wouldn't have approved.

"Miss Parsons?" Devereaux prompted, eyeing her strangely.

"Of course," she answered. "I'll do whatever I can." Mariah pushed herself upright on the seat. This time she was more clear-headed. Behind Devereaux's shoulder, Albert Lindsey ran his hand irritably through his hair and shook his head. It was then that she noticed David Conner, his cousin, and two others were missing. "Where are the others?"

"Chasing down what's left of the team," Devereaux answered. "One of the horses broke a leg and had to be put down. The lead pair snapped the first hitch and lit out for—"

"Oh, for God's sake, Devereaux," Lindsey snapped, ramming the spectacles up the bridge of his nose, "must you give her all the wretched details? She's a *lady*."

Creed slid an impatient glance to the thin man. "A

lady who's been caught in an ugly situation."

"And you're compounding that by scaring the daylights out of her. Is it your habit to frighten innocent women unnecessarily?"

Creed's jaw tightened. "I'm telling her the truth. She's part of this as much as you or me." He glanced at her bruised face. "Even more than some, I'd say."

"He's right." Mariah raised her chin defiantly, surprised to find herself defending the bounty hunter. "You needn't protect me from the truth, Mr. Lindsey, just because I'm a woman. I have a right to know." She searched Creed's eyes, suddenly glad for their steadiness. "Exactly what *is* our situation, Mr. Devereaux? Are we stranded here?"

"Only until we get that hitch fixed and the Conners get back with the team. They won't go far all rigged out like they are. In the meantime, I have several men posted as lookouts."

Mariah studied the hard planes of Devereaux's face as he three-fingered his hat back on his head. Knowing who and what he was, it seemed absurd that she should feel safer with him in charge, but, inexplicably, she did. The same person who'd brutally gunned down a man in Fort Benton had just killed again—to defend her, and she was sure she'd been lucky to get off with only a bump on the head.

Could what she'd first taken for his unmitigated arrogance have been confidence, after all? That disturbed her, not only because it forced her to look at the man in a different light, but because thinking kindly about a cold-blooded killer went against every lick of good sense she'd ever owned.

Yet, what she'd glimpsed in those teal-blue eyes when he looked at her made her question her earlier judgment about him. Shaking off the thought, Mariah asked, "Do you think they'll come back? The outlaws, I mean."

"If they do," Creed answered grimly, "we're ready for them. But I don't think they'd be that stupid." He ran a tired hand over his eyes. "Will you be all right now?"

Despite the ache in her head, she nodded.

Cullen and Lindsey followed Devereaux back out into the pouring rain to work on the broken hitch.

Mariah heard the Conner boys return with the lost team of horses as she ripped part of one cotton petticoat to replace the blood-soaked scarf at Stembridge's shoulder. Gunshot wounds rarely bled profusely unless some vital organ was damaged or an artery nicked. She suspected the latter to be the case.

Experience, and the pallor of his skin, told her he was going into shock. She applied pressure to the wound with the heel of her shaking hand. A sigh of relief escaped her after a few minutes when the bleeding stopped and she covered him with a coat. There wasn't much more she could do, except try to make him more comfortable, as they were still hours from the stage station where they'd spend the night.

Within a half-hour, the mud-wagon was underway again. Devereaux drove, with several passengers riding shotgun in the rain to make room for the wounded driver inside. The ride was considerably more uncomfortable this time, with everyone soaked to the bone and the distinctive odor of blood rank in the stifling, muggy air. The hunger that gnawed at her stomach only a few hours earlier had fled. Now, only a numb fear settled over her as the stage plowed down the muddy road toward its destination.

Nightfall found them at the small one-story soddy stage station. At the door appeared a middle-aged, bearded man dressed in brown pantaloons, patched here and there with yellow buckskin. With a poncho draped over his head and a lantern held aloft in the

47

rain, he waved to them as Creed pulled up the team.

"What in blazes kept you, and . . . and who the hell are you?" he shouted as Creed climbed down from the driver's box.

"Creed Devereaux," he called over the stinging rain. "Your driver was shot in a hold-up attempt and the guard was killed."

"Blast those murdering thugs!" the station master swore, extending his hand to Creed as they moved toward the cab. "John Lochrie's the name. My wife, Hattie, and I run this station. Who's the driver?"

"Said his name's Tom Stembridge. Do you know him?"

Lochrie stopped dead, his expression solemn. "Tom? Damnation. How bad is it?"

"Bad enough. The bullet passed through his shoulder and he was losing a lot of blood." Creed jerked open the stage door and his gaze collided with Mariah's. Fatigue had etched blue smudges beneath her amber eyes, but hadn't diminished the fire he'd seen there earlier. The bruise on her cheek had turned a nasty shade of violet-blue. Despite that, she held herself regally, as if she'd allowed none of the events of the past few hours to affect her.

Something unfamiliar and equally unwanted tore through him, skittering through his veins like heat lightning. A damned attractive woman, he thought, as his gaze traveled over her face and long, graceful neck. A perfect lady.

And . . . she was Seth's.

The untoward thought brought with it a sharp pang of guilt. For all he knew, Seth could be dying of the fever that had already claimed several lives in Virginia City. And here he was, having carnal thoughts about Seth's woman. That was a hell of a note.

An involuntary shiver raced down his back as the rain slapped against his oilcloth coat. Creed exhaled

48

slowly and offered her his hand. "Miss Parsons? Mr. Lochrie here will help you to the house so you don't get wet." She nodded silently.

An electrical charge traveled up Creed's arm when she gave him her hand and allowed him to help her down from the stage. He might have blamed it on the rain, on the chill, or the fact that he hadn't been with a woman in months. He knew better than to explore the jolt she'd given his system.

He damn well knew better.

Lochrie ducked her under his poncho and the two dashed to the house together. Creed and several others carried the wounded man inside and settled him on the simple wooden cot kept solely for use by the drivers.

"There now, Tom," soothed Lochrie's wife, Hattie, a handsome blond-haired woman in her late thirties. "Those heathens can't get a man like you down. We'll fix you up, right as rain."

Stembridge managed a smile, but Creed saw the driver's Adam's apple bob in his throat as he fought the pain in his upper chest. He stopped Mrs. Lochrie before she could walk away. "Hattie—"

"What is it, Tom?"

"You've heard me talk of my . . . my brother, Henry, back in the Dakota Territory."

"Yes," she answered gently. "Yes, I have."

Emotion clouded the man's dark eyes. "Just in case . . . if I don't . . ." He cleared his throat, dismissing the words and gathering strength. "I know you can write. I'd . . . thank you to . . . to let him know for me. Just in case."

"Phooey! There'll be no need for letters, Tom Stembridge, except to tell him you're on the mend. That one I'll be happy to write." With a reassuring squeeze of her hand, she left several men to peel off his wet, blood-smeared clothing.

John Lochrie wrapped a comforting arm around his

49

wife's waist when she came back to the common room. "It's lucky Tom didn't bleed to death before you got here by the look of his clothes," he told Creed.

"You can thank Miss Parsons for that," Creed said from his place near the roaring fire where a welcome warmth seeped through his wet clothing. He dropped his soaked hat on the horsehair settee that flanked the rag rug. "Her father was a doctor back in Chicago." He exchanged a look with Mariah that held a hint of a smile. "And . . . she doesn't swoon."

Mariah sent him an insincere smile, braced her hands across her aching lower back, and turned her attention to the couple. "I didn't do much but stop the bleeding. There wasn't much I could do in that rolling torture chamber you call a stage."

Lochrie chuckled, scratching his mutton-chop whiskers. "I've heard A.J. Oliver's mud-wagons called names before, but never that."

"Oh, my dear!" Hattie exclaimed, seeing the bruise on Mariah's face. "Look at your cheek!"

"If you've got a spare antelope steak to put on that," Creed told Hattie, "I'll gladly pay you well for one. Seth would never forgive me if I bring you back to Virginia City looking like you've been in a brawl."

Unable to resist the retort, Mariah arched one gracefully curved brow. "That wouldn't be so far from the truth, would it, Mr. Devereaux?"

"No, Miss Parsons, it would not."

"Well," Lochrie interjected, "that cheek ought to have plenty of time to heal before you get to your fella."

Creed shot him a look. "If you mean we'll have to wait because of the driver . . . that's not a problem. I can drive to the next station where we can pick up another driver."

"It's not the driver," Lochrie answered with a shake of his head. Picking up a poker, he jabbed at the fragrant pine log snapping in the fireplace. "One of my hostlers rode in from the south just before you pulled in. The ferry that crosses over the Sun River has washed out."

"Washed out?" came the collective moan from the other passengers listening nearby.

"Ain't there another one somewheres to get across?" Cullen asked hopefully.

"I'm afraid not. It'll be at least a week or two before we can get the supplies and manpower to rebuild it after the river settles down from this storm. Nobody's going anywhere but back until then. I reckon I'll have to drive you to Fort Benton myself in the morning."

Mariah felt the blood drain from her face. *"Fort Benton?* No, that . . . that can't be. I—I have to get to Seth." She turned imploringly to Creed. "Tell them, Mr. Devereaux. Tell them I can't go back. *I won't.*"

Tight-lipped, Creed lowered his gaze to the floor. He knew this country well enough to know there was only one way around that crossing. The long way.

It was no route for the inexperienced and certainly not for someone like Mariah. And, more important, no place for her to be alone with a man like him.

"Lochrie's right," he said at last without looking up.

"Right?" she cried. "What do you mean? Seth is desperately ill and you want me to—"

"You have no other choice!" he snapped, equally disturbed by the prospect.

His answer stunned her into silence, but her impotent look went back and forth between Lochrie and him.

Creed ran his fingers through his damp hair, leaving four furrows behind. "Lochrie, is it possible for Miss Parsons to stay here with you and your wife for a few days? After what happened today, I can't in good conscience send her back to Fort Benton unescorted."

"Well, I—" Lochrie began.

"Unescorted?" Mariah repeated incredulously. "And where will *you* be?"

Creed's even gaze met hers. "Tomorrow I'll ride on to Virginia City to let Seth know what's happening and check on him. There's no telegraph service yet. He'll only worry if we don't show up." He turned to the station master. "Lochrie, I'll pay her keep for the time—"

"Oh, no, you don't," Mariah interrupted. "You're not leaving me here to go on ahead alone. If you know of a way to get to Virginia City, then I'm coming, too."

"Like hell you are!"

With her hands balled into fists at her waist, Mariah met his angry glare. "Try and stop me."

"Lady . . . you're crazy."

"Because I want to be with my fiancé? How does that make me crazy?"

Creed's snort of laughter punctuated the silence that had fallen. "You have no idea what you're talking about. You wouldn't last two minutes out there."

Tears trembled on the brinks of her eyes, but she wouldn't allow them to spill over. "Don't talk to me as if I'm some foolish child, Mr. Devereaux! I may be young, but I'm not completely ignorant. Nothing in this journey has been easy and I've no reason to expect it will get better."

"It's out of the question."

"Why? Because you say so?"

"Le bon Dieu me protége des femmes têtues!" he ranted, slapping his hat across his thigh.

"Speak English if you're going to swear at me!" Furious now, she stood nose to nose with him.

"I said, God protect me from stubborn women—like *you*. Don't you see it's impossible? Forget, for a moment, the hardships of the trail. Think of your reputation."

"My reputation? Do you think I give a fig about that when Seth is lying at death's door?"

"I didn't say that," he hedged.

"You didn't have to." Now tears spilled in earnest

52

down her cheeks, but she no longer cared. Her whole body trembled like a newborn leaf in the wind. "I can see in your eyes how serious it is. He's very ill. Tell me that's not true."

He couldn't. God help him, he couldn't lie to her about something as important as Seth. "He's . . . ill. Very ill. Camp fever, pneumonia. They mean the same thing." His pained eyes met hers. "But if you think I'm risking your life to get you to him, lady, you're out of your mind."

"I'll take my own chances then," she declared impetuously. Turning to the others in the room, she asked, "Is there any man here willing to escort me to Virginia City? I can pay you well for your trouble."

Before any could answer, Creed grabbed her arm and whipped her around to face him. "What the hell do you think you're doing, you little fool?"

She clenched her jaw against the angry words she longed to hurl at the self-righteous bounty hunter. "Name-calling will get you absolutely nowhere, Mr. Devereaux. If you're not willing to help me, I'll find someone who is. There must be someone among you who is as anxious to reach the gold fields as I am."

Creed shot a killing look at every man in the room, and one by one, each wisely shrank back from her invitation. "There," he spat through clenched teeth. "Happy? Now, *Miss* Parsons, be a good girl and do as I tell you." He jammed his hat on and water flew in a spray off the brim as he headed for the door.

She followed on his heels. "Where are you going?"

"To get my horse in out of the rain!"

"This isn't finished, Mr. Devereaux—"

He turned abruptly, causing her to run smack into his chest. With a jerk, he pushed her away from him, but his fingers dug sharply into her upper arms. His eyes, the blue-green color of the hottest flame, bore into hers.

"Don't push me, Mariah. You don't know me. You don't *want* to know me. Just let this be. I'm doing the right thing here and Seth would agree with me. You know he would. Let that be an end to it." Without another word, he released her and slammed out the door into the rain.

Mariah stared at the worn wooden portal, too angry to speak, too stunned to move. She felt Hattie's arm on hers and turned toward the older woman.

"He's right, you know, dear," Hattie told her gently. "You couldn't follow him on that kind of a trip. It's rough, dangerous country—"

Mariah's chin rose with characteristic determination. "He's wrong, Mrs. Lochrie. He doesn't know that yet, but he will. If Mr. Devereaux thinks he's leaving tomorrow without me, he's got another thing coming."

Chapter Four

The rain stopped around dawn and Mariah was still awake to hear its stealthy departure. As she lay beside Mrs. Lochrie, sharing the narrow bed which her husband had generously relinquished for the night, Mariah watched the sun creep over the windowsill in the thick, white-washed sod wall.

The smell of damp, rain-washed earth lingered on the morning breeze that fluttered the lace curtains at the window. She smoothed the starched white sheet beneath her hands, admiring the home Hattie Lochrie had carved out of this wilderness. It was the kind of home she'd planned to make for herself and Seth. The kind of home a man could be proud of.

She pressed her fingertips against her tired eyelids. Sleep, except for short snatches here and there, had eluded her, despite her fatigue. In the darkness of night, Seth's face haunted her and her thoughts careened wildly out of control. What if Seth were dying slowly without her? Alone. Had she not seen men who'd lost their will to live back in the hospitals in Chicago rally when a loved one found them? Would Seth blame her if she came to him with Creed Devereaux?

She thought not.

The bounty hunter had refused to speak any more about her going with him when he'd returned from the barn. Ignoring her, he'd spread his bedroll out beside the others on the floor near the fire and shut her out by turning his back on her.

Mariah gathered a fistful of sheeting in her clenched hands. The man was infuriating! But he hadn't heard the last from her. Of that she was certain. A plan had begun to form in her mind sometime in the dark of night. All she needed was a little help.

In the outer room, the intermittent rattle and wheeze of men snoring was broken by the sound of a door being carefully latched shut. Mariah lay perfectly still for several minutes, waiting to hear boot heels moving against the floor or the fire grate opening stoked. Instead, the crunch of gravel outside drew her gaze to the window. Mariah sat bolt upright in bed and saw his dark shape cross the yard.

Devereaux!

Why, the rat! He was sneaking off before she even got up! Mariah pushed the bedclothes aside and started to dress. With a practiced hand, she slipped her new readymade Dr. Warner's Coraline corset around her waist, hooked it together and re-tightened the lacings as best she could. She winced when it pinched her and cursed the newness of the whalebone stays. Over that went her corset cover and two petticoats made of crinoline and red flannel.

She pulled a serviceable, if wrinkled, two-piece green calico from her bag as Hattie stirred behind her.

"My dear," Hattie muttered sleepily. "What's wrong? Can't you sleep?"

Mariah slipped the skirt over her petticoats and tied the drawstring waist. "Mrs. Lochrie," she began, slipping the bodice over her shoulders and keeping her voice low. "You must help me."

Hattie sat up in bed, confused and rubbing the sleep from her eyes. "Help you?"

"I wouldn't ask, but I'm desperate."

"Desperate?"

"I need a horse."

Hattie blinked as she began to understand. "A horse—? My dear, you can't mean what I think you mean."

"I mean exactly that. I have no one else to turn to. I have money. I can pay you."

Hattie shook her mob-capped head. "I can't sanction something like—"

Mariah dropped down onto the bed to sit beside Hattie. "Do you love your husband, Mrs. Lochrie?"

Hattie stared at her as if she'd lost her mind. "Well . . . of course I do, but—"

"—And if he were ill," Mariah pressed on, "desperately ill, and there was a way you could get to him to help him, you would do anything to get there, wouldn't you?"

Hattie's eyes seemed to take on a faraway look as she considered this. "I—"

"Mrs. Lochrie, I must get to Seth. I can't go back or wait here when I could be with him. You of all people can understand this, can't you? Mr. Devereaux doesn't know me, or what I'm capable of. I'm not afraid of hardship or an untraveled road. I . . . I've come a long way to be with Seth and I'm duty bound as his future wife to be there."

Hattie's eyes met hers and Mariah knew in that moment she'd found an ally.

"Miss Parsons—"

"Please . . . it's Mariah."

"Mariah. I sympathize, but even if I do sell you a horse, Mr. Devereaux will never change his mind about letting you come. I'm afraid he's dead set against it."

Hope tightened Mariah's throat. "You leave that part to me. I can handle Creed Devereaux. Does that mean you'll do it?"

Hattie let out long breath and her steady voice faltered. "I've loved my husband for more years than I care to count, dear. The thought of losing him . . . is more than I can bear to consider. I understand what you're going through." She glanced down at her work-roughened hands atop the clean white sheets. "John will think I've lost my mind . . . but this business belongs to both of us. I can sell you a horse if I'm of a mind to. And, — " she took Mariah's hand in hers — "if you're as determined as you say . . . then I'm willing to help you. Something tells me you can do it."

Impulsively, Mariah threw her arms around Hattie and squeezed her in a hug. "Oh, thank you! Thank you!" She sat back. "You can't know what this means to me. I'll have to hurry, though. I heard Mr. Devereaux leave the house a few minutes ago. I think he's planning on sneaking off before I know what he's up to."

Hattie got up and threw an old wrapper around her shoulders. "Can you ride, Mariah?"

Mariah swallowed hard. She had ridden once with Seth when she was much younger. He had found her abilities more hilarious than disastrous, but then he wasn't the one who had ended up at the bottom of a hollow, covered head to toe with leaves and too sore to walk straight for days. Still, Mariah reasoned, she'd seen enough men ride to know she could do it if she had to.

"I can ride," she lied, collecting her tapestry bag. "But, um . . . if you give me one of your gentlest mounts, I . . . well, I won't be disappointed."

The older woman gave a knowing shake of her head. "Well, then . . . Petunia should do. Be quiet now," she said lifting the latch on the bedroom door. "If we wake John, the jig will be up before it's begun."

Mariah touched the woman's arm. "Thank you Hattie. I'll never forget this."

"Mind you," Hattie returned with a fierce smile, "don't you give me cause to regret it."

"Whoa, Buck."

Creed's roan ground to a halt at the sound of his voice. The gelding's sides glistened with sweat and his sharp hooves pawed at the grassy slope of sweetgrass and goldenrod. The cool breeze tugged at them, erasing even the rushing sounds of the Sun River only a few hundred yards to the south.

Creed turned in the saddle once more to look at the ground he'd already covered. Like some bothersome gnat buzzing near his ear, the feeling that he was being followed continued to plague him, even though he could see no one.

The stands of lodgepole pine and aspen grew thicker with the altitude. To his right, a huge outcrop of granite rock stood sentinel over the valley.

Below the tree line rolled the sea of grass-covered foothills, undulating in the ceaseless prairie wind. Like a painter's canvas, the landscape below them was a boundless green, splashed here and there with the riotous colors of prairie gentian, blue flax, and Indian paintbrush. Their scents floated in the air, mingling with the fragrant crushed pine needles underfoot.

Two miles distant Creed could make out a sweeping splotch of gold and black: a small herd of pronghorns grazing a grassy hillock.

He glanced up at the sun's arc. It was nearing ten and his stomach reminded him he hadn't eaten since last night. Even then, all he'd wound up with for his efforts was a case of indigestion.

He shook his head, trying to dismiss the memory. Flipping the buckle on his saddlebag open, he pulled out a piece of pemmican. With a sigh, he bit into it and chewed slowly, savoring the bittersweet taste.

Buck dropped his head to graze in the sweetgrass at his feet and Creed was content to allow it. The truth was, Creed decided, he was tired. Bone tired. Too tired to be arguing with an ornery female who seemed bent on self-destruction. It had seemed best to leave this morning without exchanging any further pleasantries with Seth's woman. He wasn't up to another argument with her.

His encounter with Étienne LaRousse still haunted him, robbing him of yet another night's sleep. The savage pleasure he'd taken in putting a bullet between the man's eyes remained undiminished, yet, even after all these years, revenge was not the balm he'd hoped it would be. It had done little to right what had seemed wrong inside him for such a long time.

In the past four years, he'd rarely given a thought to his solitary way of life. There had always been women willing to soften his nights, most for a price. One, a madam in Virginia City named Desirée Lupone, more friend than business acquaintance, never charged him for that kindness, nor had she ever turned him away. Even the times he'd come to her half-drunk and made love to her with an almost savage intensity, she'd held him long into the night and soothed away the demons that possessed him. That had seemed enough . . . until now. Why?

Unwillingly, his mind conjured up Mariah's face; her soulful amber eyes, the way the shadows of the firelight last night had sculpted the gentle curve of her cheek and emphasized the hint of a dimple. His mental gaze drifted to her lips — too full and wide to be strictly beautiful — they were made to fit a man's mouth.

His loins tightened at the thought and his eyes slid shut with self-disgust. Could he be envious of Seth, for God's sake? Why not? Seth Travers was everything he wasn't: stable, dependable, settled. A man like that was meant for a woman like Mariah. A little house, picket fence, kids flapping around their legs like a flock of fledgling birds. He'd never wanted those things . . . had he?

A frown creased his brow. Even if he had, that kind of life wasn't meant for him. He'd chosen his path, and it didn't include a steady woman. Certainly not one like Mariah.

Just get her to Seth, you bastard. Just get her there and go see Desirée. You'll get straight again.

Like a warning, the prickle at the back of his neck came again. *Merde!*

Someone *was* following him. He heard the faint, unmistakable crack of a horseshoe against a rock somewhere behind him. He'd survived long enough to recognize that sound. But whoever it was, he wasn't being overly cautious. Any fool who wanted to sneak up on a man in rock country knew enough to wrap cloth around his horse's hooves.

Creed nudged Buck over behind the outcrop of granite and dismounted. He yanked the rifle from the boot of his saddle, poised it against the monolith and waited. Whoever it was, he'd be ready.

Mariah tightened her grip on the reins and stared at the ground where any semblance of a trail had just vanished. Where had Devereaux gone? Blast these trees, she thought. It had been so easy to follow him across the sweeping prairie. He'd been easy to spot, and it had been even easier to avoid being spotted by him in the hills and vales that rolled like ocean swells between the stage station and the foothills.

But the mountains were something else altogether, she decided, glancing at the towering pines and rocky outcropping nearby.

Without a doubt, she'd made a critical error in judgment in not showing herself sooner. What if he was so far ahead she lost him entirely? She glanced at the ground, hoping to find some sign. But the ground was littered with rocks and pine needles. If Devereaux left hoofprints, they were beyond her ability to read them.

She was no tracker. That was *his* job. She'd depended solely on her good eyesight to follow him. Now there was no sign of him — anywhere.

Overhead, a huge black-crested bluejay scolded her, diving between the branches of the trees and the huge formation of rock just ahead. Oh, for a few moments with that silly bird's wings, so she could spot him —

"Hold it right there!"

Mariah's heart staggered in her chest as the booming command echoed off the rock wall ahead. The dark shape of a man whirled from behind the rock with a gun pointed directly at her.

Devereaux!

Her horse reared and whinnied in fright. A choked cry escaped her as she clawed at the mare's neck, searching in vain for the reins that Petunia had yanked from her hands.

It was no use. She somersaulted backward over the mare's sweaty rump and plunged in a tangle of skirts to the pinestraw-covered forest floor.

The ground met her with a breath-stealing thud. For a moment, all she could do was lie gasping for air on the ground, while her whalebone stays dug into the sides of her ribs. Dimly, she heard the bounty hunter cursing as he caught and calmed her horse. But she was too stunned and angry to be grateful.

Braced on her throbbing, grass-stained elbows and knees, Mariah fought for oxygen with her head hung down between her splayed arms. Beneath her palms, she felt the low thud of footsteps on the ground as Devereaux stalked toward her.

"Maudit, woman!" he shouted. "Have you completely lost your mind?"

Devereaux's furious question held neither sympathy nor solicitation. Not that she should have expected any, she thought dazedly, staring at the tips of his brown leather boots planted only inches from her face. Reluctantly, her gaze traveled up the impossible length of his legs, past the muscular thighs and narrow hips, to see his fists balled angrily against his waist. His expression, when she had the nerve to look, was dangerously clouded.

Typical, she brooded, that he'd questioned the soundness of her mind and cared not one whit about the fact she'd just been thrown painfully from a horse. Cautiously, she pushed up off the ground, sat back on her heels, and shoved her hair from her eyes with the back of one wrist.

"Are you hurt, Miss Parsons?" she asked herself with mock sarcasm, swiping at the green stains on her white lace gloves. "Why, no, not very. Thank you for asking. Only my pride was bruised when some *lunatic* decided to point a *gun* at me."

"Lunatic? *Le bon Dieu*—you're lucky I didn't shoot you!" Devereaux shouted, towering over her.

"And I suppose I should thank you for your restraint."

"You ought to, *oui!*"

She let out a snort of laughter. "And *you* could offer me a hand up."

He folded his arms across his chest and scowled. "You've come this far without my help."

Setting her jaw, she replied, "So I have." She gathered her legs under her and stood, only to hear the tearing sound of one of her petticoats. Ignoring that, she slapped at the rumpled hem and beat it into submission.

"Well?" he fairly exploded.

Mariah flinched. Like some forbidding statue sculpted of granite, he stood waiting for her answer. It was an answer she'd rehearsed the whole morning. Perhaps it was the fall, but at the moment, her clever retorts eluded her completely. She gulped silently. "Well

. . . what?"

His eyes were blazing with anger. "Don't be coy, Miss Parsons. What the hell are you doing following me?"

She clamped a hand over her aching elbow and met his glare head on. "I think you know."

"I thought I made myself perfectly clear last night—"

"And I told you we weren't finished discussing it."

"And you decided to follow me all this way just to have the last word?" he asked incredulously.

She moistened her suddenly-dry lips with the tip of her tongue. His flashing eyes pinned her to the spot. They were beautiful eyes, she thought irrelevantly. Eyes that held the potential for great kindness and great violence. Heaven help her, the fall must have knocked her senseless to be noticing such things at a time like this! She jerked her gaze away. "I told you I wouldn't stay behind."

When he spoke again, it was with slow, deliberate fury. "Have you any idea the danger you put yourself in, trailing behind me that way?"

"I was in no danger, except, apparently, from you."

"No danger?" Shaking his head, he turned to sweep a disbelieving stare at the endless prairie foothills behind them. "Is *that* what you think? Have you heard of the Blackfeet or the Crow, Miss Parsons?"

"I—"

"—or the Gros Ventres, a particularly gruesome bunch when they're in their form. Do you have any idea what they would do to a beautiful young *femme* if they got their hands on you?"

Mariah felt heat rush to her cheeks and her gaze automatically fell to the beaded Indian choker at his throat. For the first time, real fear entered her consciousness. "I—I saw no one."

"Of course not," he snapped, ripping the hat off his head and slapping it against his thigh. "And you wouldn't have until they had their hands on you." He plunged his fingers through his windblown hair. "Not to mention the white men roaming around these hills like so many vultures."

Something cold traced a finger up her spine. "I—I had you in sight the whole time," she said a little weakly in her own defense.

"You little idiot. How could you have had me in sight when *I* couldn't see *you?*" Creed nearly shouted. The hell of it was, he realized, she truly *didn't* know the danger she'd been in. She was greener than sweetgrass and probably didn't have the sense God gave a pullet.

His imagination retraced the hundreds of dips and hills they'd crossed, knowing any one of them could have been a fatal trap. What in God's name would he have told Seth?

"Dammit," he cursed in desperation, turning away from her.

Mariah glanced down at her dirty gloved hands while the wind tore at the single braid that fell over her shoulder. He was swearing in English now and she presumed that was bad. He was, after all, correct. She *had* lost sight of him more than once and had been out of shouting distance most of the time.

Hattie had sternly warned her to catch up with Devereaux quickly, but she'd hung back, certain he'd just take her back if they were still close to the station. This was no time for self-recriminations. She'd come here with a purpose and she didn't plan to let what hadn't even happened get in her way.

"Mister Devereaux, regardless of what might or might not have happened to me, I'm here now and I'm coming with you."

A trace of a smile, an angry one, curled his lip. "No. You're not."

"You can't take me back. We've come too far."

"No distance, mademoiselle, would be too far," he replied through gritted teeth. His distaste for her was evident in his expression as he ordered, "Get your horse."

"No! I won't go back," she insisted, planting her feet. "I can't."

"Le Diable!" His already tanned face darkened dangerously and he took a threatening step closer. "Seth told me once that you were . . . how shall I say . . . willful? But I think *dangerous* would be a better word. He should have taken you across his knee years ago."

Mariah's mouth dropped open in an indignant gasp and she took an involuntary step backward. "Don't you dare—"

Taking another step closer, he taunted, "What? Scared of me now, Miss Parsons? You weren't too afraid to follow me alone out into this wilderness. Not too frightened to face men who would just as soon rape and quarter you as look at you."

Mariah went hot, then cold. She'd expected an argument from him, but never this. There was a furious, unreasonable look in his eyes and something else beyond simple anger; something that frightened her much more. "You . . . you lay a hand on me and you'll regret it—" she warned, backing up.

With a snort of mocking laughter he took another step closer. "Do you really think you could stop me, *ma petite?* A little sparrow like you?"

"I will try. As God is my witness—"

Just then, her heel caught on her ripped petticoat and she felt herself falling backward. She cried out as his steely hands clamped around her upper arms, stopping her fall. Her hands involuntarily gripped his shoulders, holding him at bay and clinging at once.

"God helps those who help themselves, Miss Parsons," he reminded, "not foolish young women who haven't a thought in their heads but what they want."

He was so close now she could feel the steamy heat from his body through the fabric of her gown, feel the angry heave of his chest brush against her breasts. A tremor raced through her, whether from anger, shock, or Creed Devereaux's touch she didn't know.

There was a subtle shift of light in those unfathomable eyes as his gaze traveled once, twice over her face, then dropped, inexorably, to her mouth. If he meant to teach her a lesson, she knew instinctively it would not be a gentle one, for there was no generosity in his expression. For the first time, she truly regretted her decision to follow him.

"Please . . ." she whispered, her dry throat constricted by fear.

"Please, what?" he demanded, drawing her dangerously closer to him. "Tell me, *ma petite,* what it is you want from me?"

"Please . . ." she pleaded hoarsely, her frightened eyes colliding with his. "I just . . . I just want to get to Seth."

Like a candle's flame snuffed out in the wind, the frightful look in Creed Devereaux's eyes vanished at her words. She might have had no less effect if she'd slapped him, Mariah thought disconcertedly.

Whirling away, Creed raked a trembling hand through his straight shock of dark hair. *Pardieu!* What had he been thinking? Not about Seth, that was certain. Damn his temper! And damn the tight, burning ache the woman incited in his loins. He drew a harsh breath and stood staring sightlessly up the tree-scattered slope.

It was useless to try to comprehend the madness that gripped him when he'd held her in his arms or what had possessed him to wonder what those full lips of hers would taste like on his. He was a fool to entertain such thoughts and, worse, a blackguard for even having them.

"Mr. Devereaux?"

Her quiet, shaken voice came from close behind him. Creed swallowed and looked at the ground, afraid to look at her, afraid his eyes would mirror his betrayal.

"You're right about . . . what you said," Mariah admitted in a voice choked with emotion. "My grandmother used to say I could be quite . . . impossible. I suppose she was right."

There was a long pause and the wind in the tall pines nearby sang through the lengthening stillness between them. Mariah watched the breeze lift his thick ebony hair away from his neck, stirring something unexpected inside her. "I didn't mean to make you angry. I only wanted . . . I just—"

"You shouldn't have come here."

Swallowing hard, she stared at him. "I shouldn't have come here—as in *after you* or to the Territory at all?"

"Take your pick."

She stared disbelievingly at his back, which was still to her. Anger swirled anew through her and she braced her hands on her hips. "What right do you have to say something like that to me? I thought you were Seth's friend."

Slowly, he turned and looked her in the eye. "I am."

"If Seth had reservations about my coming he'd have—"

"Seth has no idea what he's asking of you."

"And you do?" she retorted.

"Better than some. Better than Seth."

"What makes you so wise, Mr. Devereaux, that you know what's best for everyone? If you really were his friend—"

"—I would have put you on the next boat back to civilization and never let you pull a stunt like this!"

Mariah stared at him, knowing in her heart he was half-right about what she'd done. "I said I was sorry. But while we're laying our cards on the table, let's be honest here. You left me little choice, running off in the dark the way you did. Why, you didn't even have the nerve to tell me you were going."

68

"What good would it have done?" he asked evenly.

Her fingernails bit into the palms of her fists. "You think I should have stayed behind with Hattie and her husband, cowering there like some mouse afraid of her own shadow? Well, you're wrong—"

"Even mice know how to keep away from cats," he replied pointedly.

She narrowed her eyes. "Fine. I don't need you. I'll find someone else to take me. If you're not there to intimidate them with that miniature cannon of yours—"

"Apparently I underestimated your ingenuity, Miss Parsons. I have no doubt you could charm some poor fool into taking you there. Or at least, God knows, he'd try." He exhaled aggravatedly. "Where did you get the mare?"

Retrieving the valise from the ground, she walked toward the mare who was yanking at the tufts of sweetgrass nearby. "Hattie Lochrie sold her to me."

"Why doesn't that surprise me?" He muttered something in his patois French she suspected was derogatory about the female gender in general. Without waiting for permission, Creed stalked over and lifted her up onto Petunia's back with such force she nearly vaulted over the other side.

Mariah grabbed for the saddle horn and righted herself, then whirled to face him. At a loss for words she gasped, "Well, I never!"

"No, I'll just bet you never did," he returned, dumping the tapestry bag unceremoniously in her lap.

Her eyes narrowed. "Why don't you just leave me alone? I didn't say I needed your help to get on Petunia."

"Ha!" he scoffed humorlessly with his back already to her. "I'd like to see you mount with that contraption you've got yourself cinched into. I'm surprised you can even breathe."

"My bodily functions are none of your—" She bit

back the rest, realizing she'd nearly stooped to his level. "Ooh! You make me so mad!"

"You're welcome." Without further comment, he headed for his own mount.

"Just tell me one thing, Mr. Devereaux. Why are you so dead set against my going?"

He turned on her. "Look around you, Miss Parsons. Who do you see?"

She glanced around at the vacant hills. "Only you."

"Exactly. How do you think Seth will feel when he learns you've traveled halfway across Montana Territory alone with me?"

She rubbed at the soreness on her bruised ribs. "Under normal circumstances, believe me when I say I would agree wholeheartedly. I have no more desire to travel with you than you do with me. But what good will my reputation do Seth if he's dead by the time I get there? My being there with him could make a difference. I've seen it before with patients of my father's and in the army hospitals in Chicago — so crammed with the dying there was no room left for hope."

Creed scowled, casting about for an argument to refute the logic of her statement. She was right and he knew it. He'd never laid much credence in social mores, but a lady like Mariah Parsons damn well should.

The problem fell, Creed thought grimly, not so much with her but with himself. What had nearly happened between them only moments before when he'd held her could never be allowed to happen again. Traveling two hundred miles in the wilderness with a beautiful young woman would be temptation enough for any healthy man. But Mariah Parsons was as out of his reach as treetop berries to a hungry bear. And she would have to stay that way.

On second thought, perhaps it wouldn't be so hard. That temper of hers was enough to keep any man at bay.

He glared up at her. "If Seth's alive and well when we get there, what then?"

Mariah prayed that was true. "Then he'll understand. He trusts me, Mr. Devereaux. He has no reason not to. Perhaps it's a lack of faith in your *own* scruples that has you worried."

For an instant something flashed heatedly in those odd green eyes of his. She wondered briefly if she'd actually pricked that thick skin. Just as quickly, however, cool dismissal lurked in his expression.

"I never said I had scruples. Perhaps you should have thought of that before you followed me." He turned away to gather up his reins.

"And I think you're a liar."

Her words stopped him cold and he whirled around to face her. "You *what?*"

She wondered if she'd gone too far, but it was too late to turn back now. "Seth would never have sent a man he didn't trust after me. Perhaps it's more convenient to let people draw their own conclusions about your scruples or lack of them, Mr. Devereaux. Just as it's easier to pretend you don't care that I just insulted you."

His jaw worked. "I am used to insults, *ma petite.*"

She remembered the scene at the ticket window with that woman dragging her boys away from Devereaux as if he were dirt. And she recalled the way she'd treated him when they'd first met. Yes, he was used to insults. But instinctively she knew they cut him more deeply than he would admit. .

He swung up on Buck's back. "I'm headed into the mountains until I can find a place to cross the Sun. If the weather holds, it will take four or five days of hard riding to reach the gold fields. But it's rough travel and not for the faint of heart."

"And do you think I have a faint heart, Mr. Devereaux?"

Unexpectedly, his expression softened. "I have seen

that you do not. Do you cook?"

"I . . . beg your pardon?"

"Can you cook? If you come with me, you will do your share. I won't coddle you."

Mariah checked the flare of hope in her eyes. "Eggs are coddled, Mr. Devereaux. I, on the other hand, am more than willing to do my share. I can cook. Can you hunt?"

He tossed her a rare grin, as if to say, *touché*. "At least we won't go hungry."

At the mention of food, Mariah's stomach growled and she covered the offending spot with her hand. Creed reached in his saddlebag and tossed something to her. She regarded the brownish lump questioningly. "What is it?"

"Pemmican."

She stared at him blankly.

"The Blackfeet make it from pounded cherries, dried meat, and buffalo suet. You *eat* it, Miss Parsons."

"Oh." She invested the syllable with all the enthusiasm she could muster and bit into the edge of the lump he'd so generously identified as food. Though she'd prepared for the worst, it was quite good.

When she looked up, however, Devereaux was already urging his horse up the hill.

"Wait! Does that mean you'll take me?" She nudged her mare after him with a kick of her heels.

"Do I have a choice?" he returned over his shoulder.

She couldn't help the giddy smile of relief that curved over her lips. "Everyone has choices, Mr. Devereaux." she called.

"Peut-être," he answered, then to himself, he repeated, "Perhaps."

72

Chapter Five

In the place known to French trappers as *terres mauvaises,* or badlands, in the Missouri Breaks, the two men slowed their horses to a trot and entered the narrow chasm in the massive rock wall single-file, trailing a loaded packhorse behind. The smaller and infinitely dirtier of the two went first, signaling to a lookout perched atop the high column of rocks above them like a hawk in search of dinner.

The straggly-haired lookout smiled toothlessly, then sent out a long plume of tobacco juice in reply, which landed exactly between their two horses. "Hey, Downing — who's the dandy?" he asked with a low, mocking laugh.

"Save it, Blevins," warned the scruffier of the pair — the man named Downing. He glanced at his companion who, indeed, wore the dandiest clothes he'd ever laid eyes on. From his brocaded satin vest to the finely made black wool frock coat, the man looked as out of place as a piece of fine crystal at a slop trough. Unlike Blevins, the lookout, Downing knew better than to point that out to a man like Reese Daniels.

"Hey —" Blevins called again, still chuckling. "Where the hell is Étienne? He decide to stay behind for a little nookie with one a them smooth-skinned white whores that was shippin' in?"

Downing's shoulders stiffened beneath his grimy calico shirt, but he ignored the question. More accurately, he avoided it. Time enough, he reasoned, to explain why he had come back without Étienne. Time enough to imagine all the ways Pierre could make him suffer for letting his bastard brother die.

He'd ridden with the LaRousse brothers for three years now. It occurred to him that all those years wouldn't mean a thing once Pierre learned about Étienne. He smiled ironically. There was little loyalty among thieves.

The serpentine path to the camp led through a series of high-walled switchbacks assuring the near-invulnerability of the hideout. The light of the setting sun washed the stone walls red. Long, menacing shadows poured thickly over the towers of rock.

At the end of the path the trail opened up into a surprisingly large box canyon, littered with scrub pine, broken rocks, and graze for their stock. A slender waterfall trickled over a smooth rock spill, feeding a creek that disappeared beneath the canyon walls. Its soothing, tinkling sound belied the tension in the air as the two men trotted into camp.

Downing spotted Sam Bennett, Poke, Petey Ford, and a young Piegan outcast known as Running Fox ensconced in a heated game of cards near the cool edge of the stream. They tossed a cursory glance at the pair as they dismounted. Petey, the youngest at seventeen and the only one Downing gave a damn about, nodded in silent greeting. He was learning, Downing thought, as he turned his gaze toward the woman turning meat on a spit over the fire.

Raven was a beautiful young Blood squaw of twenty or so. A hint of a smile lit her agate-colored eyes briefly as she caught sight of Downing, but she extinguished it before the man lounging cross-legged against the willow backrest near the low fire could see.

The deadly-looking knife in Pierre LaRousse's hand stilled against the smooth sharpening stone he held against his buckskin-clad leg. He was a big man, though

74

his height was made less noticeable because of his lean, youthful build. Blue-black hair fell around his face and past his shoulders, hiding the old white scar that traced his cheekbone.

He was handsome, Downing mused, the way a fine, deadly weapon was handsome, with sharp, straight features and the rich hue of his mother's peoples' skin. Among them, he was called Red Eagle, and in deference to his long-absent mother, a lone black-tipped feather dangled from his long hair. His father's legacy, a large silver crucifix, dangled blasphemously from a chain at his neck. He spoke a curious mixture of Sioux, English, and the tongue of his father, a French-Canadian named Émile LaRousse.

Flat, expressionless eyes the color of a starless night studied the two as they approached. Downing had imagined more than once that ice would form on the half-breed's eyes if he didn't blink. He felt a sudden chill invade his bones.

"So, you 'av come, *mitakola*," LaRousse observed, regarding Daniels. *"Il y a longtemps."* He braced a forearm over his cocked knee and dangled his deadly-looking blade between his legs.

"H'llo, Pierre." The stranger slid off his mud-flecked black hat, slapped it against his equally muddy thigh, and ran a hand through his shock of white-blond hair. "You're lookin' mean as ever."

Pierre smiled and glanced at the burdened pack-horse tied to the scrub pine beside the others. Two long, heavy-looking crates straddled the pack's saddle. " 'Ave you brought what you promised?" he asked, dispensing with preliminaries.

Daniels inclined his head with a vague smile. "I always do what I say I will."

Pierre got to his feet in one fluid motion. *"C'est bon.* If zey are what you say, zen we talk. Poke! Bennett!" he yelled. "Unload ze crates and break zem open."

The two men jumped as if they'd met the business end

75

of a branding iron. Sam Bennett tossed his cards to the ground and lumbered to his feet. Two hundred and forty pounds and six feet, seven inches made him less agile than some, but gave him the distinct advantage over most men — except LaRousse. An unkempt beard covered the lower half of his face, concealing a mouthful of yellowed teeth.

With the blade of his Arkansas toothpick, Bennett sliced the rope that bound the crates and the two lowered the boxes to the ground and pried the tops open.

"Pierre —" Downing interrupted hesitantly. "I need —"

LaRousse shot a silencing look at Downing, then reached into the opened crate and lifted out a spanking new Spencer Repeater Rifle, U.S. Army issue. The walnut stock gleamed in the fading sunlight. His heartbeat quickened. There were at least twelve guns in each crate. Each of those precious weapons would bring a dear price from any of several tribes he traded with on a regular basis.

A low whistle came from the diminutive Poke, who rocked on the worn soles of his boots as he crouched beside the crates. "Holy perdition! Would'ja look at these? These here the repeaters I done heard tell of?"

Daniels smiled. "Pretty lot, aren't they?"

Entranced, the others gathered closer.

"Right out from under the Yanks' noses," Petey exclaimed in awe.

Pierre caressed the gun's smooth stock as if it were a newborn babe. *"Oui.* You 'ave done well, Daniels." He glanced admiringly at the rifle again. *"Le mitawa.* Thees one ees mine."

"Do we get one, too?" Petey asked.

Pierre leered at the youth. "Wiz gold, *mon ami,* you can buy anything." He turned and walked toward the fire.

"Hell, we gotta *buy* 'em?" he grumbled to Downing, who'd moved beside him.

"Shut up, boy," Downing snapped, leaving Petey

76

flushed and staring after him as he joined the two men at the fire.

Pierre squatted near the fire beside the woman and the Piegan, Running Fox. Pierre slid the cold walnut stock erotically against Raven's elkskin-covered breast and across her smooth brown cheek. It pleased him to see the look of fear creep into her black eyes. It made him feel stronger, invincible. As the gun did.

With the tip of his knife, he stabbed at a piece of rabbit that was cooking over the fire. The greasy morsel stopped halfway to his mouth and he looked at Downing. "Where ees my brother? 'E ees following behind?"

Downing felt his stomach shift into his throat and he swallowed hard. The scent of the rabbit made him suddenly nauseous and sweat broke out on his upper lip. "Étienne was killed," Downing mumbled. "He's dead, Pierre."

In the fraction of a second it took for those words to sink into Pierre's consciousness, Downing glimpsed a moment of something human in those eyes — a flicker of pain or disbelief or, possibly, grief.

It was quickly replaced by fury.

Before Downing could move, LaRousse was on him, flattening him to the ground with the razor-sharp edge of his knife blade — rabbit meat and all — pressed against his throat.

"Bâtard! You lie!" he snarled, drawing a fine bead of blood from Downing's neck.

"No! Pierre, listen to me!" Downing pleaded in a choked voice. "I'm sorry, it's true, but I—I swear, there was nothin' I could do. We g-got there just as the steamer was dockin'. The levee was crawlin' with people. But we didn't see nobody who would recognize us.

"That bastard bounty caught us unawares. The sonofabitch was on Étienne before we could turn around. We both took off runnin', but I . . . I guess it was Étienne he wanted. I don't reckon he—he even saw me." He felt the pressure of the blade decrease only slightly. "A-another

77

bounty come right after. Maybe they was workin' to-gether. I don't know.

"But I do know Étienne didn't have a spit's chance in hell. He drew on 'em, but the bounty shot him dead, right there in front of dozens of witnesses."

"He's quite right," Daniels confirmed from somewhere out of Downing's line of vision. "I saw the whole thing my-self. Your brother didn't have a prayer in that mob. Downing and I wouldn't have stood a chance either if we'd interfered. Besides," he added pointedly, "if we'd been fool enough to get between them, they would have killed us both and you wouldn't have had these guns."

LaRousse's hand shook slightly as he pulled the knife away from Downing's neck and eased back onto his moc-casined heels. His lip curled like that of a rogue dog who has been kicked once too often. *"Who?"* The word em-bodied a lifetime full of hate. "Who were zey?"

Downing drew his breath shakily. "The second one was that drunken *pissant,* Lydell Kraylor — that feller we run into down on the Big Horn last fall? Come outta no-wheres, after that first fella called Étienne out. Kraylor shot him once. But he ain't the one who kilt him. I ain't never seen that one before."

"Saaa-aa!" Pierre spat disgustedly, yanking the rabbit meat from the blade of his knife and flinging it at Down-ing. With a smack, the meat landed and slid greasily down his face. He dared not move to wipe it off.

"His name," Daniels interjected in a deep baritone, "was Devereaux."

Pierre felt the color leave his face. He swallowed heav-ily. *Devereaux?* It couldn't possibly be the same one. It was, after all, a common name. There must be dozens of men with that name in the Territory. Still . . . "Thees you are sure?" he asked, narrowing his eyes at the gunrunner.

"Why? You know him?"

LaRousse's face had reverted to stone, revealing noth-ing. " 'Ow did 'ee look?"

"Tall, twenty-five to thirty, dark hair . . . wears some

kind of a bone or shell choker at his throat."

The flare of LaRousse's nostrils was the only indication that he'd heard. "Eyes?" he demanded. "Did you see 'ees eyes?"

Daniels regarded LaRousse curiously for a moment. "I'm afraid I didn't get that close. They looked like any other man's eyes from where I stood."

Downing propped himself on one muddy elbow and spoke.

"I saw 'em, Pierre. They was a funny color—not blue . . . not exactly green. More like the color of one a' them turquoise stones."

LaRousse dragged the blade of his knife slowly against his buckskin leggings, leaving a smear of grease. "You saw zem and zen, *mon ami*," he asked Downing in a low voice, "zen, did you run like ze rabbit from my dead brother's body, or did you 'appen to see where 'ee went, thees bounty, Devereaux?"

Downing raked a hand defensively through his mousy brown hair as he sat up. "He followed a stage to Virginia City. He was talkin' to some woman who got on that stage, too. The ticket agent told me her name was Parsons. Mariah Parsons."

LaRousse stared unseeing at the ground for a long moment, then stood, casting his long shadow across Downing. "We leave at first light." With that, he turned and started to walk away.

"Hey, LaRousse—" Daniels inquired impatiently. "What about my guns?"

Without breaking stride, Pierre turned, and arrowed his bone-handled knife toward Daniels' chest. With a dull thunk, the weapon found its mark and the impact sent Reese stumbling backward with a mixture of surprise and horror on his face. He groaned, sinking to his knees, clutching at the hilt of the protruding weapon. A crimson stain seeped across his shirt and his rapidly numbing fingers groped futilely for the pistol at his hip.

"Mary, Mother of—" The rest was a strangled moan

and he bent over the hilt like a man in prayer.

Petey, Poke, and Bennett stared, frozen in shock. Raven backed away from the fire to cringe by Running Fox. Downing's shaking hand went to his hip, waiting for LaRousse to turn on him as well.

But the half-breed ignored him and stared down at the fallen man. With his lip curled again in a parody of a smile, he grasped his knife and tipped the gun-runner the rest of the way backward with a well-placed shove of his foot. Reese sprawled helplessly, too weak to resist, while his life's blood ebbed out onto the ground. A gurgling sound punctuated the labored rise and fall of his chest.

"*Your* guns?" Pierre repeated. "Now, Monsieur Reese, zey are *my* guns."

"Why?" Reese pleaded, clutching his chest. "I always dealt straight with you —"

LaRousse snatched up Reese's bloody shirtfront in his fists and yanked the man close to him. "Étienne was ze brother of my blood, *sacre Americaine!* And you think rifles would take 'ees place?" He spat in Reese's face and the spittle tricked down the dying man's cheek. "You are less zan nothing to me." With a shove, he released the gun-runner who slammed against the ground.

Daniels' face crumpled in pain. "I'll see you in . . . hell, LaRousse," he rasped.

Pierre LaRousse turned his back on the dying man and without a backward glance, stalked out of camp toward the high, isolated cliffs that limned the badlands. He would sing a death song for his brother, then he would find the man responsible and cut out his heart.

Chapter Six

The moisture from the damp cedar sizzled as the flames of the campfire licked it dry. Creed added several larger pieces of wood, then shoved another hunk of crystallized pine sap beneath the small pyre. The fuel roared to life, casting a crimson glow on the undersides of the aspen leaves surrounding the camp. Spires of pine forked into the midnight blue sky in inky silhouette, like giant sentinels.

Beyond these, he could hear the Sun River rushing against its banks as it flowed downstream. The water had kept them hemmed in on the north bank, its currents too treacherous and swollen to cross. Tomorrow, he thought. Surely tomorrow they would find a decent ford.

Through the flames he watched Mariah's delicately sculpted face, lit by the otherworldly light. She sat opposite him across the fire, wrapped in a blanket, eyes closed and head bobbing forward with exhaustion. The knife with which she'd been peeling a wild onion lay forgotten in the relaxed curl of her palm — the roasting pair of fat, planked trout at her feet and her earlier claims to hunger overridden by mindless fatigue.

He guessed they'd covered nearly fifteen miles today, far less than he would have covered on his own, far more than he should have pushed a tenderfoot like her. He'd suffered a pang or two of conscience over that, but he'd warned her, hadn't he?

Still, he would have felt less like a brute if she'd complained. But she hadn't. Not once. Not even when she'd nearly fallen from her horse when they'd made camp. She would have, too, if he hadn't caught her. Even then, she'd been too proud to ask for his help — too stubborn to tell him she was in pain and, until that moment, he'd been too angry with her to notice.

Unwillingly, his gaze roamed over her again as he remembered the feel of her trembling like a willow branch in his arms, the way his hands had nearly circled her small waist —

The slender stick in Creed's hands snapped in two. He stared at it a moment, surprised, then pitched it into the fire. He rose soundlessly, circled the fire and slipped the wild onion from her hand.

Her head came up with a jerk, her eyes wide, unfocused, and frightened. "Wha — ?"

He tried for a reassuring smile, but it was a gesture he'd nearly forgotten how to give. The vulnerability in her eyes had him feeling suddenly and irrationally protective. It seeped through him with a suddenness that made his heart begin to thud in his chest.

Swallowing heavily, he pointed to the pallet of blankets unfurled in the bed of pine branches ten feet away from his own bedroll. "I . . . uh, made up a bed for you."

"Oh . . . I —" She blinked and her gaze returned to him. Her hand went up to tame the burnished curls that haloed her face. "Thank you. I could have done that. But . . . I guess I fell asleep."

Creed didn't answer, but wrapped his hand in a bandanna and lifted the cooked trout away from the fire. "Hungry?"

"Not very," she replied, but the tantalizing aroma of the food reached her and she rolled her eyes. "Well, maybe I am a little hungry after all. It smells wonderful." She glanced sheepishly up at him. "I — I'm sorry I fell asleep. I told you I was going to make supper. I thought you said you couldn't cook."

He raised one dark eyebrow. "If that were true, I would have starved years ago. You become self-sufficient when you live alone." He untied the damp leather thongs that held the fish in place against the short cooking-plank. He slid one of the two five-pound fish onto a dented blue-metal plate, added a spoon and hunk of the sour-dough bread Hattie Lochrie had sent along, then held it out to her.

She looked up at him through a sweep of lashes, her expression strangely unguarded for once — perhaps, he reasoned, from exhaustion. Still, her searching gaze startled him, and an unasked question seemed to linger in her eyes.

Her fingers brushed his as she reached for the plate. Like a stroke of heat lightning, a half-memory flashed through his mind — as if this moment had passed between them before. More warning than memory, it staggered his pulse and brought moisture prickling to his palms. Yet, for a long heartbeat he didn't move his hand from hers, but held it there waiting. But for what?

A harsh sound escaped him as he released the plate. Was it insight he was waiting for? No, that wasn't part of the curse. He thought he'd become accustomed to that. Hell, until he'd met her, he'd become accustomed to a lot of things.

"Eat," he muttered more gruffly than he intended, turning his back to resume his seat across the fire. "Watch out for the bones."

Lifting the steaming fish gingerly in his hands, he nibbled away the meaty hump along the spine, then lifted out the bones in one clean piece.

The first bites only served to whet his appetite. *Dieu,* he was hungry. But when he looked up she was staring at his plate; her spoon poised uncertainly above her food.

He shoved the bite in his mouth. "Something wrong with your fish?"

"No, no," she answered quickly. She spooned a steaming bite into her mouth, sucked in a cooling breath and chewed thoughtfully, watching him. "I was just wondering . . . you're not married, are you Mr. Devereaux?"

He nearly choked. "Married? No. Why the hell would you ask a question like that?"

"Seth told me in one of his letters that many of the men out here take Indian women for wives because there are so few white women. I guess I just assumed you had one."

"Well, I don't," he said, tearing off another piece of fish with his teeth.

"How long *have* you lived alone?" she asked, still holding her spoon with that damned little pinky pointed up like some royal flag. He felt a flush creep up past his neck at the pitying way she was looking at him.

He let out a bark of laughter, but the sound held no humor. "Why? Because I eat with my hands? A barbarian, no?"

Shock erased her tentative smile. "No. That's not what I meant at all—"

He shrugged dismissively, as if she hadn't cut him. "As you say, *cherie,* I travel alone. You happen to be in possession of my only spoon." She glanced down at the dented piece of tin in her hand.

"Well, for heaven's—I didn't mean—"

"Even bounty hunters can manage utensils on occasion. Other times . . ." He dropped his attention to the fish in his hands and took a generous bite, grinning as the grease dripped down his chin.

He took devilish pleasure in playing the part of the barbarian for her. Mariah narrowed her eyes and thrust the spoon in his direction. "Here."

He stopped chewing and swiped the back of his hand across his mouth, staring at her suspiciously.

"Take it," she said. "I didn't ask to take your only spoon. You gave it to me. I can eat with my fingers just as easily as you. I'm not asking for any special treatment."

He eyed the spoon, then looked at her. With a shake of his head, he took another bite. "Keep it."

"No, I insist."

"Dieu, woman, I said keep it."

"Oh, you mean the spoon isn't what we're arguing about?" she asked.

He glanced up at her, wishing now he'd never mentioned the damned spoon. "We're not arguing."

She smiled tightly. "Good, because I find I'm too tired to fight."

He leaned back and inhaled a deep breath of cool night air, glad they'd settled it. "Good."

"No doubt that was your intent all along," she muttered.

"What?"

"Oh, nothing." She sent him a sugary smile that never reached her eyes.

Creed ran a tongue over his teeth, scowling at her, then shook his head. *Women.*

They settled into an uneasy silence and Creed forced himself to eat, the edge mysteriously gone from his hunger. She was grinding her teeth, itching to say something.

"You know, Mr. Devereaux—"

There it was. He braced himself.

"—I hardly think it will serve us to bicker this way the whole time, do you?"

The fish dangled greasily from his fingers as he spread his hands wide. "Look, can we just eat?"

"I was only trying to make pleasant conversation—"

"About the way I eat . . . ?"

"I didn't say a word about that. You cast yourself in the role of barbarian quite well all on your own, I'm sure."

He flung the fish skeleton down on the plank and wiped his mouth against the back of his sleeve as if to prove her point.

She politely ignored him. "I merely asked how long you'd lived alone. Not a terribly personal question, I didn't think, but perhaps any question is too personal for you. I merely thought . . . if we could talk, break the ice, so to speak, we could make this trip a little less . . . tense. A little more bearable."

"Tsk, tsk. Do you find it unbearable so soon, *cherie?*"

She set her jaw. "I'm *not* complaining about the riding. I knew what to expect . . ." she faltered, "more or less. But honestly, you go the entire day with hardly a word to me, barely a look to see if I'm even following along behind . . ." Her voice trailed off, and he couldn't be sure if it was anger or plain hurt that caused a tremor. The thought set him back, but only for a moment.

Then he realized what she was doing. Oh, he was on to her, all right. Just like a woman to twist things around so *he* would feel guilty for not inviting *her* in the first place. As if she had any business being here at all!

A female like Mariah Parsons belonged in some cozy little parlor somewhere crocheting doilies. She *didn't* belong here in the wilds of the Rocky Mountains with a man who hadn't touched the soft skin of a woman in months, let alone a woman who called herself a lady.

She stared at him, waiting for some kind of response. He squinted at her through the camp smoke, but wouldn't give her the satisfaction of knowing he'd been entirely too aware of her the whole damn way today. "Did you expect a running dialogue on the scenery?" he asked. "The flora and fauna, perhaps?"

A flush rose to her cheeks and her eyes snapped angrily. "No. But I suppose civility is the last thing I should expect from a man like you."

He managed an even look at her, wondering how she always got such a rise out of him. His fingers tightened on his plate. "What *do* you expect from a man like me, eh, *cherie?*"

"Perhaps any expectations I entertained are beyond you, Mr. Devereaux. How Seth could have chosen someone like you for a friend is a mystery to me. You're nothing like him."

That all-too-true observation stung. "I warned you."

Her answering laugh was brittle. "That you did. You've certainly been nothing but unpleasant since we met. I assure you, however, I don't need your *sparkling* conversation, nor your occasional concern to get me through this trip. I will manage even if you choose to ignore me entirely. In fact, I think I'd find silence preferable."

She stabbed at the fish, then chased it around her plate with the spoon. In the end, she gave up, slamming the utensil down with a clang.

Creed stared at his plate for a long time, listening to the crackle of the fire, wondering why he felt like a heel. He was right, wasn't he? She was a pain in the ass, an albatross around his neck; she was . . . a lady. He sighed. Why did she always make him act like an idiot?

She scares you, a voice answered. *She scares the hell out of you.*

"Look," he said, rubbing a tired hand down his face, "Miss Parsons—" Her eyes flashed up briefly to his. The timid, hopeful look she sent him nearly undid him. Firelight caressed her ivory cheeks and danced in her rust-colored hair turning it vermillion. His mouth went utterly dry and he found himself doing something he couldn't remember doing before in his life.

"I'm sorry," he mumbled.

She blinked, taken by surprise by his words. "I—I beg your pardon?"

He looked away. "Don't make me repeat myself."

"No. I—" Flustered, she swallowed hard. "That's a start, Mister Devereaux. Truly it is."

He shrugged. "It's been a long week and I'm tired. I'm no good at small talk." The truth was, most of the women he knew required very little conversation and the ones who did only wanted something hot and sweet whispered against their ear—words that held no pretense of social politeness.

His gaze darted to Mariah's fiery, whiskey-colored eyes and he felt his blood heat with a thought he should have been ashamed of. But he couldn't quite dredge up the emotion. He found himself wondering what it would be like to whisper something hot and sweet against her ear, if skin as pale and soft as hers would taste like —

"Small talk is merely the exchange of thoughts, the sharing of ideas, as it were, without anger," she said, breaking into his lurid musings.

Curse it! Curse his rutting imagination and his damned dishonorable hide! "Ah," he said evenly, shoving a stout branch into the dwindling fire.

"Perhaps we could . . . try it sometime?"

He looked over at her, afraid of what he would see next. Trust? Hope? But she was chewing thoughtfully on her fingernail, staring into the flames. His heart beat a little faster. "Four years," he said into the silence.

Her head snapped up. "What?"

"Four years," he repeated. "I've lived alone four years."

"Oh . . . Out of choice?"

Staring at her, he nodded. "It's my life."

She frowned. "How sad."

His heart thudded to a stop. No one had ever thought his life sad before. No one had ever given a damn one way or another. He shrugged again. "I like to be alone."

She tilted her head thoughtfully, like a little bird listening for a worm. "So do I, sometimes. But not all the time." She stared at the flames for a long moment. "I'm quite alone now, myself. My family is all . . . passed on. My mother, a long time ago, and then my father. Now," she sighed, "my grandmother. I miss them all terribly." Her eyes were watery when they met his. "But I have Seth. At least, I pray I still do."

"Seth's a fighter. He won't give in to the fever. He'll be all right."

She nodded, making herself believe him. "You're right. You've known him a long time, haven't you?"

"Long as he's been here."

"How did you meet?"

Creed pushed away from the rock and stood. "You ask a lot of questions."

Her mouth snapped shut with an audible clack of teeth. "Forgive me. I didn't mean to pry."

He scowled, wrapped his hand in his bandanna again, and reached for the steaming coffeepot dangling over the fire.

"Well, at least we've made progress here tonight, don't you think?" she said cheerily. "I don't want to spoil it. Sometimes my mouth runs on ahead of my brain."

He pointed a tin cup at her. "Coffee?"

A baleful howl rent the still night air, freezing her reply in her throat. Her plate clattered to the ground.

"Wolf," he told her, though she hadn't asked. Farther off, another one answered.

Her wide-eyed gaze collided with his. "That sounded close."

He handed her the steaming mug. "It calls its mate. Don't worry. The fire will keep them away."

She took a calming sip of the hot brew and swallowed hard. "A-Are you sure?"

He shrugged. "It's spring. They're more interested now in denning up than attacking us."

She glanced away into the inky distance once more and listened to the rhythmic chirping of the evening crickets and the chorus of frogs near the river. "Have . . . have you ever been attacked by a wolf?"

"Only once when I was riding near the Yellowstone in the dead of winter. There were five of them, desperate and half-starved because of the heavy snowfall."

"*Five?* How did you get away?"

A rare smile sparkled in his eyes. "I threw them the two brace of doves I'd just shot and ran like the devil."

With an incredulous laugh, she asked, "Truly?"

"They got the poor end of it, I think. Buck and I would have made much better eating." He tossed her a tentative smile that softened the lines of tension in his face and made him seem more . . . approachable, more human. It made her wonder why he kept that part of himself so bottled up. What had happened to make him so wary, so distrustful of everyone?

"So you ride alone most of the time," she observed. It

89

was not a question, but a statement of fact she had a hard time believing.

"Always. Except now, with you," he admitted. "And when I'm bringing a man in."

"Doesn't it . . ." — she hesitated, sliding the edge of her teeth across her lower lip — "don't you ever get . . . lonely?"

"With the songs of the wolves at night?" He shrugged. "How could I be lonely?"

Before he lied, Mariah saw the truth flit across his face. It was a wistfulness she'd never seen in him before, a longing so strong it spoke more eloquently than the ironic smile he gave her.

He glanced at the plate in his hands, then picked up his tin cup of coffee. Standing, he bent backward to stretch his spine. "We'd better get some rest. We have another long day tomorrow. I'll take these things down to the river and give you some privacy."

The soreness that had seeped into Mariah's body since she'd sat down advised her not to argue. Pride compelled her to prove she could hold up her end of the bargain.

"I can wash them in the bucket of water you drew from the river." Leaning one hand heavily on the rock behind her, she forced herself up. She swayed slightly because she'd stood too fast and she bit back a groan at the cramping of the stiff muscles in her legs.

"I don't think you're up to it tonight," he said, eyeing her suspiciously.

"Of course I am," she denied, relieving him of the dishes in his hand. But even as she walked toward the bucket, the muscles of her right leg contorted in pain. She faltered mid-step and bit her lip, praying it would pass. The torment only grew worse. The dishes fell heedlessly from her fingers and she dropped to the ground, clutching the cramping leg.

Devereaux was instantly at her side. "What is it? What's wrong?"

"Cramp—" she groaned through clenched teeth. But

she rocked back and forth, clutching her knee to her chest. Her foot curled inward at an awkward angle as the muscle pulled against itself.

"Where?" he demanded. "Show me where."

She couldn't show him. She could only clutch the offending limb as if it were on fire. She squeezed her eyes shut against the vise-like pain.

She gasped as Devereaux grabbed her foot, ripped the laces out of her ankle-high black boot and tore it off. "Oh, don't, please," she moaned, "it . . . it hurts—"

He cursed and drew her leg to him. His hands curled around her foot and pushed it from its awkward position back toward her shin, stretching the cramped muscle and massaging the tightness out. Again Mariah squeezed her eyes shut, giving in to the sickening pain.

Creed leaned forward over her leg, massaging it in long deep strokes that dug into her tender flesh.

His thumbs slid intimately over the smoothness of her stockinged leg—the taut curve of her calf, the slender perfection of her ankle—and as the tension left her, it gathered in him. Low and hard, like a blow to the gut, stirring a painful, startling ache farther down.

But it was more than lust he felt tugging at his loins. Much more than simple damned lust, he told himself. To lay his hands on her was like looking into the sun too long or pressing his palm to a hot iron and lacking the will to move away.

Le bon Dieu. He shouldn't have touched her. He knew it was a mistake, but he could do nothing else, could he? She was in pain. Well, now, so was he.

Oh, hell, he thought. Hell, hell, hell.

Mariah dared to look up at him as slowly, painfully, the agony receded. The firelight gleamed off his long, dark hair where it fell in a curtain across his face. She watched the lean but powerful muscles of his shoulders bunch and strain beneath his deerskin shirt.

He was a man of great violence and great gentleness. So unlike the other men she'd known. Different, so different from Seth.

He had a healing touch, she thought. Strong, gentle, knowing. More than that, it was almost . . . electric. The unmistakable current passed from his hands to her, prickling her skin, filling her with an emotion she couldn't name. She pressed the knuckles of one hand suddenly to her mouth.

Heaven help her, she thought, fighting back the wave of attraction that curled within her as he caressed her with his thumbs in deep, sensuous strokes. Her skin heated with a flush of guilt at the blatantly carnal thought that had just flitted through her mind. Her heartbeat quickened and she barely suppressed the cry that hovered at the base of her throat.

His hands stilled on her leg. He lifted his head and looked at her as if he'd heard her thought.

"Mr. Devereaux —" she whispered. "I —"

He glanced up, meeting her gaze with those fathomless eyes shot through with firelight. They betrayed — for the briefest of seconds — a hunger she wished she hadn't seen, a hunger she was afraid was in her eyes as well.

He kept her leg balanced between his two hands. "Better?" he asked, his voice low and even.

Dragging her gaze from his, she winced and nodded. "Much. I . . . thank you. I'm . . . I'm sorry."

He released her, his expression turning to a scowl. "You should have told me."

She stared at him, confused, dizzy with fatigue, wondering if he was actually reprimanding her for having a cramp. "Told you what?"

"That you were too exhausted to go on today. That I was pushing you too hard."

"I never said —" His pained expression trapped the lie in her throat. She dropped her hands into her lap. "I didn't want to slow you down."

"Le Diable." With a harsh, irritated sigh he turned partially away. "You did well today. Better than I expected you to. Even so, you *are* slowing me down, but I've no wish

to kill you, for God's sake." Then, as if to soften his words, he raised one dark eyebrow and shrugged. "Seth would tack my hide to his storefront if I did."

She laughed. "I'm glad to know at least you've some stake in the matter."

He didn't smile, but held her gaze intently. "It's not just your leg, is it? You can barely move."

Denying it, she sat up straighter, but couldn't help wincing at the soreness of her bottom. "I've stiffened from sitting. I'll be fine with some sleep." She drew her leg in, covering it modestly with her skirts.

"We have a lot of ground to cover tomorrow. Will you be able to ride?"

"Of course," she answered, but the thought of settling her bruised knees and bottom on that torture rack of a saddle again nearly brought on another cramp. "I'll walk if I have to."

He stared at her for a moment, then stood and reached down with one hand. She hesitated only an instant before taking it, clasping her fingers around his.

When he'd hauled her to her feet, he gestured toward her bedroll. "Go to bed before you fall down again, Miss Parsons. Get some rest. Tomorrow will come sooner than you want it to." He gathered up the fallen dishes and cups, then headed toward the rushing sound of the nearby river.

"Mister Devereaux?"

He stopped and turned, his expression hidden by shadows, but she heard him sigh. "Now that I have manhandled your lovely ankle, *ma petite*," he said, "perhaps you could do me the favor of calling me by my Christian name. It's Creed. Just Creed."

"All right. Creed," she answered, testing it out on her tongue. "I — thank you."

He might have inclined his head in reply there in the shadows, she couldn't be sure. But he turned and disappeared into the darkness without reply.

Stumbling to the bedroll he'd spread out for her, she dropped down in a loose-limbed sprawl, too tired to remove her other boot or fight with the over-tight strings on her corset. Besides, it was too cold to undress. She tugged two heavy blankets over her and lay staring sightlessly at the stars scattered across the inky half-dome above, wrestling with what had just happened between them.

A bounty hunter! Gad! She was having impure thoughts about a bounty hunter! More despicable than that, he was Seth's friend. She groaned and pulled the blanket up around her face between her fists. What did that make her? A wanton? A strumpet? Yes, all those things, but worse was the truth she couldn't deny. No man, not even Seth, had ever stirred that kind of feelings in her before — the kind that made her heart race and plunge, made her whole body heat as if it were too close to a fire, or made her long for things she didn't even understand.

She closed her eyes, watching the flames flicker behind her eyelids, feeling the crisp night air on her face. She forced her thoughts to Seth, dear Seth and his boyish, open face. He waited for her, sick — perhaps — *Dear God* — dying: then she remembered her father's strong surgeon's hand reaching for her chubby young one, sheltering, protecting her; and her Grandmother Lottie's constant reminders that life was full of the unexpected and that she should follow the road that truly made her happy.

That's why she'd come to Montana. She'd come to make a home with Seth. He would make her truly happy, wouldn't he? Until this moment, she'd always been sure of that. As sure as she could be.

But as she drifted off to sleep, it was Creed Devereaux she dreamed of, lonely, running with the wolves that bayed in the distance; silver moonlight streaking his mane of hair, he ran among the creatures of the night, seeking his mate.

Chapter Seven

The aroma of strong coffee woke him. Or maybe it was the soft groan.

Disoriented, Creed squinted an eye open and shoved his blanket down past his nose. The sky was still pink with dawn. His breath formed a white cloud in the cold morning air, then drifted up into the low pine bough overhead. The fire crackled nearby and a pot of steaming coffee dangled from his collapsible black iron tripod. Creed blinked and raised his head.

"Oooh-h," came the sound again.

Mariah.

His gaze found her. Wrapped in a heavy shawl, she edged up slowly — very slowly — from a kneeling position near her tapestry valise. She rested her hands on her thighs for a moment, massaging the stiffness he knew was there. Straightening, she raised her arms and pulled the pins from her mussed hair. One at a time, she plucked them out until her magnificent auburn mane fell loose and cascaded over her shoulders and breasts.

His lips parted. He'd never seen it down before, but even his imagination hadn't done it justice. Like molten fire, it shimmered in the sunlight, here gold, there burnished, earthy red. The curls went halfway down her back and she ran her fingers through them to get out the worst of the snarls.

His gaze followed her shuffling movements across the

camp to the leather bucket. "Ohh-hh," she moaned again as she stooped and broke the layer of ice in the bucket with one end of her hairbrush. She pulled a hanky from her sleeve and dipped it into the water. She wrung it out delicately and ran the cloth over her face and hands. Shivering with a sigh, she wiped her face on the edge of her shawl, then turned in his direction again.

Creed sank back to his bedroll, feigning sleep, but cracked an eye open to watch her. She limped back to stand near the fire, running the brush through her hair in long, sweeping strokes. His gaze roamed over her face; her pert nose, reddened from yesterday's long ride in the sun; her full, wide lips; her slender hands, following the path of the boar's bristle down her hair.

He swallowed, unable to look away. There was something intimate—erotic, in fact—about watching a woman brush her hair. He remembered the first time Desirée Lupone had let him brush her brassy red hair, having caught the look in his eye as he watched her do it. It had become part of their ritual after that when he visited her, a silent gift she gave him, knowing how he enjoyed it.

But Desirée's hair didn't hold a candle to Mariah's. His fingers itched to touch, get lost in the silky, cinnamon waves.

He blinked again. A fragment of a dream came back to him, but it remained on the edge of his memory. Only the telling tightening of his loins warned him that it hadn't been an altogether honorable fantasy. He buried his nose deeper in the blanket.

Had he finally sunk so low that all that was left to him were fantasies about other men's women? Seth's woman.

Damnation.

Four years. Four long years alone and what had he to show for it? Three men dead and how many more brought to justice? Men who meant nothing to him but a promise of money. A mercenary was what he'd become.

A bounty hunter. He said the words to himself with her loathsome inflection. And all for what? The meager satisfaction of seeing Étienne LaRousse's unseeing eyes roll back in his head? His stomach twisted at the memory. No, he had planned to make him suffer longer. Much longer.

But even that couldn't have undone his father's murder, nor made up for the dearth in Creed's life for the past four years. Seth had urged him to let go of the past, get a life for himself with a woman.

He looked at Mariah. *Doesn't it ever get lonely?* she'd asked. Was he so transparent? Sometimes he was so lonely an ache formed like a fist in his chest. Women like Desirée had slaked his physical urges, but it was a hollow satisfaction, not the kind that soothed the emptiness. He never allowed himself to dwell on it. He would always find one more man to track, one more bounty to keep him in food until he found his real quarry.

Mariah had stirred all those old feelings, feelings he'd managed to keep firmly at bay, feelings he'd just as soon were left buried along with his father.

"Good morning."

Her voice startled him out of his thoughts. He shoved the blanket aside and sat up. *"Bonjour,"* he grumbled. "You're up early."

She tightened the shawl around her. "I couldn't sleep."

He tossed the covers completely off. "You left a warm bed back with the Lochries."

She ignored the barb and flashed a brilliant smile. "Actually, waking up to the scent of pine needles and fresh mountain air is quite invigorating."

"A noble sentiment." He pulled on his boots and got to his feet, stretching his arms over his head. Automatically, he strapped his gunbelt over his hips and tied the thong around his thigh. From the corner of his eyes, he watched Mariah edge away from her rock and push herself awkwardly to a standing position. Her attempt at grace was comical. Creed folded his arms across his chest, an irreverent smile tugging at his lips.

"A little sore, are we?"

"A little," she admitted, brushing the pine needles from the back of her gown. At his dubious grin, she added, "All right — a lot."

"It will be better once you ride a while."

She blanched. "Can we please not talk about that for a few minutes? I'd rather eat breakfast while I still have my appetite, if you don't mind. Speaking of which, I found the sack of coffee, but the only food I could find in your saddlebags was pemmican and jerky. Did I, um, miss something?"

"I don't think so," he answered with a shrug.

Her face fell. "Oh. Well, in that case," she said, holding up a small black frying pan, "do you prefer your jerky pan-fried or boiled?"

He chuckled. "I don't prefer it at all when I have a choice. This country has a bounty of food, *cherie,* if you know where to look for it." He walked a few yards around the perimeter of their camp before he found what he was searching for. He stopped at a clump of delicate violet flowers on tall green stalks. He pulled several up by their roots and shook the earth from their bulb-like ends.

"Voila! Camas. The Indians roast them like potatoes. Quite tasty."

Reaching beneath the branches of a sprawling pine, he pulled a yellowish flower-shaped mushroom from under the pine tree. He tossed it to her. "Chanterelle. You can cook it with some of those wild onions we found last night."

She brightened. "Wonderful. But won't it burn if I don't use any grease? I suppose lard is out of the question?"

"Try a little of the pemmican. It's made with suet."

She made a face.

"You'll see — it works." He inhaled deeply, taking in the rich aroma of the coffee. He pointed to the pot. "Is that ready?"

"I think so. I — I mean it should be." She wrapped her hand in her shawl, filled his tin cup, and handed it to him.

"Merci." From the corner of his eye, he saw her watching him. Creed cradled the cup between his hands and blew into the steaming concoction. It was strangely thick and midnight black in color. Grounds floated around the sides like tiny warning flags.

"I thought you'd take it strong." She twined her hands behind her back.

"I do." He met her eyes and flashed her a cautious smile before he brought the steaming cup to his lips and took a sip.

Nothing could have prepared him.

The foul brew exploded from his mouth in a flume. "Bleck-hh!" he gagged, spitting the rest out and wiping his mouth with the back of his sleeve. "Good God, woman! Are you trying to poison me?"

Crestfallen, Mariah stared at him. "Too strong?"

It was a wonder the stuff hadn't already eaten straight through the tin cup. "Too *strong?* Did you put the whole bag of coffee in that one pot or what?"

"Well, of course not," she answered, with a wounded look. "I only used two cups."

"Two *cups?* Of coffee? *Alors!*"

She shrunk back a little and bit her thumbnail. "I guess . . . that was too much?"

Wiping his mouth again, he picked a stray ground off his tongue. "Not if you're serving an entire mining camp and have a few score more gallons of water."

"Oh." Her teeth worried her lip. "I — I suppose I overestimated a bit. I'm sorry."

He sent her a disbelieving frown and splashed the remainder of his coffee onto the ground. It sank there like sludgy pudding. He reached into the leather bucket and pulled a fresh handful of water to his mouth, then rinsed and spat it out. "I thought you said you could cook," he said, half-turning to her.

"I did. I mean, I can. Well," she amended, "not coffee. You see, my grandmother and I always drank tea and when my father was alive, he always insisted on brewing his own coffee." The fragrant smoke from the fire drifted on the morning air as the silence stretched between them. "I *said* I was sorry."

"Never mind." He dumped the contents of the pot onto the ground. "But I'll make the coffee from now on, eh?"

Mariah frowned. "No, I can learn. You just have to show me how. I told you I'd do the cooking."

He rubbed the bridge of his nose between his thumb and forefinger. "It would be easier and safer for all concerned if I just did it myself. Anyway," he grumbled, "I'm no good in the morning without a decent cup of coffee."

She laid a dramatic hand over her heart. "You don't say?"

Creed shifted uncomfortably, feeling like a heel for barking at her. But what the hell. She *had* nearly poisoned him. "I'm going down to the river to wash up. Do you think you can handle the breakfast?"

She arched a vexed eyebrow at him. "Surely I can manage that much." Bending down too quickly to retrieve the small black skillet, she bit back a groan. She eased herself to the ground and started cleaning the vegetables he'd collected in the bucket of water.

Creed hesitated, wondering if her boasts about her cooking abilities were altogether accurate. She must have learned to cook in order to look after her grandmother, he reasoned. He unfastened the knife at his belt and handed it to her by the deer-horn handle. "Here, you can use this."

Her warm fingers covered his for a moment as she took it. The sensation caught him off guard. The hair on the back of his neck bristled as if a cold finger of warning had stroked him there. A premonition of disaster. A band of pressure tightened around his chest and he found he couldn't take a complete breath.

Releasing her hand, the feeling vanished. *Merde,* he thought, stung by the sensation. He glanced around the clearing, then frowned down at her.

"What?" she asked, looking at him strangely. "Is something wrong?"

Wrong? His head spun. How could he tell her about the "feelings" he'd always had, these wisps of foreboding, muddled forays into the future? She'd think him a perfect fool. He used to believe that himself. In the past few years, however, he'd learned to trust his feelings, though he'd never risked telling anyone about them. Not even Seth. Certainly not her. It was a private curse he lived with and no one's business but his.

He glanced around the camp one more time. It was probably nothing, he reasoned. Sometimes he was wrong.

Sometimes.

"Creed?" The morning sun turned her eyes to gold as they met his. "Really, you can trust me with the knife."

He smiled half-heartedly at her confusion and mentally shook off the uneasiness. Gathering his soap and shaving things from his saddlebags, he hooked one finger around the handle of the graniteware coffeepot.

"Be quick with the breakfast. We've a lot of ground to cover today. I'll bring back some fresh water for the coffee." He hesitated again, then headed for the river.

Mariah squinted after him until he disappeared, then shook her head. What a strange man. Her anger was overshadowed for a moment by her uneasiness.

There were times when he looked at her as if he were seeing something or someone else, times she thought he was about to tell her something of great importance, only to see the shutters slam down around his eyes again.

She'd half-hoped after last night things would be better between them. Obviously she'd been mistaken. It wasn't as if she'd ruined the coffee on purpose. Poison him, indeed! At least she'd made an honest attempt, hadn't she?

He obviously thought she couldn't cook either. She, who'd won blue ribbons at the county fair for her apple pie and pickled watermelon relish for two years in a row before the war began. Well, she'd show him a thing or two.

Scrubbing furiously at the dirt on the camas with her

101

wet fingers, she made them shine, then started in on the mushrooms. Well, if he didn't like her breakfast, he could just go hungry.

She started to rise, but the burn in her legs froze her. Would she ever be able to walk again? She shuffled to the saddlebags and pulled out the pemmican. The mere thought of getting back on Petunia again made her nauseous. What had ever possessed her to think she could make this trip?

Of course, she knew the answer: Seth.

In her mind, she pictured him as he'd been the day he'd left: his beautiful gray eyes sparkling, eager for adventure; his sun-streaked brown hair falling in an appealing curl on his forehead. He'd been twenty-two then, full of so many dreams and plans . . .

"Have faith in me, Mariah," he'd told her, taking her in his arms that day so long ago. "I'll be so rich in a few years we can live wherever the muse takes us. San Francisco, New York, wherever you want to go. A year. Maybe two. Then I'll come back for you and we'll have a big church wedding, just the way you dreamed."

Mariah had tightened her arms around him. "I don't care about a big wedding, Seth. I don't care if we live on beans and bread our whole lives. I just want you here with me. Anything could happen out there in the Territories. I've heard terrible stories. What if I never see you again?"

"Here now," he'd crooned, smoothing her hair out of her eyes. "Nothing will happen to me. I've always been lucky. I met you, didn't I?"

"Oh, Seth." She'd pressed her face into his shirt, taking in his scent, committing it to memory. He'd been her rock, her strength for years. How would she survive without him? She needed him — and he was going.

Two years became four. She'd grown up. Changed. Through his letters, she knew he had, too. Sometimes she worried that when they met again, they'd be strangers.

Now, she might never know. He could be dead. She cursed the lack of modern conveniences as simple as telegraphs in this godforsaken country. Back in the States, she'd taken such things for granted.

She dropped her gaze to the primitive campfire and ancient, blackened skillet. There was nothing convenient about this place. Aside from its innate beauty, it was as raw and untamed as Creed Devereaux. She forced her thoughts away from him as she sizzled the pemmican in the frying pan. The fragrance of chokecherries and frying bits of dried buffalo meat billowed on the air.

The sound of footsteps came from behind her in the dry pine needles. She stiffened her shoulders, not wanting to give Creed the satisfaction of looking. "It'll be ready in a few minutes if you're hungry."

No response. His footsteps came closer and she gritted her teeth. "You'd better get the coffee going if you're in such a hurry. It'll take a few minutes to boil."

Again, he didn't answer, but merely shuffled around behind her near the saddle bags.

She narrowed her eyes. Of all the arrogant — the least he could do was exchange a polite word! After all, enough was enough. Fuming, she dropped the stirring spoon and whirled, ready to give him a piece of her mind.

The retort died on her lips and a scream rattled up from the depths of her throat.

Creed nicked his throat with the straight razor at the shrill sound of the cry. Cursing, he dropped the razor and scrambled up the rocky bank, fighting down the icy fear that gripped him. He plunged through the low-spreading pine branches that cut across his path, blood pounding in his ears.

The branches whipped by him, catching globs of the foamy lather that half-covered his face. He stumbled and caught himself on the pine-straw-littered ground. She screamed his name again and he drew his gun.

Crashing into the smoky clearing, he skidded to a stop. Mariah was perched atop a boulder across from the fire with her fists clenched over her mouth and her knees drawn up under her chin. She was gesturing wildly at the far side of the campsite.

"Aghh-hh! Creed—help! Get it away from me!"

About five feet from her, the large thorny creature that had been standing on its hind legs sniffing curiously in her direction waddled off into the brush at Creed's unexpected appearance.

He lowered his pistol with a gasp of relief. "A *porcupine?* You nearly made me slit my throat over a *porcupine?*"

"P-pa-porcupine?" she stammered, dropping her fists to her sides.

His mouth twitched.

Mariah stared at him, indignant. "Well, I fail to see what you find so humorous. It was about to *attack* me."

"*Attack* you?" His attempt at a serious expression failed him utterly. A low rumble started deep in his stomach and ended in a shaking of his shoulders.

She stared at him agog. He was laughing. *Laughing.* "Well, it was!"

He braced his hands on his knees, hung his head, and crumpled into a fit of helpless laughter. A ghost of a smile crept to her mouth at the sight of him, hee-hawing like a lunatic with that shaving soap all over his face.

"Oh, for heaven's sake," she muttered, unable to stop the chuckle that bubbled up inside her.

"It's just . . ." he gasped, rolling a look up at her and waving a surrendering hand. "It's just . . . the sight of you up on that . . . that rock like a treed coon," he said between gasps, "all b-because of a 'p-pa-porcupine'."

Before she knew it they were both laughing like children. She, perched on her rock like an idiot, he, laughing up at her from below.

"You're one to talk," she taunted between giggles. "That creature took one look at your foaming face and ran for his life." He touched his soapy jaw and they both dissolved again. Finally, Creed took a deep breath, then swiped at his face with the towel and walked toward her.

"How did you get up there anyway with all those gee-gaws you wear under your clothes?"

"Quickly, very quickly," she replied with a grin. "Hey, Creed?"

He smiled up at her through a long hank of dark hair that had fallen in his eyes. "Yeah?"

"Um, I-I don't think I can get down again."

Shaking his head, he threw the towel around his neck and reached up to her. His hands circled her waist and she braced herself against the steely muscles of his shoulders. Effortlessly, he lifted her down, and set her feet on the ground.

His hands lingered for a moment at her waist. Likewise, it didn't occur to her to move her hands from where they'd slid down his arms. She felt his thumbs tracing absent half-circles across her ribs and a tingle went through her.

Without thinking, she reached up and touched the small trickle of blood on his neck and winced. "You're bleeding."

His smile faded and he set her away from him. Blotting the nick with his towel he said, "I know. Seems to be a hazard being near you."

She forced a smile. "I have some witch hazel in my bag."

"Never mind. It's just a nick. I guess I'd, uh, better go back and—" Frowning, he sniffed, glancing around the campsite. *"Merde.* The food!"

Mariah's eyes rounded with horror at the sight of her carefully chopped vegetables flaming to a charred crisp in the skillet. A plume of black smoke erupted from the ruined breakfast. "Oh, no!"

Creed nudged the pan out of the coals with the toe of his boot. What was left of the camas sizzled and popped mockingly like bits of shiny agate at the bottom of the pan. "Charcoal, anyone?"

Mariah started at the pitiful blackened lumps and pressed her fingertips to the helpless grin creeping to her mouth. "Oh, Creed, it was going to be good. Really it was. I had it all—"

He held up his hand and shook his head with a repressed grin. "You know, jerky is sounding pretty good to me, right now." He turned and headed toward the river. "Damn good at that. But do me a favor, eh?"

She sighed contritely. "Sure, anything."

He tossed a meaningful look over his shoulder. "Don't get near it until I get back."

Chapter Eight

Hattie Lochrie settled the plump rhubarb pie onto the shelf of her new Clarion four-lidder oven and closed the door, fanning away the oppressive heat. Her gaze roamed over the simple cast iron stove with its built-in reservoir and she sighed with pleasure. John had sent back East for it. It had cost a pretty penny, she knew, but he'd insisted it was money well spent if it made things easier for her.

Lord love him, she knew he felt guilty about bringing her here to the wilds of Montana away from friends and family. But there was no need. She'd fallen for this place the minute she'd set eyes on it, just as he had. She loved the work they did, meeting people, making them feel at home, and most of all, being with John.

She rotated the sand-timer, fanned herself with the bottom of her apron, and smiled. Rhubarb was her husband's favorite. It would put a smile on his face to smell the aroma when he got back from the river with Amos. Their other wrangler, Mason, had driven the stage and its disappointed passengers back to Fort Benton earlier. Only the driver, Tom Stembridge, remained in the back room. He was sound asleep, recovering from his wounds.

The sound of a horse's whicker drew her gaze to the window. She glanced through the new four-paned glass at the yard. A tall man and his Indian squaw were walking their horses toward the house.

It wasn't unusual for travelers to stop when they were on the main road between Benton and Alder Gulch. Still, John always left her a small handgun in the desk drawer just in case there was any trouble. But she loathed guns and had yet to arm herself against some poor traveling soul who stopped by for water or a friendly word.

Hattie wrapped a shawl around her shoulders and pulled open the front door, ducking out into the sunshine. With the glare of the sun at his back, she couldn't make out his face, but he was dark-skinned and relatively clean. Probably French, she thought, walking toward them. She breathed easier.

The stranger pulled his horse to a stop near the well at the sight of her and touched his fingers to the brim of his hat. *"Bonjour, madame."*

"Good day to you," Hattie said with a smile. "I'm Hattie Lochrie. What can I do for you?"

"Eef we could trouble you for a drink from your well."

She returned his friendly smile. "You're more than welcome to help yourself."

"Merci." The man dismounted, then spoke to the squaw in French. She slid from her mare and took the reins of both horses, keeping her eyes from meeting Hattie's directly.

She was quite beautiful, Hattie thought, with her heavy, dark braids shining in the mid-morning sun. Her doeskin dress was decorated with dewclaws and small shells that rattled when she moved. Her feet were clothed in decorated moccasins that betrayed a fine hand at beadwork.

She reached for the bucket that hung from the winch hook, unlocked the rope, and sent it splashing down into the water.

"Don't bother yourself, madame," the man said with an easy smile, hauling the bucket back toward them. He removed his hat, revealing jet black hair pulled back in a tail and tucked beneath the collar of his fringed buckskin shirt.

A shiver went through her. The man's face was honed finely, with sharp, strong features that gave him a dangerous look. It occurred to her that he was part Indian, too. A half-breed. She sent a furtive look in the direction of the river, hoping to see John and Amos coming home.

"Are you headed to the gulch?" she asked, hoping to keep the conversation light.

"Could be." He slipped the tin drinking cup from its nail and scooped out a cupful of water. He took his drink first, letting water trickle down his chin. Over the rim of the cup, Hattie saw his eyes scanning the yard.

The squaw stood by silently. Her paint horse stomped a foot, shooing away a bothersome fly that buzzed around its legs.

"Ahh-hh" he sighed, splashing the remainder of his second cup on the ground. He filled it again and handed it to the squaw. Hefting the bucket, he offered it to his mount who sucked noisily at the cool water. The man slid a look at Hattie. "You are alone here, no?"

"No," she lied quickly. "My husband's in the house."

He eyed the house. "Ees a wise man who stays near 'is woman in a place as lonely as thees. I would talk wis him."

Her pulse jerked forward and her eyes darted to the river. "He's, uh, resting. I don't want to disturb him. I can answer any questions you might have."

Over the shoulder of the stranger, Hattie met the Indian girl's eyes for the first time. She wiped the back of her wrist over her mouth and shook her head ever so slightly in silent warning.

Hattie swallowed hard, backing up a step. "If you're headed for the gulch, you might consider waiting a week or so. The ferry washed out over the Sun."

His eyebrows rose fractionally and he glanced again

at the soddy. "When?"

"Day before yesterday, during the storm."

"Ze stages are not running?"

"No. Not for a week or so." She glanced at the house and tugged at the damp neckline of her faded blue dress.

"I am looking for a man 'oo was on a stage from Fort Benton that day," the stranger said. "Tall, dark-haired. 'Ees name ees Devereaux. 'E travels wis a woman."

Hattie's eyes widened, remembering Mariah Parsons and the handsome bounty hunter who'd helped Tom Stembridge. Without a doubt, she knew this man meant them no good. *John. John, where are you?*

"I don't recall seeing anyone who would fit that description. I'm very sorry." She glanced at the soddy, then smiled with tremulous bravado. "You know, I almost forgot my pie. It'll be done by now. If you'll, uh, excuse me for just . . . just one minu—"

Hattie gasped as she was brought up short by the man's steely grip on her arm. His leering smile touched only his mouth. "Your man ees gone, ees 'ee not?"

Her chest rose and fell rapidly and she shot a desperate look at the squaw, who avoided her eyes. "Take your hands off me," she demanded.

"Monsieur Lochrie?" he shouted at the empty house.

At the silence he looked meaningfully back at Hattie. "So . . ."

"I told you he was sleep—" The blade of a knife appeared at her throat and she tipped her head back avoiding it, afraid to breathe. Oh, why hadn't she taken the gun?

" 'ow rude of me not to introduce myself," he said. "Pierre LaRousse. And thees ees Raven. Say 'ello to ze lady, Raven."

Raven nodded tightly at Hattie, then glanced toward the hill where five more men were angling their horses down the slope, this lot much scruffier-looking than La-

Rousse. One was a giant and one a full-blooded Indian. The fact that the half-breed didn't bother to look around at the others told her they were together. Her heart sank and her knees gave way.

LaRousse wrapped an arm around her waist, holding her up against him. "No, *ma fille*. You must tell me what you know of Devereaux."

"I—I don't know w-who you mean."

"I can sleet your throat. Why do you protect 'eem? 'Ee ees nossing to you."

Her heart pounded in her ears. She'd heard of La-Rousse before today. He was a ruthless murderer and he meant to kill her whether she told him what he wanted to know or not. Why else would he have told her his name? So she could identify him? But he wouldn't kill her until she told him what he needed to know, she prayed. Once she did, she was dead. *Oh, John, forgive me for being so foolish.*

The other riders dismounted beside them.

"Downing," LaRousse ordered, "you and Blevins search inside. Poke and Running Fox, search ze outbuildings. Eef ee's 'ere, find him."

The men spread out across her yard like cockroaches scattering in the light. The greasy-haired giant whose clothes smelled like rotting flesh towered over La-Rousse, leering toothlessly at her. An old, well-oiled rifle dangled from his meaty fist. He licked his lips and grabbed his crotch obscenely. "Who-hoo! I'm as horny as a ruttin' boar, Pierre, an' it's been too damn long since I had anything but dark meat."

LaRousse smiled. " 'Ear zat, Mrs. Lochrie? When Bennett gets thees way, 'ees hard to hold heem back. Now tell me where Devereaux went."

"Please—"

A gunshot exploded from within the house and Hattie let out an involuntary scream. *Tom. Dear God, they've killed him!* The one named Poke appeared grinning at the door and lifted his rifle in one hand. "Found one."

"Bouffon! What good ees 'e to me dead?" Pierre demanded.

Poke looked wounded. "He aimed a gun in my nose first. 'Sides, he was already carryin' a bullet in him. He weren't no good to us."

"Sacré bleu!" LaRousse tightened the blade against her throat. "So you see, your 'usband ees dead, madame. Eet would be easier eef you just told us what we need to know."

Hysteria rose in her throat, erupting in a scream. "Joh-hh-h — nn!"

Another shot exploded in the dirt at Bennett's feet and the huge man jumped out of the way. He spun toward the sound of the shot, hitching his rifle up as he went. His gun roared, spitting flame, and Hattie saw Amos drop heavily to the ground. John, who was running beside him, stopped dead, aiming his rifle at LaRousse.

"Let go of my wife, you bastard, or I'll send you to kingdom come!" John shouted.

"John! No!" Hattie screamed as LaRousse placed her in front of him.

"And I weel sleet 'er throat — " LaRousse returned loudly. "Or you can put down your gun and we can talk." He tightened the blade against her throat to silence her.

"Let her go!"

"I'll kill her."

"Goddamn you — "

" 'Ave eet your way," LaRousse crowed and raised his elbow threateningly.

"No!" John threw down his gun and it rolled down the slope. "Wait. Don't kill her, for God's sake."

LaRousse nodded to the giant. "Go get heem, Bennett."

Bennett leered and started up the hill for John. Naively, John walked to meet him. He was met with Bennett's ham-like fist to the gut. The air gushed out of him in a whooosh and he crumpled in pain. Bennett picked him up by the collar and dragged him down the hill.

He hauled her husband to his feet and pinned his arms behind him. John's hair hung down in his eyes, his expression, dazed, agonized. Chest heaving, his look went from Hattie to LaRousse. "What do you want?"

"Devereaux," LaRousse replied. "A passenger on A.J. Oliver's stage. 'Ee was 'ere yesterday, no? Where ees 'ee now?"

John looked bewildered. "Wh-what do you want with him?"

LaRousse's smile was grim. "Answer me."

"John—don't—" Hattie rasped.

"Shut up," LaRousse ordered with a jerk. *"Where?"*

Desperate, Lochrie hesitated. "Let her go and I'll tell you."

"As you might 'ave noticed, you're not een a position to bargain, monsieur. I lose my patience." The blade nicked Hattie, drawing blood, and she inhaled sharply.

"All right, all right," John panted. "He . . . he went west toward the mountains . . . looking for another ford across the Sun River. He . . . he was headed to the gulch. Alder Gulch."

LaRousse's gaze drifted in the direction of the river, pulled by the unseen enemy. "Alone?"

"No—no, the woman went with him."

This brought a curve to the half-breed's lips. "Good."

Hattie rolled her eyes shut. It was over, she thought. Over. They were going to die now. She knew it as surely as she could feel the monster's blade against her throat.

Poke and Running Fox moved up beside LaRousse. The one called Downing hung back near the house. Raven turned her back on the whole scene and stared out across the vast rolling prairie.

"Please," John pleaded. "Let us go now. You have what you came for."

LaRousse frowned. "Oh, I couldn't do zat. You know us now."

"I swear we won't —"

"No." He scanned the endless blue dome of sky above. "Eet ees a good day to die, ees eet not, my friends?"

Bennett and Poke roared with laughter.

"Deranged bastards!" Lochrie spat at LaRousse, hitting him squarely across the cheek. John bucked furiously against Bennett's hold on him, but the huge man kneed him in the kidneys, dropping John to his knees with a strangled moan.

LaRousse slashed the spittle from his face with the back of his sleeve. "For zat," he said through gritted teeth, "you weel live — just long enough to watch us keel your wife, slowly. Eh, Bennett?"

Bennett pushed John to the ground with his foot and grunted, pig-like, tearing at the tattered belt on his filthy pants.

Hattie felt LaRousse's hand drift up to her breast, fondling her. Dimly, she heard John scream her name. Then she did the only sensible thing she'd managed to do since she'd laid eyes on the murderous heathen.

She fainted.

Mariah pulled her mare to a halt beside Creed's roan. The roar of the current was only slightly less deafening here than it had been the last few miles of the Sun River. Creed was already knee-deep in swirling eddies, surveying the forty-foot span of water for its crossing potential. Her gaze drifted involuntarily to the way his worn deerskin leggings hugged his muscular legs and the way the V of perspiration between his shoulders made the moss green shirt cling to the contours of his back.

Disgusted by her insidious curiosity, she forced her gaze to the shoreline. Petunia stomped at the river's rocky edge and yanked hungrily at the long, slippery tufts of sweetgrass, half-submerged by the spring run-off. The river spilled through the shade of giant, sheltering Ponderosa Pines, hedges of creambrush tufted with white blossoms, and glacial boulders glinting in the heat of the day.

The sun's arc indicated it was only noon, but already Mariah wished the day would end. She was still stiff as an old washboard, despite Creed's assurances to the contrary.

They'd climbed steadily, following the path of the river. He had stayed closer to her. He'd even taken pains to point out some flora and fauna along the way. Yet, he'd erected the old familiar walls around him again, and kept aloof.

In truth, she was relieved because she found she liked the other Creed she'd glimpsed earlier, the one who smiled and laughed. And that, she suspected, was a very dangerous thing.

The river narrowed significantly, though the deceptively calm centerpool looked dark and deep. The noon sun bore down on her, soaking through her numerous layers of petticoats and underthings—clothes designed for shady strolls through civilized parks and afternoon tea in cool, breezy parlors. Certainly, they weren't fit for riding through the wilds of Montana behind a man who thought the height of fashion was dead animal skins.

She tamped at her glistening neck with an already-soiled lace hanky and watched Creed edge deeper into the water, feeling for the bottom. The current tugged at him, nearly knocking him over, but he braced his legs apart and balanced one hand on a boulder.

Her heartbeat quickened apprehensively as she stared at the roiling water. She rubbed her damp palms

115

against the fabric of her skirts. *Courage, Mariah,* she cautioned herself mentally. *Courage.*

"Bottom's fairly smooth," Creed shouted, wading back to shore. "The horses can navigate it, I think. We'll cross here."

Mariah's throat tightened. "You *think?* Are you sure? It looks . . . deep."

He tossed her an irritated glance as he mounted Buck. "We've been following this river for miles with no ford more likely than this. Unless you plan to follow it to the headwaters at ten thousand feet, it's the best we'll find."

"Uh . . . h-how much farther would that be . . . exactly?" she asked hopefully.

"Two days too far." He reined the gelding around to her. "What's the matter?"

"The matter?" she echoed glancing at the dark water. "Nothing."

The truth dawned on his face. *"Maudit,* Mariah. You can't swim, can you?"

She gulped. "Well, I . . . of course. I—I've just never done this before. Chicago has bridges for this sort of thing." She was unable to summon the courage to tell him she'd never done more than paddle around in the pond near her house as a child, never in more than three feet of water, and had a deathly fear of murky, dark pools in which she couldn't see the bottom.

What good would it do to tell him that now? It was cross or suffer his endless mocking I-told-you-sos. That she couldn't abide. Besides, she reasoned, she wouldn't literally have to swim. She'd be on Petunia's back. She could do that. Surely she could do that.

He shook his head disgustedly, obviously not fooled by her bravado. "I should have known. Why didn't you tell me, for God's sake?"

Her jaw tightened. "Would it have helped my cause?"

"Your cause was a foolish one, mademoiselle. And

116

I'm the fool who brought you." He sent an uneasy look back at the tumbling river. "Well, there's nothing for it now. You'll be safe enough. All you have to do is hang on. Can you do that?"

Color stained her cheeks. "I never said I wouldn't cross."

"No, you didn't." He yanked Petunia's reins from her hands and dragged them over the mare's head. Snatching her valise, he slung it over his saddle.

He glared at her. 'Remember, just hang on to her mane and the saddle horn. I'll be right beside you." He nudged Buck toward the riverbank downstream from her and yanked the brim of his hat down low over his eyes.

Her palms prickled with moisture. Taking Petunia's mane firmly in one hand, Mariah gripped the saddle horn with the other as her mare followed Buck toward the bank.

As if she could sense Mariah's nervousness, Petunia threw her head back with a snort. Creed gave her a gentle tug and both horses edged into the icy waters of the Sun, stepping cautiously around the slippery, moss-covered rocks at the edge of the river.

Slowly, they made their way into the rushing current. Mariah felt the freezing water soak through her leather boots and tug at the hem of her dress. She ignored the impulse to hitch her skirts higher. Instead, she tightened her grip on the horse. Cold panic crept up the back of her neck as she stared into the dark pools ahead.

"You all right?" Creed shouted over the roar of the water.

She heard him, but didn't answer. Her teeth were clamped shut. Every fiber of her being was concentrated on gripping the mare with her knees. Petunia's rump angled downstream, pushed by the strong current, and knocked against Buck.

117

Mariah couldn't breathe, couldn't move. She was paralyzed with a kind of fear she'd never experienced before. It was unreasonable and she knew it. She'd get a little wet and then she'd be out of the river. All she had to do was hang on and watch the other bank coming closer. Closer. That was it. She'd keep her eyes straight ahead.

But Petunia lurched just then as the river bottom dropped out from under her. Mariah let out a shriek as she was plunged shoulder-deep into the water. She reached instinctively for Creed's arm, only inches away from hers.

Instantly, Creed fought to disengage her hand, his gelding already on the drift from her. He'd underestimated the current below the surface and even now, it pulled hard at the two horses.

"*No!* Don't hold onto me, Mariah! Hold your saddle. Hold onto the mare!"

"Creed!" she cried, tearing at his sleeve. Her breath came in short panting gasps. "Don't leave me."

"I'm right here," — he leaned toward her, trying to save her precarious balance — "but you must let go of me."

"Oh, my God!" she cried, her voice shrill with terror. "I . . . I can't!"

"You'll pull yourself off the — !"

Petunia's great brown eyes showed white as she listed sideways in the current, and Mariah felt herself being dragged from the saddle by the weight of her heavy skirts. She clutched at the saddle horn, but felt her wet hands slipping. All the while, Buck moved farther and farther away. "Cre-e-eed!"

He couldn't stop it. *Dieu,* he was right there and he was helpless to stop it! He watched her go as if in slow motion — reaching out to him with her other hand, plunging into the freezing water, her eyes wide with terror.

Chapter Nine

The frigid water closed over her scream as she disappeared beneath the swift-moving glassy surface. Creed's hand clamped around her wrist before her fingers tore free of his shirt. The current swept her around behind Buck, twisting Creed in his saddle, bringing the gelding's rump around. *God help me.* His heart pounded violently, his breath locked frozen in his chest.

He tried to haul her toward him, but he had no leverage. The dark current was a living thing, dragging her ferociously, possessively as if it had already laid its deadly claim on her.

"Nooo-oo—" he roared, feeling her slipping from his rapidly numbing fingers. Her hair floated just out of reach. "Come up," he screamed. "Help me, Mariah—damn you!"

She sputtered to the surface then, gasping, reaching for him with her other hand. She flailed with grim panic, wild-eyed with terror. "Cree-e-uhp," she managed before the current dragged her under again.

His decision was instinctive, inevitable. He couldn't pull her to him on the animal's back, but he might be able to pull her with him to the shore. Kicking away from Buck, he plunged into the freezing water. He had her only by the fabric of her sleeve. He could still feel her fingers desperately, seeking his wrist as they plummeted down the river together.

His breath came in short gasps. The icy water splashed him in the face, denying him a clean lungful of air. The far-off shoreline flew by in a blur and the whitewater grew stronger. The current twisted and tossed them violently around huge, jutting rocks. He couldn't get close enough to her. Pulled along ahead of him, Mariah hadn't resurfaced. Endless seconds ticked by like minutes. He lost all sense of time, concentrating only on surviving.

On saving her.

An undertow snatched at him and at Mariah's water-logged skirts. For a long moment it dragged him down as well, disorienting him. He whirled underwater, clinging tenuously to her sleeve. He felt the stitches give as he was dragged away.

Exploding to the surface, he gasped for breath, counting on the strength of his swimming to save them. He kicked out of the clawing undertow, finally getting in front of Mariah. By a stroke of fortune, his fingers found purchase around her wrist. It took him several horrified seconds to realize that she made no effort this time to grip him back.

Desperate, he hauled back on her with all his strength, drawing her to him. Her limp form sagged against him and her head dropped back against his shoulder.

Terror gathered in a fist at the back of his throat. With every ounce of his remaining strength, he fought the roiling flux of the water, propelling her toward the far shore. He gasped for breath as the tumbling current broke over them. Then, as abruptly as the current had claimed them, it spit them out, pushing them toward the bank.

His first stumbling contacts with the river bottom sent him crashing down into the shallow water with Mariah. Her wet clothes were unexpectedly heavy and his strength nearly gone. He dragged her onto a muddy grass bank, his chest heaving with the effort. Behind them, the river thundered like a disappointed beast, drowning out the sound of the heartbeat pounding in his ears.

He laid her on a patch of wild mint. Her body accepted the earth bonelessly. He didn't need to lay a hand on her chest to know there was no breath in her. A sinking feeling stole the remaining strength from his knees and he dropped to the ground beside her.

With a trembling hand, he raked aside the wet hair that partially covered her face. Her skin was chilled and pale, still as death.

Le bon Dieu dans le ciel! She had already left him.

"Oh, Gaa-hhh-d!" With his head thrown back in despair, the guttural, soul-wrenching cry tore from him. What good did his cursed second sight do him if he couldn't spare her life? He'd known. *Pardieu,* he'd known. He pounded a furious fist on the boning that encased her.

"Damn you, Mariah. Don't you die. Breathe, dammit! Breathe . . . breathe —" He took her by the shoulders and shook her — mindless, desperate. Her head lolled limply on her neck, her lips slack and tinged an ominous blue.

A trickle of water ran out of her mouth.

Creed froze, his eyes riveted to that small bit of hope. He shook her shoulders again and another trickle spilled out, followed by a gurgling, half-choking sound. *"Mon Dieu —"*

He yanked his knife from the sheath at his hip. He shoved her roughly over onto her stomach and flicked the tip of his knife under the waistband of her skirts, gaining access to the heavier, boned top. Edging the blade beneath the bodice of her soaked gown, he aimed for the strings of that damnable corset that had her cinched so tight she could never get a decent breath of air.

121

With one clean flick of his wrist, the deadly blade did its job, dispatching the heavy fabrics as if they were no more than candle dip. He tore the encumbrances from her, leaving her naked on top but for the transparent shift that clung to her breasts.

Tossing the knife aside, he slung her over his arms with her back to his chest and squeezed the river from her with two shaking jolts.

"Breathe . . ." he pleaded. "Breathe, Mariah—"

A coughing gag. A sputter of watery breath. Creed felt her diaphragm contract with a short, tentative gasp.

"C'est bien," he prompted. "Breathe." He crossed one arm over her chest and cupped her shoulder in his large hand. Her heartbeat bucked against his forearm and his fingertips squeezed her cold flesh—pleading, prompting, drawing her back. "That's it, Mariah, that's it."

She retched river water while he held her, then sputtered again. Shudderingly, she drew in her first clean breath in a heaving gulp.

Creed exhaled in a half-sob and squeezed his eyes shut in silent thanks. *"Oui,"* he said, pulling her hair away from her face to the back of her neck. He watched the flush of life return to her skin. *"C'est bien. C'est bien."*

Her chest rose and fell jerkily against his arm. He felt her fingers close tightly around his as a racking spasm shook her.

Finally, she moaned and dropped her head back against his shoulder with eyes closed. "Creed . . ."

"Shh-hh, *ma petite.*" He drew her fully, protectively into his lap. *She spoke his name.* Relief filled him with a shudder. His breath came in shaky heaves. "You're all right now."

"Creed." Her voice was raw and another cough shook her. "So s-scared . . . h-hold me."

"I will." He dropped his face into the curve of her

neck, his cheek in her hair. "Ah, Mariah, I almost lost you." He stroked the hair back off her forehead with his damp palm. Even as he said it, guilt flashed through him like a hot wind. She had never been his to lose.

"The water, I c-couldn't breathe," she rasped, shivering fiercely as much from shock as cold.

"I know." Closing his eyes, he drew in a ragged lungful of air. *Damn. Damn.*

She pressed her fingers against her lips. "I c-couldn't reach you. The current kept p-pulling at me—" A sob broke her words.

He cursed into her shoulder, pressing his forehead against her damp skin. "I should never have let you cross, *Dieu* . . . it was my fault." His voice cracked. "Forgive me, Mariah. I nearly killed you."

She half-turned in his arms until her cheek was pressed against his chest. She clung to him fiercely, her wet flesh fused with his, and shook her head. "My fault, not yours. I s-said I could swim. And if I hadn't—"

He let out an explosive disgusted sound. *"Swim?* The weight of your skirts would have dragged you under anyway. It was stupid of me. Stupid. I knew it. I *knew* it."

She lifted one hand to his cheek and forced him to look at her. "How c-could you have known? No one could have. D-don't do this. We both know why I'm here. Not because you wanted it." She sucked in a breath through her chattering teeth and turned her face toward the river. "I-I panicked. You saved my life and y-you don't even l-like me. You m-might have drowned yourself."

"I don't even . . . ? Ah, Mariah—" He pressed his mouth against her wet hair. "Mariah . . ." Her arms wound around his back and neck. Through his soaked shirt he could feel the fullness of her breasts. Her nipples, puckered with cold, pressed against him.

A soft, wretched sound came from his throat and he

felt the animal burn of desire welling up in him like a night sweat—irrational, uncontrollable. His lips stole over her cool temple and down her cheek, leaving a trail of heat in their wake. He gathered her protectively to him and felt her arms tighten around his back.

Perhaps it was his need for reassurance that she was alive that made him forget himself. Perhaps it was the way she clung to him as if afraid he might cast her back to the pagan river gods. Maybe it was none of those things and he was just a fool, longing for things that couldn't be.

The scent of crushed wild mint came from beneath them. He shifted slightly and she slid down into the crook of his arm. Her eyes, like pinwheels of gold, searched his face. Moisture clung to her dark lashes. Her lips trembled as she spoke his name. "Creed—"

Powerless to stop himself, he crushed his lips to hers in a hard, hungry kiss—claiming, possessing her as if she were his. She arched up to him, meeting his urgency with an unexpected desperation of her own. His hand slid down her spine to the rounded curve of her bottom. Splaying his fingers against the cold fabric of her shift, he drew her closer, until she was flush against him. Heat leapt from every point of contact and surged through his veins.

Her fingers twined in his hair at the nape of his neck, pulling him closer still. He breathed her name against her mouth and felt her lips part in welcome as the kiss deepened, shifted, descended. His tongue explored that forbidden cavern. Hers danced timidly with his, untutored to passion. A breath caught in his chest.

He wanted her. Oh, hell. He wanted her in a way he'd never wanted another woman in his life. It wasn't even a conscious thought, but primal. He was on fire, a raw blur of arousal and mindless emotion. She'd nearly drowned and he wanted to throw her on the ground and plant his seed in her.

Self-disgust tugged at his gut, overpowering the other urges that drove him to take her in his arms. *What the hell was happening between them?* She made a sound: a half-sob, half-moan when he lifted his head and broke the kiss.

"Damn," he cursed through clenched teeth.

Mariah sat up and pressed a fist to her mouth, horrified by what she'd just done. His kiss still bruised her lips. Her brain was fuzzy and whirling and heat spiraled through her despite the chill.

She couldn't look him in the eye and had no idea what to say. Should she say, I'm sorry, or I didn't mean it?

But she had. God help her, she had.

Creed raked his fingers through his wet hair. Cursing again, he shrugged out of his soaked shirt and wrapped it around her, covering her near-nakedness.

As if that gesture could make either of them forget.

Color tinged her pale cheeks and her lips were swollen and red from his kiss. He shook his head. "Mariah, that was . . . . *Dieu*, I didn't mean for that to happen."

Her eyes searched his. "I didn't either," she said truthfully. "I was just so s-scared." Another coughing fit seized her. She pulled the edges of his shirt together, glancing forlornly at the ruined things scattered around on the ground nearby. They looked as if they'd been ripped off her by an angry bear.

"I had to cut them off," he said defensively. "You weren't breathing when I pulled you out. That damnable contraption you wore would have finished the job. I had no choice."

"It's all right. I . . ." She met his uneasy gaze. "Thank you. That sounds completely inadequate, but—

He shivered involuntarily and looked away. "Look, it's freezing. Let's get warm before we catch our deaths."

She placed her hand on his bare arm and the heat of his skin warmed her fingers. "I'm all right. I'll be fine as soon as I can change into something dry."

Creed looked suddenly uncomfortable. His Adam's apple bobbed in his throat.

Mariah frowned. "What?"

"It's about your clothes . . ."

"My valise? What about it?"

"I lost it."

"Lost it?" she echoed weakly.

"It came unhooked from my saddle when I was reaching for you. The last time I saw it, it was tearing downstream, headed for parts unknown."

"Oh. Oh, my." She looked down at herself in horror. "What'll I wear? I don't even have a needle and thread to fix this."

"We'll think of something." He wrapped an arm around her and pulled her to her feet. "We need a fire. You're freezing. The horses can't be too far from here unless, God forbid, they've run off somewhe—"

The low, rumbling growl of an animal came from just beyond the hedge of huckleberries that lined the bank, cutting off his thought abruptly.

"Creed—"

"I heard it. Get back." Creed drew Mariah behind him and picked up his knife from the ground. With a silent curse, he realized his gun was safely tucked into his saddlebags thirty rods upriver.

The snarl came again, louder this time. From under a dappled green branch came a wolf, stalking them slowly on long, powerful legs. His silver and black fur stood up at the nape of his neck. His slanted, golden-eyed gaze was pinned on them. He had the look of a hybrid—half dog, half wolf. But there was only wildness in his fierce expression.

"Creed—" Mariah whispered, tightening her hold on him.

He backed up two steps, but the river was at their feet. "Yah-h!" Creed shouted, feinting forward with a slash of his knife. The wolf shied, but didn't retreat. "Yahhh! Go on!" This only made the wolf more aggressive and it bared its teeth in a snarl.

"Mahkwi — down!" commanded a voice from the opposite side of the clearing.

Incredibly, the animal responded instantly, dropping to the ground with a compliant wag of its silvery tail.

Creed's heart thudded dully in his chest. Dragging his attention from the animal to the trees, he saw a man mounted atop a magnificent brown and black appaloosa, coming toward them through the shadows at a fast trot. Behind him, he trailed two pack mules as well as Buck and Petunia.

The rider broke through the trees, fending off the lower branches with his fringed forearm. With the sun in his eyes, Creed couldn't make out his face, but his youthful silhouette was familiar as he dismounted and scratched the panting wolf behind the ears. He was a bear of a man with long, sun-streaked brown hair and a full beard to match.

"Creed Devereaux. I might 'a known it was you," said the man in a low easy drawl. "Damned careless of you to let horses this fine go an' cross the Sun alone."

"Jesse? Jesse Winslow?" Creed released a breath and his lips parted in a half-smile. *"Pardieu!* That wolf of yours nearly scared the life out of us."

Winslow's cornflower-blue eyes flicked curiously to Mariah as he reached for Creed's hand. "Last I heard, you had more lives than a cat, my friend."

"Yeah, well, I guess I just used up another couple. You couldn't have picked a better time to turn up."

Winslow's smile faded as he clasped his hand. "You're freezing, man." He turned to his pack mule and pulled several sun-warmed woolen blankets from the bundle and threw them to Creed.

"Thanks." Creed draped one over Mariah, then himself. She looked pale and ready to faint. He pulled her close and wrapped an arm around her. She accepted his support without argument and placed a hand against his chest for balance.

Jesse regarded them sideways as he rummaged through his saddlebags. The long fringe that ran the breadth of his buff-colored deerskin shirt from wrist to wrist swayed with his every movement, jangling the decorative trade beads musically. "Hell, those horses of yours came crashing out of the river like ol' satan was chasin' them. A little early in the year for a swim, isn't it?"

"We had some trouble in the crossing."

"No kidding." He pulled out a small tin of matches and stuffed them into his belt. "If anyone else had gone swimming in that river they likely would have wound up fishbait." His gaze went to Mariah and he winked. "And you come up with a mermaid. A beautiful one at that."

Creed's expression darkened. "Miss Parsons is a lady, despite the lack of wardrobe, Jesse," he said in warning. "Mariah, my old friend, Jesse Winslow."

"When he says *old*," Jesse corrected, "he's talkin' about himself, I assure you. Because I'm nowhere near as doddering as he. Anyway, I beg your pardon, Miss Parsons. Bein' out here in the wilds, I don't have much call to practice my manners. Forgive me?"

She blushed in spite of his rough but charming grin. Tugging the edges of her blanket together, she said, "I can only imagine how this must look."

Jesse untied a huge, beautifully tanned and painted buffalo robe from his mule and handed it to her. "The Blackfeet would consider this a peace offering, but I hope you'll accept it as an apology. "

Her teeth chattered and she nodded with a weak smile.

"I suggest you both wrap up in it until I get a fire going. You'll be all right for a minute?"

"We will be," Creed replied, "as soon as we get warm." He pulled Mariah to the ground with him before she fell down, then wrapped the robe around them both, fur side in.

"Right." Jesse tipped a curved silver flask out of his pocket and tossed it to Creed. "Warm is comin' right up. You two take a few pulls on that. It's bacanora—imported straight from the Utah Territory. It's guaranteed to take the chill off."

"Obliged, Jesse."

Winslow hitched a nod toward his pet. "Don't worry about the wolf." Mahkwi stood with legs braced apart and snout raised, sniffing at them suspiciously. "She'll get to know you, and then you won't be able to get rid of her." He shook his head affectionately as the wolf nudged his hand for a pat. "See what I mean? C'mon, girl!" The wolf bounded after him, and they disappeared into the thick stand of lodgepole pine.

Creed took a swallow of the potent-smelling brew, then inhaled with a long hiss. He passed it to Mariah. "Take it easy on this," he said, drawing in a pained breath. "It's nearly lethal, but it will warm you up."

He pulled the edges of the robe together. Mariah was painfully aware that their legs touched from hip to knee beneath the robe. Despite the impropriety, Mariah welcomed the warmth.

The flask trembled in her hand and she sniffed delicately at it. The fumes alone were enough to intoxicate an elephant. "I-I'm not in the habit of partaking of spirits. You don't suppose he has something milder, do you? Brandy, maybe?"

He almost laughed. "Jesse? Hardly. This is distilled cactus juice, but it does the same thing. You need it."

He was right. She was so cold she could barely hang onto the polished metal flask. Tentatively, she took a sip. At first the bacanora seemed smooth, almost tasteless.

129

But the second it hit her throat, it exploded.

"Whaugh-hh!" she gasped, fanning her mouth.

Creed laughed and took the container. "I said a *small* sip."

Her eyes watered and she nodded mutely while the liquor curled fingers of fire through her stomach. Once the burn subsided, the sensation was rather pleasant. It was undoubtedly a trick of the brew that the effect negated the painful cause. "Oh, my."

With a grin, Creed stood and walked to Buck. He unbuckled his saddle bag and withdrew a tightly wrapped oil cloth pouch. Inside were a clean buckskin shirt and an extra pair of Levis. He laid the trousers and shirt on her lap and slipped into his own dry cotton shirt and threw a fresh pair of pants over his shoulder.

"You'd best get out of those wet things. You can change under the robe. I promise I won't look." He stood with his back to her, sipping more of the fiery concoction and unlacing the front flap on his soaked deerskin leggings.

She stared up at his back. "But these are your things."

"They're all you've got at the moment. And they're a lot more practical for traveling, even if you have to roll up the legs."

Mariah shivered and cast a nervous glance at Jesse Winslow off in the woods. Quickly, she tossed the soft buffalo hide over her and peeled off her wet underthings, stockings, and shoes. Shrugging into his pants, she buttoned the fly with slow, trembling fingers under the heavy robe, then pulled on the soft fringed shirt. Though they were clean, the smell of horses, leather, and Creed's particularly masculine scent clung to the clothes. She inhaled it briefly, then with a guilty flush, threw back the heavy robe.

Creed worked the last button on his own dry pair of Levis and put on a fresh shirt. His clothes were sizes too big for her and hung on her small frame, but it was her bare toes that caught his eye. Her feet were delicate — pretty even — but reddened with the cold. Reaching into his bag again, he tossed her a dry pair of socks.

"Thanks. Do I look silly?" she asked, pulling them on.

"You look warm."

She rubbed her hands briskly up and down her arms. "They feel so good. I didn't think I'd ever feel warm again."

Creed shivered in reply, sat down on the buffalo robe, and pulled it around them again. He took another swig and exhaled sharply. "Ahh-hh. Here, have another."

She did. This sip went down easier and swirled through her with delicious heat. It made her dizzy and her vision fuzzy. "If you're trying to get me drunk, it's working." She hiccupped.

A low chuckle rumbled in his throat. "I can think of worse ways to die of the cold."

So could she. She had only to remember the frigid water closing over her, suffocating her. She swallowed another drink, then handed it back to him with a shudder. Her gaze followed Jesse Winslow's movements in the distance. "Your friend thought I was a . . . a—"

Creed shrugged, his humor fading. "It doesn't matter what he thought."

She looked down at her hands, curled in the buffalo fur. The alcohol seeped into her brain, muddying her thoughts. "It's my own fault. If all this gets back to Seth, it's my own fault."

He rubbed the back of his neck. "I had no choice about cutting your clothes off, Mariah. You have nothing to be ashamed of. Seth would have done the same in my place—"

"I wasn't thinking about the clothes," she whispered low. "I was thinking about the kiss."

He stared at her for a long heartbeat. "It will never happen again."

Something akin to disappointment shimmied through her, though she couldn't imagine why. "No. Of course not. But what if . . . what if he can tell? What if he sees it on our faces?"

"He won't. It didn't mean anything, Mariah. It just . . . just happened."

It was a lie and he knew that as well as she did. But she didn't say that. She'd never tell him how his kiss had affected her. Mariah closed her eyes to stop the ground from spinning. "No, you're right. It meant nothing. It didn't even count as a real kiss, right?"

Creed slugged down another drink. "Right."

The silence stretched between them. Creed let the flask dangle between his knees, his head bowed in thought. Was he thinking of Seth, she wondered. The man they both loved? Was he remembering their kiss, as she was, or had he truly dismissed it as if it were nothing? It was a kiss born of relief or possibly lust, after all, not of any true or even honorable emotion. She imagined he would have done the same with any woman in those circumstances. The thought stung like a thistle.

As if he'd read her mind, Creed looked up at her, his chameleon eyes reflecting the green of the shirt she wore. Perhaps the fuzzy feeling brought on by exhaustion and that brimstone she'd just drunk clouded her perception. Perhaps the stark look she thought she saw in his expression—a half-born wish he'd left unspoken—was only her imagination. Perhaps even the tingling awareness of his physical presence that curled low in her belly like warm fire was artificial.

She was aware of him nonetheless: the taut way he held himself, knuckles whitened around the flask, the sinewy strength of his forearms, the way the sun glinted silver on his dark, wet hair.

And I want him to kiss me again.

Stunned by her thought, she straightened a little too fast and the world wobbled. He was right after all. She was an idiot. And now, a drunken idiot.

The liquor had a curiously paralyzing effect and drifted through her veins like a hot, languid mist. She felt queer—slightly out of control and appallingly tired. Unwillingly, her eyes slid shut; she swayed gently against him and coughed.

He frowned. "Are you all right?"

The world seemed to tilt as she cleared her throat. "I think . . . I need t' lie down."

Creed caught her as she slipped down woozily onto the thick fur. He pulled the robe from his shoulders and covered her. "Rest now, *ma petite.* It's what you need."

She nestled into the fur, eyes half shut. "Creed?"

He smoothed the damp hair off her forehead. "Hmm-m?"

"You know what the Chinese say?" she mumbled thickly, her eyes half-closed.

"No, what?"

"—When a person saves another person's life they're bound t'gether forever. D'you think thass true?"

His chest expanded with a deep breath. "I—I don't know, *cherie.*"

She curled into a ball, nestling her head on the crook of her arm. "Creed?"

"Oui?"

"You won't leave me, will you?"

His heart twisted. "No, I won't leave. Go to sleep, *petit moineau.* Go to sleep."

Chapter Ten

Jesse shoved a larger log on the fire and watched it spiral up to the cerulean blue sky. The flames crawled along the surface of the pine and ignited it with a whoosh. He leaned back on the ground, propping himself on one elbow, and crossed his long legs at the ankle. Taking a protracted pull on the flask, he exhaled sharply and back-handed the moisture on his mustache. He smiled at Creed, who was stretched out beside him. "Here, have some more of this. You look like you could use it. Hell, Devereaux, I think you need a keeper."

Creed grunted, took a long swig, and hissed out a breath. "What's in this devil's brew anyway, Winslow?" he croaked. "Oil of asp?"

Jesse shrugged and sent him an easy grin. "Nothing so lethal. I suspect the trader who bartered this to me put a pinch or two of gunpowder in it. It's good for the blood and otherwise,"—he grinned—"deadens the mind."

Creed cocked his head in silent agreement and slugged down another drink. It had taken only a thimbleful to get Mariah pickled and while he considered himself well able to hold his liquor, a pleasant buzz already thrummed through him.

He glanced over at Mariah. He could only see the top of her head where it poked out of the buffalo hide.

She was sound asleep and that was just what she needed.

The wolf, who had placed herself between him and Jesse, edged closer, shuffling forward on all fours until her nose was inches from Creed's hand. She sniffed with covert curiosity, then yawned and lay her head back down between her paws. Creed shifted uncomfortably, glancing at Jesse. "Has your wolf had dinner yet?"

Jesse chuckled. "You should recognize that look by now, old friend. You always did have a way with the ladies."

Creed sent him a withering look. "Where did you get her?"

"From old Sun Weasel's sits-beside-him wife, Crow Woman, up on the Bear. Said the pup was big medicine for me cause she was half-dog, half-wolf and because we looked alike." He scratched his thick beard. "She calls me *Imoyinum*. That's 'Looks Furry' to the Pikunis." He laughed. "I guess she was right. Frankly, I think the old woman just wanted to be shed of the animal. Makes a damn pest of herself."

Mahkwi thumped her tail and laid her head obligingly in Jesse's lap. He grinned and scratched her behind the ears. "But she's kinda grown on me. An' I get damn few prowlers around my campfire at night, if you know what I mean."

"Personally," Creed observed with a smile, "I think you're lucky old Sun Weasel and his bunch didn't decide to lift that pretty hair of yours. I'm surprised you've kept it this long."

"Hell," Jesse scoffed, running a hand through his blond locks, "I supply his bunch and half the other Blackfeet tribes with their monthly supply of trade goods—which keep their womenfolk happy and their pipes full with twists of tobacco."

Creed sent him a measured glance. "Whiskey?"

135

Jesse looked offended. "I don't deal in that. You know that, Creed." He lifted the flask and winked. "This is my own particular poison. Besides, I got my eye on a pretty little Pikuni maiden, about this high,"— his hand sliced across his ample chest, then formed an hourglass—"shaped just so. Wouldn't do my cause any good to go getting her family all stirred up with firewater, would it?"

"You planning on settling down?"

Jesse shot him a strangled look, then laughed. "Not particularly. It's crossed my mind a time or two though."

Creed shrugged. It surprised him to hear Jesse mention a woman. Creed had known him since he was young and green, before he had carved a place for himself in the Montana wilderness. Jesse wasn't the settling down type any more than he was. He was a roamer. A dreamer. A man with a penchant for trouble.

Like you, a voice said. A lone, gray-crowned goshawk circled high on the wind currents above them, let out its shrill *kek-kek-kek,* then vanished beyond the trees.

He glanced at Mariah's sleeping form and felt a pang of regret that he had never settled down, found a woman like her. It occurred to him that he and Jesse had a lot in common. A good four years younger than Creed, Jesse didn't talk much about his family anymore. But he recognized the look in his eyes, recognized the loneliness.

"What about you? You thinkin' of settling down?"

Jesse's question pulled him from his thoughts. "Me?"

He tipped his head in Mariah's direction. "She's a pretty one, all right, even half-drowned."

Creed sobered and looked at his hands. "Hell, I almost lost her today. She wasn't . . . even breathing when I pulled her out."

Jesse searched his face. "Lucky," was all he said, but Creed knew what he meant.

"She's not mine."

The flask halted halfway to Jesse's lips. "Who the hell is she?"

Creed dug his sock-covered heels into the deep carpet of pine needles. "She's promised to a friend of mine. Seth Travers."

"The storekeeper down in Alder Gulch?"

Creed nodded, unable to look Jesse in the eye for fear he'd see what was in his heart.

Jesse whistled quietly. "I know Travers. He's a good man. I, uh, reckon there's a good reason why she's out here in the middle of nowhere with you."

Creed nearly laughed. "It's a long story, believe me. The truth is, Seth was supposed to meet her up at Benton, but he took sick."

"Hellfire. Bad?"

"Camp fever. It might even be the pneumonia. It was plenty bad when I left."

Raking a hand through his long hair, he asked, "She knows, o' course."

"That's why she's traipsing all over the countryside with me instead of staying back at the stage station like I told her to. *Merde*. She is, without a doubt, the stubbornest female I've ever run across."

Jesse took another pull on the flask, watching Creed closely. "Women. They're kinda like a jug of water to a man dyin' of thirst. A little'll keep him goin'. The whole shebang'll kill him."

Smiling, Creed took the bacanora from his old friend, but didn't drink. He had believed that once about women. Until he'd met Mariah. Now? Hell, he felt thirsty all the time and he doubted she could ever quench the burn.

Jesse stared into the flames for a long time before he spoke again. "Old Skinny Taylor down in Bannack told me about Antoine." He shook his head. "He was a good friend. I was damn sorry to hear about it." Emotion

137

tugged at his boyish features. "Your pa didn't deserve that kinda end."

Rubbing a hand over his eyes, Creed sighed. "No one does."

"What's it been? Five years? I thought I'd run into you before this, but I never did."

"I've been on the move a lot."

"I heard it was the LaRousse brothers."

Creed's fists tightened involuntarily and he took a drink as Jesse's gaze went to the choker at Creed's throat.

"Skinny said they almost killed you, too. That true?"

Creed winced, remembering. "One day, they'll both regret not finishing the job."

"You're still hunting them, then?"

Creed glanced up at him. "Only one of them, now. I put a bullet in Étienne at Benton a few days ago."

Jesse whistled low, picked a stalk from a clump of sweetgrass, and stuck it between his teeth. "I've never had the misfortune of meeting them, but he and Pierre have gotten quite a reputation around these parts in the past few years. None of it good. Word has it they were hooked up with Frank Plummer's gang of cutthroats up at Robber's Roost. I guess you heard the vigilantes hung Plummer and his deputy, Boone Helm, this past January in the gulch along with the rest of them."

Creed grunted and took another swig. "They missed a few."

"Yeah. There's always a few flies that miss the flypaper. They were tight, those LaRousse brothers. I don't reckon Pierre will take his brother's death well." He met Creed's gaze with a silent warning. "I reckon it might just flush him out of the floorboards."

"I'm counting on it."

Jesse nodded thoughtfully. "It's a dangerous business."

"*Oui.*" Creed's smile was grim. "It's a danger I welcome."

A laugh rumbled through Jesse's chest. "You're one crazy sonofabitch, Devereaux. I'd almost forgotten how much I liked you."

"What about you, *mon ami?*" Creed asked. "Been bitten by the goldbug yet?"

He let out a bark of laughter. "Hell, no. I make enough to pay my way. That's good enough for me. No, I've been here and there. Still some good trappin' up around Two Medicine Lake and Cut Bank Creek. I spent last winter with the Pikunis and learned a thing or two." He grinned. "Or three."

Creed glanced up at Jesse, envying his love of the footloose life. He knew Jesse's family were farmers back in Ohio and that Jesse had left at the tender age of sixteen for the West. He'd told him once it would have killed him to stay there. Creed believed him.

His family hadn't taken his decision well and considered him *la brébis galeuse,* the black sheep, and for that matter, so did Jesse. He'd lived with Creed and his father for the first several years, apprenticing to Antoine and learning the ropes in trading. Jesse had done well for himself.

"Have you heard from your family?"

Jesse sighed, lacing his fingers together. "Not for a few years. I suppose my father hasn't forgiven me for leaving. I guess he never will." He shrugged. "Ma, she doesn't want to cross him."

"Think you'll ever go back home?"

"Back?" He looked horrified at the notion and shook his head. "It's not my home anymore. Hasn't been for a long time now." Squinting at the shining snow-covered peaks that towered over them, he sighed. "I live here now."

Creed noticed he hadn't called Montana home either. For men like Jesse, home was wherever a bedroll could be flung on the ground. Creed thought of the

139

mud-chinked log cabin he and his father had shared near the Boulder River.

It was still standing, he guessed, though he'd spent precious little time there in the past few years. It was a place to hang his hat in the dead of winter, a place to go where the world would leave him alone.

Creed shrugged. "I don't know. Family ties can be good things to hang onto. Sometimes, I wish . . ."

Jesse frowned. "Wish what?"

Wish I had a family to go back to. Or a woman. Creed smiled sadly, clapped him on the back and stood up. *"Cela ne fait rien.* It's nothing. Must be that rotgut of yours making me sentimental, no?"

He glanced at the unloaded pack mules grazing on the river's edge and the heavy bundles of pelts and trade goods stacked under the sprawling ponderosa nearby. "You were headed somewhere today."

"The gulch," he answered. "I've got some skins to sell and I need to restock some supplies."

"You could ride along with us." As he said it, Creed realized the idea had merit on more than one level, considering what had happened between him and Mariah. "If you can wait until tomorrow. I don't think Mariah's going to be up to any more riding today."

Jesse slapped his knees and got to his feet. "Thanks. Maybe I will," he allowed, reaching for his rifle. "I think I'll go scare up somethin' for supper. I'm hungry as a bear. Get some rest yourself, my friend." He disappeared into the thicket of trees, heading toward the steep-walled canyon to the north.

Creed was tired. Suddenly, very tired. He grabbed his rifle, threw a blanket on the ground beside Mariah, and stretched out next to her. He watched her eyelashes flutter in sleep, the way her lips curved up naturally at the corners, and the smooth, freckle-spattered curve of her cheek.

Reaching out, he smoothed one finger down that

softness and watched her lips curl up in an unconscious smile. But it was what she did next that made him draw back his hand as if he'd been burned.

In her sleep, she whispered his name.

Mariah slept through the rest of that day and night, rousing only to partake of a small meal of roast rabbit Creed forced her to eat before putting her back to bed. By morning, she awoke feeling renewed and better than she had in days.

Creed set a slower pace for them that day and the next, stopping frequently for short rests and pulling up for the night while there was plenty of daylight left. She managed on the second day to build a passable fire and, with some success, took over the cooking chore of roasting the brace of rabbits Jesse had shot.

Of course, Creed kept the reins of the coffee-making and she endured his barbs about the toxic mud she'd managed to produce.

They'd crossed at a shallow ford of the Dearborn River the second day and he'd insisted she ride double with him, even though only their feet got wet. Aside from that, he'd pointedly kept his distance, staying in the lead and speaking to her only if she asked him a direct question.

Thank God for Jesse, she thought. He'd kept her company through the long days of riding, telling her stories about his travels or walking along beside her when she needed to stretch her legs. In the short time they'd known one another, they'd become friends.

Mahkwi would disappear for long periods during their days, exploring higher into the slopes that paralleled their trail, following the unfettered instincts of her ancestors. Inevitably, she would come at Jesse's shrill whistle, loping toward them on her long, graceful wolf-legs. Her wildness seemed to give her boundless energy and she was rarely even winded when she came into camp.

Often as not, she came to Creed for attention. She would lay her head in his lap and roll onto her back, demanding a scratch. The gesture of utter trust was one of the few things that brought a smile to Creed's lips. Mahkwi would send him a golden-eyed gaze, tongue lolling, basking in his touch.

The wolf's infatuation with Creed was something Mariah understood. She, too, remembered the magic of his touch, the comfort of his smile.

There were times when she'd caught Creed watching her when he thought she didn't see. A shiver of awareness would ripple through her at those times, as if she could almost feel the heat of his gaze. Yesterday, while they ate a cold lunch and Jesse entertained them with stories of grizzlies he'd known, she'd even dared to return Creed's stare. To her surprise, he hadn't looked away, but held her gaze for a long, heart-stopping moment.

Thinking back on the longing she'd seen in his eyes made her knees go weak and her pulse thud at the base of her throat. Little things, like the way he tilted his head or the way his slender fingers smoothed the piece of wood he was whittling, reminded her of the way he'd held her that day by the river. There was no denying that something had changed, shifted unalterably between them.

Mariah sighed, staring at his back as he trotted his horse ahead. As impossible as it seemed, her feelings for him were deepening. No longer could she look at him as simply a bounty hunter, an unscrupulous mercenary without virtue. Creed Devereaux was a complex man whose true depths she could only guess at. He was a man who needed more than he'd ever ask for, and one who'd doubtless given away more of himself than he'd ever admit.

By late afternoon they'd come to a broad, low-running creek that threaded through a high-walled gulch. It was shaded by dozens of cottonwood and birch and hedged by a bank of rock-bound bitterroot and bright crimson stands of Indian paintbrush. Creed had gone off on his own, under the pretense of catching fish for dinner, leaving her and Jesse to set up camp. The wolf had, not surprisingly, tagged along beside Creed, seemingly tireless after the long day's romp.

As Mariah had been doing for the past two days, she unsaddled Buck and Petunia, rubbed them down with handfuls of grass, and hobbled them near Jesse's stock. It was a chore she'd taken on voluntarily and she relished the time to be alone with her thoughts.

When she was finished, she carried a bucket to the edge of the shallow, rock-dotted creek and settled it into the water. The sun was a pool of orange, just dipping below the horizon of the western peaks in the "V" of the canyon, casting them in a pink blush. "Beautiful," she murmured, half to herself.

"It's called Wolf Creek," commented Jesse, who walked up beside her with an armload of wood, gazing at the setting sun sparkling on the water. "The Blackfeet have their own name for it. *Mahkwiyi Istikiop.*"

She smiled at the musical-sounding words. "What does that mean?"

" 'Where the Wolf Fell Down.' "

"What a strange name."

"Most of the rivers in these parts have two or three names. The ones the white men give them and the Indian names. They're usually given for a particular event someone witnessed or for a spiritual belief. The story goes that Wolf Creek got its name because a Blackfoot brave saw a herd of buffalo go right over those cliffs, followed by the unfortunate wolf who'd been chasing them."

Mariah grimaced. "How gruesome . . . *Mahkwi*

Asti—"

"Mah-kwi-yi Is-ti-kiop."

She pronounced it again and this time got it nearly right. "Well, it's quite beautiful when *you* say it. *Mahkwiyi*—that means wolf?"

He nodded with a grin.

She smiled, thinking of Mahkwi. "It's a perfect name for her. Where did you learn to speak Blackfoot?"

He stooped to gather more wood beneath a cottonwood. "A man can't trade with The People for as long as I have without learning to savvy their language."

"Are you ever afraid, dealing with . . . with—"

A frown creased his brow. "Savages?"

She hesitated. "I've read stories about the Blackfeet. They say they're a brutal, warring tribe, guilty of many atrocities."

Jesse dumped the wood near the circle of rocks he'd gathered. "You believe everything you read?"

His question took her off guard. "I—well—"

"I haven't got much personal experience with the stories myself," he admitted, arranging the wood in a pile with tinder he'd gathered underneath, "but from what I've heard, I'd advise against it, Mariah. Nobody can know a people from a thousand miles off or by sifting through what they leave behind. Those two-bit word-slingers who tell tales about the West have likely never been here and if they have, they've only looked at one side of things.

"The Blackfeet are different from us in a lot of ways: the way they live, the God they worship, the way they dress. But they laugh, have young'uns, even love same as you and me. They've had their share of war and killing, but mostly it's with their enemies—the Crow, the Cree, or the Assiniboines. They go by their own set of rules that whites don't generally understand."

He struck a match against the sole of his boot, cupping it in his hand against the wind. The tinder caught and flamed, licking the underside of the wood.

"The world of the Blackfoot is a sacred hoop—in balance with all things," he went on. "They fight to protect what's theirs, to make sure they can feed their families. They're not so different from us in that way." He fell silent while he added wood to the fire.

She handed him the last log. "I suppose I've never thought of them in that light. As people, I mean."

Jesse smiled sadly. "You and the rest of the country. There's a lot about the Blackfoot way of life I admire. In fact, I think in some ways they're more civilized than we are. Does that shock you?"

She considered it for a moment. "A few days ago, I might have been appalled," she admitted. "Now that I've gotten to know you a little better, I'm certain there must be some merit in what you say."

"Careful, Mariah, you'll turn my head." A teasing glint sparkled in his light blue eyes. "You'll find things out here are rarely what they seem. Take you, for instance."

"Me?"

"You don't look like the type of woman who'd brave a trip alone to Montana, or one who'd have a burning desire to leave civilization for this." He gestured at the wildness around them. "But here you are, going across country with the likes of Creed Devereaux."

"Yes, who could have imagined that?" she replied sardonically, inhaling the fragrance of woodsmoke.

He grinned and set his tripod over the fire. "I'd wager Creed's not exactly what you thought he was either."

The good humor slipped from her face. "Oh? And what's that?"

"A bounty hunter. A killer."

"He's both of those things."

"Yes . . . and no."

"What do you mean? I saw him gun down a man in cold blood. It happened right in front of my very eyes."

145

"Oh, I'm not saying he didn't do it. But you don't know the whole of it."

She hugged her arms. "Why don't you tell me?"

His lips curved into a half-grin as he fed the fire several larger sticks. "It's not my place to do that. If Creed wants you to know, I reckon he'll tell you."

Her shoulders slumped. "Creed doesn't tell me much about himself. In fact, if you've noticed, he's barely speaking to me. I don't really know him at all."

"Not many do. Most folks who come out here are either runnin' from something behind them or looking for a future. Not a one of 'em wants their pasts turned over by someone else's spade. A man doesn't have to talk for people to know who he is. What a fella does counts for more than all the talking in the world."

She absorbed what he'd said in silence, watching the flames gobble up the pyramid of wood. Jesse made a pot of coffee and hung it over the fire.

"You've known each other for a long time," she said, breaking the comfortable silence between them. "Has Creed always been the way he is now? He seems . . . lonely, sometimes bitter."

Jesse reached into his pocket for a packet of cigarette paper and his drawstring pouch of tobacco. "Not always. Life hasn't been kind to him and that's a fact. He's chosen a certain road and it's not an easy one. But like me, he's a survivor and I expect you're cut out of that same cloth."

"A few days ago, I would have taken offense at that," she said with a grin, "but I'll take it as a compliment today."

Jesse returned her smile. "So meant."

They sat together watching the flames in silence, content to reflect on their conversation. The lid of the coffee pot rattled with the fragrant steam that mingled with the tang of woodsmoke.

Her thoughts turned to Creed, as usual. She wondered about what Jesse had told her. What was it that drove a man to become what Creed Devereaux had become? What forces in his life had made him choose the difficult road Jesse spoke of? He wasn't an ordinary man. At least, clearly, Jesse didn't think so. If she didn't miss her guess, there was a touch of hero worship in Jesse's eyes when he spoke of Creed. What did they share and how was it they were close as brothers, yet hadn't seen each other for years?

She glanced off in the direction Creed had gone, wishing suddenly he'd come back, miraculously healed of the bitterness that had settled like a mantle over him in the past few days.

"He's fine, Mariah. He just needs some time alone, I expect," Jesse said, following her gaze.

A flush crept up her neck at his perceptiveness. It was a bit disconcerting to realize she was so obvious. "He must have had to walk a ways to find a good fishing pool." She chewed nervously on her bottom lip. "It's starting to get dark. You . . . you don't suppose anything's happened to him, do you?"

Jesse laughed. "Creed? He can take care of himself. Most of the time," he added under his breath. "By the time he gets back, we're gonna be hungry enough to eat the worms he's using for bait." Mariah laughed with him, glad to leave dismal subjects behind.

From a short distance away came a sound neither of them recognized at first. As it came closer Mariah knew it was a man's voice singing:

> *"Chante, rossignol, chante*
> 'Ow long, 'ow long 'ave I loved you?
> Never, never well I forget."

"Who the hell is that?" Jesse muttered to himself, staring in the direction of the sound.

147

"I can't see anyone through all the trees," she replied. "What's he singing?"

"It's an old voyager's song, 'Á La Clair Fontaine.'"

"What?" Mariah stared at him in surprise. "What's wrong?"

"Just to be safe. Keep quiet." He cocked his rifle.

"Oh, for heaven's sake." Indignant, she glared at his back. The first person they'd seen in days, and Jesse was getting ready to shoot him!

The resonant voice grew louder:

> "Now I 'ave lost my sweetheart,
> Wizzout any reason at all.
> Eet was just a bouquet of roses.
> Zat I forgot to geeve 'er.
> *Chante, rossignol, chante*
> 'Ow long, 'ow long have I lov —"

The man's singing stopped abruptly as his horse entered the clearing and the stranger saw Jesse's rifle pointed at the opening of his colorful blanket capote. A large crucifix dangled from his neck on a thick silver chain. He was dressed like a trapper, she imagined, though she noted he had no pack horse loaded with skins like Jesse.

His sharp, dark-skinned features gave her the impression he was a half-breed, but his smile was white-toothed and pleasant. Behind him a few paces, a squaw mounted atop a paint horse drew to a stop as well, her exquisite face devoid of any expression. A thick buffalo hide fell around her shoulders against the cold.

The breed's obsidian gaze took in the entire campsite in a glance from beneath the brim of his hat; then he spread his hands wide to show he had no weapons. "Eh, *mon ami*, so unfriendly? You do not like my song?"

Jesse's eyes narrowed. "I'm a cautious man."

"C'est bien, monsieur. So am I. But I mean you no 'arm

as you can see. We are just passing through."

"Maybe you should just keep passin' then."

Undaunted, the stranger nodded at the fire. "We could use some coffee. We 'ave traveled far." At Jesse's scowl, he laughed and added, "I will not seeng, *mon ami.*"

Jesse's gaze didn't waver. "What's your name, friend?"

The stranger's eyebrows went up in mock affront. "Ees a personal question for such a short acquaintance, no? But because the smell of your coffee stirs my 'unger, I weel tell you. My name ees Bouchard. Marcel Bouchard. Thees ees Raven, my woman." The squaw's gaze slid apathetically between Jesse and Mariah. The dewclaws decorating her blue cloth dress rattled with her every breath in the eerie silence.

"Surely we can offer them coffee," Mariah said quietly. "There's plenty. It would be rude to turn them away, wouldn't it?"

"No one ever died of rudeness," Jesse answered in a low voice.

"Don't be silly. They're just traveling like us," she whispered emphatically. "Where's the harm?"

Jesse sighed deeply, considering the logic of what she'd said. He lowered his rifle and nodded toward the fire. "You're welcome to a cup. Mariah, see if the coffee is brewed yet."

Pierre LaRousse smiled at the ease with which they'd accepted his lie. He dismounted slowly, leaving his hands visible to the pair. His gaze took in the man's blond, sunstreaked hair, his clear blue eyes and full beard. Something was wrong. Unless Downing and Daniels had been drunk when they'd seen the man called Devereaux, this wasn't him. Yet, he puzzled, he traveled with the woman. The one named Mariah. *Jesu!* He would slit Downing's throat if he'd sent him on a fool's errand.

149

It mattered little. He would find out if this was the one and, if not, he would kill them anyway. From the looks of the packs stacked on the ground nearby, there was a winter's fortune in pelts inside.

Motioning Raven off her mount, LaRousse's gaze went to the horses grazing nearby. Three riding horses and two mules.

Three.

His blood pumped harder. There was another one, but where? He swept the clearing with an intensive glance.

"Are you headed south?" Jesse asked, pouring two tin mugs of coffee.

Distracted, LaRousse swiveled his gaze back to Jesse. "East, to zee the Musselshell," he lied easily. "To my woman's people."

Jesse squinted against the setting sun and studied the design of Raven's dress. He handed them each a cup of coffee. "She's of the Blood tribe, isn't she?"

LaRousse took a sip, watching him over the rim of the cup. "You 'ave good eyes, *mon ami.*"

Jesse spoke to Raven in her own tongue. "I know some Bloods down on the Musselshell. Eagle Plume and his brother, Running Crane. Do you know them?"

Raven's eyes widened and her whole body seemed to surge forward, though she didn't take a step. "Ah!"

Before she could say more, Bouchard jarred her elbow and she splashed hot coffee down the front of her dress. Raven leapt backward, swiping at the elkskin and glancing up at the man in real fear.

The look Bouchard gave her sent a chill down Jesse's spine. Swallowing hard, Jesse passed the squaw the towel in his hand to blot the hot liquid.

"Are you all right?" Mariah asked.

Jesse doubted the squaw understood, but a solicitous tone was solicitous in any language and the woman's dark eyes met hers almost gratefully.

"Ah, she ees beautiful, no?" Bouchard said, lifting his hands in a gesture of futility toward Raven, "but clumsy, *Gauche, c'est vrai, mon chou?*"

The squaw did not bother to respond, but stared intensively at the ground. Jesse noticed the dark bruise around her left eye and wondered if it was the mark of the Frenchman's fist. Something tightened in his gut at the sight.

"Women," Bouchard went on. "A man must protect someseeng so beautiful so deep in ze mountains, no, *monsieur?"* Bouchard looked directly at Mariah. "You 'ave not told me your names yet."

"My name's Winslow. This is Miss Parsons."

Bouchard nodded, his eyes raking Mariah slowly from the toes up. "Ees a dangerous country for a *femme* with skeen the color of bleached antelope 'ide, no?" Taking in her unconventional clothing he added, "Even one as unique as thees."

"I'm perfectly safe, Mr. Bouchard," she said, unperturbed by his tone. "Especially traveling with—"

"How about a cup, Mariah?" Jesse asked, cutting her off rudely.

She opened her mouth to say so, but snapped it shut again at his strange look. "Why . . . why, no, thank you. I don't drink coffee, you know that, Jesse." His blue eyes spoke volumes, but about what she couldn't imagine.

"I meant me," he said.

"Oh . . . oh, well, of course." With her hand wrapped in her over-long sleeve, she poured a steaming cup. Handing it to him, she tried to discern his unfathomable expression, but failed.

"Thanks," he said, taking the cup. His gaze slid back to the stranger. Bouchard spoke sharply to the squaw in words Mariah couldn't make out; Raven got up and gathered the reins of the two horses, taking them to the stream for water. As she walked, Mariah noticed she seemed to be looking for something in the forest nearby. A flicker of warning skittered down her spine. She glanced at Jesse.

His mouth was a thin line. Perhaps she shouldn't have interfered when he'd advised the pair to move on. She didn't care much for the half-breed or the way he treated his wife and the tension between the two men was so thick it was nearly palpable.

Bouchard gave an exaggerated sigh and stretched his legs out in front of him. "Ahh-h. Ze coffee, madame, eet ees good."

"Then it should go down quickly," Jesse replied with thinly veiled hostility.

The man regarded him with a cool, inscrutable smile. "I'm in no 'urry, *mon ami,*" he replied. "No 'urry at all."

Chapter Eleven

Creed pulled the line up and examined the water-logged earthworm dangling from the hook. The creature wriggled futilely against its barb. Creed cursed and tossed it back into the deep pool, tightening his fingers around the line. He'd hoped at least his bad luck could be explained by lost bait—even that excuse had failed him.

He'd expected the fish to be biting at this time of day. A grandfather trout had been taunting him from the shallows, but had refused so much as a nibble.

The wolf paced nearby, here and there investigating the burrow of some animal with her snout. Above, a jay squawked noisily, fluttering from branch to branch in agitation. Creed ignored it, concentrating instead on the concentric circles of water stirred by the fishing line. The ever-widening ripples shimmered in the half-light of dusk.

He stared at his distorted reflection in the water and scowled, thanking how like those spreading circles his life had become. He was tired of running.

For the first time in years, he was tired of being alone. For the first time, he pinned a name to the feeling . . . he was lonely. He hadn't imagined he would ever admit that, even to himself. But he'd been wrong.

Mariah had proved him wrong.

Creed slid his fingers along the smooth silk line absently, glad he was here and not back at camp watching her like the fool he was. *Dieu*. He couldn't seem to help himself where she was concerned. The past few days had been hell. Being near her, but unable to touch her. He'd watched her a thousand times a day: the graceful curve of her neck when she bent over the fire; her easy laugh at Jesse's rollicking tales; the still perfection of her face when she was lost in thought.

She was the kind of woman who conjured up thoughts of settling — children, hearth, and home. Dreams he'd never dared to dream. She wasn't like any of the women he'd known, or ever imagined.

He wasn't good enough for her. He knew that. It didn't matter. She possessed his thoughts during the day and stirred a fever in his body at night. Some nights he lay staring at the stars, his body hard and aching for her. Sleep was hard to come by and when he did find it, he dreamed of her. Dreamed of holding her and covering her mouth with his and — he closed his eyes — and more.

Every day, he thanked God that Jesse had chosen to ride with them. If it weren't for him, Creed wondered how he would have kept away from her this long. He cursed the weakness of his body and his resolve. He was a bastard for wanting her and a fool for letting her come.

That thought led inevitably to another more disturbing one — Seth. The thought of seeing his old friend again in only a few days gave him a sick feeling in the pit of his stomach. If Seth had survived his illness — and he prayed to God he had — he would be waiting for his bride. Trusting Creed to bring her safe and sound, and in one piece.

He damn well would. He would give Mariah over to him and ride out of Virginia City with all due haste. He wouldn't stay around to see her married to his best friend.

154

A cool wind stirred the conifer branches above, sifting through the arrow-straight needles. A sound, a low droning buzz, began in the air. Creed's whole body grew taut, alert. He glanced at Mahkwi who seemed not to hear it.

The silk line gave a hard tug against his fingers, but he hardly noticed it. The buzz echoed in his head like the wingbeats of a thousand bees. He pressed a palm against his right ear to stop it. Straightening, he searched the darkening shadows of the trees, but knew with sudden certainty the sound came from within.

The silk tugged again, more insistently, and Creed stared at his hand as if it were no longer part of him.

Merde! He was losing his mind! It was his own heartbeat pounding in his ears.

He jumped to his feet, dropping the line in the water, and watched the grandfather trout escape like a ribbon of green into the dark shadows. Mahkwi flinched at his sudden movement and stared at him with ears pricked forward.

Suddenly, he knew. *Mariah.*

At a run, Creed scooped his rifle up and tore through the underbrush—following the river, ducking below branches, vaulting over rocks and fallen tree trunks in his path. Mahkwi shot by him in a blur, then stopped and waited for him to catch up, enjoying the running game.

But it wasn't a game.

Creed's feet skimmed the spongy ground with a rhythmic pounding, but he could only hear the rasp of his breath and the droning buzz of warning clanging in his ears. *Mariah!*

How far had he come downriver? He tried to gauge it in his mind. A mile? Two? He couldn't remember. He'd been walking just to get her out of his head.

Faster. Faster.

Ahead he could see only trees and river—nothing

that would confirm his fears. He restrained the urge to call out to her and Jesse to warn them. Of what? He didn't know exactly. But flashes of an image—obsidian eyes, an oversized silver cross—flickered through his mind the way a cloud's shadow dappled sunlit grass. His heart thudded.

Mon Dieu, don't let me be too late.

He ran for what seemed like hours, but he knew only a few minutes had passed. Suddenly Mahkwi slowed and stopped, silver mane and tail stiff with attention. Creed dropped down beside her next to the thick huckleberry hedge and forced the wolf down with a hand signal he'd seen Jesse use. A flash of red amongst the spindly trunks of lodgepole pine forty feet ahead was what had caught the wolf's eye.

His breath came in harsh rasps, not as much from exertion as from fear. Tightening his hands around the stock of his Henry, he slid the safety off and cocked the trigger with a nearly silent click and peered over the branches.

Crouched behind his cover, the man with his back to Creed wore a filthy red union suit, torn and patched at both elbows, and a pair of suspendered woolsey pants. His hat was tilted back on his head and his rifle braced casually against the ground. Creed shouldered his gun. He could kill him from here. One shot.

As he took a bead on him, the man leaned over and spit a brown stream of tobacco juice and wiped his mouth with the back of his sleeve.

When he did, Creed saw what the man was watching. Fifty feet beyond, Mariah and Jesse were standing in the campsite with two others. A squaw and a man. They were sitting drinking coffee like old friends! Creed couldn't make out their faces, but he knew. He knew who they were.

Le Diable.

Creed scanned the trees. A scant hundred feet from

the first man was another and beyond him still another. God knew how many more hovered like coyotes waiting for the kill.

Damn, damn, damn!

He lowered the rifle. To use it now would mean instant death for Mariah and Jesse. No, he had to find a way to lessen the odds against them. Propping the rifle against the dense berry branches, Creed withdrew the knife from the sheath at his belt. He glanced at Mahkwi. A low growl rumbled in her throat.

Creed placed a silencing hand over her muzzle. "Stay," he told her, but he had little hope she would. If Jesse was threatened, nothing short of death would keep her from him. Creed was sure of that. But he hoped she would give him the time to do what he had to. Then she might prove just the distraction he needed.

He started toward the red-shirted man on silent feet. Tightening his hand around the deerhorn grip of his knife, he emptied his mind of all thoughts but one.

Revenge.

Through the smoke of the campfire, Mariah glanced at Raven, who hadn't touched her cup since she'd been scalded. She was surprised to find the girl watching her. Raven's eyes widened deliberately, then she flashed a look into the forest to her left. Mariah frowned and followed her glance at the dusky forest and saw nothing but the thick timber surrounding them.

Feeling suddenly uneasy, her gaze returned to Raven, but the squaw was staring at the ground again. Mariah twined her fingers together in her lap. Bouchard drained the last of his coffee and set his tin mug on the ground in front of him.

"You are a trader, no?"

"I do some trading," Jesse answered guardedly.

157

"I am interested in some skeens. Per'aps you could show me what you 'ave. Eef zey are good, per'aps I buy."

"These skins are spoken for."

Bouchard frowned. "Zat ees too bad. My woman wants to make a winter robe for me from soft beaver pelts. From the looks of your packs, you 'ave what I want."

"I said they're spoken for."

"Ah, *oui.* So you said. You go to ze gulch, *mon ami,* to sell to ze diggers of gold?"

"Maybe."

"Maybe." He chuckled. "A cautious man. I like thees een a man. One can never be too careful." He straightened the thick leather belt that circled his Hudson blanket coat. "Myself, I always like to know where I stand, what I am up against. So, I ask you, *mon ami,* where ees your companion?"

Mariah felt Jesse go rigid beside her.

"Companion?"

The stranger tipped his head toward the cropping horses. "Three horses . . . three saddles . . . I seenk you are not alone 'ere."

Jesse's face darkened and Mariah watched the possibilities flicker behind his sky blue eyes. "They're all mine," he lied. "I won the third one in a game of cutthroat up on the Marius, outfit and all."

Mariah blinked at Jesse, wondering why he hadn't told the man about Creed. If, as she was beginning to suspect, this man meant them harm, why wouldn't Jesse tell him there was another man close by, ready to come to their aid?

"Poker, eh?" Bouchard considered this with an amused chuckle. He drained the last of his coffee and set it down on the ground precisely. "I seenk you are not good enough at ze bluff to win at cards, *mon ami.*"

Jesse eyed him coolly, refusing to be baited. "Believe whatever you want."

The stranger got to his feet. "I believe you are a liar, *monsieur*."

Jesse rose simultaneously, rifle in hand, his eyes narrowed with anger. "I don't give a bloody damn what you believe—"

Mariah grabbed his arm, terrified by the escalating tension. "Jesse, please—"

"—You're done with your coffee, now get out of my camp." He pointed the gun at Bouchard. Raven took a step back, looking nervously to either side.

Bouchard's lips curled into a smile as he spread his hands wide. "Ah, I am afraid not just yet, *mon ami*. We 'ave matters to discuss."

Jesse cocked the rifle. "No, we don't."

"Ees a very foolish thing you are doing."

"I don't think so."

"Ah, but eet ees. I 'ave five guns trained on your beautiful woman 'ere at thees very moment. Eef you kill me, she ees dead." He cocked his finger in an imitation of a gun and dropped his thumb. "Boom."

Oh, my God. "J-Jesse—"

The color drained from his face. His gaze darted to the darkening forest around them, then back.

LaRousse's laugh was grim. "You don't believe I am stupid enough to come alone, eh, *mon ami?*" He sent a small nod to the forest beyond and several approaching shapes took form in the firelight. One by one, like rats fleeing a scuttled ship, they appeared from the darkness.

A huge, bearded man wearing filthy, sun-faded clothes and a bandolier across one shoulder lumbered out of the gloom holding a shiny new repeating rifle.

From the other side, through a thicket of ferns, emerged a full-blooded Indian dressed in flesh-hugging animal skins with a huge knife sheathed at his waist. Two streaks of ocher slashed his cheeks. His dark eyes caught the firelight and glimmered like shiny wet stones.

A shorter, scruffy-looking man who was undoubtedly white-skinned under all that grime and hair came from the other direction.

Jesse's steely fingers tightened around her arm, but that did nothing to quell the tremor that went through her, making her knees wobble like so much gelatin. "Wh-what do you want from us?" she blurted to no one in particular.

"Devereaux," came the half-breed's savage reply.

Her pulse staggered. *Creed? What could they possibly want with him?* Then she remembered. He was a bounty hunter, with untold numbers of enemies — men who'd just as soon see him dead as look at him. A dull thudding started in her head and she shot a furtive glance upriver. Where *was* he?

Mariah nearly gagged from the unwashed smell of the two men who stood on either side of them with guns pointed at their heads. The Indian yanked the rifle out of Jesse's hands, tossed it to Raven, and jerked Jesse's arms brutally behind him. The giant pushed Mariah to the ground with a surprisingly easy one-armed shove. She skidded down on all fours with a gasp of surprise, but the heavy denim encasing her legs saved her knees from a nasty scrape.

"Dammit, she has no part in this," Jesse growled. "Leave her alone, LaRousse."

She started to reassure him that she was all right but his words stopped her. Scrambling to her feet, Mariah stared at him in confusion. *Did he say LaRousse? As in Étienne LaRousse — the man Creed had killed at the levee?* A sick feeling settled in the pit of her stomach. God in heaven, she was beginning to understand.

LaRousse grinned savagely at Jesse. "So, you know me."

"I should have guessed sooner. A snake can change his name, but not his colors," he spat. The Indian yanked upward on Jesse's arms, causing him to grunt in pain.

A knife appeared in LaRousse's fist as if by sleight of hand. He brought the blade up under Jesse's chin and pressed it against his throat. "Perhaps you will be ze one to shed hees skin tonight, eh? You see, you are out-manned, *mon ami*."

"Are you so sure?" Jesse asked tipping his head back away from the blade. "You said five guns. I only see three."

LaRousse's smile faltered. "Bennett," he snapped at the behemoth standing over Mariah. "Where are Blevins and Poke?"

"Hell if I know," he said, rubbing his hairy chin. "Ain't seen 'em since we split up."

LaRousse made an irritated noise between his teeth and scanned the darkness. It was then Mariah noticed the air around them had gone utterly still, but for the sigh of wind through the tops of the pines. Not a bird nor evening cricket disturbed the unnatural hush. A slight tic in his eye was all that betrayed LaRousse's uneasiness. He withdrew a pistol from beneath his woolen coat and turned back to Jesse.

"Tell me where Devereaux went."

Jesse's eyebrows raised fractionally. "Go to hell."

LaRousse drew his arm back and smashed his pistol across Jesse's face with a brutal crack.

"Oh!" Mariah gasped, horrified, as Jesse's head rocked back from the blow. Blood oozed from the cut beside his eye and a terrible welt rose immediately from his cheekbone. He staggered against his captor, then shook his head to clear his vision.

"Stop it!" she screamed, but the giant snatched her collar and yanked her back from the three men.

"Eet serves you nossing to 'old back, *monsieur*. In fact, eet could prove quite painful eef you do. Tell me where 'ee went."

161

"Bugger off . . ."

A knee connected sharply with Jesse's crotch, lifting him off the ground. His breath came out in a whoosh and his face went starkly white.

"Tell me."

Jesse gagged for air. Blood trickled down his cheek into the corner of his mouth. Gathering his strength, he spat it out on LaRousse's boot.

Pierre LaRousse's eyes widened with rage and he struck him again across the face, even harder this time. This time Jesse let out a howl of pain. His knees buckled and he slumped in the Indian's arms.

"No-oo!" Mariah screamed, only to feel the filthy hand of the giant smother her protest. She bucked wildly in his grip, but it was like struggling against a solid wall of steel. She screamed Creed's name against the giant's hand.

"*Merde!*" LaRousse stared at the limp figure on the ground, furious with himself for letting his anger outweigh his need for information. "Running Fox—get some water, wake 'eem up."

Tears stung her eyes. *This can't be happening! They mean to kill us. Oh, Creed!*

She wrenched again, but the giant's grip shifted until it almost completely covered her nostrils, too. Frantic, she clawed at his hand and kicked at his shins to no effect. He wrapped his other arm across her breast and lifted her off the ground until her feet dangled in the air. Blood pounded in her ears and she blinked at the black spots threatening her vision.

Dimly, she became aware of another sound: the thudding crash of something coming at a terrifying speed directly toward them. Owing to the darkness she could not make it out until a blur of silver and black exploded out of the trees and landed on LaRousse in a snarling ball of muscle and fur.

LaRousse's gawp of surprise was cut short by the impact. His pistol arched into the darkness as he and the creature struggled to the grass, his hands wholly occupied with the business of protecting his throat from the attacking wolf.

Pandemonium erupted all around. Startled oaths sprang from LaRousse's men. Running Fox backed furiously for the cover of the thick ferns to the right. The man called Downing, who'd been nearly hit in the attack, bobbled his gun and scrabbled crab-like on the ground to get out of reach of the snarling mass of fury at LaRousse's throat.

"Don't just stand there, Bennett, you twiddle-brain oaf!" Downing shouted at the hairy giant who still had Mariah in his smothering grip. "Shoot it!" Obligingly, Bennett flung her aside with all the accord he might give a dirty rag.

Mariah bounced along the needle-covered ground and sprawled to a stop mere inches from the fire. Despite the intense heat, she could not gather the strength to move or do any more than gulp precious air into her lungs.

The sound of a gunshot accompanied Bennett's howl of pain. She turned to see him whirl sideways, reaching futilely for the blossom of red spreading across his lower back. His disbelieving glare was aimed at Raven. The smoking gun wavered in her shaking hands.

"You—" Bennett growled thickly, too stunned to do more than stumble toward her in a parody of a lunge.

Raven aimed the rifle again and pulled the trigger, but the hammer clacked harmlessly against an empty chamber. She backed up two steps into a wall of rock. There was no terror on her face, but rather a serene acceptance of her fate as Bennett ripped the gun out of her hands and brought the butt end down on her. She ducked at the last second and he hit her hard on the shoulder instead of her skull. But a second jab caught her solidly against the jaw. Raven

163

dropped like a sack of stones to the ground.

Mariah didn't waste time wondering why the woman had joined their side of the fight. She got to her hands and knees and started toward LaRousse's pistol that lay a few feet away.

Flinging herself the last five feet, her fingers closed around the gun. But before she could pick it up, a hand yanked her sideways and dragged her into the thick ferns. Startled into complete inertia, Mariah couldn't see her assailant in the dark, but she could feel the strong length of him against her. Black spots again whirled before her eyes and a sickening sense of dread sank to the pit of her stomach.

"For God's sake, Mariah," came the desperate whisper next to her ear, "get out of the way!"

Creed. She turned in his arms. His face, hidden by shadows, was only inches from hers. "Creed! Where have you — ?"

He clapped a hand over her mouth. "Shut up and don't move from this spot," he ordered and abruptly disappeared.

Shivering, Mariah pushed herself up on her elbows to see where he went. But her hand bumped something solid and warm. She would have screamed, but her throat was too dry. She slapped a hand over her mouth to keep from being sick. It was the Indian, Running Fox, his dead eyes staring at the black night sky. His throat had been cut from ear to ear. In the thin moonlight, his blood looked thick and black against his dark skin.

Swallowing hard, she backed away, scooting further into the deep thicket of ferns. Her knee encountered the narrow pipe-bones and trade beads of Creed's choker. Her fingers closed around it and she held it to her breast.

Across the clearing, Mahkwi yelped in pain and rolled off LaRousse when Bennett clubbed her across

164

the back with the stock of Jesse's rifle. Two shots exploded out of the darkness and jerked the huge man sideways. He teetered like a broken tree and crashed to the ground.

LaRousse sprang to his feet. One side of his face was streaming with blood and the buckskin sleeve of his shirt was a mass of crimson slashes. Chest heaving, he stumbled toward the horses. From her vantage point, Mariah could see the one called Downing was already chasing down Raven's spooked pinto, frantically hopping for the stirrup.

Creed emerged out of the darkness with his gun pointed at the half-breed. "LaRousse!" he bellowed.

The man stopped in his tracks at the sound of Creed's voice. LaRousse glanced over his shoulder, but kept his back intentionally turned toward Creed, spreading his hands wide.

"Ah . . . so . . . *eet ees* you, Devereaux. You are harder to keel than I thought. I see you still bear ze mark I put on you, many years ago. Eet's a fine brand, no, for ze son of a wife-stealer?"

"Turn around." Creed's command was a deep, almost animal growl.

"I am . . . unarmed." He lifted his hands in a mock gesture of helplessness. "You would . . . shoot an unarmed man . . . in ze back?"

Mariah saw the momentary flicker of indecision cross Creed's sweat-slick face and her heart sank. With a bloodlust as foreign to her as this horrible country, she wanted Creed to pull the trigger and kill him for what he'd done.

Creed took a step forward, teeth bared like a wild animal, and thumbed the hammer of his revolver back with an ominous click. At the same moment, Downing exploded out of the darkness atop Raven's shrieking horse, coming directly at Creed.

Mariah screamed a warning—too late.

He only had time to duck and pull his arms protectively in front of his face before the horse collided with him at a full gallop. The wall of horseflesh hit him like a loaded freight wagon. His gun went off reflexively, and the bullet sliced through air. Only luck saved him from being trampled. Instead, the impact sent him flying ten feet into the air. He landed hard and rolled through the ferns.

By the time his spinning surroundings ground to a halt, he heard another horse bearing down on him. LaRousse's demon-like figure was silhouetted by the firelight, the shadows making the excitement on his face more grotesque.

There was nowhere to go. He could only watch the horse come as he braced for the inevitable impact. But another gunshot erupted out of the darkness. A startled LaRousse jerked, then bobbled in the saddle with a groan. The sudden tug on the reins diverted the horse so that instead of being trampled, Creed felt the stir of air churned up by the hooves.

Clinging to his horse's neck, the half-breed pounded out of the clearing and was instantly swallowed up by the inky night.

Creed's racing blood demanded that he follow the bastard, chase him down like a wounded badger and finish him off. But common sense prevailed. He'd left Mariah once tonight and look what had happened. Yet, like the fading hoofbeats of LaRousse's horse, the buzz in his ears still hummed like a distant memory.

Merde.

Breathing hard, Creed ran a shaking hand through his hair and sat up. His searching gaze started with the carnage around him and ended on the smoking gun dangling from Mariah's hand.

Chapter Twelve

She looked pale—too pale even in the color-robbing moonlight. Creed watched the gun slip from Mariah's fingers and drop with a dull thud to the ground. She sat down hard before he could get to her. Incredibly, she didn't faint but sat staring into the darkness.

"Mariah—" Creed sank down beside her, wrapped his arms around her trembling body, and held her close. *"Mon Dieu,* are you all right?" Comfortingly, his hand stroked the silken hair at the nape of her neck. Her arms went around him, too, searching for something solid to hang onto. He noticed, with no surprise, that her trembling echoed the shaking of his own body.

She opened her mouth and closed it several times before she could speak. "I sh-shot him. I . . . I shot a man."

"Ah, *oui.* You did well, *ma petite.* He would have killed me."

Without thinking, Mariah tightened her arms around his broad shoulders and buried her face against his chest, unable to get close enough. He smelled of woodsmoke, leather, and sweat and she filled her lungs with his reassuring scent. With a sobbing laugh, she said, "I d-didn't think I could hit him. But I wanted to. God help me, Creed. I tried to kill him."

"Shh-h. It's all right. You did what you had to. It was too dark to see where you hit him exactly, but you did some damage."

"I think I . . . hit him in the shoulder, but the . . . the gun jerked when I fired it. It almost knocked me over." She shuddered again. "Oh, Creed, he was a horrible man." She pressed a fist to her mouth trying to keep from being sick.

"Oui," Creed murmured through gritted teeth, stroking her hair. "Perhaps, if we're lucky, you've killed him."

"He wanted *you,* Creed. He came here to find you."

"I know. I'm sorry. Sorry you were caught in this."

"Caught in what? Why did he want to hurt you?"

"I killed his brother."

"The man at the fort? What did he do? Was there a bounty on his head? Is that why you killed him?"

Creed swallowed. "They're outlaws, Mariah. Both of them. Pierre is the worst of the lot."

There was more to it than what he was telling her. Something personal. *You're harder to kill than I thought,* LaRousse had said, and something about Creed being *the son of a wife-stealer.*

What did that mean?

Mariah wanted to ask him, but it was clearly none of her business. It hurt that he didn't trust her enough by now to tell her but it was plain that he didn't. She wasn't about to degrade herself by begging him for answers.

A low moan brought both their heads around toward the fire. Batting away the entreating tongue of the wolf who lay hunched beside his master, Jesse groaned and had rolled to a half-sitting position by the time they'd reached him.

One hand cradled the bloody side of his face and the other hand was sunk into the wolf's thick fur. His left eye was swollen shut and his cheek was swollen like a small lemon.

"Oh, Jesse . . ." Mariah murmured, laying a hand on his arm. "Look at you. I'll go wet a cloth in the river. The cold water should help some with the swelling."

"Oh, hell," he muttered almost unintelligibly as Mariah hurried off to search through the saddlebags for a cloth. He glanced up at Creed through his good eye. "I'm still alive. That's a surprise." He grimaced and fingered his bloody cheek gingerly. "Glad to see you made it to our little tea party, Creed." He moaned again and rolled painfully to his knees, hanging his head down between his splayed arms. "Ohh-h, I don't think I can . . . get up."

Just stay where you are for a few minutes," Creed ordered, pushing him back down to a sitting position. Tipping Jesse's head back, Creed examined it in the flickering light of the fire. *"Pardieu,* Jesse, I think he broke your cheek."

Jesse swallowed hard, looking a little green around the edges. "I've had worse. Frankly," he admitted, pressing a fist low on his abdomen, "at the moment . . . I'm more concerned with . . . another . . . part of my anatomy. That bastard's got a mean knee."

Creed tried to hide his grin. "Maybe we should have Mariah bring a wet cloth for that, too."

Jesse met his grin and winced at the pain in his cheek. "At this point, I'd take it and to hell with propriety." For the first time, Jesse's gaze took in the bodies sprawled around him. "Good God. Are they all dead?"

"LaRousse and one of his other men got away, but Mariah managed to put a slug into Pierre on the way out."

Jesse's blue eyes darkened. "Bloody hell. That breed walked in here cool as a skunk in the moonlight singin' some French love song to the trees." He cradled his forehead in his palm. "I should have listened to that little voice warning me. I never should have let him get off the damn horse. I mean, the man has eyes that would make an icicle feel feverish. But he came in with a woman, for God's sake. Hey, what happened to her anyway?"

Creed glanced around to find the Indian woman lying unconscious a few yards away and he walked over to her.

"Is she . . . dead?" Mariah asked, approaching with the dripping cloths.

"Unconscious," he answered, scooping the limp woman into his arms. He brought her over close to the fire and laid her carefully on the ground. She had a nasty bruise on her chin and the bones in her shoulder didn't feel too stable. Creed frowned down at her, wondering what they'd do with the outlaw's woman.

"She shot that . . . that man, Bennett, and saved Mahkwi," Mariah said, breaking into his thoughts. "Probably the rest of us, too."

That surprised him. Creed hadn't seen it. He'd had his hands full with the Indian at the time. Creed patted the squaw down, searching for concealed weapons and finally pulled a knife from a thong tied around her thigh. He tucked it into his belt. "Don't turn your back on her. We don't know anything about her yet. When she wakes up, we'll decide what to do with her."

Mariah nodded and turned to Jesse. "You're a sight," she said, shaking her head. "I thought . . . I was afraid he'd killed you."

He made a grumbling sound deep in his chest. "To be honest, so did I."

"God forgive me, I—I wish I'd killed him." She felt the blood drain from her face at the bitterness of her words. "I'm sorry. I was so scared for you, for all of us."

Jesse nodded. "Pierre LaRousse isn't the kind to make idle threats. He meant to kill us as sure as we're sittin' here. If Creed hadn't come along, he would have found my packs of pelts excuse enough to do it. Don't feel guilty for defending yourself. You should be proud."

She couldn't bring herself to reply. How could she be proud of almost killing a man, despite everything that had happened. It went against everything she'd been taught, everything she believed. Yet, she'd been ready to kill to save Creed's life. And the most frightening thing was she knew she'd do it again.

Gently she cleaned the blood off Jesse's face, dabbing at the jagged split next to his eye. The whole area was coming up a purplish blue. Her hand was still shaking noticeably when she produced the bottle of bacanora and soaked one corner of her cloth. She hesitated next to his face. "This is going to sting a bit."

"Ouch!" Jesse pulled away from her touch, then grinned contritely. "Sorry. That hurts."

"I'm sorry, too, because I think you'll need some stitches in that. Are you up to it?"

Jesse took the flask from her, tipped it upside down and took a long pull. "I have some trade-needles in my pack, wrapped in a piece of deerskin . . . between the, uh, bolts of blue cloth and . . ." —he winced, touching a fingertip to his cheek—"the cooking pans. I'm out of thread, but you can pluck a hair from my mule's tail. It'll do."

"All right." Mariah met Creed's gaze when she looked up. He was looking at her strangely, the way he had so many times in the past few days, in a way that made her insides go warm and her heart thud faster. Then, her gaze dropped of its own accord to his throat.

Her eyes widened at the sight of the scar on his neck. Free from the choker that had been torn from him by the Indian, she saw at last why he chose to keep his throat hidden. It was, without question, a scar made by a rope, a rope that had evidently failed to do its job well. He was alive, though someone had certainly meant to kill him.

Shock settled into her at the thought of Creed dangling from a rope, but she forced the thought away. He was staring at the ground, not wanting to look her in the eye. It struck her that he was embarrassed by the scar. She wanted to reach up and touch it to prove to him it was nothing, but she sensed he would never let her that close. And Jesse was watching.

Carefully keeping her expression blank, she took the bone and bead choker out of her pocket and handed it to him. "The leather thong is broken, but I can fix it if you want."

He stared at the necklace, turning it over in his hand, then looked up at her. *"Merci.* Where'd you find it?"

"Near the Indian. I'll be right back with the needles." Mariah felt his gaze as she gathered what she needed, including the strand of mule hair, and set to work on Jesse's eye. As she worked, she pondered the scar on Creed's throat and wondered if LaRousse had had anything to do with it. A chill went up her spine at the thought.

The bacanora muted Jesse's pain and he sat patiently waiting for her to finish. He would have a scar to remember this day by, she mused grimly, but she'd done the best she could under the circumstances. She got up and walked back to where the packs were stacked under a stand of lodgepole.

From the corner of her eye, she saw the woman by the fire move. She'd rolled onto her hands and knees and was crawling toward the ferns.

"Raven, stop—" Mariah cried out.

"Nayeyah! Nayeyah!" She got to her feet and crouched with one arm in front of her face. Her other arm, she held close to her waist.

"No, please wait, I won't hurt you!" Motioning to Creed, who had gotten to his feet, she walked slowly over to her.

"Be careful, Mariah."

"Shh-h," Mariah soothed. "No one's going to hurt you anymore."

Raven slumped back to the ground clutching her shoulder. Her head rocked back and forth against the ground. *"Aski-kiwa . . . aski-kiwa,"* she whispered over and over in a half-chant. *"Aski-kiwa."*

Bewildered, Mariah looked at Jesse. "What's she saying?"

Jesse swallowed hard and met Mariah's eyes. "It's a

Blackfoot Defiance Song. It means . . . 'I care for nothing'. She intends to die."

"Die—" Mariah echoed incredulously, glancing down at the terrible bloody bruise on the woman's chin and the shoulder she clutched. "But . . . do you think she's mortally wounded?"

"I doubt it, unless you mean her spirit. She's given up. I expect that's why she sacrificed herself tonight for our sakes. Life with Pierre LaRousse . . ." Jesse hesitated, "from what I saw tonight, was . . . unpleasant at best."

"No doubt she was with him unwillingly," Creed observed. "LaRousse is half-Sioux. I doubt any self-respecting Blackfoot maiden would go with him except under duress . . . or desperation." He glanced up at Jesse. "I speak Blackfoot, but it's been a while. Can you make yourself understood by her?"

Jesse nodded. "If she'll talk to me."

Jesse's first attempts were met with stoic silence. Raven refused to reply, though eventually she did stop the chanting and stared watchfully at them. With his hand he tentatively brushed the sweep of black hair back when it fell across her cheek. Raven flinched and one tear escaped and slid down toward her ear.

The evening wind sang through the high pines with a soothing whistle. Mahkwi limped over to where they were sitting and dropped down beside Jesse with his head on the man's leg. Finally, Raven started to talk in low, halting syllables. Jesse and Creed fell silent, listening.

"Well?" Mariah asked when she had stopped talking. "What did she say?"

"She is Raven's Wing, of the Kainahs or Blood Tribe on the Musselshell River," Jesse replied. "Her father, Yellow Shirt, was killed in battle with the Crees, or the Liars, as they call them, during the Berries-Ripe-Moon last July. Raven and her mother were hit hard by his loss, for he was considered a great man in his tribe.

173

When her mother grew ill with grief, Raven decided to make a sacrifice to the Sun for her parents."

"A sacrifice?" Mariah asked.

"It's part of her religion. She took a fine white wolf pelt she had tanned for that purpose and her best elk-teeth-trimmed gown and left camp to find the proper tree to hang them in. She traveled a few miles from camp before she found the right one and there she hung it. She sat praying for her mother to recover from her grief and for her father's spirit's safe journey to the Above People.

"Among Indians," he went on, "not even an enemy would dare disturb such a Sun Gift, nor the bearer of it. But Pierre LaRousse and his men happened upon her while she was alone there. Apparently, to no one's surprise, religion and tribal customs have no meaning to a man like him. He stole the pelt and kidnapped Raven. She has been with him ever since as his woman. No one knew where she had gone. Her people must think her dead.

"In her heart," Jesse said, bowing his head, "she believes that, too. LaRousse used her badly. She thinks we mean to kill her and she will welcome that."

Mariah shuddered and watched Raven turn her head in shame as Jesse related her story. "Has she no one now? What of her mother?"

"She doesn't know what became of her, but I know her father's people are still on the Musselshell. She told me she was promised to a young brave named Wolverine. She was in love with him. She is sure he looked for her but couldn't find her. LaRousse knows how to cover his tracks."

Mariah looked at Creed. "How far is it to her people?"

"Two, maybe three days, and," he added pointedly, "across the span of the Missouri."

"I'll take her."

Mariah and Creed both looked at Jesse.

"The tribe's summer camp is just south of the mouth of the Judith on the Musselshell," he said. "If she'll go, I'll take her there. And I'll meet you in Virginia City in a week or so."

Mariah noticed Creed stiffen and look away. She imagined it would be hard for him to say goodbye to Jesse after such a short time together. They were close friends.

Jesse spoke to Raven for a few more minutes and in the end, she reluctantly agreed to return. She tried to sit again and a low moan escaped her and she went pale.

"I think her collarbone is broken," Mariah said after fingering the spot gently. "And her jaw is badly bruised, but I don't think it's fractured. Creed, if you'll fetch what's left of my petticoat from the saddlebags, I'll tear it into strips to bind her shoulder."

Creed fetched the article and handed it to her. "You know how to set bones, Mariah?"

"I certainly watched my father do it enough and I set a few soldiers' bones at the hospital where I worked the past few years," she said, avoiding his eyes.

Creed's lips fell open. "You worked at a hospital? Seth never mentioned —"

"I never told him," she replied briskly. "Hand me that strip over there." She soaked it with bacanora and dabbed it against Raven's jaw. Raven was silent but watched Mariah closely. "There's not much to be done for a collarbone except to try to brace it back so it can heal. I'll bind her arm to her chest so she won't be tempted to use it. Jesse, you'll have to see that she doesn't."

Jesse exchanged a look with Raven and spoke to her in Blackfoot. She moistened her dry lips with her tongue, eyed Mariah warily, then nodded.

"Good," Mariah told her with a small smile, then sighed deeply. "Now . . . if you gentlemen will excuse us?"

* * *

That night, Mariah woke with a cry and sat bolt upright in the darkness. Her breath came hard and fast. In her dream, she'd been kissing Seth, but his face had changed to Creed's as her mouth met his. She could still feel the tingle his touch provoked, coursing through her like a current.

She looked wildly around her to find Raven, Jesse, and even Mahkwi sleeping calmly beside her. Then, as surely as a compass needle finds true north, she turned to see him sitting on a rock with his rifle slung carelessly across his knees, a lit cigarette dangling forgotten from his fingers. The moonlight bathed his chiseled face in blue light.

He was watching her.

He didn't say a word. He didn't have to. He knew, she realized. He knew exactly what she'd been dreaming about. She didn't know how, but he knew. It was in his eyes, in the intimate look he sent her now, as if he'd been privy, no, *part* of that dream. But . . . that was impossible.

Oh, God.

A panicky feeling choked off her breath and sent a flush of heat crawling up her neck, but she found herself unable to look away. The tip of his cigarette glowed red as he took a long, slow pull. He exhaled deliberately, then turned away from her — staring off into the darkness.

Mariah lay back down, staring up at the canopy of stars overhead without really seeing them. Her heart was like a hammer in her chest and wouldn't be still. Her fingernails bit into the flesh of her palms. She hoped for something to distract her from the awful gnawing pain growing in her chest. But it didn't help.

She was falling in love with Creed.

What in God's name was she going to do?

* * *

176

Morning broke early over the camp. After a mostly sleepless night, Mariah woke sore and stiff. It was some consolation that everyone else did, too. Creed avoided her eyes and spent the time helping Jesse make his preparations for leaving.

Jesse made the coffee—out of self-preservation—and they all shared a cold breakfast of jerky and cold beans left over from yesterday's noonday meal. By the time the sun brushed the tips of the trees, Jesse was packed and ready to go. The wolf pranced around the campsite, anxious to be on the move again. A slight hesitation in her step was the only ill effect she suffered from yesterday's battle.

As Creed made a final check on cinch straps, Mariah walked over to Raven, who stood near Jesse's horse.

Raven turned when Mariah touched her arm.

"Thank you, Raven, for everything," Mariah said, squeezing her good hand. "I'll never forget what you did for us."

A smile parted Raven's lips and the two women shared a look that transcended the need for common words. *"Haiyu, nituka."*

"She said—" Jesse began, but Mariah held up her hand with a smile.

"I *know* what she said. Some words just don't require an interpreter."

Jesse grinned and tipped his head in agreement. He took his hat off and slapped it against his thigh in a nervous gesture. "Well, Mariah . . . I sure am glad I got to meet you. And, well, for stitchin' up this ugly face of mine and all, thanks. Oh, hell . . ." He gave up and swept her into his arm in a bear hug that nearly stole her breath.

"Will we see you soon, Jesse?" she asked as he let her go and mounted.

"Soon enough. I'll be in Virginia City within a week or two. Maybe I'll even be in time to see you and

177

Travers get hitched. A weddin' is always an occasion in the gulch."

Mariah's stomach twisted at his words. Beside her, she saw Creed stiffen. "I . . . I hope so, Jesse."

Creed handed Raven up to Jesse and he settled her behind him. Mariah passed him a drawstring bag she'd filled with food enough for a couple of days. He smiled and slipped it around his saddle horn. "Thanks Mariah."

Creed handed him his rifle. "Are you sure you two are going to be all right?" He slid the rifle into the leather boot beneath the fender of Jesse's saddle. "I reckon," Jesse replied. He reached down to Creed and shook his hand. "See you in Virginia City in a couple of weeks?"

"Could be," Creed answered evasively. "It's hard to say where I'll be." Mariah shot him a questioning look which he ignored.

Jesse nodded. "Well, I'll be there, restocking my gear. Let's not let three years go by again, old friend, eh?"

Creed scratched Mahkwi behind the ears and sent Jesse a rare smile that made his face so handsome it put goose flesh on Mariah's arms. " 'Bye, Jesse," he said. "Watch your back, *mon ami*."

"And you . . ." he called over his shoulder. "Remember what your pa used to say: 'What you can't duck — welcome'." He spurred his horse and with the two mules tagging along behind, they disappeared into the thick forest.

Creed turned to Buck and gave the cinch a tug to tighten it. Mariah moved to Petunia and did the same. The mare nickered and flicked her tail across Mariah's back.

"Creed?"

"Hmm-m?"

"How far are we from Virginia City now?"

"Two and a half days if we make good time. And if the weather holds."

She cast a furtive glance at the sky. It was a perfect cerulean blue. No sign of weather at all. That was good.

Wasn't it?

A whippoorwill chirped noisily from the branch of the tall cedar rooted into the side of the creek bank. The shallow water tumbled over the round rocks in Wolf Creek with a musical sound. The wind chorused in the trees. Everything seemed perfectly as it should be, yet inside her, nothing was. She was heading for marriage to Seth, but her heart belonged more and more to the rough, rootless bounty hunter — Seth's friend.

Creed swung up into his saddle, then turned back to her. "Ready?"

She mounted and gathered up Petunia's reins. "What will you do when we get there?"

"Do?" He turned to look at her curiously.

"After you get me to Seth, I mean. Will you stay for a while or —"

"Why would I stay?" He yanked the brim of his hat down firmly on his brow.

"I — well, I thought, maybe . . . assuming Seth is all right, you'd stay for the wedding, too."

He looked off to the west at the melting snowpacks, shining silver in the morning sun. "I don't think so."

"Oh." She tried to keep the disappointment out of her voice. "Because of your job?"

He stared at her for a moment. *"Ah, oui.* My job." Clucking to his gelding, he said, "Come on. We have a lot of country to cover today."

Mariah stared after him as he loped off, then nudged Petunia forward. In two and a half days she'd see Seth.

In two days, heaven help her, she would lose Creed.

Chapter Thirteen

The country they traveled through that day was a lush patchwork of cedar, lodgepole, and alder stitched together by steep walled canyons, pastoral valleys, and glacial peaks. Dozens of lakes threaded through the high meadows, fed by streams rushing fast with the spring snowmelt. Creed remained tense and watchful and kept his rifle safety unlocked in case he needed his gun quickly. Though they saw plenty of wildlife tracks, there was no sign of LaRousse.

As they descended, the temperature warmed, though at seven thousand feet Mariah could still see her breath in the air. She wore a blanket wrapped around her shoulders for most of the day and despite the clear sunny sky, wondered if Montana truly ever experienced summer.

They rode hard and made up some of the time they'd lost on the trail. By mid-afternoon, Mariah insisted they pull up so she could stretch her legs. A smell like rotten eggs wafted toward them as they came to a stop in a wide, grassy canyon. Even Petunia threw her nose up in the air, wiggling her lips in disgust.

"What in the world is that smell?" Mariah asked when Creed pulled up beside her.

"Hot spring."

"Really?" She'd certainly heard of the geological phenomenon, but had never seen one. "Where? Can we see it?"

He threw her the sort of patient look one gives a gawky tourist, then grinned in spite of himself. "You really want to? From the smell, it's close by."

She nodded enthusiastically and followed him on foot through the rough brush toward the odor. In less than two hundred yards, they found it. Steam scuttled across the surface of the small rock pool of sulphury, crystalline water. At the heart of the spring, a slippery-looking mound of minerals coated the rocks. He hung back while Mariah walked toward the water.

"Be careful," he warned. "Some of these get very hot."

Dipping her fingers into the edge of the pool, her eyes slid shut. "Oh-hh . . . heaven. Is it . . . usable?"

"Drinkable, you mean? I suppose, but I'd rather use it for baths." Creed laughed, seeing the plotting wheels spin in her head. "Don't get too used to it. We haven't got time for one."

Mariah's lips drew into an exasperated pout. "Are you sure? Look at me. I'm filthy." She plucked at the grimy buckskin shirt. "These clothes of yours could probably walk the rest of the way to Virginia City with no help from me." She plucked a dandelion from the pool's edge and blew it playfully into the air. "I don't know how you can even stand to be near me anymore."

Creed would have laughed if he'd found any humor in her comment. His expression was carefully blank, but his body went hard, watching her. The afternoon sun lit her from behind, catching the drifting fluff in the air around her like a crown of sliver. His gaze fell to the artless way the shirt clung to the contours of her breasts as she lifted her arms to catch the seedlings and he found himself contemplating what it would feel like to pull her into the vaporous water with him and wrestle her clothes off.

Hell. It wasn't a hot soak he needed, but a dip in a frigid mountain stream.

"Oh, Creed! Look!" She was pointing to a rocky

ledge thirty feet up where a Bighorn ewe and her lamb balanced on a precarious notch of rock staring down curiously at Mariah. The lamb was newborn, perhaps not more than two weeks old, yet had the agile footing of its mother. Farther up, several males glared down regally from atop the cliff. They sent a shower of rocks down on the female, sending her and the young one scrambling to another vantage point.

Mariah's cheeks were flushed with excitement and her smile broad as the morning sky as she walked back to the horse. "Weren't they wonderful?"

The sheer joy in her expression sent a bolt of heat through him. How long had it been since he'd looked at a newborn lamb and ewe with such unabashed pleasure? He remembered once such sights had struck him that way. When had he become so jaded that he'd forgotten these things? His heart thudded irreverently at the womanly sway of her hips when she walked.

"I've never seen horns like that," she commented as she gathered up Petunia's reins, sublimely oblivious to his attention. "Are there many of those sheep out here?"

"Thousands," he answered, mounting Buck as an excuse to tear his eyes from her. "You should see the males in the fall if you think that was something."

"Tell me," she demanded, swinging up on Petunia. "It must be wonderful."

He yanked the brim of his hat down over his eyes. "You can hear it from miles away. It's like the sound of rifle shots echoing down the canyon walls, only it can go on and on for hours. The males butt horns over and over, crashing against each other with a force you'd think would knock them senseless."

"How very odd. What are they fighting over?"

Creed's gaze lingered on hers for a moment before he answered. "A female, of course. It's mating season." He clucked to his horse and started off in time to miss the color that rose to her cheeks.

It wasn't what he'd said, but how he'd said it that had made Mariah blush. She kicked her horse and caught up with him. "How barbaric. And what do the female sheep do while all this 'head-bashing' is going on?"

"Run like hell, *cherie*. But they can't run far enough. The male rams are merciless. They will chase a ewe 'til she can barely stand." A wicked grin caught the edge of Creed's mouth. "He won't give up until he has her."

"Hmm-m, poor ewes," she murmured feelingly.

"You think so? It's all part of the dance of life, *ma petite*."

"Well, I'm not a sheep, of course, but it all seems rather unromantic. A woman likes to be wooed."

"Ah, but of course." He looked at her thoughtfully. "Did Seth woo you?"

Petunia stumbled over a rock, nicely covering the jolt his sudden question sent through her. "Seth?" A frown creased her brow as she considered it. "Well . . . come to think of it, not exactly, no. Not in the standard wooing-sort-of-way, at least. We knew each other for years. We grew up together, though he was five years older than I. I've known him all my life. I suppose he never felt that he had to . . . woo me. What was between us just . . . was."

A grunt of skepticism rumbled from deep in his chest.

"But," she amended quickly, "that doesn't mean I didn't love him just the same. I did." Mortification crept up her cheeks. "I, I mean, I *do*." Her gaze flicked to Creed.

"So," he asked, staring straight ahead, apparently altogether missing her slip of the tongue, "you've always been in love with him then?"

With a smile of relief, she answered, "I don't suppose what I felt at twelve could be considered true love. I had a schoolgirl crush on him to be sure. Why, there wasn't a girl in the county who didn't have eyes for him. He was considered quite a catch before he left for the Territory. In fact, I was sure he'd be married by the time I grew up." Mariah's gaze scanned a blossoming hedge of blackberries as they passed it. "Of course, he wasn't.

"I was fifteen when my father passed on, leaving only my grandmother and me. Seth . . ." she sighed, "was like a knight in shining armor riding to my rescue. He saw me through it all, the funeral, the arrangements, moving me into my grandmother's house. And afterward, we started to see more of each other."

Creed sent her a sidelong glance. "But he didn't court you?"

Something in his tone irritated her and she tightened her grip on the reins. "Court me? No . . . we always seemed to get along. I helped him at his father's store, we'd go for walks, picnics . . . if that's what you mean. It was . . . well, easy to be together. Comfortable. Like an old slipper, you know?" She almost groaned aloud. That wasn't the analogy she had intended at all. It had just—

"Ah, so old slippers are romantic to a fifteen-year-old girl, eh?" Creed asked with more than a hint of sarcasm. "What about a young *femme* of twenty?"

Her cheeks grew hot. "I didn't mean that the way it sounded."

"No? How did you mean it then?"

Her eyes widened. "Are you . . . questioning my feelings for Seth?"

"Are you?" he returned evenly, sliding his gaze to her.

She took several breaths. He'd hit too dangerously close to the mark about her fears concerning her fiancé, but she wasn't about to admit it. "Of all the nerve! I thought you were his friend."

"I am." He kept his stare aimed at the glaring patch of snow on the mountaintop to the west but his jaw was set in a firm line.

"Really? You're not acting like—" A cold thought

struck her. "You're not trying to tell me he's . . . he's found someone else, are you?"

Creed laughed sardonically. "No, *mon petit moineau.* Even if he had, it wouldn't be my place to say."

Anger muted her sense of relief. "Then why—?"

"You were only fifteen when he left you."

"Sixteen!"

"Ah, *mais oui,* almost an old crone—" He bent at the waist in a mocking bow. "I concede the distinction."

Mariah jerked her horse to a stop. "Just what are you implying, Mr. Devereaux? That I was too young to know my own mind?"

"Perhaps too young to know what grown men and women need from each other."

"Need? Are you speaking of—" she gulped, hardly able to bring herself to say the word, "—carnality? Because if you are—"

He grabbed Petunia's reins and pulled her closer to him. "I'm talking about the fire that consumes two people and forges a bond between them, not some comfortable old shoe to take on and off at whim."

"And you're so worldly! What makes you such an expert on love? How would you even know what it feels like? I'll bet you've never let a woman get close enough to love you," she taunted, dancing dangerously close to the flame she saw igniting in his eyes. "You keep yourself walled off from the world like a well-guarded palace secret, perfectly content to spend your life chasing after shadows and men who mean nothing to you—"

Creed's rugged features grew stony and he pulled up close to her so their horses were head to tail—until his knee was crushed warningly against hers. "Watch yourself, Mariah."

"—and for *what?*" she ranted on, ignoring him. "For *what,* Creed? So you can die young one day on a lonely mountain with no one to care? A senseless hero?" She jerked back on the reins to escape his closeness, but

Creed nudged Buck with his knees so the gelding followed Petunia's movements step for step.

"Stop that!" Lashing out with her arm, she tried to shove him back, but he grabbed her wrist and held it away from him.

Her pulse throbbed in her ears and she glared at him, trying to yank her hand away. "I have news for you, Mr. Devereaux! Even if my love for Seth *is* as comfortable as an old slipper, it's more than *you're* ever likely to have with a woman. What Seth and I have together . . . is special and there's nothing you can say or do to diminish tha—"

His mouth crushed down on hers with the lightning speed of a rattler's attack, smothering her words and sending shock waves through her. His hand wound around the back of her neck and he pulled her halfway over to his saddle, throwing her completely off balance. She made a useless noise of protest against his lips, but he only used the opportunity to invade her mouth more fully.

He plundered her like a miner seeking out treasure, exploring and ravaging the sensitive cavity. Her traitorous body responded with a tremor that started as a vibration in her throat and swelled to a crescendo all the way to her toes.

He'd kissed her before, she thought wildly, that time by the river. But this wasn't a kiss. It was a hungry, calculated assault on her senses that sent flames shooting down her limbs, effectively robbing her of breath, strength, and all coherent thought. His mouth slashed over hers, first one way then the other.

"Kiss me back, Mariah," he demanded. She gasped for breath, but found herself sharing his. A lady should be revolted by his brutish actions, she thought desperately, but she found herself a willing victim in his arms.

Creed's eyes were river-dark with passion, aflame with something even more dangerous. "I—I don't—"

His mouth claimed hers again before she could refuse him, demanding a response. Resistance bled away and she clung insensibly to the front of his shirt and the whipcord strength of his arms. From deep in his chest came a low, primal sound of possession, while the violent pounding of his heart beat a heavy rhythm against her fingertips. Their bodies fit together like two halves of a whole. Somewhere, in the deepest recesses of her soul, a long ago memory stirred, tumbled, revived.

Her tongue mated with his, dancing across the smooth surface of his teeth, then back again. The dark stubble on his face rasped against her sensitive skin, but she hardly noticed. His fingers wound tightly in the skein of hair at the back of her neck, drawing her closer still.

His free hand slid down to cover one breast, kneading it roughly and causing her nipple to bud like a new flower. Mariah arched mindlessly up to meet him, caught in the whirlwind of sensation. She didn't think to stop him when his hand strayed from her breast to follow the curve of her waist down her hip. He cupped her bottom and pulled her closer, pressing her intimately across his iron-like thigh.

Disturbed by the movement, Petunia stamped a foot and took a step away from Buck, breaking the spell between her and Creed. His arms tightened protectively around her and he slid her fully onto his lap. A growl rumbled in his chest as he tore his mouth from hers.

To her everlasting disgrace, she followed his retreat like a hungry bird wanting more, but he stayed just a heartbeat out of reach. His breath was ragged as hers, and his blue-green eyes were edged with flame as they searched her face.

"You see, *ma petite?*" he whispered, "The flame does not much resemble the comfortable old slipper, does it?"

A hot flush crept up Mariah's neck. His question required no reply. The answer was plain enough in the wanton way she'd responded.

She stared at him, gathering her wits, aghast at what she'd just done. No simple rationalization, no half-baked justification could explain nor excuse what had happened between them. What they'd done was wrong. Horribly, terribly wrong. They'd betrayed Seth.

They'd betrayed themselves.

Pressing her fingers hard against her swollen lips to keep from sobbing out loud, she tried to sit up. His arms detained her.

"Mariah—"

His eyes were filled with the same regret she felt, but she couldn't think about that. "Please," she said in a thick voice, "just put me down."

He didn't move for several long seconds. A cool gust of wind sighed through the nearby pines, tossing her hair, fanning her warm face. The saddle creaked as he shifted, releasing her. She slid off the horse and dropped to the ground. Her shaky knees nearly buckled, but she caught her balance and stumbled to Petunia.

After several missed attempts, she gathered up the mare's reins and grabbed hold of the saddle horn. But she couldn't force herself to lift her foot as far as the stirrup. Instead, she sagged against the leather and pressed her damp face against her arm. Her chest rose and fell shakily, giving her away. Creed appeared behind her, bracketing her shoulders between his hands.

"Don't—" she gasped, but he didn't let her go. Slowly, he turned her to face him, but she focused her eyes on his tooled leather belt buckle.

"Mariah, I'm sorry. So damned sorry."

She nodded miserably, swiping at the moisture on her cheeks with the edge of her too-long shirt sleeve. Blast it all, she hadn't meant to cry. "I think . . ." she said, sniffing, "we'd better hurry and get to Virginia City, before we end up hating each other." *And ourselves.* Creed swallowed hard and dropped his arms. "I think you're right." He bent down and cradled his hands for her foot. She stared downward for a long moment before allowing him to help her up onto Petunia.

Without another word, Creed swung up onto Buck and kicked him into a lope. Behind him, he heard Mariah's horse follow, but he only stared straight ahead. *Hell and damnation!*

Night after night, day after day, he had coached himself in restraint. We're almost there, he would tell himself. A few days and no one would have been the wiser. Especially not Mariah.

Why then had he done it? *Why?* To prove a point? At whose expense? Seth's? Mariah's? His own? No, it wasn't to prove a point.

It *was* the point.

That kiss wasn't about Seth or anything else in the world they were headed toward. It was only about them, about the power that leapt between them like an electric charge whenever they touched—whenever their eyes met.

You're a damn fool, Devereaux, falling in love with a woman you can never have.

A fool? *Peut-être.* But she was right about one thing: he'd never let a woman close enough to feel what he felt for her right now. He'd spent his life avoiding the kind of pain his father had gone through after losing Creed's mother. Now, he understood it in a way he never had before. And he knew that after Mariah, he'd never risk it again.

By late afternoon, the mild temperature had plunged and a strong, glacial wind from the north scoured the hillsides and laid the carpet of sweetgrass and wildflowers nearly flat. The sun sank behind a massing wall of gunmetal-gray clouds to the northwest, beyond the snowcapped bitterroots. The clouds were eighteen miles off, Creed guessed, and moving with incredible speed. That kind meant only one thing: snow. Possibly, God forbid, a Norther.

Sacre bleu! Was *nothing* going right on this trip?

He pulled his horse to a stop to get his bearings. Buck pranced nervously and blew out a steamy breath. It meant certain death to be caught in the open during one of these storms. A cave, even a small one, might be enough to shelter them, but he didn't remember ever seeing one in this area.

"There's a storm coming," Mariah announced, pulling up beside him. Her cheeks were red and her eyes were watering in the wind. Only her hands and face were visible outside the buffalo robe.

"We'll catch our deaths if we get wet in this cold weather," she said, watching the fast-moving front.

"It's not rain you smell, Mariah. It's snow."

Her amber eyes blinked in disbelief. "In *June?* Snow in June? Good God."

"We'll have to find some shelter. Quickly."

"I suppose it's too much to hope for a town nearby?" she asked hopefully, glancing gloomily at the thick forested land around them.

"There's a cabin. But it's still four, maybe five miles south of here on the Boulder River."

Shivering, Mariah pulled her robe more tightly around her. "Are you sure? You don't sound sure."

"I'm sure that's where it is. I'm not sure it's still standing," he answered over the roar of the wind.

"How long since you've seen it?"

"Three years or so."

She rolled her eyes. "What makes you so sure there's a cabin there at all?"

"Because it's mine." He gathered up his reins. "Try to

stay right with me, Mariah. Don't lag." He kicked Buck with his heels, sending him into a lope.

"*Lag?* I don't lag!" Mariah called after him indignantly, nudging Petunia in the ribs. The mare gave a nervous little buck before starting off after Creed, but Mariah grabbed the saddle horn and hung on. "I may not ride well," she muttered, "but I don't lag." *Damn you.*

The weather bore down out of the north on the countryside like a white stampede. The bitter temperature had dropped even further by the time they reached the Boulder River. It had started with driving, freezing sleet and turned into a blizzard. Petunia and Buck struggled on with heads bowed against the driving snow.

The tanned hide of the buffalo robe Jesse had given Mariah was encrusted with icy snow, but the thick fur kept her relatively warm and dry. Only her fingers were numb with cold.

Creed, on the other hand, had donned a thick blanket-capote and wrapped a woolen shawl around his shoulders and head. Both were soggy and wet. He'd freeze to death before he asked her for help, Mariah decided. And it was getting worse.

"Creed!" The wind nearly swallowed her shout. "Stop—"

"We're nearly there," he called back stiffly, hunkering down closer to the gelding's neck.

She nudged her horse up beside his. "You'll freeze before we get there, you big idiot. We can *share* the robe. It's roomy enough for two."

He looked up, considering it. A violent shiver raced through him. "Good idea." But his hands were almost too cold to put the plan into action. Mariah dismounted and fitted her foot into his stirrup. Awkwardly, Creed pulled the sodden blanket from his shoulders and laid it across Buck's neck. He reached an icy hand down and helped her up behind him and she wrapped the fur around them both.

He let out a sigh of relief as she wound her arms around his waist and pressed herself against his back. "Thanks," he muttered, covering her hand with his icy one. "Feels better."

"Don't get any ideas," she shouted close to his ear. "I'm only doing this so you don't freeze to death and leave me here to find my way to Virginia City alone."

"How considerate of you."

"How much farther is it?"

He reached for Petunia's reins and found his fingers too numb to hold them. He passed them back to her.

She pulled them inside the robe. "I said how—"

"Not much farther."

The dampness from his capote seeped through her shirt and she shivered. "Can't you be a little more specific?"

"Sorry. This area's grown up some since I was here last. It can't be more than a half-mile or so."

Thirty minutes later, Creed pulled up his horse. The storm was worsening. Everything was white. The land, the trees, the air . . . his face. The howling wind erased even the familiar sound of the river, though he could just make it out ahead.

The cold air tore at his lungs with each breath. He remembered his father telling him the story about finding his old trapper friend, Abe Walker, frozen stiff in the Bear Paws, curled up in his buffalo robe, still clutching his old Hawkins rifle. He'd looked like he'd just gone to sleep. Creed's heart pumped harder, pushing the thought from his mind, denying that would be his fate.

"We're lost, aren't we?" Mariah's breath came warm against his ear.

He swallowed heavily. Damn. He was too turned

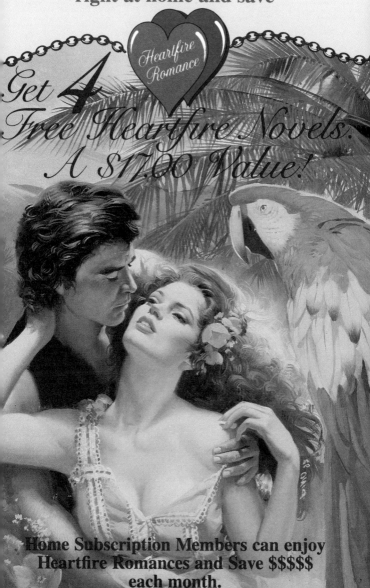

ENJOY ALL THE PASSION AND ROMANCE OF...

Heartfire

ROMANCES from ZEBRA

After you have read HEART-FIRE ROMANCES, we're sure you'll agree that HEARTFIRE sets new standards of excellence for historical romantic fiction. Each Zebra HEARTFIRE novel is the ultimate blend of intimate romance and grand adventure and each takes place in the kinds of historical settings you want most...the American Revolution, the Old West, Civil War and more.

SUBSCRIBERS $AVE, $AVE, $AVE!!!

As a HEARTFIRE Home Subscriber, you'll save with your HEARTFIRE Subscription. You'll receive 4 brand new Heartfire Romances to preview Free for 10 days each month. If you decide to keep them you'll pay only $3.50 each; a total of $14.00 and you'll save $3.00 each month off the cover price.

Plus, we'll send you these novels as soon as they are published each month. There is never any shipping, handling or other hidden charges; home delivery is always FREE! And there is no obligation to buy even a single book. You may return any of the books within 10 days for full credit and you can cancel your subscription at any time. No questions asked.

Zebra's HEARTFIRE ROMANCES Are The Ultimate
In Historical Romantic Fiction.
Start Enjoying Romance As You Have Never Enjoyed It Before...
With 4 FREE Books From HEARTFIRE

TO GET YOUR
4 FREE BOOKS
MAIL THE COUPON BELOW.

FREE BOOK CERTIFICATE

GET 4 FREE BOOKS

Yes! I want to subscribe to Zebra's HEARTFIRE HOME SUBSCRIPTION SERVICE. Please send me my 4 FREE books. Then each month I'll receive the four newest Heartfire Romances as soon as they are published to preview Free for ten days. If I decide to keep them I'll pay the special discounted price of just $3.50 each; a total of $14.00. This is a savings of $3.00 off the regular publishers price. There are no shipping, handling or other hidden charges. There is no minimum number of books to buy and I may cancel this subscription at any time. In any case the 4 FREE Books are mine to keep regardless.

NAME

ADDRESS

CITY _____ STATE _____ ZIP

TELEPHONE

SIGNATURE _____

(If under 18 parent or guardian must sign)
Terms and prices subject to change.
Orders subject to acceptance.

HF 103

Heartfire Romance

GET 4 FREE BOOKS

HEARTFIRE HOME SUBSCRIPTION
SERVICE
P.O. BOX 5214
120 BRIGHTON ROAD
CLIFTON, NEW JERSEY 07015

AFFIX
STAMP
HERE

around even to be certain of that. The snow blotted out every familiar landmark. He nudged Buck forward a few more steps. Visibility was ten feet and closing.

They would have to find shelter soon . . . or die.

Chapter Fourteen

Creed closed his eyes, willing himself to concentrate on something besides the painful numbness of his fingers and the slick of frost forming on his face. He was trying to picture a place which, out of long habit, he shunned the way a wise man did a house riddled with pestilence. To call it up intentionally, to own it, he thought, was the height of desperation. But desperate was precisely what they were.

He visualized the cabin, detail for detail, saw himself approaching it in the snow. *There was the huge ponderosa pine sheltering one corner of the roomy log cabin. The small shed for stock thirty feet away.*

The image flickered like a shadow, fading.

Focus, Devereaux. Concentrate!

Mariah shook him from behind. "Creed! What are you doing? Don't go to sleep for God's sake!"

"Quiet," he snapped. "I'm thinking." *There above the door in a place of honor, the pair of deer antlers — his first kill — now whitened with age.*

"The snow's drifting around Buck's knees! We need to keep moving!" The pitch of her voice told him she was on the edge of panic.

There — the path that led to the feeder-creek and the odd rock formation: an old man bent with the weight of a heavy pack — along the north shore.

"We're lost. You can tell me the truth, Creed."

And the ancient broken tree lying at right angles to the earth pointing directly at the cabin.

Her arms tightened around his middle and she dropped her forehead against his back.

He opened his eyes, leaving that magical place in his mind behind. "No, we're not lost. Unless the curse has failed me at last."

He turned Buck sharply right and headed through an unlikely thicket of trees that opened up onto a creek where the banks were tufted with snow. They had only followed it for five minutes before spotting the rocks, the fallen ponderosa, then the cabin tucked safely beneath a sprawling pine and a ring of younger trees.

Le bon Dieu. He felt Mariah's sigh of relief more than he heard it. Pulling to a stop at the door, he helped her down; then, with deliberate, stiff movements, he dismounted. Brushing the snow off the rough-hewn handle, he pushed open the unlocked door. It creaked in protest and he ushered Mariah inside the dark cabin.

Their steamy breath mingled in the dark room. He rubbed his hands together and blew on them until he could grip a match.

Clumsily, he touched the flame to the wick of the glass-domed coal oil lamp on the small table near the door. The glass rattled against the metal in his shaking hand as a soft yellow glow filled the room.

Her lips were tinged blue with cold and she was shivering despite the heavy robe that still enshrouded her. His face was covered with rime of white. He could feel the glacial cold heavy on his lashes and eyebrows and still numbing his cheeks. He wiped his face against his shoulder but found no relief in the stiffened fabric.

"H-how did you do that?" Mariah asked, clutching her hands to her sides.

He stared, confused. "Do what?"

She shook her head. "How did you find this place? How did you . . . know which way to come in all that whiteness?" She took a step closer to him, staring as if he were some creature in a side show. "How did you know?"

He dropped his gaze to the neatly stacked wood by the fireplace and started piling it on the fire grate. "It's my home, remember?"

"It didn't matter out there. You could have been ten feet away and not seen it. You would have needed divine guidance to find it."

He shrugged, rubbing his hands together.

"What curse?" she pressed.

His throat tightened. "What?"

"What *curse* were you talking about? You said, 'unless the curse has failed me at last'."

He ground his back teeth together. "Did I say that? I only meant my faultless sense of direction, *ma petite*. Now," — a shiver poured through him — "why don't you let me get this fire going? Then I'll have to take care of the horses and you can get out of those wet things."

Mariah frowned, clutching her arms. "You're not going to tell me, are you?"

"Tell you what?" he nearly shouted in exasperation. "I got us here, didn't I? Let's just leave it at that."

"Fine." She frowned and turned away. He could deny it all he wanted, she fumed, dropping the heavy buffalo robe into one of the two pelt-lined willow chairs flanking the fireplace. There was a good deal more than sheer coincidence in the uncanny knack he had for knowing things. She was curious about it, but she'd be damned if she'd grovel at his feet for the truth.

Her clothes were wet where she had leaned against Creed. She shivered, rubbed her upper arms and looked around the cabin. It was a small but comfortable one-room structure that smelled musty from years of disuse.

Dominating one corner was a pelt-covered bed. It was built from sturdy, unpeeled lodgepole pine logs and was, she noticed with some dismay, large enough for two. Unbidden, her body heated fractionally at the sight — a reaction born as much of anticipation as fear. Preferring not to dwell on that, she turned her attention to the rest of the room.

From the thick-beamed ceiling hung several pairs of willow snowshoes, baskets, and bunches of dusty dried herbs. A bighorn ram's curly horns crowned one of the four-paned glass windows by the door. Finely tanned pelts of beaver, black bear, and lynx covered the lime-chinked walls, adding an extra measure of insulation.

She ran her hand over the smooth surface of the scarred slab-table in the center of the room. Her fingers left a trail in the dust and stopped on an exquisite hand-blown blue vase at the center of the table. She picked it up, examining the fine craftsmanship. The house had once had a woman's touch, she decided, glancing at the faded blue curtains and the braided rag rugs.

Her eyes were drawn to a pegged shelf on the wall. There, beside an old steeple shelf-clock which had long since wound down, was a punched-tin frame containing a small oil portrait of a woman. A beautiful woman with Creed's black hair and unusual-colored eyes. The resemblance was extraordinary.

"Solange Devereaux." Creed's voice came from right behind her. "My mother."

Mariah whirled around guiltily and replaced the vase on the table. "Oh. I — was just . . . she's very beautiful."

Creed's eyes darkened as he brushed the soot from his hands. *"Oui.* She was. Beautiful and fragile. Just like you."

"That sounds more like an accusation than a compliment. What happened to her?"

"I told you," he said, holding her gaze, "this country's hard on women, Mariah. My mother was headstrong, and in love with my father. She thought she was up to this kind of life, too. But it killed her. Sucked the life right out of her."

Like it will you, his unspoken words rang out.

Mariah's eyes smarted at the stark pain she saw in his face and she tamped down her flare of anger. "I'm sorry, Creed."

"Don't be. It was a long time ago. I didn't tell you to get pity—"

Her mouth dropped open. *"Pity?"*

"—I told you for your own good." He gathered up a coil of rope hanging by the door and started tying it around his waist.

Tears of frustration stung her eyes. "Oh, really? My own good? As if it's news to me that I'm unwanted here. You've been trying to get rid of me since the moment I stepped off the boat."

He whirled on her. "And you've been trying to kill yourself since then, too."

"I have not!" she choked out. "Things have happened, yes, but unlike your mother, I'm still here, and very much alive in case you haven't noticed."

He cinched the rope's knot with a vicious tug. "Oh, I've noticed. Believe me. I'm not made of stone, Mariah. I've noticed."

Without another word, he yanked open the door, with its gust of freezing air, and slammed out. Mariah stared at the whirling snowflakes as they drifted to the floor and melted in miniature puddles. She sank down onto the bench beside the table, dropped her head on her folded arms, and gave in to the wrenching tears that had been threatening all day long.

She cried for herself and for this awful mess she'd gotten herself into. She cried for Creed and his stubborn, angry need to shut her out. And finally, she cried for Seth, whose only fault in all this was that he loved her.

That was how Creed found her when he came back from putting the stock up—hiccupping in long, gulping sobs that nearly broke his heart. He lowered the saddlebags to the floor and untied the rope that had kept him from getting lost in the whiteness. His fists,

198

numb with cold, curled at his sides.

Damn you, Devereaux. Now look what you've done! She'd been beaten up, nearly drowned, almost murdered, and through it all, she'd held up like a trooper—never complaining or whining, never blaming him. But he'd sharpened his tongue on her and with a few well-placed thrusts he'd finally put her over the edge. It wasn't her fault that they were in this situation. It was his. He reached out to touch her shoulder.

"Mariah?"

She jumped at the contact and turned swollen eyes up to him; then, embarrassed, she dropped her face in her hands.

"Don't . . . don't look at be." Her nose was clogged from crying and her m's came out sounding like b's.

His gut twisted. "I'm sorry. I didn't mean to make you cry, *ma petite.*"

She shook her head hopelessly. "It's not just you. It's—it's" she hiccupped—"everythink."

He knelt down beside her, rubbing a hand comfortingly over her back. "Everything?"

Lifting her hands palms up, she cried, "You were right. I should never have cub. I've been nothig but trouble to you—"

"No, I shouldn't have said that."

"I'b so tired I can't see straight, you hate be—"

"I don't hate you—"

"—and look at be. Look at *us!*" Creed ran a self-conscious hand over his stubble of beard. "In two days," she went on with a sniffle, "I'b going to see Seth—*if* he's alive . . . and *if* we survive this damb weather. And here I ab . . ."—she let loose another sob—"wearing your filthy clothes, looking like subthing subbody dragged under a wagon frub Illinois. What's he goig to think?"

Creed's hand slowed on her back. He knew she was talking about more than her clothes. She was as worried as he was about what Seth would think when they rode in together. There was nothing to be done for it now.

Hell and damnation.

He went to the dresser and took out one of his mother's neatly folded linen hankies, and handed it to her. "Here. Blow."

"But . . ." She looked at the delicate initials, "S. D.," embroidered into the folds. "It's . . . it's your buther's!" A new gush of tears broke free.

"I know it's my mother's," he said, patting her shoulder awkwardly. "Just blow."

In between sobs, she did.

Dieu, he hated it when women cried. He felt so . . . helpless. He slipped outside the door for a moment with two buckets and came back with them full of snow. He dumped them into the cooking pot that hung over the fire, then went back for two more. When he'd filled the pot, he strung a blanket up across the room, separating the bed area from the rest.

Flipping over the old steel tub propped in the corner, he set it beside the bed and filled it with the warm water.

He dug up an old bar of tallow soap and set it with a towel and an old flannel nightrail on the bed.

When he'd finished, he took Mariah by the arm and led her to the curtained-off area. "Strip," he ordered, gaining a wide-eyed reaction from her that put an immediate, if shocked, halt to her tears.

"Wh-what?" She clutched the neckline of her shirt tightly in her fist.

"I mean, after I leave." He was only slightly irritated by her vast look of relief. "It's the best bath I can offer under the circumstances. It will . . . make you feel better. I'll be out here if you need anything." He started to back out of the makeshift room.

She nodded with a sniff and relaxed her death-grip on her shirt. "Creed?"

He ducked his head back in. "What?"

200

"Thank you."

"Yeah." Muttering, he retrieved two more buckets of snow and tossed them in the pot. He ran a hand over his face, deciding he could stand to get acquainted with a little water himself. Pouring some of the heated water back in a bucket, he stripped off his shirt and pulled his shaving things out of his saddlebags.

With one ear, he listened to the sounds of Mariah bathing. Each splash of water fed his overactive imagination and bit by bit dispelled the chill that had settled into his bones. He pictured her there, naked and wet, water rivulets coursing down the curve of her —

With an oath, he plunged his frost-bitten hands into the warm water, but even that painful distraction was little help with Mariah Parsons four feet away in the beautiful altogether.

Damn, damn, damn.

Mariah stepped hesitantly out of the tub, casting a brief look at the thin blanket separating her from Creed. He was standing only ten feet away. She could hear the splash of water, the tap of his straight razor against the washbasin as he finished his own ablutions. In her mind's eye, she pictured him with his shirt off and it shamed her to realize she wanted to do more than just fantasize about it. She had the craziest urge to touch his damp skin, feel the smooth play of muscle beneath it and the dusting of hair above.

Shivering, she dried herself quickly on the flannel blanket he'd left. The fire had yet to take the chill out of the air. She still had her hair to wash and didn't relish the idea of turning into an icicle while she did it.

Slipping the nightrail over her head, she rolled up the sleeves and kneeled over the tub. She poured water over her head with the bucket, then started to soap up her hair.

The soap squirted out of her hand and hit the floor

with a slippery thud, skidding under the curtain. "Oh, for heaven's sake." She cracked an eye open, groping for the lost bar, but the soap seeped into eyes and she slammed them shut.

"Ow, ow-ow—" she whispered, rubbing at her eyes with the cotton sleeve of her nightrail. Blindly she reached for the flannel blanket she'd left on the floor beside her, but she gasped when her hand connected with Creed's.

"Here," he said, wiping her eyes with the edge of the blanket. "Let me help you with this."

"Creed, you shouldn't be—"

But he was already massaging the soap through her hair. "Shouldn't be what?"

It took her a few long seconds to answer. "Doing this." She braced her palms on the edge of the tub. The tips of his fingers slid over every inch of her scalp in gentle, sensuous strokes. He squeezed the soap through her hair, lifting it and massaging it over and over. Soap suds gathered at her temple and slipped down her cheek. His finger caught the rivulet and slowly scraped up the side of her face, away from her eyes.

An ache curled low inside her, a need for more of his touch. Wantonly, she leaned back into his hands and her lashes closed over her cheeks. A shiver of anticipation traveled up her spine as his fingers slid lower, to the base of her neck where he massaged away the tension of the past few days.

"Mm-mmm. Doesn't it feel good?"

His voice was husky and deep. *Yes, oh yes.* A sigh escaped her. "But it's not . . . decent."

"No." She heard the smile in his voice. "Probably not." His fingers spread sensuously through her hair again, sliding deliciously against her scalp.

She lost herself to the sensation. It felt so good to let someone help her, pamper her—to just give in to it.

Finally, he said, "Lean over." She did. He dipped the bucket in the water and poured the warm water over her head, following its path with his hand. She held her breath when his fingers brushed the sensitive curve behind her ears. His steely thighs brushed flush against her rear for a moment as he leaned over her and it was suddenly, startlingly clear exactly how indecent their position was. Her heart thudded heavily until she thought the tub might echo its sound.

Never had a man touched her the way he was — with gentle, aching tenderness, with sheer male need. It made her heart swell and pound, her throat clog with an emotion she'd never known.

Creed squeezed the water from her hair, helped her up, and towel-dried her hair on the flannel blanket.

She opened her eyes and swallowed hard at her first real look at him. The top half of his long johns hung down around his hips. Her gaze was even with his bare chest and his flat, brown nipples in their nests of black hair. His chest rose and fell with a chaotic rhythm. Until that moment, she hadn't noticed that his hands still lingered on her shoulders. His skin was hot and smooth beneath her hands.

Her gaze moved up. He'd shaved and his hair was wet and finger-combed. The clean scent of soap lingered on his skin. His eyes, dark with hunger, burned into her and she prayed the roaring sound of the wind would drown out the cannon-like pounding of her heart.

If she hadn't touched him, perhaps nothing more would have happened, but she reached out and brushed a finger across the blue beads at his throat.

Pinioning her hand at the wrist, he brought her knuckles to his lips. His mouth, hot and wet, caressed her skin with the barest brush of his tongue. Her eyes slid shut when he turned her palm over and repeated the gesture.

A thousand sensations chased behind his touch — a melting ache, a trembling fear, and worse — a hunger that nothing but his touch seemed to fill.

"Creed—"

"This is wrong," he muttered, pulling her toward him, twining his hand in her wet hair.

"Is it?" she asked, so flush against him she could once more feel the rock-hard evidence of his desire.

"I don't give a damn anymore," Creed ground out, covering her mouth almost violently with his own. She met him more than halfway, pulling his head to her, arching her body against his in need of even more closeness. There was no stopping it this time. No turning back. A throbbing pulse beat echoed in her brain and vibrated down her body.

She'd never known it could be like this between a man and a woman. He was a burning fire that raged in her. He stroked her the way a flame strokes the wood it's about to consume—seductively, passionately ablaze. To welcome the conflagration he'd ignited inside her was to leave behind her expectations, but to deny it was to deny her heart. And that had become too painful.

The days of pent-up longing exploded. His hands, hungry and strong, roved across her body insistently, holding back nothing. With each touch he branded her as his. She'd known it would come to this since the moment she'd laid eyes on him, since the first time they'd touched. Now, he wasn't waiting for consent, or even asking for it.

Chapter Fifteen

His hands tore at the tiny pearl buttons that marched down the front of her nightrail until she felt his rough palm curve around her breast, lifting, caressing. With a sigh of pleasure, she dropped her head back, exposing her throat. He didn't hesitate to oblige — his mouth was on her, burning a fiery path of moisture down her neck, exploring the hollows with his tongue and claiming the one just below her ear.

A shiver rolled through her that had nothing to do with the chilled air. One-handed, he pushed her night-rail down over one shoulder and lifted her breast to his mouth, suckling her with barely restrained savagery. His teeth slid over the delicate areola, sending shafts of pleasure through her. Arching toward him, she dropped her head back again with a moan. Never had she felt anything close to the sensation that was spilling through her blood, rocketing through her nerves. Then, with an abruptness that stole her breath, he left her breast and renewed his attentions at her ear, invading it with his tongue.

"Do you have any idea," he breathed, "how beautiful you look in the firelight?"

Her knees buckled as a tremor chased through her and he pressed her back against the fur-covered wall. Her chest rose and fell in a chaotic rhythm. Plunging her fingers into his hair, she directed his mouth back to hers. Creed slanted a kiss across her lips, driving, hungry, as if any space between them was too much. His hands glided over her, first caressing, then worshipful as his fingers explored the curves and secret places that made her a woman. Every touch seemed to melt her. Her bones ceased to exist.

"Touch me, Mariah," he demanded raggedly. Creed dragged her hand down past the V of hair that disappeared below his waistband. He felt her hesitate above the metal buttons, afraid for the first time.

"Ah, *Dieu*, Mariah, *tu me rends fou* . . . you drive me crazy," he breathed raggedly against her cheek.

"Creed . . ."

He tore open the buttons on his Levis himself, pushing them downward over his hips until he kicked them off completely. With a moan, he slid his thigh between her legs and pressed up intimately against her. A tremor went through her and he lifted her up off the floor in his arms.

Mariah's nightrail crept up her thighs, followed by the tortuous caress of his fingertips trailing higher and higher. Fire raced along her skin, tingling wherever he touched her. He was fire and ice, sanity and madness. Leaving behind her last vestige of coherence, Mariah let herself go.

Creed wrapped his arms around her slender back, drawing her nearer. He needed her in a way he'd never needed a woman, with a burning, furious passion so intense it scorched his resolve and laid waste to whatever honor was left to him.

He no longer cared.

She was his. He knew that as surely as he'd ever known anything. He knew it in that moment of surrender when he felt the give of her body against his. He knew it in the way his own body pounded out of control. Her uncertainty at touching him only fueled his fire and drove him mad with desire.

He lifted her higher in his arms, tugging her nightrail out of his way. She wound her arms around his neck and her legs twined around his. With the cushion of lynx fur behind her, he strained against her, exploring her body with his mouth, his hands — tasting, taking — ravenous and barely controlled. She uttered a startled sound when his fingers dipped into her slick depths to find her hunger equal to his. Her breath exploded in a gasp as he prolonged the exquisite torture.

She trembled. He felt his control slipping. She writhed against him, demanding an end to the torment. He never wanted to let her go.

With a moan she slid her head backward against the wall. "You're killing me."

His mouth found the curve of her shoulder. "I haven't even begun." He slid her down until her feet once more touched the floor and ran his hand down the smoothness of her belly. "Touch me."

Hesitantly, she did. He groaned as her hand closed over him and she pulled away. "Did I hurt you?"

His heavy-lidded gaze rose slowly to meet hers. "Oh, God, yes. But don't stop," he begged. *Dieu*, don't stop."

A woman's smile curved her lips. With silken fire she stroked him, caressed him as he had her, driving him to the brink of madness. She explored his neck, his temple, his mouth with her tongue, leaving a trail of moisture cooling against his heated skin.

The heavy timbers of the cabin creaked and groaned with the power of the storm outside, but within, the tempest between them raged even stronger. When he could stand no more, he lifted her into his arms.

The pelt-covered bed met his knees from behind and they dropped down on it, making the rope netting creak. He rolled her onto her back, and slid her trembling body under him.

Spreading her legs apart with his knee, he entered her with as much restraint as he could manage. She gasped from the sudden, sharp pain and her eyes flew open wide. He went still inside her and crushed her mouth with his until the pain passed. She gasped when he freed her, pressing her cheek desperately to his.

"I hurt you." It wasn't a question. He knew he had.

"Yes, but for God's sake, don't stop."

Her whispered plea nearly made him lose control. Blood was pounding in his head. He began to move inside her, slowly at first, then with an ancient rhythm that made him forget everything—the smoky scent of the fire, the groaning storm outside faded in the distance. He knew nothing but her—the soft, sweet feel of her around him.

Her soul tangled with his as surely as her body did. His lungs struggled for air, but she crushed her mouth down on his. Soon the only air they took was from each other.

Mariah gasped, her senses reeling. His flesh was taut and warm under her hands. She couldn't think, didn't want to think beyond the man who was loving her. His scent was primal and his skin tasted of salt and her. He pushed her arms up over her head, twining their fingers together. With his body gleaming with a sheen of passion, he rose over her like a sculpted Greek statue. But no statue this—his muscled flesh was warm, his eyes alive and on fire for her.

It was almost more than she could bear. She turned her head and squeezed her eyes shut to keep the sob that rose in her throat from escaping. She pressed her hips into his—seeking, needing. His thrusts became stronger, harder, taking her higher, ever higher in her flight from reality. The tension coiled tightly low in her belly, spiraling upward. Flaming, powerful, exquisite.

"Open your eyes, *cherie*," he rasped. "I want to see you."

The look on his face put her over the edge. The too-tight coil inside her exploded like an overwound spring.

It transcended anything she'd ever known and a cry tore from the depths of her soul. Lights exploded behind her eyes. It was pain and ecstasy, fear and trust, sin and heaven.

Creed felt her contract around him and lost his last wisps of control. Giving in to it, he allowed the sensation to overtake him as his rhythm quickened. Then, with a groan of completion, he spilled himself into her and slumped over her slender, damp shoulder.

They lay collapsed on one another until sanity returned. Creed's arms were still around her and he lay sprawled with one leg across hers. Finally, he raised his head from the comfort of her shoulder. He frowned as his fingers brushed at the tears on her cheeks.

"I did hurt you."

She tightened her arms around him. "No. It was—" her voice choked with emotion. "I didn't know it would be like that."

"Neither did I."

Surprised, she blinked. "You didn't?"

He shook his head and kissed her nose.

"It's not always like that?" she asked, brushing a reciprocal kiss along his temple.

"Not like that. Never before. Never, before you." His finger traced the tracks of her tears to the hollow of her throat where her heartbeat pulsed in a steady thrum. He rose up on one elbow and looked at her. "Then . . . the tears are because—"

She pressed a finger to his lips. "Don't say it. I don't want to think, not yet. I just want to hold you."

His mouth dipped down to hers, brushing her lips with the barest of touches, once, twice before settling over her in a kiss so achingly tender she thought she would die if he let her go. For a long time, he didn't.

The smoky smell of the fire hung lazily in the air and the shadows danced along the ceiling. Outside, the storm went on without them, burrowing harder into the mountains. She wanted to forget the storm, forget the world outside this cabin. The thought of facing it again made her stomach tighten in a knot. When he rolled onto his back, bringing her over on top of him, she forgot about all that.

Slowly, she trailed kisses along his cheek and down his throat until her lips met the smooth beads of the choker at his throat. She felt him tense as she pushed it downward, and pressed her lips against the scar he kept hidden from the world.

A shudder of panic went through him. "Mariah—"

"What?" Her amber eyes met his.

"Don't. It's—"

"—part of you." She kissed him again.

"An ugly part." He was afraid to look at her.

"No. No part of you could be ugly." Her lips trailed upward again. "It's a rope mark, isn't it?"

He opened his eyes, determined to see her reaction. "Yes. It's a hanging scar. Few men live to carry one."

Her mouth drew into a tight line as her eyes surveyed it. "To think someone could do this to you. Try to—"

"How do you know I didn't deserve it?"

Her eyes never wavered. "I know. It . . . it must have been a mistake."

Her simple declaration of faith touched him. He rolled his eyes shut and rubbed the pad of his thumb against the nape of her neck. "Most women who saw this shrank from it," he said, lifting the choker to hide the scar. "Men drew their own conclusions, mostly bad. I got tired of trying to explain it."

Her fingers caressed his cheek. "You don't have to explain it . . ." She shivered suddenly, but Creed wasn't sure if it was the chill air or what she glimpsed in his eyes.

He reached across and pulled the edges of the buffalo robe up and over them, cocooning them in warmth and wrapping his hand around her back. *"Oui, ma petite,* I

210

do. You were right. It was a mistake. My mistake. It cost me my father and the past four years of my life."

She dropped her forehead to his shoulder and he drew her closer. She didn't ask him . . . somehow, he knew she wouldn't. But it had suddenly become important to him that she know — share that part of him as she'd shared everything else.

"It was Pierre LaRousse," he told her, "and his brother, Étienne."

Her eyes rose to meet his. Creed watched the play of emotion flit across her expression — surprise, disbelief, anger.

"Oh . . . oh, Creed."

He swallowed and a shudder coursed through him at the memory. "They were already well established killers by the time they found my father and me camped along the Yellowstone, but we never expected that their hatred for my father would lead to . . . I suppose we underestimated Émile LaRousse's powers of persuasion."

"Émile?"

"Their father." Creed sighed deeply. "He was a trapper, and, years before, had been my father's partner."

"They hated each other?"

Creed nodded. "Most of the hatred was on Émile's part. My father only felt sorry for him."

She was quiet, waiting for him to go on.

"Years ago, while they were still partners, Émile took a Sioux wife named Otter Woman. She bore him two half-breed sons, Pierre and Étienne. Émile was a good trapper, and when he was sober, a good father to his boys. But he was a hard man and when he drank, he would beat Otter. She stayed with him because she couldn't bear to leave her boys and she knew he'd never let them go.

As they grew older, the boys would go off trapping for weeks at a time with Émile . . . leaving Otter alone, often without food to see her through."

211

Creed gritted his teeth and Mariah felt him tense beneath her. "My father watched over her. They were friends. Not lovers." He flashed an angry look at Mariah that made her recoil slightly until she realized the anger was part of the memory.

At last, he looked at the ceiling again with faraway eyes, remembering. "My father had a wife—my mother—back in Missouri, whom he was devoted to. But when Émile drank, he accused Antoine and Otter of betraying him behind his back. He would beat Otter and, when my father interfered, traded blows with him, too.

"Their partnership was finished long before it ended, but my father stayed for Otter's sake. When she decided to leave Émile, he helped her. Émile had the two boys with him on a trapping run. When he returned home to find her gone . . ."—Creed's fingers tightened on the back of Mariah's neck—"he went mad. Chased them across the countryside, swore he'd kill my father for running off with her."

Mariah raised her head from his shoulder to see the pain in his expression. "What happened?"

"He never got her back—her Sioux family made sure of that. My father became the object of Émile's hatred and over the years, he passed that venom on to his sons. They grew up believing my father was responsible for Otter's leaving."

Son of a wife-stealer. You are harder to kill than I thought. LaRousse's words came back to her in a rush. It was all starting to make some kind of horrible, twisted sense.

"In the intervening years," Creed went on, "my father brought us here to live from Missouri. My mother, Solange,"—his voice deepened conspicuously on the word—"came from a wealthy family. They were against her coming. Even my father was against it."

"Why?"

He nodded his head toward the storm outside. "Look

around you. Winters are hard. *Life* here is hard and it kills most everything that's beautiful, except the mountains." His gaze drifted vacantly to the ceiling again. "But my mother wanted to come. She was in love with my father and he with her. The time apart—the trapping seasons—had become too difficult. So at last, she convinced him.

She lived and died here two years later of mountain fever. My father always blamed himself for bringing her. And, for many years, so did I."

"But . . . they loved each other," she argued with the logic of a woman who had only tonight begun to understand what that could mean.

"Yes, they did. But it wasn't enough to save her, was it?"

She fell silent, absently stroking the silken hair on his chest.

He raked a shaky hand through his damp hair. "At any rate, after she died we went into trading, with the Blackfeet and the Shoshone, and, sometimes, the Northern Cheyenne down along the Bighorn and Yellowstone. That's where . . . they found us that day— Pierre and his brother."

She traced her finger along the furious pulse at the base of his throat, waiting.

His eyes slammed shut. She could feel a tremor move up through his body like a small earthquake, but guessed it was the combined pounding of their hearts. He drew her head down flush with his shoulder so she wouldn't see his face and tightened his arms around her in a gesture that made her heart ache for him. "You don't have to tell me—"

"No," he whispered. "I want you to know who I am. *Why* I am."

She nodded against his chest.

"Until that day, I had never seen the two of them, only heard my father speak of them with remembered

213

fondness. Émile had died several years before in a knife fight and we'd heard bad stories about the brothers, but my father didn't lend them much credence. Pierre and Étienne grew up around him. He loved them as if they were his own, because they were Otter's.

"So when they confronted us there along the river, my father welcomed them into our camp. It was his last mistake."

Mariah tightened a hand over his clenched fist. His chest heaved as if he'd been running and his eyes shone with an abiding hatred she'd seen there only twice before.

"There were others with them," he went on. "Pierre turned a gun on us and another one threw a rope over a cottonwood branch. My father didn't believe at first what they intended to do. He talked with them as he would have to me. But it only seemed to infuriate Pierre." Creed looked down at their intertwined hands.

"I tried to fight, but there were too many. They tied our hands and put us on our horses. Finally, my father pleaded with them, not for himself, but . . ." his voice choked, "for me."

Mariah's stomach twisted as she listened to the unbearable memory he'd kept locked away for so long.

"Pierre obliged him by letting me watch my father go first. I'll never forget the look he sent me before they kicked the horse out from under him." Moisture gathered behind his closed eyelids and he squeezed them tighter. " 'I never thought it would come to this, boy', he said. 'I never thought — ' "

Creed shoved himself up to a sitting position, leaving her alone on the stiff-haired buffalo fur. His chest heaved as if he couldn't quite catch his breath. Mariah lay silent, not even touching him. She had the sense he wasn't there with her anymore, but reliving it again, with all the pain that came with it.

The firelight flickered across his profile, deepening

the darkness in his face. His voice was almost fragile, as if it might splinter into a thousand pieces if he went on.

"He didn't . . . die right away," Creed continued almost in a whisper. "They made sure of that by the way they tied his knot. I saw him choke . . ." He dropped his head into his hands. "The . . . look in his . . . eyes—it seemed like forever before . . . before he stopped . . . moving. And then he . . . he was dead. Just like that. A lifetime gone, snuffed. And those . . . those bastards were grinning. *Laughing.* I had never wanted to live more than I did at that moment. I wanted to . . . kill them with my bare hands. To rip them apart piece by piece for what they'd done. But—" His hand went automatically to his throat as if he could feel the rope there still and he stared at the crackling fire.

"The next thing I knew, they were whooping and riding their horses around mine until my pony bolted. I saw them ride off laughing even as the rope . . . cinched around my . . . my neck." He was breathing furiously. "I was of little consequence to them. Just a loose end. I understood that as I felt myself kicking for the ground that wasn't there . . . felt the life ebbing out of me.

"I don't know how long it took for everything to go black, disappear. Seconds, minutes. Then—" His brows dropped, remembering. "Then, I was somewhere else. I was outside of myself. I saw—"

He stopped short, the strange look gone from his eyes, and he turned to her with a blank expression.

"What?" She sat up beside him, wrapping her arms around him as if she could protect him from the pain. "What did you see?"

"Nothing." He stood. His body was perfection in the firelight, his face was still as carved marble.

"Something," she prodded.

His fists tightened and he turned to her. "I didn't

mean to—you'll think I'm crazy."

"Don't tell me what I'll think."

"It *is* crazy." He walked to the fire and shoved another log in, sending up a cascade of sparks. For a long moment he watched it. At last, he turned back to her. "It . . . it changed me.

"Changed you . . . how?"

"You've seen me. You know what I am."

She'd never seen him so vulnerable. She searched for the right words, praying she wouldn't abuse the trust glimmering in his eyes. "I've seen that you're a good man. A kind man."

He laughed harshly. "I'm a killer."

"No. That's not what you are. I thought so, at first. But I was wrong."

His body relaxed a fraction, as if he'd been waiting for a blow that hadn't come. "I am what I've become. And I'm not the same man I was . . . before."

"I didn't know you then. I only know what I see." She shook her head. "I only care for the man I know now. It doesn't matter what you were before—"

He turned to her, his eyes soft and pleading. He sat on the edge of the bed. "You asked . . . how I knew how to find this place in the snow."

She nodded slowly.

"And how I knew to come back to camp when La-Rousse was there, though I didn't see him?"

She stared unblinkingly.

"And the first time I touched you and I felt . . . it was so strong it nearly knocked me over and I knew . . . I knew we'd end up right here where we are."

"Yes." It was all she could say, because she'd felt it that day, too, as she still did every time they touched.

"It's a legacy of that . . . that day. Something I never wanted, something I can't control. It just comes and . . . I know things. Things I shouldn't know. The first time it happened was about two weeks after my father's death. I thought I had lost my mind.

"I was in Virginia City and I shook hands with a farrier who had just finished shoeing my horse. When I touched him, an image flashed through my mind of his leg pinned beneath the wheel of a wagon. Of course, I said nothing to him, but three days later, it happened. A wagon rolled over him, pinning his leg. He lost it."

Mariah could see the pain it cost him to know such a thing. To know and not be able to stop it. "Go on."

"It's been like that ever since. I see things; sometimes it requires a touch, sometimes not. Sometimes it's only a feeling, not an image. Crazy, huh?"

Mariah sank back against the pillow, trying to absorb what he'd just told her. She understood now what he'd meant. If anyone else had said these things, no doubt she would have reacted with fear or disbelief. But it was Creed telling her, and she'd trusted him with her life. Nothing he could say would ever change that. She shook her head slowly. "No, I don't think you're crazy. Some might call it a gift."

"I never have," he said softly.

"Without it, Jesse and I would both be dead."

His gaze dropped to his hands. "I know."

"What happened to you, Creed, that day?"

He fingered the curly hide beneath his hand. "I've never talked about it. I'm not sure I can tell you. I'm not sure I believe it myself." She watched him in silence.

"I was dying, I could feel . . . my life . . . leaving me. It couldn't have been more than a few seconds, though it felt longer. Much longer." A tremor went through him, though he didn't seem to notice it. His knuckles went white around the buffalo fur. "I saw myself kicking, dying, as if . . . as if it was someone else. I remember a moment of pity for the one who was dying. I wasn't afraid. There was only this light. I . . . heard my mother's voice, sensed her beside me. She spoke to me . . . something in French, but I've never been able

217

to remember her words."

He swallowed hard and looked up at her. "Then I saw a man ride up and cut my . . . cut me down. I felt myself falling. When I opened my eyes, the man was leaning over me, shouting at me to breathe." He lifted his eyes to hers. "That man was Seth."

Mariah braced a trembling palm against the hide, her mind whirling. "Seth? *My* Seth?"

"Oui, ma petite. Your Seth. He was heading through there for Alder Gulch when he heard the shouting. He got to me just in time to see them ride off, leaving me swinging. He cut me down and ripped the rope from my throat. Forced me to breathe again."

No.

"He buried my father and stayed with me until I was strong enough to ride. Then he invited me to come along with him to the gulch. We've been friends ever since." Creed shrugged, staring at his hands. "He didn't even know me. He could have ridden away from that kind of trouble and left me to die. I was almost there." Creed looked up. "But he didn't." Creed took a halting breath. "I owe him my life. Ironic, isn't it? It's only because of him that I'm here with you now."

"Oh, God." Mariah's eyes slid shut in misery. Now she understood.

"Well put." Creed's fists flexed, searching for something to punch. "So here we are, the three of us. Whatever destiny brought me back, Seth is a part of it, has been since that first moment. And now . . . I've betrayed him." Creed pounded a fist into the hide, sending up a cloud of dust. "He saves my life and I've spoiled his woman."

A coldness icier than the air outside the cabin crept over her. *I'm not his woman anymore. Can't you see that, Creed? I'm yours. Always and forever.* She forced herself to face reality. He'd spoken no words of love. Nothing to make her think he wouldn't give her back to Seth when

218

they got there. Nothing to bind them but what they had shared with each other tonight. But that, for her, was enough to last a lifetime. Her voice, when she spoke, was barely audible. "Spoiled?"

His gaze met hers. "You were . . . *une jeune vierge*. A virgin."

"And did you think I wouldn't be?" She damned the catch in her voice.

"Of course not." He furrowed his hair back with both hands. "Hell. It's pretty obvious I wasn't thinking at all. If I had been, we wouldn't be in this situation."

She turned her head away sharply and gazed at the fire. "Are you saying you're sorry we . . . about what happened?"

"Sorry I made love to you? Or sorry I ruined you for Seth?" he countered.

She glared back at him, afraid to choose one over the other. Afraid to hear the truth.

His eyes locked with hers as he moved toward her from across the bed. Like a stalking animal, he came closer. She watched him come, but found she couldn't move. With two hands he took her shoulders and shoved her down on the buffalo hide. He hovered over her, a fierce breath away, while his eyes roved over her face and hair as if he were memorizing her.

"No, Mariah." His mouth dipped down to cover hers. His lips were gentle, pleading. "How can I be sorry about making love to you," he breathed along her jaw, "when I want you again already?" He pressed himself against her. "When you can do this to me by just being near you—"

"Creed—"

He lowered his mouth to hers again, silencing her, sending her mind spinning away from the rights and the wrongs of his kiss. When he lifted his head, his gaze locked with hers. "I don't regret this, *mon bijou*. Not tonight. Not tonight."

Need overrode reason. Passion thundered through them like the storm raging outside. What was done was done, there was no undoing it. Not tonight, not tomorrow.

Not ever.

He dropped his mouth to her breast again, sucking, pulling hard on the beaded rosy nub. His teeth rasped the sensitive skin, inflaming her.

"Oh . . . Creed . . ." She wanted . . . she needed . . . all of him. Sinking her fingers into thick ebony hair she pulled him closer to her breast. She gasped as his fingers dipped past the triangle of hair curled at the apex of her legs and found her once more, stroking her to the brink of madness.

Reaching down, her palm skimmed the muscles of his abdomen until they brushed the silken heat of him. He let out a low sound and flexed his hips against her hand.

"Ah, *Dieu*, Mariah . . . yes . . ."

She stroked him as he had her, until he groaned and turned her over onto her back. His knee impatiently thrust her legs apart. She welcomed the invasion, ached for it. His tongue laved her breast, abrading her nipple with fire, then trailed upward until his teeth closed tantalizingly around the lobe of her ear.

"I won't hurt you this time," he promised against her ear, tormenting the inside of it with his tongue.

She twisted until her mouth found his and she told him with her kiss that it didn't matter. With a groan, he deepened the kiss and entered her in a quick, certain thrust. While his hips moved against hers, the hair on his chest rasped against her breasts, creating an unbearable friction.

She hooked her ankles around the backs of his legs and drew her knees up, urging him closer, closer. Her hands moved against the flexing muscles of his back to the thrusting movements of his hips, awed by the sheer animal power of him.

Slow first, then faster, they fused like tinder and flame, exploding into a brilliant burst. A cry tore from deep inside her and he captured it with his mouth, finding his own release only seconds later. He pulsed within her, slumping over her shoulder with a groan.

Arms and legs entwined, they lay exhausted and sated, without saying a word, until sleep stole over them.

Dawn came with the gentle patter of rain on the roof. The fire snapped and popped with fresh wood and the scent of it filled the cabin. Groggily, Mariah realized that Creed's body was no longer curved around hers. Opening her eyes, she rolled over beneath the buffalo robe and reached for him, only to find him gone. She sat up.

He stood at the window, watching the rain through the wavy panes of glass. His back was to her. He'd pulled on his Levis, but his back was bare. The early morning light washed over him, defining the smooth muscles of his powerful back and arms. Her attraction to him hit her like a rolling wave, making her body tighten all over again with desire.

"Creed?"

The only indication he had heard her was a slight inclination of his head, but he didn't answer.

"Creed?" she repeated, throwing her feet over the edge of the bed. "Are you all right?"

"Go back to sleep, Mariah."

She unwound the nightrail from her legs and stood, wincing a little as she did. "I'm not tired."

"You should be," he said, still looking out the window. "I kept you up last night."

"I didn't mind. How long have you been up?"

"A while."

"You can't look at me this morning. Is that it?"

Creed turned around at that. His gaze started at her bare toes and traveled up until he was looking her in the eye. "No. It's myself I'm having a little trouble with."

Her gaze fell to the floor. "What shall we do now?"

"Do?" Creed knew what she meant. Dammit, he knew, but he had no answer. "Nothing."

Shock held her silent for a few moments. "Wh-what do you mean?"

"You belong with him, Mariah. Not me."

"You can say that after what we've done?" Her voice quavered. "Did it mean nothing to you?"

He sighed heavily. It was a question he'd been wrestling with for hours. Solutions seemed as scarce as sunny skies. "I don't regret making love to you, Mariah. In fact, you're probably the best thing that's ever happened to me. But I do regret that I've betrayed Seth . . . and you."

"Me? No, you're wro—"

"Seth trusted me with you. You trusted me to bring you to him. Now, look what I've done." He raked a hand through his sleep-tumbled hair.

Mariah stared at him. *"You've* done? What about me?"

"It was my fault. I could have stopped it."

"I didn't *want* you to stop. My God, Creed, can't you see what's happening to us?"

"I didn't mean for this to happen."

She shook her head in confusion. "Of course not. Neither did I. But it *did.*"

He hated himself for what he was about to say. But there was no avoiding it. "There's no future for us. I have nothing to offer you, Mariah. You've seen what I am. What kind of a life could we have together? I'm nothing but a bounty hunter—"

"There's only one man you're after and we both know it," she replied steadily. "He may be dead already."

222

"Maybe. Maybe not. He could kill me tomorrow. Then where would you be? You're a lady, Mariah. Seth—he's the kind of man you need."

"And you know what that is, do you? What it is I need?"

"Better than *you* seem to, yes."

She'd walked up behind him and turned him fiercely by the elbow. "Do you feel nothing for me?"

His insides twisted. God, he wished it were true. Wished what had happened between them had been no more or less than that little shred of himself he'd shared with Desirée Lupone back at The Nightingale, but he knew it wasn't. Not by a long shot.

A deep breath did little to ease the ache in him. He felt torn and bloody inside and he doubted he'd ever be whole again. "It doesn't matter what I feel. Seth trusted me to bring you to him. That's what I'm going to do."

"And what," she asked defiantly, "shall I tell him on our wedding night?"

That stopped him cold. It wasn't as if he hadn't thought of it. What *would* she tell him? Should she lie? But Seth would know, just as Creed had known she'd been a maiden. *Merde.*

"I'll go to him, if you want," he said at last, turning toward the fire. "I'll tell him I took advantage of you."

"You'll what?" She stared at him as if he'd just turned into a piece of furniture.

"I'll tell him it wasn't your fault. I . . . I seduced you when you were vulnerable." His gaze traced the lovely curve of her cheek and ended on her lips. "He'll believe me. Any man in his right mind would believe it."

Her mouth tightened. "How noble of you, but it's hardly the truth."

"Close enough."

Not nearly close enough, she thought with a sharp pang of guilt. "No." She walked toward the fire and slumped into the robe-covered chair.

223

"Why not?" he asked, pacing away from the window. "It would work. Seth would forgive you. I know he would."

She turned to look at him, angry. "I don't know what I'll do yet, but I won't let you take the blame for this. Whether you want to believe it or not, what happened between us wasn't a seduction. It was . . . inevitable. And we both know it." She watched the flames blacken the underside of the river rocks that lined the fireplace. "Even if . . . if it meant nothing to you, it meant . . . something to me." *It meant everything.*

Creed's heart twisted with an almost physical pain. *Don't do this to me, Mariah. You're tearing me up inside.*

"Don't be a fool. Don't throw away what you have with Seth because of one night with me. It would be a terrible mistake."

"Would it?" she asked, staring at him.

Creed stood watching her for a long minute and finally returned to the window. "The snow is nearly gone. The rain's letting up. If we leave soon, we can be in Virginia City by tomorrow evening."

When she didn't answer, he looked back at her. She was walking toward him, her fingers working open the buttons of her nightrail. Pop, pop, pop, they flicked open until the gentle swell of her breast appeared.

Creed swallowed, fighting the tightening in his groin and an erratic pounding in his chest. "Mariah, what are you — ?"

She didn't answer. Instead, she stopped in front of him, her eyes locked with his, and slipped the gown first off one shoulder, then the other until it pooled in an ivory puddle at her feet. Heat soared through him like a Chinook wind. Hands still at his sides, his eyes widened, taking in the perfection of her body backlit by the morning light coming through the window.

He shuddered as she reached up and trailed her fingers down his bare chest and across his sensitive nipple.

His eyes slid shut on a moan. *"Dieu,* don't . . ."

"Does this feel like a mistake to you, Creed?" she whispered, touching the moist tip of her tongue where her fingers had been.

"This doesn't change anything," he warned, breathing deeply, inhaling her touch.

"No," Mariah whispered against his skin. "It doesn't change a thing." *But everything is changed.* "Make love to me, Creed. Make love to me one last time in the daylight. Don't talk. Don't even think."

With a groan, he scooped her in his arms. Dropping his mouth heatedly against hers, he gave up his good intentions and gave in to the inevitable force that bound them together as surely as a magnet to steel.

"Just love me, Creed," she whispered against his ear. "Just for a little while. Soon enough, we'll have to say goodbye."

And one last time, he did.

Chapter Sixteen

"Gentlemen, take your positions!" shouted the tall, bewhiskered man on the wooden stoop of one of Virginia City's newest hotels, The Missouri House. The man's distinguished black frock coat—minus tie—and tall gray hat set him apart from the begrimed collection of miners who shoved and jostled for prime positions in the circle near the brim-full watering trough.

The dozen or so men did not seem bothered by either the ankle-deep mud—which carried the distinct odor of horse dung—nor the fading daylight, but were furiously stuffing chaw inside their cheeks and tossing last minute wagers of antelope bags filled with gold dust at the tally man. This fellow scribbled rapid notes in a leatherbound notebook atop a metal scale in his lap.

Wide-eyed, Mariah steered Petunia around the crowd of rowdies, dodging the spectators who had gathered for the event and who gawked from every stoop and balcony close at hand. Whores in skimpy, shock-bright costumes dangled out the windows of a half-painted brothel in a lascivious display of skin and cleavage, shouting ribald encouragement at the miners.

"Git that little bugger fer me, Harry, you sweet thang," one counterfeit blonde drawled, "and ah'll give ya one fer half-price t'night." She winked and shook her ample bosom at a handsome, tow-headed miner who whooped and tossed both his purse and his hat into the melee.

Shock suffused Mariah's cheeks with heat, but before she knew it, a drunken man collided at full stagger with Petunia's considerable flank. Knocked senseless — if, indeed, he'd any in the first place — the sot sent her a silly grin and pitched face-first into the muck at the horse's feet. It was a comically artful fall which the mare took with stoic good grace as she sidestepped the fallen man.

Mariah gasped, certain the man would drown, but his equally inebriated companions lifted him by the arms and dragged him across the street, as they roared with laughter. Together, they staggered toward one of the dozens of saloons firmly entrenched in the town's business section. The sound of hammers striking nails and the screech of saws echoed through the evening air in a discordant cacophony.

Words failed her as she evaded another swerving pedestrian. A feeling of despair took hold and she gathered the edges of Creed's blanket capote tighter around her.

This was Virginia City?

This — this . . . *Gomorrah* was what she'd traveled halfway across the country for? It was beyond reckoning, much worse than anything she could have imagined. She'd heard, of course, that mining camps were, well, rowdy. But this . . .

She sent a dismayed look at Creed who, for the first time since they'd left the cabin, was half-smiling beneath the brim of his hat. He'd pulled his horse to a stop and settled back to watch.

"Are you certain we're in the right place?" she shouted over the din. "There isn't, by any slim chance, some mistake?"

227

He actually laughed. "No, *ange*. This is it. Home sweet home. What do you think?"

Her vocabulary wasn't up to providing an answer. "Whatever are they *doing* over there?" she asked, pointing to the group of men near the trough.

"It has to do with an unlucky, eh, . . . *cafard, mon chou.* A cockroach."

Cockroach? Before she could reply, the man in the frock coat raised a revolver high over his head and cocked the weapon as the last of the bets were recorded.

"Gentlemen—" he called with a grandiose sweep of the gun, "take aim!"

The pistol exploded and a collective roar rose from the crowd around the circled men. From within that circle came not cheers but the revolting sound of spitting as each miner took his luck hawking brown juice at a madly scrambling cockroach who'd been unceremoniously dumped from a jar.

With all due seriousness of purpose, the contestants chomped on their wads of tobacco, oblivious to the streams of brown dribbling down their chins. They laughed raucously, elbowing each other with good-natured shoves.

"Hey, you little scum picker!" shouted one of them at the beleaguered insect. "C'mere! I got a little sumpin' for ya!" He let loose with a stream of brown juice that landed squarely across the toe of a second man's mining boot.

The thick-waisted man jumped back and yelled, "Proctor, your aim's so poor ya couldn't hit the ground with yer hat in three tries!" He let loose with a wad of his own aimed dead at the other's boot. It found its mark with a satisfying splat.

Several bystanders slipped in the mud, adding to the bedlam before a cheer went up for the miner who had christened the cockroach with a well-placed gob of tobacco juice.

The winner, a scruffy-looking fellow, thin as a bed slat, was hoisted in victory onto the shoulders of several others and hauled over to the tally man to collect his share of the winnings. Others, who'd had the foresight to wager on him, surged in that direction as well. The rest of the crowd began to disperse, heading into various saloons and newly built bawdy houses that lined the street. Mariah drew her gaze from the sight, appalled to admit she'd found the whole affair somewhat fascinating but she couldn't help but wonder what had become of the poor cockroach.

Beside her, Creed lounged on Buck with one knee thrown over the saddle horn and his chin cupped in his hand. He was grinning. "Enjoy that, did you?"

"Enjoy it?" she said huffily, casting a condescending glance at the crowd. "Hardly! That was the most . . . disgusting sight I've ever—why, how grown men could be so easily entertained at the suffering of some poor dumb creature is—"

The rest caught in her throat. Her eyes widened at the sight of the thin, blond-haired fellow not fifteen feet from her, holding a fat bag of dust. He, too, had stopped in the middle of slapping the winner on the shoulder to turn and stare open-mouthed at her.

Mariah's heart rose to her throat. The well-trimmed mustache was new, the face more gaunt than she remembered and a shade paler than looked entirely healthy, but those gray eyes—she knew them as well as her own.

"Seth?"

He took a step toward her. His mustache twitched in a smile—the charming one that had always sent her heart to her toes.

"Good Lord. Mari, is it really you?" A cough rat-

229

tled through his frame, but he didn't take his eyes off her.

A strange mixture of joy, guilt, and relief knotted her throat. Seth was alive and standing right there betting on a cockroach! *Oh, thank God, thank God.* "Of course it's me," she cried, sliding off Petunia into the mucky street. Her boots sank deeply. "Who in the world else would ride halfway around the country to see you?"

Seth met her before she'd taken two steps and gathered her in his strong arms. "Good Lord, I was about to send the cavalry out after you two." He pressed a hand to the back of her head and tenderly drew her to his shoulder.

From his horse, Creed watched Mariah go to him and felt his insides tear apart. He gritted his teeth and told himself he had no rights to her. None at all. But it didn't help. Damn, how was he going to get through it?

His thoughts were not far from Mariah's own. She tightened her arms around Seth and hugged him tight, wishing their reunion could have been the simple one he'd planned.

"When I didn't hear . . ." Seth pulled back to see her face. "Thank God you're all right. You are the stubbornest darn woman—"

His head dropped toward her and for a moment Mariah was certain he was going to kiss her full on the mouth, but his lips slid across her cheek disappointingly in a chaste buss.

She blushed profusely and so, to her surprise, did he, as the men gathered curiously around him. Her eyes were drawn inevitably to Creed. He was watching her, his mouth set in a grim line with no hint of pleasure at seeing his old friend again. *Don't look at me that way, Creed,* she begged him with her eyes. *Please.*

230

Turning back to Seth, she forced herself to speak. "I—I heard you were very ill. Are you . . . I mean, you look well. A little pale, maybe . ." Emotion tightened her throat. Her gaze swept over the smile lines around his eyes and the upturned corners of his mouth she remembered so well.

"I'm nearly as good as new," Seth reassured her, brushing a strand of hair from her eyes. "Let me look at you, Mari," he said, holding her at arm's length.

She brushed a hand self-consciously over her loose auburn curls and cast a forlorn glance at her travel-stained denims, rolled up at the ankles, and over-sized shirt she'd knotted at the waist. "I can explain about the clothes—"

His gaze roamed over her face. "You've turned into a real beauty, Mari. Just like I knew you would."

She let out a teary laugh. "Oh, Seth, it's so good to see you." She threw her arms around his neck again and buried her face against his shoulder.

Seth's gaze focused on Creed and he pulled Mariah along with him as he extended a hand and a smile to his old friend.

"Creed—" Seth said, loosening his hold on Mariah.

Creed forced a smile and slid off his horse. "Seth."

Seth wrapped both hands around Creed's. "By God, you're a sight for sore eyes. I expected you days ago, but no stages came through and then we got word about the trouble up there at the station—"

"About the robbery? Ah, *oui*. It was a hell of a trip," Creed confirmed.

"I want to hear all about it." Seth glanced at Mariah and shifted the conversation to Petunia. "Don't tell me you rode all the way here on horseback, Mariah?"

231

"Nearly," Creed answered for her, "but it's a long story." Her dark eyes held his for the briefest of seconds, then went to Seth. "Time enough to tell you later. You look halfway human again, partner."

Mariah shot Creed a confused look which he ignored.

"A darn sight better than when you left, I imagine," Seth answered, wincing at the memory. "But I'm nearly as good as new. Listen, I — how can I ever thank you?" He slapped Creed across the back. "A fellow couldn't have a truer friend. I could never repay you for what you've done for me." He hugged Mariah and she managed a tremulous smile. "For us."

Heat crept up Creed's neck and he cleared his throat. He was losing her. God, she was just going to slip away from him and he was letting her go. He shrugged and smiled at Seth. "I'm just glad to see you back on your feet again, *mon ami*. Look's like Sadie took good care of you."

"That woman's a national treasure," Seth admitted with a grin, "and she makes a mean chicken soup. Her husband, Wade, looked after the store for me."

The burly man Seth had been standing with moments ago came forward, swiped his hat from his head, and wrung the brim in his hands. "This yer Miss Parsons, Travers?" His gaze roamed with awed politeness over Mariah as he solemnly declared, "It were worth the wait, friend." That elicited a roar of laughter from the group surrounding them and slaps on the back for Seth.

A redheaded Scot with a flaming beard leaned toward her, grinning happily. "Ach, an' Seth here has been pinin' after ye for days now since he got his feet under him." He punched Seth in the shoulder good naturedly. "Aye, an' we had to put the twist to his arm to get him outta tha' shop o' his this even'. Just

232

to get his mind off his worries, ye ken? Didn't we, lads?"

A murmur of agreement rumbled around them, but most of the men stood apparently tongue-tied by the sight of a single white woman who wasn't a fallen dove.

Belatedly, the Scot lifted his scruffy, flat-billed cap. "Rory McPheerson, lassie, at yer service. Finest blacksmith this side of the Divide."

"Pleased to meet you, Mr. McPheerson. Should I need the services of a blacksmith, I shall certainly know where to come." McPheerson grinned delightedly and backed away. He was replaced with several others who sheepishly came up and paid their respects.

"All right, all right, boys," Seth told them, "Miss Parsons has had a trying trip. She's too much a lady to tell you she's too tired for this now. There'll be plenty of time for all of you to meet her later. Right now, I'm sure what she wants is a quiet room all to herself."

He took her by the elbow. "Come on, Mari, let's get you settled down at *The Virginia*. It's the newest hotel in town—safe and clean for single ladies. You'll be comfortable there. Do you have any baggage?"

Her head was spinning and she looked helplessly up at Creed. "Baggage? I, uh, well, no. Actually, I sort of *lost* a bag on the way here and—my other things were . . . um, ruined. Hattie was supposed to ship my trunk on when the stages started running again." Her gaze flicked briefly to Creed, who was toying with the reins in his hands and avoiding her eyes.

"Anyway, these were more practical to ride in," she rushed on, babbling with an attack of nerves. "I mean, what with all those rivers and brush and all, well, Creed thought—"

"No worry," Seth cut in, looking a bit bemused by the whole explanation. "I run a mercantile, remember? Though readymade dresses, I'm afraid, are in short supply in a mining camp. There is a seamstress in town—the wife of one of the miners—the hurdy-gurdies have been keeping her employed of late."

"Bon, you two go on then," Creed said, mounting Buck. "I'll catch up after I stable the horses down at Denton's Livery."

Mariah felt a twinge of panic at the sight of Creed on his horse. What if he just rode away and she never saw him again? Lord, why had she thought she could *do* this?

"You're not coming with us?" she asked in her calmest voice as he gathered up her mare's reins. "Don't you need a room as well?"

Seth shook his head. "You'll stay with me as always, of course. I've got plenty of room."

Creed's shrug was noncommittal. "We'll talk about that later."

Her heart sank. He was going to leave. She could see it in his eyes.

"Listen, the Benders invited me to supper tonight. I'm sure she won't mind two more," he told Creed. "You know Sadie—she always cooks enough for a regiment."

Creed's expression eased a bit. "I know. I'll try to make it. I have some, uh, things to take care of tonight." His eyes studiously avoided Mariah's.

She shook her head. "Oh, and I couldn't go anywhere looking the way I do. I—"

"You look beautiful, Mari, and Sadie can't wait to meet you," Seth said. "She doesn't give a tinker's damn about things like that. You'll see. Besides, you'll have time to rest up at *The Virginia.* Even a hot

234

bath if you want one."

Mariah's eyes flicked to Creed to find him staring uncomfortably at his feet. "A bath . . ." she repeated. "Yes, that would be nice."

"Seven o'clock at Sadie's, Creed." Seth slapped him on the shoulder. "Try and make it. I want to hear all about your trip."

"Pretty boring stuff, *oui*, Mariah?" Creed said, meeting her gaze at last. "She can tell you everything you need to know. You two go on. Tell Sadie not to hold dinner for me."

Mariah tried to smile, but her face seemed to crack. Instead, she just watched him ride down the street without her.

Creed followed Wallace Street past the rows of shops and houses toward Van Buren. The sound of a concertina playing "Sweet Betsy from Pike," poured out the door of *The Bale of Hay,* a lively house of gambling and drink already crowded with customers.

The streets were alive with miners and the even scruffier pilgrims who worked for a daily wage headed home after working since dawn on their claims, lugging pickaxes and gold pans. The fragrant scents of a bakery drifted on the evening breeze, mingling incongruously with the pungent dried fish and raw meats hanging in the open air stall of a Chinese grocer.

There, amidst all that humanity, Creed had never felt more miserably alone. Walking the horses slowly, he allowed the noise of the crowded street to cushion his raw emotions. He was in no particular hurry to be anywhere, he mused glumly, except maybe to cozy up to some bar and get roaring drunk.

But Seth expected him to come to Sadie's tonight,

and it wouldn't help Mariah's cause any to show up soused, looking as wretched as he felt. But he could hardly stomach the thought of trying to swallow dinner while watching Seth and Mariah together.

Hell.

He'd seen it in her eyes. She was scared. She wasn't any more ready to meet Seth there on the street than he was. It was all Creed could do to look Seth straight in the eye.

How could he have let it happen?

How?

Dammit, he hadn't meant for things to go that far with Mariah, but it had all seemed to slip out of his control. He had never felt for a woman what he did for her. She was the most beautiful, independent, argumentative woman he'd ever—

You love her.

He slammed his eyes shut at the unbidden thought. "No," he said aloud.

Admit it, Devereaux. You're in deeper than you ever wanted to be. Just because you're not good enough for her doesn't change the facts. You want her. And not just in your bed. In your life.

"No!" he nearly shouted, causing a miner ahead of him to leap out of Creed's path with an alarmed look. *Hell.*

He gave Petunia's reins a yank and scowled. They'd had this discussion in the cabin. He'd never mentioned the word *love,* but then neither had she. They were bound together by the simple fact that they'd survived the harrowing trip down from Fort Benton. He suspected it was gratitude, not love, that Mariah felt for him. It was a natural thing that they should become closer for it. She was young, impressionable, and he'd taken advantage of that. Stolen her most precious gift. For that, he'd never forgive himself.

He'd lost control. Lost the edge that had kept him going these past few years. Now, he was about to lose not only the best friend he'd ever had, but the only woman who'd ever meant anything to him as well.

He wanted to scream, howl at the moon at the injustice of it all. Instead, a quiet desperation stole over his soul. Creed kicked Buck into a trot, glancing at the dozens of new buildings under construction along the muddy street. A blue-smocked Chinese with a black queue dangling beneath his basket hat was putting the finishing touches on the sign above a new cooper shop:

A.K. KNOPF COOPERAGE AND WOODWORKS

BARRELS, BUCKETS, COFFINS

MADE TO SPECIFICATION — AFFORDABLE PRICES

It was amazing how much a town could change in just the two weeks he'd been gone, he mused. New buildings were being erected at a pace of a hundred a week. Green lumber, cut and freighted into the gulch by ox-team freight wagons, were stacked in strategic piles along the road. The hillsides had long since been stripped of the alder wood which had given the gulch its name, leaving them desolate and barren.

The main thoroughfare spanned five hundred feet of mud and horse dung that looked as if a hog had rooted it up. Older one-room shanties made of logs, mud, and stone lined the avenue like so many toadstools sprouting out of the fertile Montana soil.

A wagon rolled by in the mud, loaded with a lonely coffin, bound for Cemetery Hill. The driver played a soulful mouth harp in lieu of a funeral procession. The dead man apparently had few friends.

Creed watched it pass, wondering if that was the way he would end someday, then he pulled to a stop at Denton's Livery. Dismounting, he tied the two horses to the hitching post outside the wide double doors. The fragrance of ripe horseflesh and clean straw drifted to him as he pulled open the set-in door.

"Well, if it ain't Creed Devereaux." The middle-aged Missourian in worn overalls glanced up from the gelding's hoof he was doctoring and grinned. "I see you ain't got yerself kilt . . . yet."

One corner of Creed's mouth turned up. "Disappointed, Hasty?"

Hasty Denton dropped the horse's hoof with a thud and brushed his weathered hands against his denims. "Well now, that's a downright ungenerous remark comin' from a man who wants me to look after his hoss." He slapped the mare on the withers and sent Creed a wicked grin. "Less'n you got me writ up in yer will."

"I'll be sure to remember to take care of that," Creed allowed, extending his hand. "I have a couple of horses to board this time. You have the room?"

"Reckon as how I do. I thought you was up Fort Benton-way pickin' up Travers' sweetheart."

Creed plucked a stalk of hay from a manger and stuck it between his teeth. "That seems to be common knowledge around here."

"Travers is a popular feller. I reckon some folks didn't think you had that kinda kindness in ya, pard."

"Maybe I don't," Creed mumbled in reply.

Hasty harumphed. "Anyway, Travers, he was in a real tizzy about you two after hearin' what happened at the stage stop."

Creed's brows drew into a frown. "You mean about the stage robbery?"

"Nah. About John Lochrie an' his wife."

Creed's body went rigid. "What about them?"

"Dead. You didn't know? Dead as doornails, them

238

and their help.

Creed felt as if he'd taken a physical blow to the gut and he struggled for air. *John and Hattie, murdered? Le bon Dieu.* It didn't seem possible. Then his mind raced to yet a more horrifying thought. *Mariah . . . if she'd stayed there like he told her . . .*

"Yeah," Hasty went on, "they was kilt by some somvabitches who, ah . . . took turns with the woman a'fore they strangled her." Hasty shook his head and his lips drew into a grim white line. "It were downright indecent what they done. Kilt them some driver who'd been shot once before, too, who was layin' abed in their house." Hasty shook his head in disgust.

Creed braced one hand on the splintery wood of the stall and rubbed his temple with his fingertips. "When? When did it happen?"

"Oh, week or so since they died . . . it appeared."

Just about the time Pierre would have started after me. A sick feeling rose in his throat.

"Got the sad word when the A.J. Oliver coach finally come in yestiddy evenin'. Real shame. Nice folks they was, too. Bought some hosses from me a while back."

Damn LaRousse. Damn him to hell! He slammed his hand against a thick wooden beam. He'd find that son of a bitch and kill him if it was the last thing he did!

Hasty frowned and reached up to untether the horse's lead from the wall. He clucked to the mare, who ambled down the wide corridor to her stall. "The Lochries personal friends o' yourn, was they?"

Creed stared sightlessly at the rough grain of the barn wood, his jaw working. "You could say that."

"You know who done it, don't ya?"

"I've got a damn good idea." He raked a hand through his hair, started to turn away, then remem-

239

bering his initial purpose, turned back. "Hasty, my horses are tied up outside. Brush them down and give them an extra ration of oats and don't scrimp on the hay, *oui?* They've had a rough couple of weeks."

Hasty nodded. "You got it. You know the rates. Dollar a day, four bits fer oats, another two fer rubdown. Hay's included in the price."

"Bon," Creed said and shook his hand, but he wasn't really listening. He was thinking about La-Rousse and how long it would take to find him again.

"How long?" Hasty asked.

Creed's head jerked up. "What?"

"The *horses,*" Hasty said. "How long they gonna be here?"

"Oh." Creed ran a hand over his beard-roughened jaw. "The mare, Petunia, belongs to Seth's fiancé, Miss Parsons. The gelding's named Buck, and I'll be leaving within the next day or so."

"Right'o. Say—you got an idear about them good folks' killers—talk to Sheriff Fox. He'll be wantin' to hear what you got to say. I hear they's a ree-ward fer the murderers," he said, but Creed had already turned away. "Evenin' to you, Devereaux."

"Evenin', Hasty," he muttered, and walked out.

Mariah jumped at the sound of the knock on her door and realized she'd been staring vacantly at her reflection in the looking glass. Outside the window, the sky had grown quite dark and she wondered how long she'd been sitting there thinking.

"Mari, it's me." Seth's voice came from the other side of the door. "Are you ready?"

She plaited the last of her still-damp hair into its braid and tied it off with the strand of fringe Creed had torn off his shirt for her that day by the river. Her fingers hovered on it for a few seconds before she got up and pulled the door open for Seth.

"I'm as ready as I'll ever be, considering," she said, smiling brightly into his gray-blue eyes.

"Considering what? That you're the most beautiful girl Alder Gulch has ever laid eyes on?" He crossed the threshold and withdrew a bouquet of bright orange flowers from behind his back.

"Lilies—" she whispered, taking them. "What a . . . sweet thing to do. Thank you, Seth." She reached up and kissed his cheek. His arms caught her before she could withdraw.

"Mari, it's so good to see you."

His breath was warm and sweet against her forehead and she could smell the spicy scent of his shaving soap. Her gaze traced his face from his strong jawline upward. Though partially hidden by his mustache, she knew the corners of his mouth turned up even when he wasn't smiling, giving him a perpetually boyish look.

The years had deepened the grooves in his cheeks that appeared when he smiled; his nose was strong, aquiline, but she'd always thought it suited him. His hair, sandy brown and streaked blond by Montana sun, was cut neatly and combed back, away from his face. All in all, it was a face anyone would love. And he was smiling down at her, believing that she did just that.

She thought of the hundreds of times she'd fantasized about him doing this when she was younger. *I do love him. I do.*

Not the way you love Creed.

It doesn't matter. I'll make it work.

He doesn't make your heart pound, does he?

Shut up.

He doesn't make your breasts ache just to be near him,

241

does he?"

Shut up, shut up!

"When you wrote to tell me your grandmother had died and you were coming here, I admit I had serious doubts," he said. "Virginia City is nothing like Chicago. I was afraid you'd hate it."

"Montana's the most beautiful country I've ever seen — truly."

A pleased smile creased his cheeks. "I love it here, too. Virginia's growing fast and families are moving in. We'll be happy here, Mari." His gray eyes darkened as his hands roved over her shoulders. "May I . . . may I kiss you, Mariah?"

Her fingers tightened around the bouquet and she smelled the fragrance of the crushed stems. Seth's mouth hovered a breath away. *Don't ask me. Just kiss me. Long and hard and prove me wrong about us, Seth.* Instead, she simply nodded.

His closed lips brushed hers softly with tender reverence and moved across her mouth with a bristle of whiskers, tickling her nose.

Please, let me feel something. Let my pulse race, my knees buckle. Anything.

She wrapped her arms around his neck and pressed herself closer, brazenly urging him to deepen the kiss. She felt his mouth slacken in surprise, but he responded by touching her lips with the barest of brushes with his tongue. A tremor went through him as her lips parted, welcoming his kiss. She felt the evidence of his desire hard against her as he pulled her closer.

She was reminded of the comfortable old slipper she'd so foolishly mentioned to Creed. Kissing Seth was comfortable, even pleasant, she admitted. But it didn't weaken her knees like Creed's kisses did. It didn't rob her of breath and sanity.

God help her, it didn't do that.

Abruptly, Seth ended the kiss, pulled back to look at her and swallowed hard. "Ah, Mariah." Passion and a hint of surprise thickened his voice, made his breath come fast. "You can't know how long I've wanted to do that. You're so . . . so lovely. You've grown up, Mariah." His fingers brushed down the side of her cheek. "I want us to be married right away. The circuit preacher from Bannack is coming through here next week. I know you always pictured a church wedding, but I'm afraid this place has no church yet. But I'll make it nice for you, Mari, I promise."

Slowly, she pulled herself out of his arms. Her head spun at the thought of all of his plans. He looked at her with such trusting eyes, how could she lie? She couldn't and she knew it.

Confusion furrowed his brow. "What's wrong, Mari?"

Her throat burned. "Seth," she said softly, withdrawing her hands from his, "I'm sorry but . . . I can't marry you."

Chapter Seventeen

"You *what?*"

"I said, I can't marry you." Mariah hugged her arms to herself.

"I heard what you said. I . . ." His expression was frozen in shock. "I just don't . . . My God, Mari, why not?" He stared at her for a long minute. When she didn't answer, he asked, "Is . . . is there someone else?"

She walked over to the window and peered through the wavy glass pane. Outside, life went on as usual. The streets were thick with people, the sun had set, the moon had risen. But inside, she felt dead. *Someone else?*

"Not anymore," she answered. "There was someone, though. Briefly. I thought . . ." She turned to him. "I thought I was in love with him."

"Were you?"

"I . . . I'm not sure." No, she told herself, this was the time for honesty, not half-truths. "Yes. Yes I was."

"I see." He turned away, plunging his fingers into his thick, wavy hair.

She felt something crack inside her. *I'm sorry, Seth, so sorry.*

"And now?" he asked in a strange voice that didn't seem to belong to the Seth she knew. "Are you still in love with him?"

Her finger traced down the window frame as it blurred through her tears. Outside, the noisy ebb and flow of humanity echoed the beat of her heart. "It's over."

"Are you certain?"

She nodded. "Quite certain. But there are things about me you don't know. I—I'm not the same girl you left behind in Chicago."

He exhaled sharply. "I'm not the same either, Mari," he said, taking a step toward her. "Everyone changes. Everyone . . . makes mistakes."

"No. You don't understand—"

He took her by the shoulders from behind. "I understand that I love you. That I've always loved you. Jesus, Mari, we practically grew up together. We've been intended since I can remember. I never wanted to marry anyone but you. Don't you . . . love me anymore?"

She whirled to face him, tears streaking her cheeks. "Of course I do. I've always loved you, Seth—" *But not the way I love him.*

Relief flooded his face. He took her by the upper arms and drew her close. "Ah, Mari, then I—I don't understand. If you love me . . ."

His earnest expression broke her heart. "There are things about me you should know. You have a right to know. I—I've *done* things—"

He put a finger to her lips. "No. I don't need to know anything else. Look at me." He tipped her face up to his. "Four years is a long time to be apart. Things happen—"

"But—"

"—so be it. I'm looking at you. Not at the young girl I left behind. Your letters all these years have kept me going. You haven't even seen the plans for

245

the house I'm going to build for us, or . . . or seen my store yet. I've made a success of it, Mari. I did this all for you, for us. So I could take care of you, make a home for you. It's *you* I want. I want you to have my children. I want to raise them with you."

She bowed her head, unable to meet his eye. "Oh, Seth, I don't deserve you."

"Oh, hell," he muttered. "That's just not true. I've certainly . . . well, I've made my share of mistakes here," he said, pushing his hand through his swept-back hair. "You can ask Creed if you don't believe me. He's seen me at my worst." She closed her eyes, willing herself not to turn away at the mention of Creed.

"Look," he went on, sliding a hand over her shoulder and down her arm, "I know it'll take some time to . . . to get to know one another again, to be truly . . . comfortable. I probably shouldn't have kissed you that way. But I couldn't help myself. God, just to look at you, I . . ."

He moistened his dry lips with his tongue and tipped her chin up so she was forced to look at him. "Say you'll marry me, Mari. Whatever's happened in the past, we can put it behind us. None of that matters anymore.

"I'll make you happy," he went on. "I promise I will. I'll take care of you. You'll never have to worry about anything. You'll see." His fingers toyed with her sleeve. "Just give me the chance. You'll make me the proudest man in Montana."

She released the breath she hadn't realized she'd been holding. She'd tried, hadn't she? She tried to tell him.

We'll put the past behind us. That's what he said. Maybe, just maybe it was true.

Besides, what good would it do to tell him it was

Creed she'd so foolishly fallen in love with? It would probably destroy him—them. And what was the point of that? It was kinder to let him think it was another man in her past.

And easier to let him think its over.

It *was* over, she told herself firmly. Creed had made it all too clear there was no future for her with him. She was alone in the world, except for the man who'd always been her best friend.

Friendship is important to a marriage, isn't it?

So is passion.

She shut out the thought. It's all for the best. It would hardly be awful being married to a man like Seth—a man who loved her unconditionally. She could be a good wife to him. She *would*.

She would forget about Creed Devereaux, put him out of her mind. Forever. She'd be the best wife to Seth he could ever want. And he'd be happy, too.

At least someone should end up happy in all this.

"Mariah?" Seth was waiting for her answer.

She felt her mouth quiver into a smile. "All right. All right. If you still want me, I'll be proud to marry you, Seth."

He sighed deeply and wrapped his arms around her. "You won't be sorry. I promise you. You won't be sorry. I love you, Mari."

For four long years she'd waited for this moment, to hear him say those very words. Now here he was and those same words broke her heart.

She hated herself for what she'd done and what she was doing. His lips brushed her neck and the clean, masculine scent of him filled her senses. She tightened her arms around his back, remembering his solidness, his strength. He was a man she'd always been able to lean on.

The problem was, she'd finally discovered she could stand on her own.

The Benders' house was situated at the far end of a muddy thoroughfare called Van Buren. The wood-frame structure was separated from a livery on one side and a mud and stone house on the other by a white picket fence. The enclosure boasted ten feet of winter-browned grass and a garden full of rose bushes, red with buds. Raw wood boxes of blooming geraniums sprouted below the waxed-muslin windows.

As she and Seth mounted the wooden steps, the door swung open. The light from within was partially blocked by the broad-beamed figure of a woman in the doorway, brandishing a wooden spoon. Her voice reminded Mariah of a rusty foghorn. "Well, I declare!" the woman cried, planting her fists on her hips. "Is this—?"

"It sure is, Sadie," Seth answered, grinning broadly.

"Saints be praised and hallelujah!" She turned and hollered back into the house. "Wade, look who Seth's brought to dinner." Without waiting for her husband, Sadie hurried down the steps and pulled Mariah into her arms in a bone-crunching hug. "Land sakes, child! You've had us worried sick. What kept you? Seth was about to round the vigilantes up again and set out a'lookin' for you."

"I—I, uh . . ." Mariah mumbled against the woman's ample shoulder.

"Heavens to Betsy, where are my manners?" She let Mariah go, rocking her backward on her heels. "Here I am a'huggin' you an' we haven't even been introduced formal-like. But then I feel as if I know

248

you already. Seth, here, has talked about you so much."

Mariah nodded, unable to gather a coherent thought. Seth coughed beside her.

"Come in, come in," Sadie boomed, "we'll do our talkin' inside where the chill ain't gonna put frost on our teeth."

Seth leaned close to her ear. "Don't let her scare you. She's a lamb." He straightened and smiled broadly again as Sadie's husband reached a hand to him. Two strapping teenaged boys appeared at their father's side, gaping curiously at Mariah.

Without breaking stride, Sadie rapped each on the head with her spoon. "Catchin' flies with yer mouth ain't gonna win you any points with womenfolk, boys. It ain't terrible attractive. C'mon inside, now."

Mariah stifled a smile as the boys, properly chastised, stumbled back into the house, their mouths firmly closed.

The house was, indeed, warm with a fire burning in the huge stone fireplace that took up the better part of one wall. Most of the furniture was handmade; colorful rag rugs decorated the floor, adding to the coziness. Kerosene lamps brightened the corners and the plank table was set with a mishmash of plates and dishes that suited the house just perfectly. The tantalizing aroma of roast venison made her stomach rumble.

Her gaze went to the smudge of flour on Sadie's cheek and the long white apron that covered her faded blue calico gown. She was plentifully built, with strong hands that Mariah could imagine pushing a plow. There was, however, a grace about Sadie despite her rough manner—an economy of motion that belied her size.

"This here's my husband, Wade Bender," Sadie went on, taking control of the introductions. "And my two boys, Jarrod and Jason. Say hello, boys."

"Hullo," they mumbled in unison.

"Miss Parsons — it's a pure pleasure to meet you at last," Wade replied in a gallant, soft-spoken voice. He held an ornately carved pipe clamped between his teeth. As slender as Sadie was broad, Wade had thinning brown hair and spectacles. His face was gentle, with laugh lines around his eyes and a neatly trimmed beard showing the first touches of gray.

A smile eased the tension of Mariah's mouth. "The pleasure's mine, Mr. Bender."

"And o' course, I'm Sadie Bender," his wife went on, "but I only go by Sadie. Anything more formal just makes me feel old."

"Hello, Sadie." Mariah awkwardly took her proffered hand and Sadie pumped her arm up and down. She sent a helpless look to Seth, who simply grinned.

"Howdy-do, Miss Parsons."

"It's just Mariah, please," she insisted. "I apologize for my inappropriate appearance." She glanced down at her still-grimy pants and shirt, which Sadie seemed not to notice.

"Ain't nothin' inappropriate about you, young lady. You're lookin' mighty fit after a trip like you must have had."

Relief swelled through Mariah. "Seth has told me what a help you were to him when he was ill. I wish there was some way to thank you."

"Pshaw," Sadie retorted with a wave of her hand, urging Mariah into a horsehair sofa near the fireplace. "Friends help friends in times of need. Nothin' more to it. Yer bein' here at last is thanks

250

enough. But to be sure, Seth's lucky to be here at all.

"There were times, girl, I thought I'd be a'showin' you his grave when you came. That fever were the dad-blamedest affliction I ever did see, burnin' him up like a pyre and Wade and me packin' him with blockhouse ice cut from the Missouri last winter."

"Truthfully," Seth admitted, sheepishly, "I don't ever recall absorbing the effect of that particular remedy. I don't recall much of anything for nigh on a week, except the distinct impression that I would shake myself out of my bed."

"Oh, Seth," Mariah whispered.

Sadie shook her head. "That quack of a doctor tried oil of wormwood, vermifuge, quinine . . . even jalap-of-turpentine." Waving her hand disparagingly, she said, "Then he gave it up altogether, leavin' us to our own resources. Goldenseal. There was the ticket. And my teas—feverfew, yarrow and hyssop. Right as rain after forty-eight hours, he was. He's still a mite peaked though, and he can use a hand at the store with the heavy work for a few days." She looked up at Seth. "Speakin' of which, where's Creed?"

"He's back, too." Seth sat down next to Mariah. "I hope you don't mind that I invited him to come tonight, too. He had some things to do, but he said he'd try to make it."

"Try? He'd *better* come or he'll miss my bramble-berry pie. An' ya know how he hankers after my pies. Jarrod," she ordered, rapping the youngster on the arm with the wooden spoon, "set another place for Miss Parsons and Mr. Devereaux."

The boy jumped out of the chair he'd been lounging in, eyes wide with expectation. "Creed's comin'? Think he'll tell us any more stories about

251

the Innocents Gang, Pa? Or the way he caught up with Black Jack Jesson up in the north country?"

Wade sent his younger son a patient look and took a thoughtful pull on his pipe. Smoke curled in a blue wreath around his head. "Aren't you tired of hearing those tales yet, boy?"

Stricken, Jarrod exclaimed, *"Tired?* No, sir. I don't reckon I'll ever get tired of hearin' Creed talk about it. I want to be a bounty hunter someday, just like him."

"When pigs fly," Sadie mumbled, wrapping a dishtowel around her hands to pull a pan out of the oven.

"It's *Mister Devereaux* to you, Jarrod," Wade instructed in a fatherly tone. "And maybe, just maybe, Mr. Devereaux doesn't find it as fascinating to talk about his line of work as you do."

That was the understatement of the year, Mariah thought.

Seth grinned. "Jarrod plagues Creed whenever he comes over until he's forced to recount at least one hair-raising adventure of his 'illustrious' career. But he doesn't really mind. He's taken a shine to the boys."

She tried to imagine Creed plying the boys with tales of derring-do. It was so out of character, it made her smile. But then, there were undoubtedly sides to Creed she'd never even seen.

Seth's hand slipped over hers and he gave her a covert squeeze. It lasted only long enough to make her heart jump, then Wade called him over to look at a new mail order pipe he'd added to his collection.

While Jarrod set the extra places, Mariah glanced at his older brother, Jason, whose mind was clearly not on criminals. His gaze seemed fastened with

252

some tenacity on the shape of her legs beneath the heavy denim Levis.

But for the sweet moonstruck expression on his face when his gaze met hers, she might have been offended. Color flooded his neck and blossomed in two splotches in his fair cheeks. Without a word, he bolted from the room with a mumbled excuse about going for more wood. Jarrod followed him out the door.

Sadie smiled and shook her head as she removed the roast venison and partridges from the warming oven and set them on the table. "Don't you pay him no mind, Mariah. Jason's sap's runnin' high these days. Hasn't got his mind on much but the opposite gender."

Mariah rose and walked into the cozy kitchen area where Sadie was pouring a batch of piccalilli into a glass bowl. "How old are the boys?"

Sadie raised an eyebrow. "Jarrod's nearly thirteen. Jason's fourteen, goin' on twenty-four. Ah, it goes by too fast, Mariah. Seems like those two was sprouts just yesterday."

Though now it seemed a lifetime ago that she'd been that young and naive, Mariah remembered sending lovestruck looks of her own at Seth. Had it only been four years? She watched Sadie pull a puffy, golden-edged yorkshire pudding from the oven.

"They're wonderful boys," Mariah said, picking up the tray of relish and setting it on the table. "Handsome, too."

Sadie nodded. "Thanks, darlin'. You an' Seth . . . you'll have a fine batch of younguns, too. Real lookers, they'll be."

Mariah faltered, clattering the bowl against the planked table. The room grew suddenly warm. *Chil-*

253

dren. Yes, she'd always wanted children. She knew Seth did, too. But not now. Not yet.

She felt Sadie's hand on her arm and turned to find her looking at her with concern. "Are ya all right, dear? You look a mite . . . tuckered."

"I'm fine." Mariah ran a hand over her hair. "I'm just . . . it's been a long day."

Sadie patted her hand with a shake of her head. "O' *course* yer tired, and ya got a bride's jitters. And here I am talkin' about younguns. Sometimes my mouth runs on ahead of the cart. Ya know, it hasn't been so long I don't remember what it's like."

Mariah glanced up at Seth, who was deep in conversation with Wade. "I guess I am a little nervous."

Sadie lowered her voice. "And rightly so. Young thing like you. My heavens, and after a trip like you must've had . . . and what with not seein' yer man for nigh onto four years. You got every right to feel a little ruffled.

"But let me tell you this—Seth, he's a fine man. One of the best I know. You remember that. And if you ever need anyone to talk to about . . . womanly things . . . well, you just come to Sadie. I may have a voice that would shake the last leaf off'n a fall tree, but my ears aren't half bad." She patted her hand again and turned to finish putting dinner on the table.

Mariah found she liked Sadie Bender very much. It was heartening to know that she'd have a friend here in Virginia City. And seeing a family like this gave Mariah hope that she, too, could have this kind of contentment.

Without Creed.

From across the room, Seth caught her eye and smiled. It was a private smile, one she imagined

254

husbands and wives exchanged every day. A lump formed in her throat as she returned it. Yes, she thought, I love him. I can do this. I can make it work.

Mariah picked up the water pitcher and filled the glasses at each place. Jason and Jarrod returned with armloads of wood just in time to hear the knock on the door. Jarrod got there first and yanked the portal open.

Mariah looked up to see Creed standing on the stoop. Her heart stopped, then raced. His black hair was still damp and his jaw freshly shaven. His choker stood out against his tanned face and complemented the teal chambray shirt beneath his blanket capote. His fingers toyed absently with the string on the box he was holding.

Creed's eyes found hers before the cool air from outdoors reached her and as if he'd touched her, a shiver went down her spine. She set the pitcher down heavily against the table, but couldn't move her gaze from him.

"Creed!" Jarrod cried, cuffing Creed's arm.

Creed pulled his hat off and smiled tightly at the boy. "I think you've grown another inch since I left, Jarrod."

The boy beamed and his brother pressed forward to shake Creed's hand. "H'llo, Creed," he said formally in a voice that cracked on the last word.

"Jase?"

"High time you got here, Creed Devereaux," Sadie boomed, giving Creed a hug. "You were about to miss the vittles."

"Not likely, Sadie. You're the best cook in the gulch and it's been a while since I had a home-cooked meal." He glanced at Mariah. "Campfire coffee excluded, of course."

Mariah's gaze flicked to him and she forced a smile. Seth took Creed's hand with both of his. "Ah, Creed," he interjected with a laugh. "I should have warned you about Mariah's coffee. Her father wouldn't let her near the pot."

Clearing her throat, Mariah admitted, "I'm afraid my coffee receipt is becoming somewhat infamous," she said, looking at Sadie. "It's been compared quite favorably to rattlesnake venom."

Wade and Seth laughed, but Creed's attempt at a smile was tellingly poor. He wasn't remembering the coffee, but the river incident that had followed it and the moment he'd realized he was in over his head with Miss Mariah Parsons.

Sadie just shook her head at Mariah and said, "Don't you worry about that, honey. Coffee's easier to figure out than men."

Creed handed Sadie the box. "I stopped at the Mechanical Bakery on my way here—a loaf of bread. Yours is better, but I didn't want to come empty-handed."

Sadie sent him a pleased smile. "Thanks. You won't find anybody in this house turnin' away food. In fact, this brace of partridge here is Seth's contribution. He's become quite a crack shot, Mariah. Why, he can shoot the eye off a fly at a hundred paces. I've never seen anything like it."

"Well, a shopkeeper should have *some* redeeming qualities," Seth allowed modestly.

Sadie patted his arm. "More'n yer share, dearie . . . Dinner's on so why don't we all set down before it gets cold?"

While the others were heading toward the table, Seth stopped Creed with a hand on his arm and a serious look in his eye. "I haven't had a chance to thank you properly yet for everything you did."

"Yes, you have. Besides, seeing you on your feet again is thanks enough. I never realized what a stubborn cuss you are, Travers. I thought I was going to have to tie you down to keep you here."

Seth shook his head, running two fingers over his mustache. "Hell, I barely remember arguing."

"You look good. A hell of a lot better, at any rate."

"Virginia's buried a few men who had the same thing I had. Nevada City, even more. They weren't lucky enough to have Sadie doctoring them with those God-awful teas," he added with a smile.

Creed glanced at the plump woman bustling around the dinner table, setting out the food with Mariah. Seth's gaze was on the younger woman.

"Mariah's turned into a real beauty, hasn't she?"

Creed followed Seth's gaze and swallowed hard. *"Oui."* In buckskins, denims, or silk, Mariah Parsons was the prettiest woman he'd ever laid eyes on. A real swan, he thought, remembering back to the first time he saw her aboard that steamer at Fort Benton. That day seemed so long ago.

"I hope she didn't give you too much trouble. Thank God you brought her with you on horseback instead of leaving her at the stage station," Seth said quietly. "You probably haven't heard what happened to the Lochries."

"Hasty Denton told me over at the livery."

Seth shook his head. "I kept imagining that you two were among them, but they told me only one woman was found." He pushed his dark blond hair back. "I haven't told Mariah yet. I didn't want to upset her. Who the hell would do something like that?"

"One guess," Creed answered grimly.

Seth frowned, but before he could reply, Sadie

257

called them from the table.

"Are you two gonna stand there jawin' all day, or are you gonna set down and partake of these vittles?"

Seth forced a grin. "Well, partake, of course." He slapped Creed on the back and they headed for the table.

Despite his protests to the contrary and the wonderful aroma of the food, Creed found his appetite decidedly lacking. The sight of Seth and Mariah sitting together was almost more than he could bear. More than once, their eyes caught and held for a moment, but she looked away before he could guess what she was thinking. They hadn't discussed her impending marriage to Seth since that morning at the cabin. He thought it best to avoid talking about options where there were none.

Despite the fact that his best friend was sitting only two feet away, he wanted nothing more than to take Mariah in his arms and taste the sweetness of those lips one more time, savor the feel of her arms around him and the nearly mystical rightness of their bodies fitting together.

He scowled at his nearly full plate, wondering at the sort of bastard he'd become.

The feast of roast venison, yorkshire pudding, greens, and piccalilli seemed to vanish without much help from him, and no one but Mariah seemed to notice.

Everyone was anxious to hear about their trip. Creed let Mariah do most of the telling—from her near-drowning, to LaRousse's attack on their camp, to the blizzard that had nearly killed them.

Seth's expression went from pale to grim upon

258

learning of their ordeal. His knuckles went white at the part about LaRousse, his raging fury held barely in check. Sadie and Wade were equally shocked.

For their part, the boys were riveted to the tale, Jason pelting her with questions and comments along the way. He was particularly fascinated with Jesse's wolf-dog and the Indian woman, Raven.

Creed listened with half an ear, toying with his food. It was excruciating to sit there so close to her without being able to touch her. It had taken him two hours to work up the courage to come tonight. In the end, it had been for her sake that he had—avoiding her and Seth would only create suspicion. He didn't know what she'd decided to do about Seth, but he had no intention of standing in her way any more than he already had.

The fire had burned down in the grate by the time they finished dessert and Wade got up to stoke it while Sadie and Mariah cleared the table. Wade returned with a bottle of brandy, poured Seth and Creed a shot, and filled the ladies' glasses with dandelion wine Sadie had made the previous summer. The boys lifted glasses of water.

"Here's to Creed and Mariah, surviving a trip that would have been a trial to Job himself. We thank you, Creed, for bringing Mariah home to Seth safely," Wade said softly.

"Here, here," Seth agreed and took a sip of his brandy. "And here's to friendship."

Heat crawled up Creed's neck, but he managed a smile. Wishing fervently for a hole to open up in the floor and swallow his black soul, he slugged back half his brandy. The smooth liquor burned a comforting path of fire down his throat and his gaze flicked to Mariah. Her back was rigid as a spruce plank and she stared sightlessly at the untouched glass of dandelion wine in her hand.

"And here's to Seth and Mariah," Creed said, knuckles going white around the stem of the glass. "To the future . . . to happiness." Mariah's gaze rose suddenly to his and held for one brief, bittersweet moment.

"Thanks, Creed," Seth said, his voice thick with emotion. "Listen . . . I, uh, guess this is as good a time as any to announce it. Mariah and I will be married before the circuit preacher from Bannack when he comes through next week."

Creed concentrated on breathing normally while the others at the table offered their congratulations. He forced himself not to look at Mariah. If he did that, not a soul in the room would miss what was in his eyes.

He'd known it was coming, but imagining and hearing it first-hand were two different things. He wanted to run, bolt, get on Buck and ride so damn far he wouldn't have to think of either one of them again.

But what he did was to reach across the table and shake Seth's hand. "*Bon. Très bon, mes amis.* I am . . . happy for you both."

Mariah leaned back in her chair and avoided Sadie's curious stare. She felt sick. Sick at heart. She would have given anything to be the one to tell Creed her decision instead of letting him hear it here in front of everyone. The pain she saw in his eyes told her what he'd never been able to. He *did* care about her, even if he'd never been able to tell her. It was killing him to see her with Seth, but he was too damnably honorable to do anything.

But wasn't that what she loved about him? If he had betrayed his best friend without conscience, would she still feel the same way? Would he still be the man who owned her heart? It was a stupid question, one for which she already knew the answer.

"Creed," Seth said, with a serious look, "I want you to be my best man."

Chapter Eighteen

Creed froze. His hand tightened around his glass. "Best man? *Moi?*"

Seth grinned. "Of course *you*. Who else would I ask to stand up for me?"

Creed let go of Seth's hand and shot a look at Mariah. She, too, sat perfectly still, lips parted in shock. It gave him little comfort that she hadn't known about this either. The room seemed to shrink with all eyes trained on him. He gripped the edges of the smooth pine table.

"*Mon ami,* I—" he began haltingly, spreading his hands. "I'm honored that you would ask me, but I—I plan to leave in the morning."

"Leave?" Seth repeated, incredulously. "You just got here."

The muscles in Creed's jaw bunched. "I have some ends to tie up."

"You mean Pierre LaRousse?" Wade asked, tamping down the tobacco in his pipe. Creed nodded.

"But Miss Parsons said she shot him," Jarrod argued, leaning forward. "Maybe by now he's got worms crawlin' in and—"

"Jarrod—" Sadie warned.

"—or maybe another bounty hunter found him and strung him up by his—"

"Jarrod!"

The boy slumped back to his seat. "Aw, shucks. Sorry."

Seth looked back to Creed. "Well, he could be right, you know. Pierre LaRousse may very well be dead. And whatever trail he might have left has long been erased by the snow and rain."

"I know."

"Creed," Seth said gently, "you've been after him for four years. In all that time you've only seen him once. Do you think, if he's alive, he'll be any easier to find this time?"

"Maybe," Jason suggested quietly, "he'll come here, after you."

That pronouncement was met with stunned silence. The possibility had occurred to them all, but none had ventured to say it. Jason sank back in his seat, embarrassed.

"It's a possibility, Jason," Seth admitted, "but he'd be a fool to come near the gulch. People know him, and he's wanted from here to Deer Lodge and God knows where else."

"That's never stopped him before," Creed said.

"I have no argument with your cause, Creed," Seth continued. "You have more reason to go after him than most. But to ride out blind . . ." He shook his head. "Look, stay the week. You can see how things are going at the store . . . you *are* half owner you know and believe it or not, you're doing pretty well, partner."

Mariah drew in a breath. *"Partner?"*

"Didn't Creed tell you?"

Her golden eyes widened with accusation. "No, he didn't."

"We invested in the store together a few years ago. He's turned a nice profit. We both have."

Partner. Her heart sank. She'd been foolish to expect he'd walk out of their lives, never to be seen

263

again. But a *partner?* That meant she'd have to see him over and over throughout the years.

The fire crackled in the silent room and the two boys watched the conversation bounce back and forth with eager faces.

"It's just a week, Creed. Stay. It would mean a lot to me if you'd be my best man. I'm sure Mariah feels the same way." He touched her elbow. "Tell him, Mariah. He *must* be a part of our wedding. After all, without him, we wouldn't be standing here at all. You'd still be on the levee at Benton wondering what had become of me."

She looked uncomfortably from Seth to Creed. Dear God, how different her life might be if only Seth had come for her! If only she had never met Creed and fallen hopelessly in love with him. But there was no help for it now. She moistened her lips with her tongue. "I—um, of course. We want you to be a part of it." She looked up at him, meeting his gaze. "Please stay, Creed."

Creed's eyes held hers for a long moment, until the pressure in his chest became unbearable. If he didn't get out of here right now, he might hit something.

"I'll sleep on it, *mes amis,*" he answered, getting up from the table. "I took a room down at *The Exchange.*"

"Now what'd you go and do a fool thing like that for?" Seth asked. "You always stay with me above the store."

"Truth is, I needed a bath tonight before I could come near Sadie's dinner table." He clapped Seth on the shoulder. "I'll come by in the morning."

Sadie and Wade stood as he took his hat and coat off the coat tree. Creed bent down to give Sadie's cheek a buss. *"Merci,* Sadie." He kissed the tips of his fingers. "Delicious as always and kind of you to let me barge in."

Sadie's expression was serious for once when she

took his hands in hers. "Creed, yer always welcome, you know that. We're just glad yer back safe."

"*Merci.*" He nodded and reached for his hat and coat. "See you and Mariah in the morning, Seth, *oui?*"

"*Oui, mon ami,*" Seth answered with a slight frown.

Mariah felt the word *goodbye* form a lump in her throat. She simply watched Creed walk out the door, leaving only the cold air to swirl in his wake and seep into her soul.

She looked up to find Sadie watching her curiously again, a sympathetic smile touching the corners of her mouth. Mariah forced a bright smile back, but it occurred to her that it was much easier to keep secrets from men than from a woman like Sadie.

"C'mon, dearie," Sadie murmured, threading her arm through Mariah's. "What say I show you how to make a pot of coffee?"

Sleep held no solace for Creed. Nor did the half-empty bottle of red-eye, he decided, but he poured another glassful until the amber liquid spilled over the brim. Staring blearily at the widening circle of moisture spreading on the green felt table, he wondered how much more he'd have to drink before he stopped thinking altogether.

The bar, which occupied the bottom level of the *California Exchange Hotel,* was filled with loud voices, choking with smoke, and stifling with the odors of hard-working miners who struck gold more often than they took baths. Streams of men trickled in and out of the Hurdy-Gurdy in the back room where the chesty, blond-haired women, known to the locals as "Teutons" for their Germanic origins, danced with a man for four-bits a ticket and if he was lucky, he got an evening of sport later on at some other location.

Creed closed his eyes, listening to the wheeze of the hurdy-gurdy man's concertina and the peculiar harmonies of a jug blower. He recognized a slightly off-key rendition of "Joe Bowers" and what Creed thought might be "Seeing the Elephant" — a forty-niner's song about coming around the Horn.

Creed slugged down his drink and poured another. He had decided against going to his room. He had no wish to be utterly alone tonight. However, neither had he invited company. His table was empty but for him, and that was the way he wanted it.

Creed tipped his chair back on two legs, leaning into the corner. The room seemed to sway a little with the motion.

"Can ah interest ya'll in a game of chance, suh?"

Creed rolled his head toward the sound. His narrowed gaze fell on the man standing near his table holding a deck of cards fanned open. His brocaded silk waistcoat with its over-sized gold watch fob, his slicked-back hair, neatly trimmed goatee, and charming smile all labeled him a card sharp.

He'd seen the type before. Mining camps like Virginia attracted them by the dozens, all of them waiting to bilk some poor miner out of his hard-earned dust. In fact, he'd watched this one do just that for the past hour or so.

"Erastus Field is mah name," the man drawled. "Five card stud? Monte? You call it, ah play it."

" 'Zat right?" Creed slurred, slugging down the last of his drink. "I just bet you do."

"Ahhh," the man sighed expansively. "A gentleman of the French-Canadian persuasion. Am ah right, suh?"

Creed lowered his chair to the floor, glaring. "My origins are none of your business, *monsieur.*"

Field's gilded southern smile faded slightly. "Why, all I meant to infer, suh, is that they'uh excellent card players. Nothing more. I, mahself, have been up against some of the most talented French Canadians in these here parts."

"Not interested." He tipped the bottle once more and filled the glass to the rim. The man was beginning to irritate him.

"Ah beg to differ, but you look like a man in need of a diversion. And ah have just the one close at hand, if you catch mah meanin'."

"Perhaps your diversions are better left up your sleeve," Creed replied, pinning him with a deliberate look.

The gambler snapped his deck of cards shut with a scowl that reddened his pale face. "Are you calling me a cheat, *suh?*"

"I am not calling you anything. Yet." Creed stood up and banged his thigh against the table, off balance. The noise of the saloon drowned their voices and not a man noticed the escalating violence.

Field took a step closer, glaring. "A gentleman does not take such charges lightly."

Feeling reckless, Creed replied, "Pistols at dawn, *monsieur?*"

Field paled. "Duelin' has been outlawed, suh, in case it hadn't come to your attention. Though that wouldn't greatly surprise me." His gaze fell to the beaded choker at Creed's throat and his fringed buckskin trousers. "It appears you've been spendin' your time with Injuns more than with *decent* white folk."

Creed's fist gathered at his side. It itched to connect with the holier-than-thou expression on Erastus Field's face. He didn't need any more excuse than he already had. "Field," he said, stepping around the edge of the table, swaying again from the delayed but potent effects of the red-eye, "I suggest you walk away while you still can, because I'm about to hit you."

Field foolishly laughed and raised his clenched fists, taking a ridiculous bent-knee stance. "You could try. Bettah men than you have. But ah hardly think a drunken Indian-lover has much chance of—"

Creed slammed a fist into the other man's jaw before he could dodge the punch. Erastus Field hung suspended in the air for a prolonged second, eyes glazed by shock, then pitched backward like a pole-axed deer, crashing into the center of the card game behind him.

Chips flew and the table broke in half with a splintering explosion. When the dust cleared, the room had grown deafeningly silent. On another day, such an event would have been an invitation to a brawl. But as Creed stood over the man, flexing his bleeding hand, his thunderous expression dared anyone to repeat the challenge.

There were no takers.

Creed couldn't be sure if he was relieved or disappointed, but he backed out of *The Exchange,* throwing a five-dollar gold piece on the bar for the damages, and slammed out of the swinging louvered doors. By the time they'd swung shut, the noise within resumed as if it had never abated.

Ten minutes later, he found himself staring at the red-painted double door entrance to The Nightingale. Through the waxed muslin windows, which adorned most of the hastily built structures in town, he could hear the sound of mens' laughter and the plinkety-plink of the piano Desirée had shipped clear from Salt Lake last spring. It was the only one in town and drew its fair share of music-hungry men, but clearly wasn't The Nightingale's strongest hold card.

The doors burst open, washing Creed in golden light as a man and a scantily clad blonde tumbled out the door, laughing.

"*All* night, Proctor? Are you sure she said *all* night?"

"Sweetcakes, with the color I just struck, I could keep you all week."

The woman squealed and the pair disappeared into the shadows. Creed stepped around the sawdust-filled brass spittoon that decorated the muddy stoop and entered the brothel.

The parlor was crowded with whores—Chinese, American, French—lounging beside men on velvet covered settees and ottomans. Two muscle-bound bouncers stood with arms folded across their chests, eyeing Creed. In the back corner, the gray-haired Negro piano-player, Oleander Smith, looked up and tipped his chin up in acknowledgement. Creed nodded back.

An S-shaped *tête-à-tête*, fringed extravagantly in the same deep red as the rest of the upholstery, held two couples getting better acquainted. Spittoons punctuated each corner and the Persian carpet Desirée had shipped from New York City covered the center of the floor.

"Wipe yore feet, handsome."

The husky sound of a woman's voice came from behind him. He turned to see Lula Mae, a voluptuous brunette whose once-pretty face had been scarred by smallpox. Her costume never changed: black net stockings, red silk bloomers, and a suggestively-laced corset over her filmy chemise. Lula Mae smiled seductively while he wiped his feet on the dog-shaped boot scraper by the door.

"It's been a long time, honey," she crooned, her red lips set in a fetching pout. She took a step in his direction. "Where've you been?"

"Around." Her heavy perfume wafted around her like an evening mist. It wasn't unpleasant exactly, but he preferred something more subtle. Unbidden,

269

Mariah's sweet scent filled his memory and his body tightened all over.

"I don't suppose I can talk you into tryin' me out tonight instead of Miss Desirée," she murmured. Spreading her arms wide she twirled slowly for his inspection. "It just so happens my dance card is wide open." Laughing, she draped herself across his side and pressed her breasts up against his chest.

He swayed slightly with her assault, feeling the effects of his drinking, then extricated himself. "Not tonight, *cherie.*"

"Ooh," she crooned with a wink, "I lo-oove it when you talk French to me, Devereaux."

He couldn't help but smile at her persistence. "Is Miss Desirée . . . entertaining, Lula Mae?"

With a frown, she plucked at the laces on her satin-edged corset. "Well-l-l . . ."

"Depends on 'oo ees asking, *blonde,*" came a heavily accented voice behind him.

Creed turned to find Desirée smiling genteelly at him from beside a pair of heavy velvet drapes. Dressed to the nines in her signature red silk gown, Desirée Lupone bore little resemblance to the whores she employed. Her apparel set her apart from the others as surely as her beauty did and he wondered for the hundredth time what a woman like her was doing in this kind of a life.

Though her piled-high hair was tinted a brassy red, her pale, freckled skin proved it had once been genuine. She wasn't much older than he—thirty-three or four at most—but the life had aged her, hardened what he imagined had once been soft and innocent.

Despite that, her makeup wasn't garish or overdone, nor was that of any of her girls. The kohl around her eyes was applied with a light hand, as was the lip tint that reddened her mouth. He supposed the class she lent to the place was one of the reasons why The Nightingale had grown into one of the most popular brothels in the gulch.

"Desirée." Creed stepped forward to take her out-stretched hands. "You look beautiful . . . as always."

Her gaze raked and read him in the same instant. He'd known she would. He'd never been able to keep anything from her. "And you . . . *mon ami*," she returned, "you are too 'andsome for the world's good, as always."

She tossed a look at Lula Mae and continued in French. "Shall we . . . go somewhere more private?" Nodding toward the whore who was feigning indifference, she added, "You know what they say about little jugs having big ears? Little whores are worse."

He followed her, somewhat unsteadily, upstairs to her private bedroom, a place where he knew few men were ever allowed. The comfortable room, done in muted blues and greens with tasteful furnishings and a minimum of clutter, was in direct contrast to the rest of the house with its garish trims and colors. Her only concession was the intricate brass bed that was, by design, the focal point of the room.

He stared at it, for the first time uncertain why he'd come. He swayed indecisively, then took off his hat and hung it on the brass ball of the bedstead.

"It's been a long time, Creed," she continued in French. Desirée stopped in front of him and slid her hands inside his capote, spreading her fingers across the wall of his chest.

He allowed the touch, sucked it in the way a parched man would rain. He felt the room tilt, and with it went perception. The red-eye surged through his veins, heating his blood. Suddenly, it wasn't Desirée's brassy red hair he saw, but the burnished chestnut color of Mariah's; sable eyes turned whiskey-colored and guileless. His muscles felt aflame with his aching need and his heart thudded heavily against

271

her fingertips.

Brushing the V of hair-dusted skin at his throat, she undid the sash that tied his capote. Sliding the garment off his shoulders, it landed in a heavy heap on the floor.

"You're cold, *mon chou*," she whispered against his skin. "But you don't need that coat to warm you."

Her touch sent passion through him, exploding in his blood like a brushfire. His body tightened as she pressed herself against him, purring like a hungry cat.

Without thought, Creed cupped her face with both his hands and pulled her mouth up to his. There was no gentleness in his kiss. It was a hard, volatile plunder—tongue, lips, teeth grinding together in a seeking, mindless need. It had been building in him all night and even smashing his fist into Erastus Field's face hadn't assuaged it. He wanted to show her, prove to her, beg her . . .

She tightened her arms around him, pulling him closer. Creed's breath came ragged and hot. With a moan, he slid one hand down her back to her derrière, forcing her hips against his and filling his other hand with her breast.

No, wait. Just wait a goddamn minute.

Pulling back a fraction, he gave himself a mental shake.

That's wrong. His sodden brain struggled with the situation. The breast in his hand was more voluptuous, the figure fuller, the lips not nearly soft enough. Realization struck him like a bucket of icy water.

Creed jerked back and took her wrists in his hands, pulling them away from him. His breath ground in his chest like the wheels of a runaway train. Desirée was staring at him, her open mouth still bruised by his kiss, a half-lidded expression of surprise and hurt in her eyes.

"Jesus." He cupped her face and dragged his thumb across her cheek. "I'm sorry, Desirée." He let her go and raked his fingers through his too-long hair. "I need a drink."

After a moment, Desirée sighed heavily and nodded. "What are you drinking?" She stepped toward the cluster of crystal decanters on her dresser. The stopper of the bottle rattled in its nest.

He was tempted to request cyanide, but he said, "Whiskey will do." He slumped heavily onto the comfortable tufted settee near the fireplace.

He let out a long breath that drew Desirée's glance from the decanter in her hand. She steadied the tremble in it and released a sigh of her own. She'd seen trouble on Creed Devereaux's face before. Often. Trouble followed him like a shadow.

Or, perhaps he went looking for it.

It didn't matter. Trouble was always what brought him to her. And she had decided long ago she'd take Creed Devereaux any way she could get him.

But tonight was different. *He* was different. The trouble in his eyes was not the kind she'd seen before. It was woman trouble. He hadn't been kissing *her*. She'd known it from the moment their lips touched. She'd been in the business too long not to recognize it, but not so long that the loss of a man like Creed Devereaux didn't hurt.

She handed him the cut-crystal glass and sat down opposite him in the velvet upholstered slipper chair. Sipping her bourbon, she endured the ache inside and waited for him to speak.

Creed swallowed the drink in one gulp and grimaced as it went down. He sat forward, bracing his forearms on his knees. His head hung between his arms. His temples throbbed, his chest ached, and his hand burned. But none of it mattered. When he spoke, he spoke in French. "I shouldn't have come here tonight, Desirée. I'm drunk."

"I've seen you drunk before."

"I'm very drunk."

"This I know, too, *cheri*." She sipped her bourbon, watching him carefully. "What happened to your hand?"

He glanced at his bloody knuckles and smiled. "It ran into an idiot's face."

Desirée's mouth curved upward. "You don't sound contrite, love."

"It felt good to hit something."

"Yes." She set her drink down on the marble-topped teakwood table and went for a clean cloth. Dipping the edge in the bourbon, she went to sit beside Creed. "Let me see."

He gave her his hand and she dabbed the cloth against the bloody cut. He winced, but kept his eyes trained on her beautiful white hands.

"So, *cheri*," she said, trailing a gentle finger down the side of his face. "Do you want to talk about it?"

"I don't know. I don't even know why I'm here." He shrugged helplessly. "I had nowhere else to go."

Another woman might have been insulted by such a comment, but Desirée wasn't. She no longer whored for a living. Her girls did that for her. She'd become a successful madam first in Salt Lake, then in Virginia. Her relationships with men were absolutely her choice now and there were few who interested her.

Of those few, only Creed owned her heart. If, tomorrow, he asked her to marry him, she'd leave this life behind in a second. Lock, stock, and velvet cushion. But fantasy was never her strong suit, so she'd given the possibility little serious consideration. A man like Creed didn't come to a woman like her for a lifetime commitment. The most she could hope for was friendship, and that's what she offered him now.

Lifting her arms, she pulled the tortoiseshell pins from her hair, one by one. In a cascade of flame, her burnished tresses uncoiled to her waist. Creed's gaze followed every movement. She reached for the embossed silver hairbrush on the table behind the settee and handed it to him.

"Here. Perhaps we'll both think better if you brush my hair." When he hesitated, she asked, "You like it, no? It soothes you, no?"

One corner of his mouth curved in answer. Lifting her hair off her neck, his fingers brushed against her skin. She allowed the shiver his touch never failed to produce, and she inhaled deeply. The boar bristles sank into her hair at the crown and he drew the brush down in long, gentle strokes. She closed her eyes and sighed. The piano music from below drifted up through the floor.

"You have beautiful hair, Desirée. But you know that, don't you?"

"I've been told. Yet, I think . . . not as beautiful as hers."

The brush paused mid-stroke. "Hers?"

"There is a woman, no? Is that not what I see in your eyes? What I tasted just now in your kiss?"

The brush moved through her hair again. "Yes."

"And she troubles you, *cheri?*"

"Yes." She heard him sigh slowly as if relieved of a great burden.

She wound her fingers together in her lap, inhaling his nearness, the masculine scent of him she always found such a powerful aphrodisiac. "So, who is she?" The brush massaged her back as he drew it downward.

"She's . . . not mine. She belongs to Seth."

"Ahh . . . Seth." A sigh lifted her chest. "Tell me, does she still?"

"Still what?"

"Belong to Seth." Her eyes caught and held his. His bleak expression told her what she wanted to know. She turned around again. "So . . . you're in love with her, *ma beau*."

"It doesn't matter."

"Is that what you think?" Desirée laughed softly, tipping her head back languorously with the pressure of the brush. "It is the only thing that *does* matter, *cheri*."

He stroked the hair back away from her face, silent. From outside her door came the sounds of a couple fumbling with a doorknob down the hallway, laughing.

"Does it surprise you that a whore would speak of love?" she asked, ignoring the intrusion.

"I've never thought of you that way, Desirée."

"I know. But that's what I am," she replied without apology. "It hasn't always been so. I was once young and in love." She glanced up. "I can remember what it's like."

"Was it with your best friend's fiancé?" he asked bitterly, stroking unintentionally harder.

She stopped his hand with hers. "No. He was married."

Creed stared and she smiled. "Are you shocked?"

"Did you know?" he asked. "Did he tell you?"

With a shrug, she answered, "Of course. His marriage had been arranged — it was a matter of money. They had nothing in common, least of all love. They even lived separately, because together, they fought constantly. They had been married eight years when he met me. We fell madly in love and before I knew it, his child grew inside me."

Creed's jaw tightened at the thought of what she must have gone through . . . a woman alone. "What happened?"

She hugged her arms to her chest. "It was . . . months before he could get his wife to agree to grant him a divorce. Then, at last he did. But before he could make it final, he was . . . he was killed in a riding accident." After all these years, her voice still trembled at the memory. "He'd been on his way to me."

Creed's hands brushed her shoulders. "I'm sorry."

She got up and crossed the room, staring into the flames as if she couldn't bear to be comforted. "There was nothing for us. His wife made certain of that. My family was shamed by what I'd done. They turned their backs on me completely. Which is how I ended up . . . doing this."

The fire crackled in the silence as Creed turned over what she'd told him in his mind. "You had his child?"

Pride eased the sadness on her face. "Joel's fifteen now. He lives in a boarding school back East. He knows all about me, of course, but it wouldn't do for his friends to know." Her chin rose a fraction and she smoothed the wrinkles from her red silk skirt. "Someday, he'll attend a university. He's a brilliant student. He wants to be a physician."

Creed's gaze roamed over her face. "That's why you do this?" He gestured broadly around him. "For him?"

Her mouth curved upward and she faced him. "If you think I regret the life I've built, Creed, you'd be wrong. I don't regret a minute. I did what I had to do. I survived. And I've turned a pretty profit in the process.

"If you ask me if I'd change anything today—if I'd go back and pick another man, a safer man—the answer would still be no." She took a deep breath, her eyes fierce and bright. "I loved him and I would do it all again,"—she snapped her fingers—"like that. My only regret is that I haven't had him all these years. If I could change one thing, it would be that."

Slowly, she walked over to the settee and sat down beside him. She didn't touch him, except with her gaze.

"What you must ask yourself, *mon chou*, is if you can imagine your life without her. Tomorrow? A year from now? Ten? What will you regret then?"

Creed stared at the drink in his hand, rubbing his thumb around the rim until a keening note sounded, then he tipped the glass and slugged down the remaining whiskey. It burned through him like the lingering heat of a banked fire and spread lethargy through his limbs. He slumped against the tufted sofa back, staring at the fire. "It's not as simple as that, Desirée. Seth loves her, too."

With a knowing smile she smoothed a hand through his dark hair. "She is a woman to love, yes?"

"Yes," Creed stood and swallowed down the desperation rising in his gut. "She is. I told her to marry him."

She shook her head. "Did you? Men can be so stupid."

He glared at her, pressing a hand to his throbbing head. "I'm right about this, Desirée. We're as far apart as Montana is from Chicago. She's a lady, I'm—"

"You're what?"

"Nothing." He lurched around the sofa, wrenching his hat off the bedstand and his coat from the floor. "I'm nothing except for the dishonorable fool I've become. It was a mistake to think I could have someone like her even for a minute."

Desirée didn't get up. She only watched him try, unsuccessfully, to shove his arms in his coat. "Is that what she says?"

He shot her a twisted smile. "They asked me to be the best man at their wedding." He let out a bark of laughter as he shoved his hat on and gave up on the coat. "Best man. *Me.* Isn't that a hoot?"

"Did you say yes?"

He shot a disgusted look at his muddy boots. "I didn't say no." He wrenched the door open, bracing his hand on the frame to steady himself. With his back to her he said, "I'm sorry for coming here tonight, Desirée. I'm sorry, I . . . oh, hell, I'm just sorry." Without turning around, he disappeared out the door.

She shook her head, listening to the fading sound of his footsteps. "Men can be so stupid."

Chapter Nineteen

"What makes you so sure it was LaRousse?"

Creed squinted through the brilliant morning sun at Sheriff Jim Fox. They were nearly the same height, Fox an imposing forty pounds heavier than Creed, with a gut that hung over his belt. The Sheriff stood ankle deep in the fetid mud outside his office, glaring at Creed as the hammers pounded in a nearby structure and the morning traffic rumbled by on the street behind him with a dull roar.

Creed rubbed his throbbing head, trying to keep it from exploding. "I told you. He was following me. He had to go though the stage station to track me. He probably tortured the information out of Mrs. Lochrie before he murdered her. That's how the bastard works."

Fox placed three dirty-nailed fingers near his mouth and nodded. "I have a WANTED dodger on him, as I reckon you'd know, fer another killin', up Deer Lodge way. But I got no evidence he was anywhere near the Lochries when this happened. Just your sayso, an' you weren't there neither. No witnesses left alive, apparently. You say you winged him a few days later?"

"Miss Parsons did." Creed squeezed the bridge of his nose between his thumb and forefinger. "I found blood on his trail, but there's no way to know how serious it was."

Fox grunted and patted his stomach. "Too bad you didn't follow him."

Creed sent the man a killing look. "I told you, if I *could* have, I *would* have."

Fox's inky eyes narrowed. "Don't get testy on me, Devereaux. I'm just commentin'."

Creed counted to ten. Slowly. "So, are you going to do anything about it?"

"Hell . . ." He scratched his chest and sent a wad of tobacco juice flying into the mud. "I got five killin's a day right here in Virginia to deal with. Claim jumpers, back-stabbers, just plain mean sons of bitches too drunk to hold their tempers."

He started walking toward Dillard's Cafe and Creed followed. "But based on your suspicions, I'll see that Professor Dimmesdale inks up another dodger on that printin' press of his and sends it out to Nevada City and the surrounding camps. And . . . I'll up the bounty on him by seventy-five dollars. That enough incentive to get you off my back, Bounty?"

Blindly, Creed grabbed the man's shirtfront and slammed him against the nearest log wall with a heavy thud. "This isn't about money, you *imbecile!*" The hammer of Fox's Colt clicked next to Creed's abdomen. He felt the cold nudge of steel.

"You're this close to a jail cell, boy. Or a bullet in the gut. Unhand me *now.*"

It took Creed five full seconds to swallow his fury and release Fox. He cursed his lack of control and the pounding hangover that had frayed his patience to a thread.

The sheriff shook his worn flannel shirt back into place, holstered his gun, and yanked at the sleeves of his union suit. "*Now* . . . I'll tell you what I *ain't* gonna do. I *ain't* sendin' a posse out on a blind goose chase on yer say-so, Devereaux, after a half-breed who's as elusive as a goddamned ghost. You *got* that?"

Creed ground his teeth. "I've got it."

"And the next time you call me an imbecile," — he poked a finger into Creed's chest — "you'd better be prepared for Judge Colt to argue the point with you."

Creed was just angry enough to consider tempting fate, but a shout from behind them stopped him.

"Sheriff!"

A squat man in a bowler hat and window-pane plaid wool pants hurried up the street just ahead of a gathering mob.

"Sheriff, you better come. There's been a killin'."

Fox's heated expression darkened further. "Dangit, Edward, I ain't had my coffee yet," he growled. "Take the body over to MacGrudy's and tell him I'll be over later."

"It weren't the usual sort of killing, Sheriff," Edward told him, wide-eyed. "This feller were lynched and that ain't all."

Fox cursed. Pushing away from the wall, he sent Creed a final warning look and hurried toward the men. Creed followed.

The crowd parted for them, revealing a two-wheeled, mule-drawn cart. Inside was a blanket-covered body.

"Anybody know who it is?" Fox demanded, pulling back the blanket. He grimaced and replaced the covering, but not before Creed had gotten a look.

"Lydell Kraylor."

Fox looked up as Creed spoke. "You know him?"

"I had the misfortune, *oui*. I saw him last at Fort Benton, taking the credit for killing Étienne La-Rousse."

The crowd murmured loudly around them. Fox held up his hand. "Who found him?"

A stooped-over miner with scruffy hair and beard stepped forward. "It were me. Name's Karl Brown," he announced loud enough for everyone to hear. "I found him." His weathered face creased with pride. "Swingin' from that cottonwood branch up in Stinkin' Water Valley with his neck stretched fer him. Then looks like they used him fer target practice. Stole ever' scrap of money and valuables off 'n him, too."

Fox and Creed exchanged looks. "You see any sign of the scoundrels that did it?" Fox asked.

"They was long gone by the time I got there, but . . ." Brown fished a piece of paper out of his pocket and handed it to the Sheriff. "He had this note a'pinned to his chest with his knife. I cain't read so I don't rightly know what it says. But I figgered it might be important."

Fox took the bloody note, inspecting the knife hole at the top of it. He read it briefly, glanced at Creed and folded it up again.

"Wal, what'd it say, Sheriff?" one man asked.

"Yeah," another chimed in.

"Ain't you gonna tell us?" a third man queried. "We got a right to know. We could all be in danger from this thievin' scallawag."

Again, the crowd swelled with noise.

"Boys, boys—" cautioned Fox, pushing his hands down against the air in a calming gesture. "Don't get yerselves all het up over nothin'. Ain't nothin' in it pertainin' to none of you. This here note is evidence in a murder. As such, I aim to keep it under wraps until the villain or villains are caught. Edward, Brown—you two take the body over to the undertaker's shop. Tell him I'll be along directly. The rest of you boys, break up and get to work. The day's a wastin'."

Reluctantly, the crowd broke up, scattering like so many wind-blown seeds toward the staked banks of Alder Creek. Fox turned on his heel and almost ran into Creed.

"Well?" Fox demanded, stepping around him and continuing on toward his office.

"What did the note say?"

"Why should I tell you?"

"Because it *pertains* to me," Creed said through

283

clenched teeth. "Doesn't it? It was LaRousse, wasn't it?"

"I never said." Fox kept on, slogging through the stinking mud.

"Sheriff!"

Fox skidded to a halt and turned around. *"What?"*

"You looked up at me when you read it. *Me.* No one else. What did it say, dammit?"

Fox scowled, adding deep lines to his forehead. He handed Creed the note. "I reckon it could be about you, and it might be from LaRousse, but it ain't specific."

Creed unfolded the crimson-smeared note and read: *"Kraylor's first. The woman is next. You're last."*

Creed struggled for air and crumpled the note in his fist and swore. It was too much to hope LaRousse had died. It made perfect twisted sense. Kraylor had taken a piece of Étienne back at Fort Benton. Whoever had told Pierre about Creed had told him about Kraylor, too.

Damn, damn, damn!

Now he was after Mariah.

Creed looked up to find Fox watching him. "Well, *now* what do you say? It's not just me. It's Mariah Parsons, too."

"You got no grounds to prove—"

"The hell I don't! Can you read, Sheriff?" He shoved the note under Fox's nose. "He all but signed his *name.*"

Fox's jaw tightened and he grabbed the note out of Creed's hand. "I can read just fine, Devereaux. How's yer hearing? I said I'll do what I can. If you're so all fired set on seein' justice done, why don't you mount up and go a'lookin' yerself?"

Creed shook his head with disbelief. "And what about Miss Parsons? Are you going to protect her?"

Fox hawked a wad of juice into the street. "I'll tell Travers about the note, warn them to be wary—"

"Wary?" Creed's laugh rang with sarcasm. "Ah, *bon—*

that's good. That's very good, Sheriff. A lot of help against a lunatic like Pierre LaRousse." A freight wagon lumbered past them, nearly running them down, but neither man budged.

"You got a better idear?" Fox asked with a sneer.

"Oui. Keep this note to yourself. Seth and Miss Parsons plan to marry next week. This will put a kink in things and I don't want that to happen. I'll watch her. If LaRousse is close by, who better than me to find him? He'll be looking for me."

"All right. If he is close by, you'd be wise to stay around people. It's hard for a bastard like that to make a move in a crowd. I'll let my deputy know about it and tell him to keep his eyes peeled." He stuck his hand out to Creed in a gesture of truce. "Okay?"

"Okay."

Fox nodded and started off for the café. "Better get you another pair of eyes, son," he called over his shoulder. "In the back of yer head."

Creed fingered the handle of his gun. "Right."

"Of course, I'll help you in the store," Mariah told Seth indignantly, pushing away from the dill pickle barrel she'd been leaning against. "Don't be silly." She picked up a feather duster and started to work on the tall shelves full of tinned fruit, milk, and meats.

Seth watched the fabric of her shirt pull tightly across her back and outline her breasts in profile. Without thought, his body quickened with desire. It seemed all he had to do was look at her and he started acting like a foolish schoolboy. It was funny how their roles had reversed. In many ways, she was the same girl he remembered back in Chicago—stubborn, willful . . . but the young girl who'd trailed after him like a faithful puppy was gone. Now, the woman she'd become was much more appealing. Though he'd loved her always, what he felt for her now bore no resemblance to the fraternal feelings he'd harbored in the early years.

"Look at these shelves," Mariah scolded, waving away the dust drifting down beneath her feather duster. "When was the last time you dusted?"

"Merchandise moves too fast to gather much dust," he argued, frowning at the cloud.

"Well, the shelves are enough to give a person an attack of asthma!"

"Oddly enough, none of the miners who patronize my store have mentioned it. Now, Mariah . . ." he told her firmly, "Don't try to change the subject. I won't have my wife working behind a counter. I didn't bring you all the way out here so you could—"

"You didn't bring me here at all. I insisted on coming, remember?"

He squeezed the bridge of his nose between thumb and forefinger. "True, but—"

"And if you'd had your way," she went on, sweeping dust off the neatly stacked shelves, "you would have had me wait another four years before I saw you again."

He laughed and shook his head. "As I recall, you were all but on the train to St. Louis by the time I could answer your letter, informing me of the time and place to meet you. True?"

She sniffed. "Well, yes, but I knew you'd say no if I gave you half a chance."

He walked up behind her and took her shoulders between his hands. His breath was warm against her ear. "It wasn't for lack of wanting you, Mari . . . I've missed you like the devil. It was knowing you were coming that kept me going through that fever." His lips brushed her throat and she stiffened.

"Seth—"

"God," he whispered, trailing moisture along her neck with his lips. "You're so beautiful."

"Seth . . ." She wiggled out of his hands. "Don't."

He pulled back and regarded her seriously. "I'm sorry. I'm rushing things again, I know."

"No. No, it . . . it's not that." She toyed with the feathers on the duster, unable to look him in the eye. "It's just . . . what if customers walked in and saw us like that? What in the world would they think?"

"They'd probably think I'm a lucky so-and-so . . . which I am." He sighed, taking a step back. "But that doesn't change how I feel about your working here. This is hard work and you're not up to—"

Her eyes flashed up to his in challenge. "Hard work? *This?* Riding halfway across Montana, ten hours a day on the back of a horse, fording rivers . . . making coffee . . . now *that's* hard work. This,"—she gestured at the stock-laden shelves and mining tools hanging from the walls of Travers' Mercantile—"this is a cinch."

He crossed his arms. "No."

She crossed hers. "Yes."

"No."

"Yes."

"You two having a lover's quarrel so soon?"

Mariah jumped at the sound of Creed's deep voice. He was leaning on the door jamb, his arms against his chest. Her heart rose to her throat and lodged there. He looked tired. His eyes were bloodshot and he'd nicked his freshly shaven jaw in two places. It seemed he'd slept no better than she.

He flipped open the lid of his pocket watch and shook his head. "Let's see, what's that? Sixteen hours and thirty-five minutes," he said lightly. "Not bad."

"We are not having a lover's quarrel," she retorted, folding her arms. "Are we, Seth?"

Seth rolled his eyes for Creed's benefit. "Hell's bells! I told you she was stubborn, didn't I?"

"Stubbornness has nothing to do with it. He just thinks I'm too *delicate* to work in his store." She made a face to tell them both what she thought.

Creed snorted and slid his hat off.

"What's wrong with 'delicate'?" Seth asked, genuinely confused.

"Nothing," she replied, "if you're a china teacup. I'm a grown woman. And I won't break from a little exertion! Exactly what do you propose I'd do all day while you're here working, Seth? Twiddle my thumbs? Stroll down the muddy street and windowshop for pickaxes? . . . Goldpans? Perhaps a new flannel shirt to complete my wardrobe?" She hiked up her trousers and yanked against the rope belt. "You're the one who's being stubborn. Tell him, Creed."

Creed hid a grin and rubbed his jaw.

Seth scowled. "Don't involve Creed in our disagreement, Mari. This has nothing to do with him."

"Oh? He *is* part owner, isn't he?" she pointed out. "You *are* a partner—isn't that what you said last night?"

Creed's eyes dueled devilishly with hers. "Silent partner."

"Now there's a redundant statement," she muttered, plucking at a loose thread on the sleeve of her shirt.

He pushed lazily away from the door and strolled toward her. "You shouldn't provoke the only man in the room who's on your side, Mariah."

She looked up in surprise. "Are you? On my side, I mean?"

Creed glanced at Seth, who was frowning over the whole exchange. "Actually, yes. I think it would be a good idea to let her work here with you, *mon ami.*"

Seth unfolded his arms. "Judas priest, Creed—"

"Think about it. You can use the extra help, she's willing, and it will keep her out of trouble. And God knows," he said, glancing at her, "she knows how to find that." He forced a grin to one corner of his mouth.

Mariah pressed her lips together to refrain from retorting. Well, she could hardly argue with him after everything they'd been through, though she did think it unfair to blame it all on her. After all, hardly any of it had been her fault!

"Granted," Seth admitted with a chuckle, smoothing down his mustache with his thumb and first finger. "But I had in mind something more . . . domestic, Mari. Such as staying at home . . . having our babies."

An uncomfortable silence filled the air. Creed looked pointedly at the floor and rubbed his temple. A picture of Mariah with babies playing around her flashed through his mind. But the little girl nearest her leg had thick, dark hair and startling blue-green eyes. The image made him inhale sharply and stare out the open door.

"You know . . . *babies?*" Seth interjected into the lengthening pause. "Small people who say 'goo, goo — gah, gah?' "

Mariah twisted her fingers together and tried to laugh. "Babies . . . of course . . . there will be plenty of time for that, Seth. We're not even married yet, for heaven's sake. I'm simply talking about right now. You're still not fully recovered from your illness. You need me here."

Creed shrugged with feigned indifference. "She's right, you know. And I can help you out with some of the heavy work. Until the wedding, at least."

Seth and Mariah spoke in unison. "You're staying?"

He nodded. "Yeah, just until the wedding."

"Well, for crying out loud, when were you going to tell us? That's wonderful, Creed," Seth said, pumping his hand. "I can't imagine getting hitched without you there. Mari, isn't that wonderful?"

Mariah cleared her throat, her face flushed — not with pleasure, but a kind of dull, foreboding shock. "Yes, um . . . we're both so glad you'll be there."

Creed gave what he hoped was a nonchalant shrug. "A week either way won't change much."

Seth clapped him on the shoulder earnestly. "Good. Then after the shop closes up, I'll take you both to the site I picked out to build our house."

The house. *Pardieu,* Creed swore silently. He'd almost forgotten the house Seth started drawing up plans for when he'd gotten word Mariah was coming. A house for the two of them to build a life together . . . as man and wife.

"You're building a house?" Mariah asked.

"We. *We're* building one. It'll take a little time to build, but you're going to love it, Mari. I've incorporated some of the latest amenities in the design . . . running hot water, a built-in bathtub framed in cherry wood. It's all on order from St. Louis. Until then, we'll have to make do with the little apartment I have here."

"That's . . . that's wonderful, darling. I can hardly wait to see the plans." She turned to fuss with something on the counter that didn't need straightening.

"All right, then. I'll see you later," Creed answered, settling his hat back on his head. "Keep your eye on her, eh, *mon ami?*"

Seth grinned with the smitten look of a man in love. "I will. Hey, get some rest today, Creed," Seth advised. "You're looking a little rough around the edges."

Creed rolled his eyes as he continued out the door, waving a silent goodbye. The sunshine made his head throb but he refrained from holding it between his hands.

Le bon Dieu, he wished the cost of oblivion wasn't so painful.

Down the street, he heard the sound of men's voices spilling out of The Bale of Hay saloon. The thought of a little 'hair of the dog that bit him' didn't set well with his queasy stomach, so he veered toward Dillard's Café. He'd have breakfast and some strong coffee. He needed a clear head if he was going to —

Creed came to a halt in the ankle deep mud as if he'd slammed up against an imaginary wall. No particular sound or motion confirmed his reaction — only the familiar warning tingle at the back of his neck that had his heart pounding. One hand automatically dropped to unhook the safety strap on his revolver. He whirled around, half-expecting to feel the burn of a bullet plowing into him.

A freight wagon rolled noisily by him, loaded with lumber from the south. Creed pushed along the length of it with his hand as it passed, glad for the momentary cover.

Against the skeletal backdrop of the half-finished town, the street behind him was crowded with men, wagons, horses, and a half-dozen mongrels sniffing at the refuse gathering in the street corners. The ever-present din of hammers and saws echoed in the clear morning air.

Creed searched the faces of the men behind him: the hopefuls, the philanderers, the cynics, and the dreamers . . . all of them emigrés to Virginia nurturing dreams of gold. Their reasons for leaving their pasts behind were as varied as their faces. But they all had one thing in common:

None bore the slightest resemblance to the half-breed devil, Pierre LaRousse.

Creed exhaled slowly, sliding his gun fully back in its leather cradle, and cast one more quick glance around him. Nothing. The term 'sitting duck' came to mind and he swore silently. Perhaps it was just nerves. Perhaps not.

Clamping a hand to his temple, he rubbed it and headed for the café. If he was going to be a target, he preferred to be one with a clear head.

One hundred yards away, atop the flat, false-fronted roof of Lott Brothers' Emporium, Pierre LaRousse looked down the barrel of his shiny Spencer Repeater Rifle until the sight leveled on Creed Devereaux's forehead. His finger tightened over the coil-action trigger, feeling the spring give in fractional clicks.

"Boom."

"What in hades are you waitin' for?" muttered Downing, who was crouching beside him. He shot a nervous glance around them and shoved the dirty tail of his duster out of the way of his holster. "You got him dead to rights, Pierre. Just . . . do it and let's go."

LaRousse's mouth twisted into a sardonic smile. He eased his finger off the trigger. "No."

Downing stared at him as if he'd just lost his mind. *"No?* Whadya mean no? I thought that was why—"

"No." LaRousse turned and pressed his back against the wooden wall of the false-fronted building. His shoulder length black hair curtained his face. "Ees too quick. Too easy. But,"—he chuckled, watching Devereaux turn and continue on down the street—"I could 'ave killed 'eem just now. Did you see?"

Downing looked at him oddly. "Yeah, I saw."

"Eet was beautiful, no?"

"No." Downing slumped beside him, scratching his arms. "I want to get out of here, goddammit. This town gives me the crawlin' jitters."

The half-breed eased the hammer down on his gun with an ominous click. "Perhaps you 'ave lost your nerve, *mon ami.*"

"This ain't a *game,* Pierre," Downing nearly shouted. "They got them WANTED dodgers tacked up ever' which way, with our faces plastered all over 'em. The longer we stay here, the better the odds somebody's gonna recognize us. And in case it ain't come to yore attention, we ain't as many as we used to be. Devereaux took care of that."

Pierre's black eyes took on the cold glint of malachite. "My *attention?*" He ripped the neck of his buckskin shirt open to reveal his bandaged left shoulder. "You zink I could forget thees? You zink I could forget what 'ee did to Étienne, or to my father? *Saaa-aa!* You 'orse's ass! I forget nothing."

Downing sat back in a silent stew, staring at the bottomless blue sky overhead. For the second time since heir close escape by the river four days ago, he had he feeling of impending doom. Pierre was becoming more and more irrational.

He was the one who'd come up with the harebrained scheme of following Devereaux into Virginia—dogging his trail into this booby trapped hellhole that boasted one of the strongest vigilance committees this side of the Mississippi. The same town where only months ago they lynched every living member of Henry Plummer's Innocents Gang, except, he mused uncomfortably, the ones they didn't find. Hell, it was only a matter of time before it all caught up with them.

He scraped a boot heel irritably against the wood-shingled roof. He should'a left that night Pierre rode up behind him, bleedin' all over himself. He should'a rode off and not looked back. That business with the Lochries had turned his stomach and watchin' the pleasure Pierre took out of tormenting that old bounty hunter, Kraylor, hadn't done much for his appetite neither.

Even though he'd had no actual hand in either one of those killin's and only one of the others of which they'd been accused, he'd been ridin' with LaRousse too long to come off smellin' like anything but stinkweed.

Pierre got to his feet and headed toward the back of the roof where the ladder was pitched against the alley wall.

Downing scowled, getting up slowly to follow. Past was past and the truth was—it pained him to admit it—he had nowhere else to go.

Except straight to hell.

Chapter Twenty

Four days.

Four hellish days since they rode into town, Creed thought, watching Mariah hesitate, then lean over the counter to kiss Seth goodbye on the cheek.

"I won't be long," she told him. Seth trapped her hands and pulled her closer to give her a kiss of his own.

Creed's grip tightened around the iron-rimmed hogshead full of crockery he was rolling across the floor and anger pumped through him like a fast-working poison. Dammit, what had made him think he could go through with this farce? Four days of working side by side, the three of them . . . together. He sighed in frustration. It would be laughable if only he could find the humor in the situation.

His gaze roved over the glove-like way Mariah's new gingham dress fit her—smooth and tight around waist, breast, and wrist, a layer of petticoats hiding her rounded bottom. The sight of her in proper woman's clothes stirred his blood and made it damned hard to concentrate on work.

"Maybe I should walk you down there," Seth suggested as she swept the apron over her head and slipped into a woven shawl. He rounded the counter, his persistent cough shaking his shoulders. "I don't like you walking unescorted."

"I'm just going to Emaline Fitzwilly's shop for a fitting," Mariah said, tying the black ribbon on her new straw bonnet. "I have to pick up the gown for the party tonight and have the last fitting for the . . . um, wedding gown." Her eyes flicked to Creed's, then quickly away. "Besides, it's only a few doors down."

"The end of the block."

"Seth's right." Creed said, straightening. "Let him walk you down there."

Mariah frowned at them. "You both have your hands full with this new shipment. I can certainly find my way to the end of the—"

Creed tilted the hogshead to the floor with a thud. "I'll take her."

Her face reddened. "You will not! Look, you two, if I'm going to live in this town, I'd better get used to walking around like everyone else."

"Everyone else isn't a woman." Creed moved a stack of pickaxe handles out of his way and watched that peculiar stubborn glint light her topaz eyes.

"You act as if I should be afraid of my own shadow," she argued. "The miners I've met have been nothing but gentlemen to me. You two give me more trouble than all of them combined."

Providence sent Jason Bender barreling through the door at that moment. "Hi, Seth, Creed." He stumbled to a stop at the sight of Mariah. "Oh, h'llo, Miss Parsons. Gosh, you look . . . awful pretty today, ma'am. I mean, you *always* look pretty, but today you look 'specially . . . that is . . ." His voice drifted off into an embarrassed mumble.

"Why, thank you, Jason," she said, with a pointed look at the two men. "I'm glad *someone* noticed I'm not in buckskins anymore."

"Oh, for . . ." Seth bit back the rest and rolled his eyes heavenward.

She ignored the look Creed gave her. "What brings you in this morning, Jason?"

"Ma sent me with a list of things to pick up." He handed a slip of brown paper to Seth.

Seth perused it and nodded. "I think we can fill this. And while I'm doing it, why don't *you* walk Miss Parsons down to Emaline Fitzwilly's dress shop. Perhaps she won't mind someone more neutral. There'll be two bits in it for you."

Jason's mouth opened and closed in a good imitation of a polliwog. "Me? Oh, *yessir.* You don't have to pay me nothin'. I'd be most honored to walk Miss Parsons down fer no money a'tall."

Mariah gave the *basque* of her bodice an irritated tug and smoothed a hand down the blue gingham, realizing she'd been outmaneuvered. "I can't think of a more pleasant companion. Come along, Jason. Let's leave these two worrywarts to their fretting."

Watching them disappear out the door, Seth shook his head. Holding his fist over his mouth, he half-coughed, half-laughed. "God, I'll say one thing. Life will never be boring with her."

Creed turned his head toward Seth. "No. I don't suppose it will." He put his shoulder to the hogshead and rolled it over in the corner, then took a crowbar to the top. The wood splintered against the force.

"You know, Creed, I've been thinking . . ."

"Uh-oh . . ."

Seth laughed. "Well, it was my thinking that got us this store, wasn't it?"

Creed dug into the barrel and pulled out a sawdust-covered water crock and blew it clean. "As I recall."

"And this store has made you a man of means, no?"

Creed shrugged and dug out another piece. "What's your point, my wordy friend?"

Seth strolled over to the barrel and leaned against the wall of shelves with his arms folded across his chest. "I was thinking . . . why don't you leave bounty hunting behind . . . settle down here and become a real partner in the store. Not a silent one. You're good

this, Creed. You've been on the road for years now.
's amazing that you're still in one piece, considering
he kind of life you've led."

Creed frowned and reached into the barrel again.
Mariah's right. You are a worrywart. I'm content
/ith my life just the way it is."

"Are you? Maybe it's time to settle down. Find a
/oman."

Creed shot a look at him. They'd had this discussion
»efore, but then the stakes hadn't been so high. "That's
ight for you, *mon ami*. Not for me."

Seth stared at the crock in Creed's hands. "Why? Is
t LaRousse? He's most likely dead."

"I don't think so. It would take more than one bullet
o kill a bastard like him."

"Maybe . . . just maybe it's time to let it go," he suggested softly.

"I'll know when it's time," Creed snapped. He ran a
1and through his hair, leaving bits of sawdust there.
'Look, I . . . I didn't mean to shout. I just . . . thanks
or the offer. But the truth is, I'm thinking of cashing
)ut."

Seth blinked in surprise. "Jesus, you can't be seri-
)us. You mean quit? Why? You're making money doing nothing."

"Exactement. And I don't feel right about that. Besides, it will be yours and Mariah's now. You don't
need me taking food off your table."

"For God's sake, Creed, I hope you don't think that's
what I meant when I asked you to come and work
here. I didn't. I mean, I couldn't have gotten this place
off the ground without the money you invested. I just
wish we'd see more of you."

Creed gave a tight smile. "It's something I've been
thinking about anyway. Shopkeeping's not in my
blood."

"Bounty hunting is?"

"I have to finish with LaRousse once and for all."

Seth nodded, fingering the stack of heavy denim pants sitting on the counter. "I know. You have to do what you have to do. But don't cut yourself off here because of that. You may change your mind later."

"I don't think so."

Seth sighed. "Before you say no to everything, hear me out. There are rumors of a new strike up in a place they're calling Last Chance Gulch. Quartz mining. I hear the syndicates are looking for investors to come in on the ground floor. They intend to bring in crushers to get the gold out of the rock. I've been thinking of staking some of my profits there. If you've no interest in the mercantile, maybe we could pool our money—"

The bell over the door jangled before Creed could tell him no. He looked up to find Jesse Winslow, blond hair wild and windblown, standing spread-legged by the open door, holding his rifle in one hand and a tight rope on Mahkwi in the other. He looked every bit the mountain man he was reputed to be.

"Jesse!" Creed set the crock on the counter and strode over to shake his hand. *"Pardieu,* what are you doing here?"

Jesse's grin showed as a slash of white through his beard. He clasped Creed's hand. "I told you I was coming in to restock after I took care of our little friend. I just made better time than I expected. I had the wind at my back and songs of 'Nightingales' loomin' ahead." He sent Creed a wink. "Didn't figure it was time to dawdle. Howdy, Seth."

"Jesse." Seth grinned and shook his hand, too. "It's been a while. How's the trading going this year?"

"Can't complain. My packs are full of skins and empty of pots and pans."

"You're in luck, because we just got a full shipment in today." Seth cast a nervous glance at the wolf, who was sniffing curiously at Seth's crotch. "I see you've, uh, picked up a stray along the way."

"Mahkwi, mind your manners," Jesse told him

sharply and the wolf obediently repositioned her head under Creed's hand for a stroke. "She's a pet, but you don't wanna tangle with her if she gets her dander up."

Seth backed up a few steps toward the dilly-smelling pickle barrel. "I'll, uh . . . remember that.

"I see that knock on the head she took hasn't dulled her instincts," Creed said, scratching her behind the ears.

"Nah . . . but, ya know, it's been mighty unfriendly since I got into town. Folks are dodgin' right and left to get out of our way." With a puzzled shrug he added, "I mean, I've *got* her on a short rope." Mahkwi yawned broadly in reply, showing off her razor-like canines.

"Yeah, what's wrong with people in this town any-way?" Seth commented with one eyebrow arched.

"Did you find Raven's people?" Creed inquired.

Jesse nodded. "The fellow she was intended to had just returned from a hunting party and there was a big celebration going on. Raven's return sent the festivities into the next day. Her uncle, Medicine Wing, who happens to be a chief among the Kainahs was, needless to say, very pleased to get her back and promised me good trading with the Bloods as long as sweetgrass grows along the Musselshell'."

The bell over the door jingled again as several miners came in to browse. Seth nodded to them and turned back to Jesse. "Quite an impressive promise coming from a Blood chief," he observed. "While we're on the subject of gratitude, Jesse, I'd like to add my own. I owe you a debt for what you did for my fianceé and for Creed. Not only by the river, but with regards to that bastard, LaRousse."

Jesse shrugged and shook his head. "I can't take any credit there. If it hadn't been for Creed's sneaking up on them, Mariah and I would both have been crow bait."

"Well, you're just in time for Mariah's and my engagement party tonight at Hasty's Livery. We're to be married in two days."

Jesse glanced at Creed, who was studying the floor. "That so?" He extended his hand to Seth. "I'm happy for ya, Travers. Congratulations. She's all right . . . for a city girl."

Seth laughed. "Thanks, I think. Speaking of the city, I've been holding a letter for you for over a month." He walked around the counter and reached into a cubbyhole beside his gold scale and blower. He pulled out an onion-skin letter. "It's got an Ohio postmark."

Jesse's easygoing expression faded and he reached for the letter. He turned the missive over in his hands several times as though he didn't want to open it. "It's . . . from my folks, I guess. Had it a month you say?"

"Near that." A customer motioned to Seth for help with a grain order and he excused himself, leaving Creed and Jesse alone.

"Are you going to open it, *mon ami?*"

Jesse smoothed his hand over the paper. "It's been three years since I heard a word from home. I reckon Pa laid down the law to my ma. We didn't part on the best of terms." Carefully, he tore the letter open and unfolded it. While the store filled up with customers, he read. His face drained of color and he sat down heavily on the crate behind him. Finally, he crumpled the paper in his fist.

"Bad news?"

Jesse turned to him with stricken eyes. "It's from my ma. My younger brother . . . Zach, was . . . killed at a place they call Chicamonga Creek, fightin' for the Union." He sent a puzzled look up at Creed. "He was a farmer like my old man. The land ran in his veins the way wandering runs in mine. What in the hell was he doing fighting in the war?"

Creed tightened a hand around his shoulder, feeling the steely tension there. "I'm . . . sorry, Jesse."

He stared at the paper in his hands as if it was a

300

venomous snake that had just bitten him. "She says Pa took sick with the news. There's nobody to take care of the land and it's goin' fallow." His sky blue eyes met Creed's with a look of disbelief. "She asked me to come home,"—he laughed bitterly—"for my old man's sake."

Jesse had rarely spoken about his family, but Creed knew there were hard feelings between Jesse and his father.

Jesse pushed away from the crate, rubbing his palms against his doeskin trousers, leaving damp slashes behind. "In all these years, never once did I hear from him. He's never forgiven me for leaving the farm, goin' off on my own. And now she wants me to give it all up and come home. For him."

"Perhaps she asks for herself as well."

With a frown, Jesse turned on him. "I swore eight years ago, when I left, I'd never go back."

Creed folded his arms tightly across his chest. "Time has a way of mocking the promises we make to ourselves," Creed said, remembering his own unkept vows. "The mountains will always be here, *mon ami*. They're the only promise written in stone."

Jesse sat back down on the wooden crate, cradling his head in his hands. His breath came in long, shuddering sighs. Mahkwi settled her head in his lap.

"It should have been me. Zach would have stayed home where he belonged if I'd been there. He could,"—his voice choked—"he could barely shoot a squirrel out of a tree. His hands were made for a hoe, not a gun, dammit!"

The war in the East had seemed a long way off until this moment when Creed watched it inflict its tragedy on Jesse. It was easy to forget the hell the States were enduring when Montana was on fire with gold fever. But few who came were left untouched by the destruction.

Outside the door, he could hear the sounds of the busy thoroughfare, the wagons, the random shouts that mingled with the pounding of hammers. Life went on.

Reaching for a bottle of whiskey under the counter, Creed poured Jesse a drink and handed it to him. "What will you do?"

He stared at the amber liquid swirling in his glass before he slugged it down. He grimaced and wiped his mouth with the back of his sleeve. "I don't know. How can I stay?" His fingers dug into the wolf's fur. "How can I go?" He glanced up at Creed, then fleetingly at Seth who was with a customer. "And what of you? What will you do now?"

Creed knew what he was asking. To imagine Jesse hadn't seen what was happening between Mariah and him was impossible. A blind man could have seen it. "LaRousse is still alive. He killed Lydell Kraylor just outside the gulch." He lowered his voice. "He's after Mariah now, too."

Jesse cursed roundly. "Does Seth know?"

He shook his head. "I didn't want to delay their wedding plans. I'll tell him then."

"I see." His hands tightened around the empty glass. "Damn, what a mess."

Turning away from him, Creed corked the whiskey bottle and shoved it under the counter. "For the past four days, I've been closer to her than a tick on a dog's ear, without her knowing. Nothing. Not a sign of the bastard. I think he's waiting to draw me out in the open."

Jesse regarded Creed soberly. "So?"

"So, I think I'll have to give him what he wants. I told Seth I'd stay for the wedding. Then I'll go."

"Need some help?"

Creed pulled his revolver from its holster, checked the rounds, and slid it back. "You've got problems enough of your own."

"LaRousse made himself my problem, too, remember?"

"Merci, mon ami. I can handle him. This time, I intend to finish his worthless hide." He laid a hand on
Jesse's shoulder. "I've got to go get Mariah. She'll be
finished at the dress shop soon. Will I see you tonight?"

"I don't know. Maybe. I have some thinking to do."

"Bon. Au revoir, mon ami." Creed turned and walked
out of the store.

"A little tuck here, and another one . . . just so,"
said Emaline Fitzwilly in a sing-song voice as she ad-
justed the garnet-colored *basque* of Mariah's gown. She
tugged at the tight-fitting muslin hugging Mariah's
waist until it did what she wanted, then marked the
tuck with the dressmaker's chalk that dangled from the
sterling *chatelaine* pinned at her belt.

Mariah stood on the footstool with arms held
straight out, feeling lightheaded from staying in one
position for so long and from the unaccustomed pressure of the corset. It was cutting sharply into her ribs
at her waist.

"Ahhh—" the seamstress sighed. "We're nearly
there. Just another minute or two. Mercy, I wish I'd
had some white muslin or nainsook for your gown,
but, you know, there hasn't been much call for white in
this town. Raise your arm, dear."

Emaline prodded Mariah's drooping arms up again
and clucked around the tiny steel pins she'd stuffed in
her mouth. "With a figure like yours, Miss Parsons, it
pays to take a little extra time with details. You look so
beautiful in this color, why, your man won't even know
what hit him when he sees you."

Emaline prattled on as she'd been doing for the last
half hour about the latest town gossip, but Mariah
wasn't listening. Two words kept ringing in her mind.

Your man.

Her fists tightened around thin air at the despairing

thought. It had been four days since she and Creed had arrived. Four days during which they'd barely had one moment alone. There were things she wished she could say to him. Things that needed saying. And though he seemed to always be nearby, he was disinclined to talk to her at all, except in monosyllables.

She missed him. Missed his laugh, his friendship, and most of all, his touch. Night after night, she'd lain awake wondering if she was doing the right thing in marrying Seth. Night after night, what sleep she got was punctuated with aching dreams of Creed holding her, making love to her.

The room grew suddenly warmer as a guilty flush spread through her limbs. It was an impossible problem, one for which she supposed there was no real answer. Was it fair to shackle Seth with a woman who could never love him fully, the way he deserved to be loved?

On the other hand, perhaps that kind of love would grow between them over the years. After all, she grew up loving him. She could surely recapture that feeling again, couldn't she?

Mariah looked up at the jingle of the little bell over Miss Fitzwilly's shop door. Three young women burst through the door, laughing at something one of them had said. They wore strident-colored calico day dresses, rich with coal tar dyes.

Behind these three was one of the most beautiful women she'd ever seen, tall and buxom with copper-penny red hair and freckled, honey-colored skin. Her violet-colored dress was made of the finest muslin, lavishly tucked and draped with a wide skirt buoyed by stiff crinoline.

"Oh, Desirée—" Emaline Fitzwilly murmured as her head came up abruptly under Mariah's arm, nearly knocking her off the stool. Emaline's face flushed bright red and she took the pins from her mouth in one hand. "Hello, girls."

The three young women stifled the last of their giggles and said hello to the dressmaker, eyeing Mariah curiously. Two of them wore cheek rouge and one had kohl around her eyes.

Why, they were soiled doves, Mariah realized with a start. She nearly lost her balance again and her eyes widened. They hardly resembled the trollops who had been hanging out the windows of the brothel that day she'd ridden into town. They just looked like four friends out for a morning of shopping. Two of the girls looked the same age as she. The other seemed even younger!

"Ah," said Desirée in a thick French accent, "I'm afraid we are early."

"No, no. I'm running late," Emaline fretted. "You've come for the girls' dresses, of course, and they're ready."

Desirée nodded and glanced up at Mariah again. "It can wait. If you would prefer, we could come back . . ."

"We're nearly finished here, aren't we, Miss Fitzwilly?" Mariah asked diplomatically, stepping down from the stool. "Why don't you just go ahead and help these ladies while I change."

"Yes, I suppose so," Emaline admitted, wringing her hands. An awkward silence stretched among the five women for a few seconds, then Emaline cleared her throat. "Um . . . Miss Parsons, this is Miss Desirée Lupone and uh . . . her . . . employees, Angel and Daisy and . . . uh, Lula Mae."

"Miss Parsons." Desirée sent her a curious smile. Mariah nodded back stiffly.

"Isn't this a pretty gown, girls?" Ermaline asked. "It's her weddin' gown. Miss Parsons is marrying Seth Travers in a few days. Sadie and Wade Bender are throwing them an engagement party tonight. Miss Parsons is going to be the belle of the ball, with that gown I stitched up for her, if I do say so myself."

305

The doves cooed appreciatively, but Mariah was shocked at the casual way in which her personal life had become fodder for Emaline's gossip mill and she pressed her lips together.

Desirée's brown eyes widened and she paled visibly at the mention of Seth's name. " 'Ow fortunate for you," she said. " 'Ee ees a fine man, Miss Parsons."

Mariah blinked. "D-do you *know* Seth, Miss Lupone?" Certainly she could not . . . surely Seth hadn't —

"Ah, *oui,* I know 'im. He runs one of the most successful mercantiles in town. Even *we* must patronize shops, Miss Parsons."

Color crept to Mariah's cheeks and she stared blindly at Emaline's hand-crank Wilcox and Grubs sewing machine. "Oh, I didn't mean . . . of course you do."

Desirée tilted her head in a graceful gesture of understanding and tightened her fingers around the string of her glass-beaded reticule. "Ees's all right, *cherie.* I know many men 'ere in Virginia City in . . . other ways. Seth, 'ee ees not one of them."

There was something in the woman's dark eyes — a sadness, an accusation — that made Mariah distinctly uncomfortable. Perhaps it was her imagination. After all, she'd never laid eyes on her before. Then again, Mariah mused, perhaps it was simply her own guilty conscience reminding her that she and Desirée Lupone were not as far apart as she wanted to think they were.

Anxious to be out from under her scrutiny, Mariah excused herself and slipped into the curtained dressing room a few feet away. It took several minutes to unfasten the dozens of hooks and eyes along the bodice and slip out of the skirt.

On the other side of the curtain, she listened to Desirée's girls "ooh" and "ah" over Emaline's latest creations.

For her part, Emaline rambled on, filling the girls in

on all the latest talk from the grisly lynching of a stranger whom no one seemed to know, to the fact that the apparently notorious Jack Slade had, in one of his drunken rages, shot up the spanking-new glass windows of the Mechanical Bakery for the second time, nearly hitting a miner named Levander Marchand in the process.

Slade's beautiful young wife, Alison, had — Emaline assured them — poured her husband back onto a buckboard and taken him home without so much as a blink. Word was, the merchants, to a man, were threatening to arrest him if he didn't change his drunken ways, but quick.

Mariah sighed and tried to shut out Emaline's ramblings. She pulled on the simple blue gingham day dress Emaline had made for another customer who had run off with "some foreign man" and gotten herself hitched before Emaline got her money. The gown, as it happened, fit Mariah perfectly.

She was gathering up the wedding gown in her arms when Emaline's voice drifted back to her.

". . . hear that good-lookin' bounty hunter, Creed Devereaux, is back in town. That feller ever going to marry you, Desirée?"

Chapter Twenty-one

Mariah pricked her finger with a pin. "Ouch!"

"You all right back there, Miss Parsons?" Emaline called.

Creed and Desirée Lupone? Numb, she stuck the digit in her mouth and tasted blood. "I-I'm fine. I just . . . jabbed myself is all."

Emaline went back to her gossip. "My, my . . . that bounty hunter's a handsome devil. I suppose you heard about the other night? He hit a man at the *California Exchange* without an ounce of provocation."

"Oh, she knows," one of the girls chimed in. "Why, he came by to see her that very night it happened, knuckles bleedin' an' all."

Mariah's heart sank to her toes. Creed certainly hadn't wasted any time grieving over her. Apparently he'd no sooner gotten into town than he was with that . . . that—

"Nope," the girl went on, "he don't see no one but her when he comes to the Nightingale—"

"Lula Mae—" Desirée snapped. "I think you girl's 'ad better get back, 'adn't you? Cook said she ees serving a special tonight—*boiled tongue . . .*"

The trollop gulped audibly. "Oh, M-Miss Desirée . . . I didn't mean—"

"Off with you. *Allez, allez!* I will take care of ze rest."

As the girls tripped over one another to get out the

308

door, Mariah swept back the curtain and sent a frosty glare at Desirée Lupone, who had the audacity to look apologetic.

Creed and the whore. She felt sick to her stomach. Of course the madam wouldn't want her girls talking about her clientele. Bad for business. Particularly when she's especially fond of one certain customer.

Mariah focused her gaze on a lone spider climbing up the dressmaker's wall and tried to breathe normally. "Miss Fitzwilly, I'll need a bill on these dresses."

Emaline seemed unfazed by what had just occurred and she fluttered a hand. "Mr. Travers will take care of all that, Miss Parsons, don't you worry. Oh, that blue gingham looks divine on you, my dear. Simply divine," she said, taking the maroon gown from Mariah. "And the one you picked out for your engagement party tonight is all ready for you." She lifted down a gown protected from dust by sewn-together flour sacks and handed it over the counter to her.

Engagement party, Mariah groaned silently. That had been Seth's brilliant idea. He'd invited everyone — friends, customers. *Creed . . .*

"Thank you," she answered briskly, feeling Desirée Lupone's eyes on her, burning into her back. She fought the urge to turn around and tell her what she thought. "Will you need another fitting on the maroon?"

"I shouldn't think so." Smoothing the wrinkles out of the skirt, Emaline laid it across the counter. "I think I have all I need."

"Very well. Tomorrow then." With her back stiff as a church pew, she turned to go. She hadn't taken five steps before Emaline resumed her prattle.

"Of course," Emaline continued to Desirée in a confidential voice, "you heard about the awful thing that happened up North to that couple managing A.J. Oliver's stage stop — Lochrie was their name, I think."

Mariah's hand froze on the brass doorpull.

"Oui, oui, 'oo 'asn't?" Desirée answered impatiently, clucking her tongue. *"Épouvantable.* Terrible. Now, Emaline . . . I really must be going."

Mariah turned back to the busybody. "Wh-what did you say about the Lochries? Did something happen to them?"

Emaline's face lit up like a holiday lantern at the prospect of enlightening her. "Mercy, yes, dear. You mean you haven't heard about it? Well, of course, you've only been here a few days yet. But it happened almost ten days ago. Why, they were both killed. Horribly, I might add, by some savage who, word has it . . ." she cleared her throat, "—well, there's no gentle way to put it—he had his way with the woman before finishing her off."

Hattie and John murdered? Mariah felt the room sway and she grabbed a coat tree for support and knocked it into the raw wood wall with a bang. She struggled for breath, but the blasted corset cinched off her air.

Desirée grabbed her arm before she could fall. *"Le bon Dieu,* Miss Parsons, are you all right?"

"I—n-no. Was . . . was it Indians?"

Emaline drew conspiratorially closer. "It's possible, though there wasn't an arrow on the place. Whoever it was had a fine hand at carving though."

"Oh, Gawd—" The words choked off in her throat. She pressed her fingers to her forehead. *Hattie dead? It couldn't be.* It seemed only yesterday that Hattie was selling her Petunia; telling her how happy she was living there and how much she loved her husband. Nausea churned Mariah's stomach. Who could have done such a thing?

Only one name came to mind.

Pierre LaRousse.

"Oh, dear, oh dear," Emaline fluttered, fanning her hands like an old hen. "Perhaps you should sit down.

Your color's quite gone, dear. Goodness, I had no idea they were *friends* of yours." She minced closer. "They were, weren't they? Friends, I mean?"

"*Sacré bleu,* Emaline!" Desirée snapped. "For once, mind your own business."

Shocked into silence, Emaline snapped her galloping mouth shut.

Desirée helped Mariah to a chair and pushed her head down between her spread knees. "Zere, deep breaths. Zat's eet. You won't faint now."

Mariah stared at the floor, gulping air. She felt the blood rush back to her head and her vision clear. *Everyone knew about this. Everyone but me.* If that was true, it meant Creed and Seth had intentionally kept it from her. Behind her, Desirée stroked her hair lightly with one comforting hand. *Desirée Lupone, Creed's whore . . .*

Abruptly, Mariah pushed the woman's hand away and got to her feet. Her defiant look went from Emaline, who was staring wide-eyed at her, to Desirée, whose expression was closer to resignation than sympathy.

"I h-have to go," Mariah told them, backing against the door, making the little bell at the top jangle.

Neither woman tried to stop her.

She turned and yanked open the door, rushing outside into the cool air. She hurried across the rutted street, hugging her finished gown, barely noticing the wagons rolling by. Head down, she fought down tears while anger rose in her like autumn sap.

Hattie and John dead and Creed and Seth knew. They both must have known for days, but no one had told her. No, she had to learn it from the town blabbermouth and Creed's strumpet! She swiped at her eyes with the back of her sleeve and stomped through the drying mud.

Anger and grief duelled with a stinging hurt. And what a fool she'd been! Why, she'd probably meant nothing more than a convenient roll in the hay to Creed Devereaux. Her cheeks burned at the thought. He'd turned her away to go back to Desirée Lupone—a woman whose red hair was so glaring, she could probably stop carriage traffic on Chicago's East Side!

Mariah stepped up onto the sidewalk, her heels clacking an angry rhythm against the boards. If she'd been looking where she was going she would have seen him, but as it was, she collided with his massive chest with a smack and nearly fell on her bottom.

Creed grabbed her upper arms, steadying her. *"Maudit,* Mariah, it helps to walk with your eyes open." He tossed his cigarette to the boardwalk.

Mariah gasped and wrenched herself from his grasp. "You!"

Creed looked behind him in confusion, then spread his fingers across his chest. *"Me?"*

"Don't you touch me," she hissed, brushing past him and knocking away his outstretched hand and starting off again down the boardwalk.

"What the hell—?" Creed had to wait for two rank-smelling miners to pass before he could follow. She'd been crying, dammit, and he meant to find out why. He caught up with her in five strides and took her by the arm again. "Mariah, where do you think you're going?"

"To my room. Let me go."

"Not until you tell me what's wrong."

Her eyes flared gold as she whirled on him. "Why don't you ask your little friend Miss Lupone? You two seem to share everything else."

Creed felt the color drain from his face. "Desirée?"

Her face crumpled again. "Ooooh! So you even admit it, you . . . you *scoundrel.*"

At a loss, Creed shook his head. "Admit what? I don't know what the hell you mean."

"Don't you swear at me, Creed Devereaux. You

have no right . . ." Her voice broke and she turned her face from him.

"All right, all right, *ma petite—*"

"And don't call me that either. I'm not your *petite* anything!"

Creed cursed silently. "Did Desirée say something to you?"

Mariah gave a choked laugh. "With the town's resident gossip monger on duty? She hardly had to."

His jaw tightened and she started off again, her heels beating a tattoo against the boards.

"Je m'en fou!" he swore, stopping her again. "There is a misunderstanding here somewhere . . ."

She looked up at him incredulously. "A misunderstanding? Is that what you call it? Let me go, Creed Devereaux, or, so help me, I'll scream."

With a shake of his head, his green eyes pleaded with her. "Mariah—"

A scowling young swain, seven inches shorter than Creed with a full red beard, stepped up to Mariah and gallantly scooped off his slouch hat. "Is this fellow bothering you, Miss?"

Mariah's mouth snapped shut as she appraised her rescuer. She swiped at her eyes. "I . . . yes . . . yes, he is. He—he won't let me pass."

Creed rolled his eyes. "Ah, Mariah . . ."

The redheaded fellow glared at Creed. "Unhand this woman, sir."

"Sacre bleu!" Dropping her arm, Creed whirled on the man. "Listen, you little pipsqueak—" Mariah escaped down the sidewalk and disappeared into the crowd.

The man balled his fists in a show of might. "Ladies walk unmolested on our streets, no thanks to fellows like you, sir." The miner danced in front of him.

Creed picked the man up bodily and sent him crashing into the log wall of Pfouts Store with a sickening thud. As he slid down the wall, Creed glared at him fiercely. "Next time you rescue a damsel in distress, *mon ami,* make sure she is in need of rescuing."

He started off after her without a look back at the men who were gathering around the fallen knight. It took him until he reached the front stoop of *The Virginia* to catch her and when she heard him coming behind her, she raced up the steps. But he was too fast for her.

"Mariah, wait!"

She turned on him again. "What do you want from me?"

"Answers."

"Answers? How about questions? For starters, why didn't you tell me about Hattie and John being murdered?"

Creed ground his teeth together. It was inevitable in a town this size that she'd find out before the wedding. He hadn't told her because . . . well, because he didn't want to see her hurt or remind her that she'd come close to meeting the same fate.

"You knew and you kept it from me," she accused, hands on her hips. "Why? Did you think I was too 'fragile' to take it?"

He looked at the ground, knowing she was right to be angry. "No. I would have told you, but I didn't want to upset you before your wedding."

Her throat swelled with tears. "How dare you presume to choose what I should and shouldn't know? I'm sick to death of people protecting me from myself! All my life, my father, my grandmother, now Seth and you . . ." She turned to go, but he stopped her.

"Stop that!" she hissed glaring at his hand on her arm.

Releasing her, he stammered, "Mariah, I'm . . . I'm sorry about keeping it from you. You had every right to know. I was wrong, *mais oui?*"

She stared at him, too angry to speak for several

seconds. "Was it LaRousse?"

There was no keeping that kind of news from her. "I think so. He must have been looking for me."

She took a tremulous step back, leaning against the rough wooden wall. "And if . . . if I'd stayed there, he would have killed me, too."

"Oui." Creed's tortured eyes met hers. "Thank God you were too stubborn to stay."

"Oh, yes, thank God . . . indeed." She turned to go, but his voice stopped her.

"Mariah, I know you're upset about the Lochries, but that's not why you're so angry. What else?"

She sniffed and kept her face turned away.

"What the hell did that old biddy say to you?"

She sent him a haughty look, bordering on tears. "I hardly think I need to remind you of your exploits. You are, after all, the talk of the brothel. Not to mention," she added with a sniff, "the dress shop."

He took a step back, as though she'd punched him. "Mariah, I know Desirée, I admit, but—"

"Know her," she parroted with a bitter laugh. "In a strictly biblical sense, you mean."

Creed's expression darkened and he took her elbow again, this time dragging her into the lobby of the hotel. "Come on."

"What are you—? Let go of me." She tripped on the carpet inside the door, but he held her up. Her feet barely touched the floor as he whisked her past the two leather-covered settees parked in the lobby. "Creed!"

"We're going somewhere more private to discuss this before someone hears us fighting and gets the wrong idea."

The desk clerk watched open-mouthed as Creed dragged her across the foyer toward the hallway to her room. The rail-thin man cleared his throat timidly. "Uh . . . Miss Parsons? Is . . . uh, is everything all right?"

"She's fine," Creed snapped, cutting off her gasp of protest. "Mind your own damn business!"

The desk clerk drew in his chin and resettled his wire-rimmed spectacles on his nose.

Mariah's skirts tangled with Creed's trunk-like thighs as he hustled her toward her door. His fingers cut into her upper arm. He yanked her to a stop in front of room sixteen. "Where's your key?"

"You're hurting me," she told him, looking pointedly at his hand. When he let her go, she released the breath she'd been holding.

"You're not coming in," she said defiantly. "And how do you know this is my room? Have you been following me? Is that how you happened to be standing outside the dressmaker's shop today?"

"What if I have?"

She searched for the proper curse, but failed. "Well, don't. I don't want you following me."

With a look that would have put goose flesh on a snake's skin, Creed backed her into the door and placed one arm on either side of her shoulders, effectively trapping her, yet leaving a hand's span between them. The gown in her arms slid to the floor unnoticed. There was a restrained violence in his eyes, the kind that made her fear for her safety and sanity.

Mariah gulped and pressed her back against the hard surface behind her. Her pulse, already rapid from running, cranked up another notch and a low ache started in her belly. He smelled of fresh air and male sweat, and there was just a hint of alcohol and tobacco on his breath. He didn't touch her.

He didn't have to.

Simply standing this close to him made her limbs turn to gelatin and had her thinking thoughts she'd sworn never to think again. Damn him, damn him!

"What you want, Mariah, is not always what's good for you." His whiskey-raw voice slid inside her bones and kindled an irreverent heat. What made it all the worse, she thought, was that he could still make her react like this after everything she'd just learned about him.

It made her want to sit down and cry her eyes out, or scream at the sky. But she could barely breathe, so she simply stared at him with her trembling chin held high.

"Now," he went on, "you will tell me what has you so upset." He inched threateningly closer. "Tell me."

Her lip quivered. "How c-could you?"

"How could I what?"

"Go to that . . . that woman after . . . after . . . what we—" She dropped her gaze to the floor. "You were barely in town before you ran to her bed."

Creed blinked and his scowl deepened. "Who told you that?"

"What does it matter?"

"Desirée's a friend, Mariah—"

She snorted.

"—and I did go to see her that first night, after Sadie's. But not for what you think. I was drunk. We only talked."

Her gaze leapt to his like a wild flame. "Talked? You must think I'm very naive to believe—"

He slammed an open palm against the door next to her ear, rattling it in its frame and making her jump. "You can believe whatever you damn well please," he growled. "And since when am I answerable to you, anyway? *Sacre bleu!* You're the one marrying another man. If anyone has the right to be jealous, it's me!" He shoved away from the door and paced to the opposite wall, banging his hand there, too, as if that would assuage the irreconcilable rage inside him.

"Jealous!" She gathered herself to her full height. "You *told* me to marry Seth."

"Mais oui, but I don't have to like it." The words

317

rushed out before he could stop them and the two of them stared at each other in stunned silence.

Like a plant reaching for sunlight, Creed's gaze drifted to her breasts, which rose and fell rapidly beneath the blue gingham fabric of her gown. A fleeting memory of his fingertips drifting over those soft breasts tightened his groin and made him wish he'd never gotten this close to her again.

He looked at her, his face registering guilt.

Mariah sucked in a breath as his gaze took her in. As if she could hear his thoughts, she knew what he'd been remembering. She was remembering it, too.

What are we doing? she wondered. *What makes us think we can leave each other and forget what was between us? There will never be another man who will make me feel this way.*

Never.

Creed jerked away from her, pacing back and forth in the narrow hallway, grinding a fist into his palm. "Don't look at me that way."

Tears welled in her eyes. "What way?"

"I can't give you what you want," he nearly shouted, then braced his hands high up on the wall and hung his head between his arms. "But, goddammit, Mariah, I'm only human. You're tearing me apart."

"And you're alone in that, I suppose? As usual. Do you think I'm not hurting as well?"

"What we did was wrong. Dead wrong."

"Not if you love me." It was out before she could call the words back.

Creed's fists curled at his sides as he spun to face her. "Seth is like a brother to me. He saved my life. He trusted me with you. I betrayed him." He grabbed her upper arms and rattled her as if he could shake some sense into her. "Look at me. Take a good, long look at the man you see. A man who would betray a friend like I did. I have nothing to offer a woman like you. Seth can give you everything. There

318

is no choice here, Mariah."

Her eyes flamed in the dim hallway light. "It's so easy for you to talk about choices. What choices do I have? Do you think I want to hurt Seth? Do you think I meant to fall in love with you? Believe me, it was the last thing I intended. But it happened, God help us, it *did*." Creed's eyes flashed up to hers as if to deny what she'd said, but she rushed on.

"Some things are out of our power to control. You of all people, with that gift of yours, should believe that. It's what brought us together." Her hands went to grasp his arms. "I love you, Creed. Damn your honor! I love you and you love me. Look at me and deny it."

Creed's mouth was only a kiss away, and his gaze searched hers the way a starving man would covet a crumb of bread. His breath, sweet and warm, whispered across her skin in uneven bursts. Reaching up, he slid his hands into her hair and raked through her swept-back tresses as if he were memorizing the feel of her, drawing her fractionally closer to his lips. But his eyes, dark as a wind-tossed sea, betrayed his turmoil. She felt herself drowning.

No. She was lost already. Didn't he know? Couldn't he see? None of those things he thought were so important to her mattered at all. But this . . . this did.

His thumb traced almost reverently across her parted lips before he shook his head and slammed his eyes shut.

"Creed." The word was a whisper, a plea.

"No." He wrenched himself from her arms, pushing her back against the hallway wall. "No, dammit. Forget me, Mariah. I have nothing to offer you. It's over."

Before she could reply, he turned and strode down the corridor. She watched him go, until he disappeared around the corner, until all she could hear was the sound of his boot heels ringing against the lobby floor and receding out the door.

Mariah sank back against the wooden door for support. Tears squeezed out under her shut eyelids and spilled down her face, unchecked. She could do no more.

It was over. All of it. Over.

Downing plucked a stem of hay from the haystack and picked at a piece of jerky stuck between his teeth as he watched shadows of evening creep up the barn's rafters. The two men Pierre had recruited into the gang from the Cottonwood Ranch, Quincy and Snake, snored quietly ten feet away, hands folded corpse-like across their chests.

The temperature had dropped with the sun, but despite that, beads of sweat glistened on Pierre's forehead and stained the front of his shirt. Downing wondered absently if Pierre's shoulder was festering. He found the possibility decidedly encouraging.

Crossing his legs at the ankles, he watched La-Rousse polish his precious Spencer for the fourth time today. Sucking at his teeth with his tongue, Downing shook his head at the half-breed's obsession with the weapon and looked down at his own sorry old Henry with a sharp twinge of resentment.

"There's another two dozen of them beauties back in camp, in case you forgot," he said, drawing a heated glance from Pierre. "I reckon as how Petey will figger us for dead by now. Might just take it into his head to sell them rifles himself."

"Saa-aa! You seenk too much, *mon ami sans dessein.* You talk too much, too."

Downing sighed, deciding it prudent not to take offense at being called stupid. He wasn't so stupid he hadn't picked up a few words of French from Pierre's ramblings. LaRousse could call him anything he wanted. He'd decided to get the hell out. He was sick and tired of waiting for Pierre to make his move. Finished with hanging around the gulch like a tethered mallard, waiting for someone to take a potshot at them.

Hell, he couldn't even sneak into a brothel and take advantage of bein' in town, for fear of bein' recognized. No, Pierre had definitely gone over the edge with Devereaux, and he had no intention of followin' him.

"Maybe I should take a stroll outside now that the sun's goin' down. See if I can spot her."

"I know where she ees." His cloth glided up and down the gun's stock the way a man's hand would caress a woman's back. "I know where zey both are."

It shouldn't surprise him that Pierre had his ways of finding things out. He wondered for the first time if Pierre had picked up a fifth man without telling him. It was no skin off his teeth. He shifted tacks. "Well, I'm hungry, an' I'm sick of jerky," he said, getting to his feet in the steep-roofed loft. "I'm gonna go find me somethin' to eat."

He heard the click of the Spencer's cocking mechanism and looked up to find the rifle pointed at his belly. "What the hell—?"

"Seet down and keep your voice down. No one goes anywhere tonight."

If he thought he stood a chance, Downing would have jumped the son of a bitch right then and there. After all, if he had a fever, maybe he was weak. Downing's gaze assessed the half-breed's blazing black eyes and decided against anything impulsive. He'd never seen a weak bone in LaRousse's body and he dared not assume a little fever might diminish him. He dropped back to the hay pile. "What are we doin' here, sittin' like a pair of fools up in this loft? Somebody's gonna find us here sooner or later."

"Later will be too late," Pierre replied.

Downing pounded his fist in the hay, sending up a cloud of chaff. "You know somethin' I don't know? Well, you just come out an' say it."

Pierre eased the hammer of his rifle back down and smiled. "Tonight, *mon ami sans dessein,* Étienne's dess will be avenged."

Chapter Twenty-two

"Honey, yer as nervous as a cat teeterin' over the edge of a washbasin," Sadie told Mariah, and patted her hand. The woman gestured at the crowded hallway of Hasty's Livery which had been transformed into a dance floor for their party, complete with punched-tin candle holders hanging on long chains from heavy pine rafters. Brighter lanterns dangled from nails above the empty stalls. The stock had been moved outside for the party.

"It ain't all these people, is it?" Sadie asked over the din. "Shucks, these is just folks like you and me. And they're all here to wish you and Seth the best."

"I know," Mariah answered, playing with the silk-tasseled ends of the scarf Seth had given her tonight as a gift to match her new dress. Draped around her neck, the rust-colored silk felt smooth and soothing against her skin.

She drew in the sweet smell of hay which seemed to overpower the earthy scent of the men. The quartet of musicians by the barn doors had warmed to their task an hour ago and were playing a reel that had everyone on the dance floor lined up in pairs. A handful of the buxom Teutons, or Hurdies, had made an appearance to do what they did best. Despite the presence of these and the dozen or so wives who had moved to Virginia City, the dancing lines were made up mostly of men.

Some of them she'd met in Seth's store during the past week, others she had not. Sadie had said that Virginia City never let a good excuse for a celebration get by and their impending wedding was as good as any to turn an ordinary social into a party. Since nearly everyone in town knew the bridegroom-to-be, the place was packed to the rafters with men, noise, and music.

Mariah's throat tightened, watching Seth take congratulatory slaps on the back from the men near the punch table. Guilt tore at her insides. He looked so happy. She should be, as well, but she felt nothing that even came close.

She turned back to Sadie. "It's just . . . I don't know any of these people and Seth is so at home here. I wonder if I'll ever really fit in." She set her punch down on the plank table beside them, which was laden with fragrant desserts.

"Virginia's got its wild side," Sadie murmured as she smoothed a hand down her Sunday-best black bombazine dress. "And it ain't fer everyone. But you'll do here, gal. This town needs women. You've got grit and that's what it takes. You'll settle in all right once you and Seth get hitched." She flashed Mariah a smile. "And don't forget, you got me fer a friend."

"Thanks, Sadie. That means more than I can tell you."

The candle holders cast star-shaped rays of soft yellow light across the crowded dance floor as Seth and Sadie's husband, Wade, made their way back to the table through the noisy throng.

Seth looked so handsome, she thought, with his dark blond hair swept back from his face and his new fawn-colored frock coat a perfect complement to his tight-fitting brown trousers. Seth Travers was any woman's dream.

Any woman but her.

Mariah forced her hands to her sides where they

twined in the fine russet fabric of her gown and took a deep breath. I *do* love him, she thought, watching him approach her with that same emotion evident in his eyes. I love him for what he is, for the man he's always been to me. I love the kindness in his eyes and the way he has with people.

What about passion?

No, not passion. But a warm kind of—

Passion, the voice insisted. *What about passion? The kind you feel when Creed is close. The kind that sends electricity rolling up from your fingertips at his touch. What of that? Is that warm feeling enough to make a marriage work?*

What did it matter what she'd felt with Creed? She sighed deeply. He was walking out of her life and she had to let him go. Instinctively, she knew she'd never feel the same way with any other man again. And that truth had her stomach tied in knots.

"Darling," Seth said, slipping an arm around her shoulders, pulling her close.

She inhaled the clean masculine scent of him. His lips brushed her ear and he lowered his voice so only she could hear.

"My friends are all green with envy over you," he said, "but I didn't need them to tell me what a beauty you are, Mari. You look ravishing tonight." He dropped a chaste kiss on her cheek and a ripple of guilt rolled through her.

"Are you having fun?" he asked. "I didn't mean to neglect you. Some of the boys were just talking about Alex Davis' appointment as the new judge of the Virginia City Court."

"Your fiancé is being modest," Wade told Mariah as he wrapped an arm around his wife. "Now that Montana has been officially declared a Territory on its own, some have even been suggesting that Seth would make a good mayor."

Mariah forced back the emotions roiling inside her, emotions that had nothing to do with Wade's news.

"Oh, Seth, that's wonderful. You would. You'd make a wonderful mayor of Virginia City."

"He'd make a darn fine mayor if you ask me," Wade agreed, "and I'm not the only one who feels that way."

Seth frowned. "I don't know. It's never been a goal of mine. After all, I'll be plenty busy with the store, not to mention my new wife." He gave her a squeeze. "And I've talked to Creed about investing in some other business ventures up north. I'll have my hands full, I think. Speaking of Creed, where is he? He told me he'd be here tonight."

Mariah tensed and eased away from Seth. "I—I don't know. I haven't seen him since earlier this afternoon." Unconsciously, she'd been looking for him all evening, too.

"Oh," Sadie said, "he's probably primping that handsome face of his. He'll be along." Without a pause, she reached out and beaned her younger son, Jarrod, on the head with the flat of her palm as he snuck yet another sweetcake from the table beside them.

"Ouch! Ma!" He rubbed the spot with a frown and dropped the treat.

His mother shook her head in vexation. "Boy, you've got a leg as hollow as an old sycamore tree. Yer gonna make yerself sick eatin' all these sweets. And I reckon ever'body else here might like to have a taste or two."

Jarrod's charming grin mimicked his father's. "I'm a growin' boy, Ma. You say so yourself."

"You'll be growin' right outta this here barn if I catch you at that sweet table again," she warned with a threatening glint in her eye. "Now, I saw Jilly Stevens with her folks over by the other doors a few minutes ago. Why don't you go snag her for a dance?"

Jarrod sent Sadie a horrified look. "A *girl?* Yuck." He drifted off, mumbling to himself about the dangers of consorting with the enemy.

Sadie grinned at Seth and Mariah. "Goes by fast, don't it? Today, girls are the enemy. Tomorrow, he won't be able to live without 'em."

"Miss Parsons?"

The voice from behind her made Mariah turn around. Standing there beside a few other men was Nate Cullen, one of the passengers on the fateful stage from Fort Benton.

"Mister Cullen, how wonderful to see you again."

He tipped his hat and squashed it to his chest. "I was about to say the same, ma'am." He reached for Seth's hand and shook it. "Howdy, Travers. Your lovely fiancée and me met aboard the A.J. Oliver mudwagon that was to bring us down here. As you know, we didn't make it the whole way. I reckon we was all lucky to get out of that mess alive, considerin' how it ended."

"Yes," she answered, her smile faltering. "I suppose we were."

Nate chuckled at the memory and rubbed his jaw. "Truth be known, I'm surprised you and that feller Devereaux didn't kill each other on the trip down the way you two was at odds."

Mariah forced a smile. "Yes, Mr. Devereaux and I have certainly had our differences. But they're . . . they're behind us now."

Seth's expression grew serious and he tightened his arm around her. "Creed's been a good friend. The best. He went far beyond what he had to, to get Mariah home to me. I'll never be able to repay him."

Nate shook Seth's hand again and offered his congratulations, as did several others. Mariah plucked the fabric of her gown away from her throat, wondering if she were the only one who felt overly warm. Her smile seemed frozen on her lips and panic began to finger along her spine.

Everyone had expectations about her and Seth, and seemed so certain they were the perfect couple. Even Seth seemed to have forgotten the misgivings she'd had. He'd never brought it up again and neither had she—nor had she forgotten his vow to forgive her whatever had come between them.

But could he?

More to the point, *should* he?

The grizzled fellow on the mouth harp whined out the tune to "Red River Valley." Soon the concertina, saw, and guitar players joined him, sending the strains of the bittersweet song up to the rafters. Finally, Seth leaned in to her and grabbed her wrist.

"C'mon, darlin'. If they finish this song before I get you in my arms, I'll have to make them play it all over again."

He drew her out onto the dance floor and enfolded her in his arms. She tried her best to block out everything but the dancing. She'd already noticed the difference in the Territory's version of a waltz. It was nothing so stilted as was practiced in Eastern salons, but a flowing, loose-limbed movement that seemed to lift hearts and ease spirits.

To her dismay, the dance did none of those things for her. Instead, she found herself comparing the smoothness of his palm to the roughness of Creed's; the firmness of Seth's chest with the steely strength of Creed's. The gentleness of his touch with the possessiveness of the bounty hunter's. She felt as if she were dancing with a brother, not a lover. And suddenly, she knew that was all she would ever, could ever, feel for Seth.

Mariah dropped her forehead against his shoulder trying to hold back the tears that threatened to spill down her cheeks. It was impossible. Impossible. She couldn't do it to him. She couldn't marry him when she loved Creed.

Oh, Seth, Seth, I'm so sorry.

Misinterpreting her movement, Seth drew his arm tighter around her waist and soothed it up and down her spine. "Ah, Mari. I can't wait until Tuesday. Have I told you today that I love you? I know I've told you how beautiful you look." He tipped her chin up so she'd have to look at him. "Hey, what's this? Tears?"

She shook her head. She couldn't tell him now. Not tonight, among all these people. She'd wait until tomorrow. It would be time enough. Still, she had no idea what she'd do, where she'd go. Back, perhaps. Back to Chicago. She could get work in a hospital, maybe working in one of the factories. A knot formed in her throat.

"Mari?"

She looked into his serious gray eyes and her heart tore. "I'm sorry," she said just loud enough for him to hear, but she meant it for everything she'd done and hadn't done.

She cleared her throat. "It's nothing. I'm just a little overwhelmed by all of this. Meeting all your friends. Don't mind me, Seth." She tightened her hand around his and pulled him closer. "Let's just dance. Just for tonight. Let's dance."

And they did. For the next hour they hardly missed one. As the evening wore on, Creed's absence became more conspicuous. She found herself wondering if he would stay away completely because of her. Perhaps he hated her after all. And why not? She'd come between two men, good friends. How could any of them ever be the same again?

The barn was crowded and noisy and a bit warm. A headache fingered up the back of her neck and she asked Seth if they could sit the next one out. Before they could get through the crowds to reach the punch table, however, she saw Sadie and Wade heading toward her with a slightly green-faced Jarrod in tow. "Sadie, Wade, are you leaving?"

"Jarrod's feeling a little puny,"—Sadie sent him a peeved look—"I wonder why . . . so we're takin' him home. I'm sorry we'll have to miss the end of the shindig, darlin'."

"That's all right," Mariah told her. "I'll see you tomorrow. I hope you feel better, Jarrod."

With a hand clutched to his belly, the boy gave a halfhearted groan in reply. They said their goodbyes and she and Seth headed for the punch bowl. Her eyes went wide at the sight of Jesse Winslow standing near the door.

"Jesse!"

His grin faded as his eyes found her. He surveyed her kindly, down the length of her new gown and back up to her face. "Mariah. You look . . . well, you look . . . wonderful."

She felt her cheeks grow warm and she smiled back, feeling at ease for the first time all evening. Her gaze took in the bruise that was healing on his cheek, reminding her of that night by the Wolf River. Putting the thought out of her mind, she spread her full skirt wide with her hands. "Not exactly denims and rope belts?"

He took her hand and kissed it gallantly. "Dear lady, like a flower in a field of stones, your beauty needs no ornamentation."

Embarrassed, she laughed. "Why Jesse, I never knew you to be poetic. What a lovely thing to say."

"Yes, lovely," Seth commented dryly, standing beside her with a possessive smile.

"Seth told me you were back," she said, squeezing Jesse's hand. "I'm so glad you came tonight."

"I only came for a few minutes. I just wanted to wish you my best."

His sky blue eyes bore into hers and she sensed he knew more than he was saying. Of course he did. He'd seen her with Creed in the mountains.

"Dance with me, Mariah? You won't mind missing one dance, will you, Seth?"

Seth grinned and raised a speculative eyebrow. "Should I trust a man who plies my woman with poetry?"

Jesse's sun-tanned cheek dimpled appealingly as he

took her hand and pulled her toward the dance floor. "Never."

Creed stood near the wide double-hung doors of the barn. He ran a finger beneath his choker and straightened the fringe on his buckskin traveling shirt. The hallway was warm with body heat and he was glad he'd left his capote back in the room. He found himself wishing he'd stayed there with it.

He'd made his decision after seeing Mariah in the afternoon. He was leaving. Tonight. It was only a matter of time before more than simple words passed between them. A deep breath filled his chest. They'd been only inches from disaster today.

The memory tightened his gut and sent fresh pain shooting across his chest. He'd wanted to kiss her. God help him, he almost had. He could still feel her breath, warm against his face, and smell the sweetness of her hair. It had almost killed him to tell her to forget him, but it was the only thing to do. As long as she held out any hope for them, she could never get on with her life.

It was a relief, really. Now that the decision was made, he had some semblance of peace. He would go, she would stay, and perhaps they would be happy. Despite what she thought she felt for him, he knew in time she would reclaim her feelings for Seth. Yes, they'd be happy together. Seth would make sure of it.

Ruthlessly, Creed ignored the voice that told him it would never be so.

His gaze scanned the crowd, unconsciously searching for her cinnamon-colored hair, but if she was there, the crowd swallowed her up. Just as well. The plan was to speak to Seth and get out. Creed had already paid Hasty for boarding Buck. All he had to do was saddle up and go back to *The Exchange* for his things.

He headed toward the clutch of men standing near

the punch bowl. Seth intercepted him on the way.

"Hey, Creed!" Seth elbowed his way through the noisy crowd, holding a cup of Haymaker's in his hand. "Where the hell have you been, partner? I almost thought you weren't going to show."

Creed didn't smile. "Seth, I need to talk to you."

Seth eyed him with a speculative frown. "Sure. You want some of this punch first? It's got quite a kick."

Creed shook his head and scanned the dancers. "Where's Mariah?"

Seth frowned. "Dancing with Jesse Winslow. Why?"

"Look . . . I came to tell you I have to leave town."

"Leave? What do you mean? Before the wedding?"

"Yeah. Something's come up."

Disappointment and anger tightened Seth's jaw. "Something?"

"LaRousse."

"I thought . . . you've heard from him?"

"*Oui*, in a circular way. I've kept it from you because I didn't want you to worry—"

"About what?"

"Mariah."

Seth staggered back a step and his punch sloshed onto his shirt. "What the hell are you talking about, Creed?"

Creed told him about the note and his reasons for wanting to keep the whole thing quiet. "But it's been five days, and nothing. I think the bastard's waiting. It's me he wants. If I stay here any longer, I'm only putting Mariah in danger. I'm riding out tonight. I'm going to find him and end it between us."

"Are you crazy? You're putting yourself in the thick of it by leaving town. How can you know where he is? He could be out there just waiting for you to do something like this."

Creed looked at the floor. "Sheriff Fox got word that LaRousse had been spotted up at Cottonwood Ranch," Creed lied, referring to the infamous hangout to gamblers and thieves not twenty miles from Virginia. "I'm heading there."

Seth's eyes narrowed. "You heard this today? Fox is up in Deer Lodge on official business. Has been for the past two days."

A silent curse tore through him. He should have known better than to try to lie. Seth could read him like a book. "His deputy told me. *Maudit,* Seth, what does it matter how I found out?"

"You should let Fox handle it," Seth replied flatly. "It's his job."

Creed's eyes darkened. "No," he growled and thumbed toward his chest. "I'm going to kill the son of a bitch or he's going to kill me. Either way, *c'est finie.* It's over."

Seth shook his head at a loss for words. Finally, he said, "Then I'm going with you."

"Merde, you are more a fool than I thought."

Seth rankled at that and Creed put a hand on his arm. "Stay. Stay here with Mariah. She needs you, *mon ami.* You have a future together. I have . . . nothing to lose. I have to do this. Alone."

Seth plunged his fingers into his hair. "Have you told Mariah?"

Creed shrugged and glanced around them. "Tell her for me, will you? After I'm gone. I don't want to spoil the evening for her. And keep her close, Seth. Don't let her out of your sight, *oui?*" He held out his hand and Seth took it grimly. Like a punch, Seth's touch traveled up his arm and nearly made Creed wince. He swallowed hard and looked his old friend in the eye. "You're a lucky man, Seth. I wish you all the best."

Seth regarded Creed for a long moment. He felt as far from truly understanding what drove the man as he ever had. Creed was an enigma, like a wandering rogue wolf.

They were friends. To death they would be friends. It pained him to think it would come to that. But

Creed was driven by guilts even Seth didn't fully understand.

"*Au revoir, mon ami,*" Creed squeezed Seth's hand in parting.

"*Au revoir, mon frère.*" Seth watched him turn and melt into the crowd. Walking to the punch table, Seth poured himself a generous cupful of the rum-spiked punch and tossed it down his throat, trying to dispel the uneasy sadness that had settled in his chest.

It didn't help.

"Will you go home then?" Mariah asked Jesse after he told her about the letter. So many had lost so much in that War, she reflected, and coming West didn't seem to be much of an escape.

Jesse looked thoughtful as he spun her across the dance floor to the strains of "In the Sweet By and By." He released a long sigh. "For a while. Maybe it's time they gave up the farm, since they have no one to follow after them. With Zach gone there'll be no grandchildren to inherit the land."

"You may have children one day," she suggested gently.

"Me?" He shrugged. "I'm not the marrying type. My brother was the settling down kind. I like being rootless."

Mariah looked up at him with a sad smile. "That sounds familiar."

He nearly smiled. "You mean Creed?"

She almost denied it, but finally, she nodded.

"I guess you know he's leaving," he said, as his fingers tightened around hers.

She nodded. "After the wedding."

Jesse looked down at her. "He didn't tell you?"

Her step faltered. "Tell me what?" she asked. Her pulse accelerated as a prickle of warning ran up her back.

He nodded toward the other side of the room and

334

she caught sight of Creed's back. Her stomach took a plunge. He was shaking Seth's hand as if . . . She pulled Jesse to a stop. "What do you mean, *he's leaving?*"

"He's riding out tonight. He told me late this afternoon. Said he had some ends to tie up with Pierre La-Rousse."

At a loss for words, she watched Creed fit his hat back on his head and start for the door. She sent Jesse a desperate look. "Now? You mean right *now?* Without even telling me?"

He nodded slowly. "Mariah, I don't know what's between you and Creed. It's none of my business, except you both seem more miserable than any two people I've ever seen who care about each other."

Her gaze followed Creed out the barn door, back where the stock was kept in the corrals. "Damn him." A shadow of anger, swift and dark, swept across her face. "Damn him." Why did she care? After all, they'd said all there was to say today. Was there anything left?

Yes, by God, there was. A simple goodbye would have sufficed, but no—he wouldn't even give her that.

"Jesse, I hope you'll forgive me." Her attempt at calm came out raspy with emotion. "I have something to do."

He nodded and squeezed her hand. "I'm sorry, Mariah. Sorry it didn't work out. I probably shouldn't have said anything."

Squeezing him back she said, "I'm glad you did. You're a friend, Jesse. Thank you."

Jesse shook his head as he watched her go, wondering if he'd done the wrong thing. He didn't think so, but it was done. Swearing silently, he made his way out the front doors and headed for The Bale of Hay. He had an appointment with a bottle of whiskey.

The yard was empty when Mariah reached it, but for the horses shifting in the lodgepole pine pens behind the livery. With the party in full swing, any dance-weary soul seeking air would go to the street instead of the less fragrant corrals.

The only person she saw was Creed, tightening the cinch on Buck's saddle at the far end of the pen beneath the shadow of a sprawling cottonwood. Her feet covered the ground between them soundlessly. She stopped a mere ten feet from him but he was too preoccupied to hear her.

"Coward."

Creed jumped and whirled around guiltily. His handsome features seemed pale in the blue-washed moonlight. "Mariah."

She walked slowly closer, her lips tightly compressed. "How could you?"

Dropping his gaze to the ground, Creed searched for an answer that didn't sound asinine. He failed.

"You would have left, just like that, without saying a word to me. Wouldn't you?"

"Mariah—"

"*Wouldn't you?*"

"*Oui.*" He turned back to knot off the latigo and unhook his stirrup from the saddle horn. "We've said all there is to say, I think."

"We haven't said goodbye."

He stood stock still with his back half-toward her. "Goodbye, Mariah." Hearing her indrawn breath of outrage, he turned just in time to catch her wrist as she swung at him with an open palm. He gripped her hand tightly in his fist and drew her up with a jerk. Her thighs collided with his. "Don't."

Their faces were only inches apart. Her eyes flashed with anger and tears in the moonlight. "You deserve it."

"Undoubtedly. But I don't want us to end this way. Not now."

"No, you'd rather sneak away under the cover of darkness than risk giving me a decent word of farewell. Am I such a shrew that you can't face me anymore?"

"No, *ma petite,*" he said fiercely, his eyes blazing into

hers. "It's myself I don't trust." The heat of his hand clasping hers scorched her, but he didn't release her. Instead, his other hand came up to hold her other arm, clamping down over the row of mother-of-pearl buttons that seamed her sleeve.

Her breath came raggedly, as if she'd been running a long way. Blood pounded in her ears like a drum. His eyes searched her face, reaching into her very thoughts.

He cinched his fingers tighter around her wrist. Anger twisted his voice. "What is it you want from me?"

"A little honesty would do."

"Honesty," he repeated bitterly. *"Eh bien, ma petite,* let's be honest. Look at me. I am the man you see, standing before you, saddling his horse. That's who I am."

"That's only half the truth and you know it. You're just too busy running away from life to know what you're leaving behind. I may not have your gift or 'curse,' as you call it, but I know you better than you do."

He shook his head. "Do you? Then do you know what it would do to me to stay and look in the mirror every day and know that I've betrayed the two people who mean the most to me?"

"So you run?" she asked, curling her fist. "From me? From Seth?"

He dropped his gaze to the silken scarf around her neck. "I guess running is what I do best."

She sighed deeply. "I didn't come out here to stop you, Creed. I know I can't."

"Jesu! Why then? What do you want?"

"I wanted you to know," she finished, choking back the emotion that threatened her voice, "that what happened between us wasn't only your fault. It happened because *I* wanted it, too. I think you've taken on all the blame and that's not right. I don't want you to go feeling guilty about me or what you've done to my life. I'll be all right. No matter what happens. But I'm . . . sorry that you regret the night we shared, because I never will."

Regret it? Creed thought, crumbling inside. She was the best thing that had ever happened in his life and if he only had that one night of holding her in his arms . . . if that was all he was ever meant to have, it would be enough. But he couldn't say it to her. He would never tell her that.

Mariah watched the play of emotions across the moonwashed planes of his face. He didn't have to speak. She understood now. How would she ever go on without him?

Somehow, she would have to.

Reaching one hand up to his cheek, she wiped away the moisture that slid down his face. "I . . . I came to let you go . . . to say goodbye. Say goodbye to me, Creed."

Her gentle touch dissolved his will to stop what was inevitable between them. They met halfway and his mouth covered hers in a tender kiss that washed away the bitterness between them. Their tongues mated in a final dance, seeking, no longer to incite, but to resolve.

He drew her to him, wrapping his arms around her, pulling their bodies together until they were as one. Fused by heat and the destiny that had given her to him for a moment, he held her. He wanted to memorize her: the soft give of her breasts against his chest, her lips, so warm and sweet under his; the way she fit in his arms as if he were holding the other half of himself. *Dieu*, how he'd miss her!

Mariah cherished the feel of his heated lips on hers, his hands moving across her back, and the hard strength of him that would be forever emblazoned in her mind. His lips slanted across hers, settling more deeply against her mouth, filling her mind, and senses and heart. One kiss, one kiss and he would go; a shadow on her soul. Forever. Forever.

Behind them Buck nickered a warning. Too late—too *damn* late—Creed looked up to see Seth Travers standing not ten feet away, a look of utter disbelief written on his face. Creed pulled away from Mariah with a curse.

"Mariah . . . Creed," came Seth's stricken whisper. "My God!"

Chapter Twenty-three

Mariah's hand went to cover her reddened mouth. "Oh, my God. Seth."

Seth stared open-mouthed at the two of them, his fists working at his sides.

"Seth, it's not what it looks like," Creed began lamely, knowing any excuse he could offer would sound like a blatant lie.

"Jesus," Seth whispered in a breathy hiss. "And I didn't even see it . . . didn't even suspect." His bewildered, accusing look went back and forth between Creed and Mariah and he shook his head. "What a damned idiot I am. I should have known."

Creed took a step forward. "Seth."

"Son of a *bitch*," Seth snarled in dawning realization.

Creed reached out in a helpless gesture. "Seth, let me try to—"

His face darkened. "My *friend!* The man I trusted with my life, with my *woman*." A cough rattled through him, but he didn't seem to notice.

"We were saying goodbye," Mariah told him in a small voice.

A bitter laugh escaped him and his lip curled. "Goodbye? Is that what that was? That's . . . that's a hell of a goodbye kiss if you ask me."

Creed lowered his eyes, unable to bear the accusation in Seth's. His fingernails dug into his palms.

Then, Seth nodded as if he had suddenly figured it all out. He stared at Mariah. "It was him, wasn't it? He's the one you were talking about when you said you couldn't marry me. Isn't he?"

Mariah faced him, silent, her mouth quivering and her eyes bright with tears.

"*Isn't* he?"

"Yes. But—"

Seth took two steps and threw a punch at Creed's jaw so unexpectedly, it connected with a smack of bone and flesh, knocking Creed nearly off his feet. His black hat went sailing to the ground.

"No!" Mariah cried, covering her mouth with both hands.

Pain rocketed up Creed's jaw and stars flashed in front of him. Staggering to a stop, he wiped a hand across his mouth and it came back bloody. He shook his head to clear it, but Seth forced him to back up as he came toward him again. Creed dropped his hands deliberately to his sides, showing him he didn't mean to fight.

"You bastard," Seth growled, his eyes bright with hurt. "How could you do it? You knew how I felt about her. You *knew*."

He shook his head helplessly. "I never meant for it to happen. You've got to believe that. I'm sorry. So sorry."

"You're sorry, all right. You're the sorriest excuse for a friend,"—Seth's fist smashed into Creed's shoulder, once, twice, driving him backward—"I've ever known." Creed took the bruising punches like a man who believed he deserved the punishment. Horrified, Mariah watched, unable to stop it.

"C'mon, c'mon, you bastard," Seth baited with teeth bared. "What happened on the way from Benton anyway? Did you only kiss her, you son of a bitch, or did you screw her, too?"

Mariah gasped. "Seth!"

Anger worked its way up Creed's throat. "Stop it, Seth," he warned between gritted teeth. "Don't say another word you'll regret. I'm leaving tonight. It's over between her and me. It's been over since before we got here. I'm not going to fight you."

"Oh, yes, you are." His fist connected again with Creed's stomach and despite his readiness for it, the punch knocked the wind out of him and sent a sickening pain radiating through his torso. He doubled over, grabbing his gut.

"Seth, stop, for God's sake—" Mariah pleaded, grabbing his arm.

He whirled, throwing her off and she stumbled backward. "For *God's* sake? What about my sake? What about me, Mariah? Did you think about me when he was—Jesus, did you think about me at all?"

She shrank back from his wrath, hardly able to believe it was the same man she'd known all her life, unable to bear the pain of betrayal in his eyes.

"Dammit, Seth—" Creed warned in a half-groan as he straightened. "Leave her alone. It wasn't her fault. It was . . . mine. I seduced her."

"Creed, no," Mariah cried.

Seth advanced on him again, ignoring Mariah. "I'll just bet you did, you rutting bastard. What's the matter, wasn't Desirée Lupone enough for you? Did you have to go and make a whore out of *my* woman, too?" He started to throw another punch but this time Creed deflected it with his steely arm.

Rage shadowed his eyes. "Shut up, Seth. Or I swear to God, I'll—"

"What? You'll hit me? C'mon. I want you to try, Creed, because, frankly, I feel like killing you." He launched himself at Creed and sent them both crashing into Buck. The gelding snorted in fright, tossing its head, and sidestepped the two bodies that had fallen under its belly.

Seth's fist found Creed's cheek with a dull smack, grinding his head back against the straw-littered ground. Creed groaned, grabbing two handfuls of

Seth's white collar in his fists. Creed threw him off balance with a well placed knee and Seth rolled off him, giving Creed time to stagger to his feet.

There was dirt and straw in his hair, and Creed's face bled from two nasty cuts. Swaying on his feet, a hot green flame of fury burned in his eyes. He released the leather holster thong around his thigh and unbuckled his gunbelt, dropping it to the ground. "Damn you—"

"That's a good one . . ." Seth swung again, but this time Creed ducked and landed a telling punch of his own in Seth's unprotected belly. He doubled over, clutching his stomach with one bloody hand, coughing and gasping for air.

"Enough!" Creed rasped, standing spraddle-legged before Seth. "Enough. Don't make me hit you again."

Seth's head came up and he glared at him through the hank of blond hair that had fallen across his eyes. "You already hit me below the . . . belt . . . you bastard, when you took my woman. I know you fight dirty. Let's see you try without that . . . that *jezebel* standing behind you."

Mariah staggered back a step, as if he'd hit her physically. "Oh God, please . . . please . . ."

"Even God can't help him now," Seth slurred, and she watched in impotent horror as he lowered his head and tackled Creed, sending him crashing against the lodgepole rails of the fence. The wood splintered under their combined weight and the rail crashed down. The horses penned there herded toward the far side, eyes white with terror as the two men landed in the dirt.

Seth and Creed pummeled each other bare-knuckled about the head, shoulders, and stomach in sickening, meaty thuds. Back and forth it went, the two men rolling from one side of the paddock to the other trying to knock each other senseless. They banged against the livery wall, collapsed against a spare carriage wheel, and came dangerously close to the hooves of the frantic horses prancing in the pen.

Finally, they rolled back under the fence. Creed snapped Seth's head back with a well-aimed blow, sending him sprawling sideways in the dirt. In the next second, Seth dragged himself to a standing position, but Creed was slower to get up, groaning as he rolled to his feet.

Several men tumbled out of the barn doors, drawn by the sound of the fight. More followed, filtering into the yard beyond the circle of lantern light.

"Here, now," Hasty called in disbelief, "what's going on, you two?"

"Stay out of it," Seth ordered, waving the old man away with one arm as if drunk. "This . . . is between me . . . and him."

Hasty shot a look at Mariah and his expression descended into a scowl. Helplessly, Mariah turned back to the two men she loved.

"Get up," Seth demanded, his chest heaving. "I'm not finished . . . with you . . . yet, you low-down, stinking polecat."

Creed's breath, too, came in puffing gasps. "You're gonna . . . have to do better than that to . . . to keep me down."

Tears streamed down Mariah's face. She could see no end to it until they killed one another and it seemed that was just what they intended.

The two men circled each other like wary alley cats, waiting for an opening. Their faces and knuckles were raw and bloody, their clothes torn and filthy. Seth swiped the blood from his mouth and sent Creed a killing look. "I should have let you . . . hang, you bastard."

Creed's eye was half-shut and he blinked to clear his vision. Sweat streamed down his face and dampened his shirt. *"Oui?"* he rasped, chest heaving like a blown racehorse. "Why the h-hell . . . didn't you? Nobody . . . asked you."

Seth shook his head. "Damned if . . . I c-can remember." He flailed at him, too weak anymore to do much harm, but it didn't take much at that point to hurt Creed. He grunted with the blow to his chest, back-pedaling to keep his balance. He came back swinging, his fist connecting with little strength against Seth's stomach. It was enough to send Seth to his knees holding his ribs.

Creed shook his aching hand, cradling it to his battered chest. His wobbly legs refused to cooperate with his brain, and he fell against the trunk of the cottonwood, clutching it for support. Sliding down the rough bark, he sprawled with his back against the base, too tired to move, too damned sore to even attempt it.

By now, the crowd they'd drawn had grown. Several men went immediately to Seth, who had lowered himself to the ground and rolled onto his back.

Torn between the two of them, Mariah went to Creed, who sat alone in the dark, his head tipped back against the tree. His eyes were closed. Cuts ravaged his cheek and mouth, sending rivulets of blood down his face and under the choker. His knuckles were crimsoned and split and a walnut-sized swelling had already started on his right hand.

"Oh, Creed . . ." she moaned, "dear God, look at you."

Holding up his left hand, he stopped her just short of touching him and shook his head, his breath still coming in raspy bursts. "Don't . . . if you ever mean to . . . hold your head up in this town again . . . don't come near me. Go to Seth. He needs you."

"*You* need me. You're hurt."

He squeezed his eyes shut and gritted his teeth. "No, I'll be . . . all right." He motioned to Seth with a slight lift of his chin. "His heart's b-bleeding all over the ground."

What about yours? she wanted to say. *What about mine?* His final rejection stung like salt on a festering wound. There was no undoing what had been done. She could see that in the accusatory looks the men sent her when it

345

became apparent what, or rather whom, Creed and Seth had been brawling over.

She looked back at Creed, the man who still thought first of her and Seth after all that had happened, and her heart swelled with love.

Impossible, unwanted love.

Slowly, she got to her feet, pressing a hand to her churning stomach. "I'm so sorry, Creed. I wish I . . ." She didn't finish. What could she say to make up for the terrible damage?

Nothing.

He winced, shifting his back against the cottonwood bark and turned his face away. "Go, dammit."

Her feet felt weighted with lead as she walked over to Seth. He lay on his back in the middle of the yard, being ministered to by Hasty and two others. They sent her a hard look, but she gave it right back, daring them to lash out at her. It was all a well played ruse. If they'd spoken to her, she would have crumbled. Instead, they removed themselves a few feet away to give her and Seth a moment to talk.

He had straw in his hair and blood in his mustache from a split lip that was already swelling. She dropped down beside him and tentatively reached out to touch the one spot on his jaw that wasn't bruised.

Sensing her, he opened his eyes and stopped her from touching him by clamping a hand around her trembling wrist. "Why? Why, Mariah? I loved you. I thought—"

She shook her head, helpless to answer that simplest of questions. "I don't know. I'm so sorry. So, so sorry. I never meant to hurt you this way. I tried to tell you. It just . . ."

"Happened," he finished, dropping her wrist with a flick of self-disgust that edged near tears. His swollen eyes slid shut. "I guess I'm not as forgiving as I thought. I should have known. My best friend. God, what a perfect fool you must think me. What a perfect fool I *am*."

"Oh, no. Not you, Seth. It's me. Any woman would

be lucky to have you."

"I didn't want *any* woman. I loved you." His chest hitched with an emotionally charged breath and he threw an arm over his eyes. The murmur of low voices nearby told her the crowd was growing. Tears rolled unchecked down her cheeks. She didn't care what they thought. God, if she could only take away the pain in his eyes.

Groaning, he rolled to a sitting position and drew one knee up. Cradling his forehead in the palm of his hand, he said, "I think you'd better go now . . . before I say something else I'll regret."

She choked back a sob. "Oh, Seth . . ."

From beneath a sweep of brown lashes, his gray-blue eyes had turned to ice. "I mean it. Get out of here, Mari."

The wounded rage in his voice sent her scuttling backward. She got to her feet, ignoring the pointed looks from the gathering crowd. She turned to Creed and found him being tended to by one of the Hurdies. He answered the woman's questions in soft tones Mariah couldn't make out, but pointedly avoided meeting Mariah's eyes.

She felt panic creeping up her neck. She wanted to run and hide. Oh, what a horrible mess she'd made. Creed and Seth enemies, beating each other bloody — all because of *her.* God, how could she ever live with herself after this? How could she ever face either one of them again? Or anyone in this town, for that matter. If only she hadn't gone to Creed. If only she hadn't kissed him. If only . . .

Mariah started walking, stumbling really, without thought to her destination. She pushed her way through the crowds huddled near the door, not meeting anyone's eye. The music was still playing farcically and some were still unaware of the fight. She started running blindly through the wide barn hallway, past the gaping stares and confused looks of Seth's friends.

Reaching the other doors she ran out into the night, without stopping for her shawl. Where should she go? Home? To her hotel room? Her first muddled instincts said: *Go and crawl under the covers.* The darkness seemed the only way to hide from what she'd done.

She headed down the wide, rutted street — Van Buren — past the Wells Fargo office and the darkened Lecture Hall that shared a wall with a Chinese Laundry. For a half-block, the street was unlit and virtually clear of the strolling pedestrians that peopled the roadway a mere thirty feet farther on.

Three men walked twenty feet ahead of her, laughing and singing a silly drunken song. She hung back, hoping they wouldn't notice her. The last thing she wanted was to attract attention to herself, alone on a dark street.

The crunch of footsteps close behind her made her glance back sharply. From the corner of her eye she thought she saw a figure melt into the dark shadows. Her eyes widened. Fear pulsed through her like a sharp pain and she quickened her pace, trying to convince herself she had imagined the movement. A cool breeze ruffled her hair, but she hardly noticed the chill. A sort of numbness had settled in, muting everything but the lonely ache inside her.

For the first time, she wondered where she was. Virginia City seemed different in the dark — seedy and dangerous. As she hurried toward the business district ahead, she welcomed the sight of the gaming houses, saloons, and brothels that lined the block, spilling their light across the rutted thoroughfare.

Men by the dozens wandered in and out of these oases of companionable noise, ever in search of the perfect game or drink or warm body.

Two grizzled miners, a year's worth of Montana dirt on their clothes, leered as she passed them.

"Hey, sugar," one of them called. "Lookin' fer someone?"

She pressed her lips together, hoping they would leave

her alone. A woman unescorted on the streets of a mining camp at night? She knew what they were thinking. Her teeth chattered involuntarily. Clutching her arms, she hurried by the men, but not before the taller of the two snaked a hand out to grab her and jerked her to a stop. Hearing the fabric of her dress tear, she screamed.

The man who held her laughed raucously with his partner, displaying a mouthful of rotted teeth as he pulled her closer. His breath reeked of alcohol and tobacco chaw. "Whoa-haw, what a set o' lungs. Where you goin' in sech a hurry, girlie? You look mighty gussied up to be out on yer lonesome. We kin fix that, cain't we, Joe?"

Joe nodded, displaying the same lack of dental hygiene as his friend. His gaze drifted down to her breasts and his watery blue eyes widened.

Heart pounding, she clawed at the first man's hand, drawing blood.

"Yeo-ow!" He wrenched her hand away from his, repositioning his grip.

"Stop it!" she shouted. "Let me . . . go!"

"Oooh-hooo!" he hollered, enjoying the fight. "She's a feisty li'l kitten, eh, Joe?" He gestured obscenely with his hips. "Hey, I got th' money, if you got th' honey." He and his partner guffawed drunkenly at his little rhyme. The other fellow grabbed her other arm and together they hustled her past an open doorway.

Mariah kicked at them, trying to pull free. It was useless. Even dead drunk, they outmatched her puny ability to fight.

"Let 'er go, *mes amis*," a woman's voice demanded from a few feet behind them.

The men swerved to a halt and turned around to see Desirée Lupone standing on the stoop of The Nightingale, a cocked derringer in her hand.

Mariah's breath came fast and hard as she stared at the woman, garbed in elegant scarlet. It was too incredible. Desirée Lupone helping *her* after the awful things Mariah had said about her.

"Let ze girl go and we won't make a fuss, eh?" she repeated. "Thees one ees not for sale." The two buffoons looked from the gun to each other and dropped Mariah's arms.

"Aw, hell, Miss Desirée," said the first. "You ain't gonna hol' this agin us, are ya? We was jes' havin' some fun with this li'l she-cat. She one of yorn?"

"Eet ees enough to know zat she's not yours. Go 'ome and sleep it off, *mes amis.*" The men stumbled off, leaving Mariah standing alone in the crescent of light cast from the brothel's open door. "Come 'ere, Mariah," Desirée said quietly, reaching a hand out. "Come inside wis me."

Shaking, Mariah did as Desirée asked, not caring that it was a brothel. Gratitude knotted in her throat and stung her eyes as she reached for Desirée's hand and walked through the red-painted doors.

She didn't notice the silk-tasseled scarf slip off her neck and float behind her to the ground. Nor did she see the man emerge from the shadows to claim it. His long ebony hair fell like a crow's wing over his scarred cheek as he bent to retrieve the fallen bit of cloth.

Pierre LaRousse fingered the fine fabric between his fingers and cursed. Nothing had gone right tonight. He'd planned on taking her from Travers at the end of the party, when most of the guests had already made their way home.

But the fight had changed all that. *Le Diable!* Though it had given him immense pleasure to watch Creed Devereaux take a beating at the hands of the shopkeeper, he'd thought for a moment she would play right into his waiting hands. But his shoulder made him slow. He'd missed his chance.

Sweat beaded his upper lip and he pulled a hand across his hot, aching shoulder. The infection had grown worse and it hurt like hell.

In the shadows across the street, he watched the nervous tip of Downing's cigarette glow in the dark. The cowardly *lapin* meant to run. But if he did, he wouldn't get far. No rabbit could outrun him and he wasn't foolish enough to count on one man for his plan. He had help.

His eyes narrowed as another thought came to him. Fingering the silk in his hands, he started across the street as a new, even better plan fermented in his mind.

Chapter Twenty-four

Desirée poured steaming coffee into a translucent china cup, laced it generously with whiskey, and handed it to Mariah. The saucer clattered in Mariah's hand as she took it. The madam poured herself a whiskey, neat, and sat down beside her on the green velvet settee.

"There, there, *cherie*," she soothed. "You 'ad a leetle scare ees all. You'll be all right."

Mariah's red-rimmed eyes met Desirée's. "No, I won't. Nothing will ever be all right again."

" 'ere, dreenk up, *mon petit chou*. Thees weel make you feel better."

Mariah took a sip and nearly choked on the fiery taste of whiskey, but as it burned a path down her throat, she felt it seep comfortingly through her veins. She sighed, exhausted, drained of everything, it seemed, but the ability to breathe.

"Ze streets of Virginia City are not ze place for you alone at night, *cherie*," Desirée scolded gently. "Thees you know, yes?"

Mariah sniffed and nodded, taking another long sip.

"So! Why you are alone? I sought you 'ad a party tonight. To celebrate your *fiançailles* . . . eh . . . your engagement to ze shopkeeper."

Tears started again. "I did. Oh, God, I made a horrible mess of things."

Desirée watched her carefully, leaning back against

the green velvet. "You . . . 'ad a fight wis your man?"

"Oh, worse. S-So much worse than that." Choking sobs erupted from her throat and Desirée took the coffee away from her lest she scald herself. Mariah hadn't meant to blurt out her troubles to this woman, but she couldn't seem to help it. Desirée wasn't at all the woman she'd expected and her soothing voice just seemed to break down Mariah's carefully erected misconceptions.

"Sometimes . . . eet 'elps to talk." She handed her a hanky edged in lace with the letters D. L. embroidered on one corner. It smelled of expensive perfume.

Mariah sniffed and dabbed her eyes. "It's all my fault."

"What ees?"

"Everything. I never meant to hurt him. I loved him. I loved them both."

"Ahh-h. I see."

"No, you don't. You can't. I was supposed to marry Seth, but I couldn't. I just couldn't, knowing I . . . I was in love with another man."

"You mean Creed, yes?"

Mariah's eyes flashed up to Desirée's in surprise. "How did you know that?"

Desirée rose and crossed to the dark window, looking out over the street. " 'Ee's a friend of mine, *cherie.*"

"I know. He—he told you about . . . *us?*" A sickening sensation rolled through her stomach.

" 'Ee didn't 'ave to tell me. I could see it on 'ees face that 'ee 'ad fallen for someone."

Mariah watched the pain flit across Desirée's face and suddenly it struck her. "You love him, too, don't you?"

Desirée took a long sip of her whiskey, glanced out the window, and nodded.

"Then . . . why are you being so . . . kind to me?"

The woman shrugged and turned a smile on Mariah. "Why not? We don't compete for ze same man, *cherie.* I was never in ze race. I 'elp you because . . . 'e cares for you. And I am 'ees friend."

Mariah slumped in the seat. "You're wrong. Creed

353

hates me."

"Eef you seenk zat, you are ze one 'oo ees wrong."

Mariah pressed the hanky against her red nose. "It doesn't matter anymore. I've ruined everything. Creed doesn't want me. He has some stupid idea that marrying him would ruin my life and besides, he wouldn't intentionally hurt Seth for anything."

Desirée crossed the room and sat down beside her again. "Why don't you tell me what 'appened, *cherie*. Zen we can theenk of what to do."

In the yard behind Hasty's Livery, Creed forced himself slowly, painfully up off the ground. His ribs throbbed sharply with every breath. The Teuton hurdie, bless her soul, had given him something to stop the bleeding from the cut near his eye and mouth, but his face felt like chopped steak.

The worst, however, was his right hand, which he cradled against his chest. From the way it was swelling, he decided he'd broken it against Seth Travers' jaw.

Merde.

Woozy, he staggered and braced his left hand against the cottonwood to steady himself. Twenty feet away several men, including Nate Cullen, were helping Seth to his feet. He glared over at Creed, sullen-mouthed.

"Seth —"

"Shut up! Just shut up, Creed."

"I'm damned sorry," he said, swaying on his feet.

Seth's jaw tightened. "Do me a favor, okay? Stay away from me. Just get the hell away from me." Two men helped Seth walk back to the barn, leaving Creed standing under the cottonwood, alone.

He dropped his gaze to the ground and pressed an elbow against his aching ribs. Hell.

Hell, hell, hell.

Pain traveled up his chest as he leaned down to retrieve his hat and gunbelt, which he fastened on one-handed. He walked over to Buck and gathered up the reins.

"You still figure on a'leavin' tonight, bounty?"

Creed turned to find Hasty a few feet away.

"Don't look to me like you should be ridin' anywheres, movin' like you are."

Carefully, Creed pulled the reins over Buck's head and fitted his foot into the stirrup. It took four tries to actually haul himself up into the saddle one-handed. Creed bent over the horn, catching his breath. Hasty was right, but he wouldn't make it back to the hotel on foot.

"I'll be all right," he said, straightening at last. Reaching into his pocket, he pulled out a twenty-dollar Liberty gold piece and tossed it to the liveryman. "Sorry about the fence."

Hasty caught it with a frown and nodded. "It ain't none of my business what happened here tonight, but I'm right sorry to see two friends beatin' each other bloody that'a way."

"*Moi aussi,* Hasty. Me, too. *Au revoir.*" Creed gave Buck a nudge with his knee.

"You take care o' yerself, boy," the man grumbled as he rode past him. Creed didn't answer, but aimed Buck in the direction of *The California Exchange.*

Every step his gelding took sent pain rattling through Creed's chest and arm. He groaned, wondering absently if he'd actually fractured a rib or two as well.

He rode past a dozen saloons and houses of ill repute before he passed The Nightingale. Slowing his horse, he glanced up and saw the lamp was lit in Desirée's room. For a moment, he considered going in to tell her he was leaving. But he didn't have the heart for another goodbye.

Five minutes later, Creed filled the porcelain bowl on the washstand in his room with water from the pitcher. He pulled the cool moisture up to his face with one hand, over and over, until the clear water turned pink with his blood. Then, wiping his face off with a thin linen towel he lowered his throbbing hand into the cool liquid.

A hiss of pain escaped him as the water seeped against his bloody knuckles and cooled the heat in his hand. His attempt to flex it sent a sharp, sickening pain rocketing up his arm. Damn. His gun hand.

Absently, he pulled his army Colt out of its holster and hefted the weight of it in his left hand. Pulling back the trigger, he pointed the weapon at the door. His arm shook, making the tip waver.

He uncocked the gun, letting it drop disconsolately to his side, and he closed his eyes. Mariah's face invaded his mind and a surge of pain poured through him, making his eyes burn the way his hand did. Who could have predicted it would end this way for the three of them?

You should have, you idiot, a voice said. *The minute you put your hands on her on the levee. You should have known then it would all end badly.*

He swallowed hard and looked up into the small, spotted mirror hanging over the washbasin. He hardly recognized the face that stared back at him. The difference went beyond the cuts and darkening bruises that abraded his face. He'd changed. Gone soft, letting his emotions — for once in his life — rule his mind. And look what he'd come to.

Cursing the fickle vision that seemed to desert him when he needed it most, his mind drifted over the days he and Mariah had shared in the mountains — seeing the flare of anger in her eyes that first day when he'd pointed the rifle at her and sent her somersaulting over her horse's rear; the sparkle of laughter over the porcupine and the burned food; the first moment at the river, holding her in his arms, when he realized he was falling in love with her. *Le Diable.*

Slowly, he holstered his gun, listening to the sibilant sound of gunmetal mating with leather. Something on the floor near the door caught his eye. A rust-colored

iece of cloth . . . he must have walked right over it
when he came in.

His heart shuddered to a stop. Yanking his hand out
of the water, he crossed the floor in two long strides. He
went to pick it up, but he knew already what it was. Mariah's scarf. The one she'd been wearing tonight.

Unwrapping it, a folded piece of paper fluttered out
and he caught it before it fell to the floor. He shook the
missive open with one trembling hand and read the
childish scrawl written there:

THE SPRINGS OF STINKING WATER VAL-
LEY, TONIGHT. HER LIFE FOR YOURS. COME
ALONE OR SHE DIES.

L.

A crushing weight pressed down on his chest and he
sat down heavily on the edge of the bed, crumpling the
note in his hand. Dear God, he'd forgotten all about the
bastard tonight after fighting with Seth. He'd let her
walk away alone. He hadn't tried to stop her . . . protect
her. Of course. It was the opening that scavenger sonofabitch had been waiting for. Cold, mouth-drying fear
gripped him as he thought of LaRousse's hands touching Mariah. Damn him, he thought. Damn his bloody,
wretched soul.

Creed lurched away from the bed, only to be brought
up short by the pain in his ribs and hand. The note
dropped unheeded to the floor and he steadied himself
against the bedstead. Taking a few shallow breaths, his
muddled brain cleared.

Wait. How did he know LaRousse wasn't bluffing?
What if she were sitting in her room right now and . . .
But how did he have her scarf?

How, indeed?

If it were all a lie, there were only a few places she
would go. He would check them out first, he decided, fitting his hat on his head and reaching for his capote. As he yanked the door open and slammed out of
his room, he took refuge in that small hope.

The lights at the Benders' house were still on by the time Creed hauled Buck to a stop and slid off. He'd already ridden by Hasty's which was closed up tighter than a drum. Seth's apartment was dark, her room at the hotel, empty.

Pounding up the steps, he made enough racket to wake the dead. Wade Bender appeared at the door wearing a nightshirt and a frown.

"Creed—what the hell . . . ?"

"Is she here?" he asked breathlessly.

"Dear God, what happened to your—"

"Is she *here*, goddammit, Wade?"

Sadie appeared at her husband's shoulder. "Is *who* here?" She gasped at the sight of Creed's mangled face.

"Mariah. Did she come here after—?"

"We haven't seen her since the party, son. What's going on?"

"Jesus . . ." Creed muttered raggedly, his breath clouding white in the cool night air. He cradled his throbbing right hand against his chest.

"Has something happened to her?" Wade pressed.

"I don't know . . . yes . . . I—I checked her room . . . she wasn't there. Where else would she go?"

"Isn't she with Seth?" Sadie asked, confused.

"No. That's one place I'm sure she isn't." He turned to go, pounding down the steps again.

"Wait—where are you going? You're not fit to be riding," Sadie called after him.

Wade followed him down. "Creed, for God's sake . . ."

He hauled himself painfully onto the saddle again and reined in the prancing gelding. "LaRousse has her, Wade. I'm going to get her back."

"*What?* Are you sure? Let me come with you, Creed. Just give me a minute to get dress—"

"No. He said to come alone or he'll kill her. I believe him. Don't come after me, Wade. I'm going to get the

358

astard this time . . . or die trying." Without waiting to ear his reply, Creed kicked the gelding into a lope and re down the road.

Wade turned back to Sadie, ashen-faced, and shook is head. "Dear God."

"This here the place, miss?" asked Pete Loudin, the uscular bouncer whom Desirée had sent along to walk lariah safely to her destination. He stopped in front of bustling, saloon-fronted hotel. Light, music, and oise spilled from the drinking house. A pistol retorted om within, causing her frayed nerves to unravel fur-her.

She looked up at the wooden sign over the hotel stoop: *California Exchange Hotel.* "Yes, this is it. Thanks, Pete."

"You want me to come with you?"

"No. That won't be necessary. I won't be long." *He may ot even let me past the door.*

Pete nodded and lit a cigarette. Mariah pushed open he swinging saloon doors and bypassed the drinking oom. Slipping past the registration desk, she thought ack to Desirée's words and prayed she was right:

"Men are stubborn fools when eet comes to under-tanding what ze 'eart already knows, *cherie*," she'd said fter Mariah had told her what had happened. "Creed oves you more than 'ee can bear to love. Eet frightens a nan as strong as 'ee to be made weak by such a thing. But what 'ee doesn't know, ees your love will make him tronger. Don't let 'eem run from you. Eef you care bout 'eem, go to 'eem, quickly, before 'ee gets away."

Stopping before his door, she noticed it was partly pen.

"Creed?" No answer.

Pushing the portal with her foot, it swung open. He vasn't there. The lamp was still lit and his saddlebags vere beside the bed. A pinkish bowl of water sat on the washstand, a towel carelessly dropped on the floor.

Tension frizzled up her spine. Something wasn't right. Glancing around the room uneasily, her eyes fell to the crumpled piece of paper on the floor. Picking it up, her eyes scanned the page.

At first, she didn't understand what it meant. "He life for yours?" she repeated out loud. "Come alone or she dies. *L.*" The paper trembled in her hand. *LaRousse.* Pierre Larousse? Did the 'her' in the note mean *her?*

Did Creed think LaRousse had her? But how could he believe—?

Her gaze fell to the rust-colored silk tangled in the gray woolen blanket at the foot of the bed. Her scarf. She felt around her neck. Panic tightened her throat. She'd lost it and LaRousse had picked it up . . . using it to trick Creed into thinking . . .

He was riding right into a trap!

Clutching the silk and the wrinkled note, she bolted from the room. She had to help him. But how? She'd never find her way to Stinking Water Valley in the dark. And even if she did, how could she fight LaRousse? She needed help.

Her mind raced over the possibilities. Sheriff Fox was in Deer Lodge until tomorrow. *Jesse!* But where was he? She didn't even know where he was staying.

There was one other man. Please, God, she prayed. Let him help me. Let him help Creed!

Seth sat in the dark. Only the moonlight shone vaguely through the waxed muslin windows. It was enough to guide the bottle in his hand to the rim of his glass. The darkness suited his mood. In fact, oblivion would have suited it better. He was working on that.

"Here's to nothing," he muttered, lifting the amber liquid to the moonlit window. He lowered the glass to his lips as footsteps sounded on the wooden stairs outside his door. Narrowing his eyes, he slugged down the drink and prepared to ignore whoever it was.

A fist pounded on his door, making him jump in spite f himself. "Seth! Seth, please let me in."

He scowled at the sound of her voice and tipped the ottle against the glass once more.

"Seth! I must talk with you! It's me, Mariah."

He almost laughed. Almost. "I wouldn't have uessed."

"You *are* there. Seth, please."

Standing shakily, Seth crossed to the door, bottle in .and. He opened the door to find her wide-eyed and reathless.

"What do you want, Mari? Did you come to gloat? Rub it in? Announce your wedding date to my best ex-riend?"

She bit her lip and brushed past him into the room. He swept his bottle up into the air as he bowed low to .er.

"It's dark," she said, pressing a hand to her thudding .eart. "M-may I light the lamp?"

"Afraid of me?"

"Of course not. I need to talk with you."

He shuffled to the chair and slumped down. "A little ate for that, don't you think?"

Fumbling with a match, she lit the kerosene lamp on he table. The wick hissed and filled the room with a soft ight. Turning back to Seth, she saw afresh the damage he'd done tonight. His nose, cheek, and mouth were wollen and split. She bit her lip to keep from crying.

"You're a gutsy one, coming here when I'm not even completely drunk yet." He tipped back the glass and lowned the fiery swill with a grimace. "Say what you nave to say and get out."

"Seth, it's Creed," she blurted. "Something terrible nas happened."

His eyes took on an altogether new sort of anger. "Where have *you* been all night, angel? That's yesterday's news. Too bad Dimmesdale's newspaper isn't ready to go to press for another month. He could have had a field

361

day with our little *ménage à trois* tonight, don't you think?" He swept his hand through the air to indicate the headlines. "WRONGED SHOPKEEPER MAKES ASS OF HIMSELF AT ENGAGEMENT BASH OVER FICKLE FIANCÉE!", he shouted.

She inhaled sharply and sat down on the chair beside him. "You have every right to hate me. I don't blame you. But, Seth, I . . . I didn't come here for myself. I came for Creed—"

He shoved away from the table, knocking his chair to the floor with a bang. "Well, you needn't have bothered."

"It's not what you think. He's in terrible trouble."

"Only if he comes near me again."

She stared at him for a moment, then handed him the crumpled up paper.

"What the hell is—?"

"It was in Creed's room along with my scarf. Read it."

"I don't—"

"Read it, Seth!"

His eyes dropped to the paper. He read it and reread it, then looked up at her. "What is this?"

"L. for *LaRousse.* Pierre LaRousse. Don't you see? He's laid a trap for Creed with me. Creed thinks LaRousse took me. I was safe all along, but he doesn't know that. Creed's gone there alone. You have to stop him before LaRousse kills him."

A fleeting look of dread flickered in his eyes before he shuttered the expression. He tossed the paper on the table. "No, I don't. I don't owe Creed Devereaux a damn thing. He can ride into the camp of old Satan himself for all I care and I wouldn't lift a finger to help him."

Shaking her head, she said, "You don't mean that."

"The hell I don't."

She took a shuddering breath. "You're angry. I know you are and with every right. But Creed is . . . *was* your best friend. He never meant to hurt you. You must know that."

His icy gray eyes met hers and he grabbed for the

362

whiskey. "Get out, Mariah. I haven't finished my bottle."

Blood pounded in her ears. "He needs you."

"*I* needed you!"

Mariah felt the color drain from her face. "Oh, Seth . . do you hate me so much you'd let Creed die?"

He stared at her without a trace of forgiveness in his eyes, then turned back to his bottle and filled his glass with the clear amber liquid.

She grabbed the crumpled note and moved to the door, shaking her head. "Maybe I was wrong about you, after all. Maybe you can live with yourself if he dies. I know I never can." Turning, she disappeared out the door.

Seth listened to her footsteps clanging down the wooden steps until the sound disappeared. He closed his eyes and slugged down the whiskey then flung the empty glass across the room. It shattered into a thousand pieces. Just like his heart. Damn them, he thought. Damn them both.

Chapter Twenty-five

On the street, Mariah ran smack into the black-haired bouncer, Pete, who was waiting for her. Steadying her with his hands, he frowned down at the desperate look on her face. "Miss? Are you all right? What in tarnation is going on here? First you run out of *The Exchange* like your tail's on fire . . . now—"

She clutched his arms. "Pete, do you know where the Stinking Water Valley is?"

" 'Course. Everybody knows. Can't come into the gulch from the north or west without passin' through it."

"Can you take me there?"

"Now? I don't think . . ." The pounding of hoofbeats coming up behind him drew his eyes away from her.

"Mariah!"

She whirled to see Wade Bender and Jesse Winslow tearing up the street, shouting to her. She ran out to meet them. "Wade!"

Vaulting off his horse, Wade grabbed her by the arms, looking as if he'd seen a ghost. "You're all right! Where have you been? Creed told us—"

"You *saw* him?" she cried. "Where is he?"

"Going after you . . . or . . . so he thought. Hell."

"You let him *go?*"

"He thought the bastard had you! We all did. He rode off before I could stop him. Something about having to go alone. But I couldn't let him. I ran into Jesse on my way here. Where were you, Mariah?"

"I—I was with Desirée Lupone."

Pete stepped into their circle. "Will someone tell me what's goin' on?"

"Does Seth know about this?" Jesse asked.

"He knows," she answered. "He won't help Creed."

"*What?*"

"Never mind. You won't change his mind," Mariah told him. "We're wasting time."

Jesse scowled and reined in his prancing appaloosa. "What do you mean, we? You're going to go to your room and stay put."

Her eyes flared. "No, I'm not. I'm coming with you."

"Not a chance," Wade told her, mounting his roan. "We can't be worrying about you when we're after a man like LaRousse."

Pete fingered the gun holstered at his hip. "You're goin' after Pierre LaRousse?"

"If we're not too late," he said. "Get her to her room."

"Jesse, please, wait—"

"We'll find him, Mariah. Now, go on."

Heart sinking, Mariah watched as Wade and Jesse galloped off down the street, Mahkwi running at their heels. Beside her, she felt Pete touch her arm.

"Miss?"

Desperate, her eyes settled on the row of horses tied up outside a nearby saloon and particularly on the white-stockinged chestnut. The butt of a rifle protruded from the scabbard beneath the saddle. They wouldn't leave her behind. She had to go and find Creed. She had to help him. None of this would have happened if it hadn't been for her. Crossing to the hitching rail, she threw the reins over the chestnut's head and slipped her foot in the stirrup.

"Miss!" came Pete's shocked whisper. He looked over his shoulder. "What in tarnation do you think you're doin'?"

"Taking a horse." She swung up on the mare, hitching her skirts up out of the way, leaving the white ruffles of her pantalets showing.

Pete let out an exasperated breath and grabbed the reins. "Holy Smokes! You can't do that. That's horse stealing."

"So shoot me," she said fiercely, yanking the reins around toward the street, "or join me. But whatever you do, get out of my way."

Pete jumped back as she kicked the horse's flanks and galloped off down the street after the others.

"Holy smokes," he muttered. Pacing back and forth in the middle of the road, he watched her disappear into the blackness. Then, with an uneasy look toward the saloon, he kicked at the dirt and grabbed a dun horse.

"What the hell are you doing, Loudin?" he muttered to himself as he mounted and kicked the stolen horse into a lope after the woman he'd been sent to watch.

Pulling Buck to a halt under a stand of cottonwoods lining the nearby creek, Creed leaned over his saddle horn. His breath came in short, painful gasps. Sulphurous fumes from the nearby springs only added to the nausea rising in his throat. He twisted his left hand in Buck's mane, pressing his other forearm against his throbbing rib.

Sweat trickled down his cheek and between his shoulder blades, soaking through his elkskin shirt to his capote. Peering into the darkness, he tried to guess LaRousse's position. He pictured Mariah, terrified and alone, waiting for him. If LaRousse had touched her . . .

Creed ruthlessly checked the feeling. Emotions had gotten him into this trouble in the first place. It was his fault she was here. His fault she'd become tangled in this whole mess. To get her out, he'd have to use his head, which at the moment, was anything but clear. Uncorking the top on his canteen, he took a long drink and surveyed the dark landscape ahead.

The Stinking Water Valley was a sprawling bottom land that bordered the gentle swell of the Ruby Mountains. With numerous smaller hot springs dotted through it, he knew the main springs were another halfmile up the valley in a ravine of rocks and gnarled pine.

Above him, the half-dome of stars winked mockingly and the full moon painted the land under the trees in long shadows. Steam rose eerily off the surface of the water as it fingered into the cold night air. The only sound that broke the silence was the quiet gurgling.

Pierre LaRousse was a madman, but he wasn't a fool. The spot he'd chosen to meet was well protected from surprise assault. Nearly impenetrable. The advantage was LaRousse's. He was waiting somewhere ahead, with the darkness and fog to hide him. There was only one approach. The direct one.

There was only a slim chance he'd get Mariah or himself out of this alive, he thought futilely, but he had to try. He was, after all, the one the bastard wanted. Tonight, it would end. At last.

He nudged Buck forward, pressing deeper and deeper into the nightmarish fog shrouding the river. The cool breeze swam through the mist like a capricious child, opening brief rifts of moonlit clarity, only to close around behind him again like a trap door. The sound of Buck's hoofbeats echoed like thunder in the silence.

He slid his revolver out of his holster and eased the trigger back. Cradling it in his left hand, he dropped it to his side, blinking back the sweat trickling down his brow.

Just ahead, the fog swirled away. Standing in his path, he saw Pierre LaRousse, looking like Satan incarnate, feet planted, rifle primed and pointed at Creed's chest. The eagle feather tied in his long, loose hair fluttered silver in the moonlight, flicking the streaks of black war-paint slashed across his cheeks. His eyes shone brightly with an unnatural light.

Buck snorted and half-reared at the sight. Creed pulled him to a stop.

"So . . . you 'ave come, Devereaux." LaRousse's voice held a sinister rasp. "I knew you would."

Creed's hand tightened around the gun. "Where is she?"

LaRousse smiled. "Put down your gun."

Creed smiled and instead, raised the tip of his gun toward LaRousse. "We are both men with nothing to lose tonight, Pierre. Send her out to me and let her go. Then, you can do what you want with me."

Pierre sauntered a step closer. "Ah, 'ow noble of you. Just like your father. But you see, your father was a fool. And so are you, *mon ami sans dussein.*" His laugh reminded Creed of the yip of a coyote.

The tip of Creed's pistol wavered. Suddenly, he knew. She wasn't here. *Le bon Dieu,* she wasn't even here! It had all been an elaborate bluff to—

A rope sailed over his head from behind and cinched around his chest and shoulders before his dulled reflexes could react, yanking him painfully sideways. He cursed, scrambling for a hold on the saddle, but felt himself falling . . . heard the gun in his hand retort and the bullet pull wild, pinging off the rocks somewhere in the darkness.

The ground came up to meet him with a breath-stealing thud that sent agony crashing through him. Blackness swooped in on him, like the ebony wing of a bird of prey, snuffing out sight and sound and pain. *She was safe,* came his last fleeting thought. *At least she was safe.*

They rode in silence, four abreast, with Mahkwi at their heels. Only the soft plodding of the horses' trotting hooves against the spring-softened ground disturbed the unearthly quiet of the Stinking Water Valley.

Wade and Jesse had given her a thorough tongue-lashing and then agreed to let her come — when they realized, first, that there was no time to turn back and second, that she might actually prove useful in holding the horses for them when the time came.

She didn't argue. Nor did she promise to stay behind when they found him. *If* they found him.

Squeezing back the thought, she inhaled deeply of the fetid, sulphurous air and fought the panic rising in her throat. They *would* find him. They had to.

Crossing a stream, they moved closer to the thick tendrils of fog encasing the edge of the valley. She glanced at her companions, each lost in his own thoughts; Wade, whose jaw hadn't stopped working once, fidgeted with the gun at his hip; Jesse, whose brooding mien lent him a particularly dangerous air; and Pete, who stared unblinkingly ahead, no doubt wondering what he had let himself in for.

The fog thickened as they went, making the going more treacherous. Strangely, not a night bird or insect broke the uneasy silence. Only the moonlight, it seemed, dared intrude on this unholy place.

Far ahead, the high pitched whine of a gunshot stopped them short. A single shot — followed by a deathly silence.

"Creed!" Mariah breathed, surging forward.

Jesse reached for her reins. "Mariah, don't."

"But—"

"Get off your horse," he said, pulling his rifle from its scabbard. "Now."

She complied shakily and the others followed suit. All had agreed on their paths and now, silent, carried out the plan. Handing her their reins quietly, Pete and Wade started off at a soundless run, veering to the east.

"Stay here," Jesse, reiterated, and disappeared with the wolf into the fog-shrouded darkness to her right.

For a full two minutes, she stood where she was told, trying to imagine what had happened . . . Creed bushwhacked, lying wounded . . . or dead. Her heartbeat pounded through her like thunder.

The crack of a twig nearby made her whirl around. She searched the darkness, but the fog obscured everything. One of the horses nickered and she clamped a hand over its nose to quiet it, then held her breath.

Someone was out there.

Tugging the heavy rifle out of the scabbard of the stolen horse, she wrestled with the cocking lever until it clicked. She wouldn't wait here like a frightened mouse until it was over.

Moving away from the horses, she went in the direction she'd seen Jesse go. In the distance, she could hear the faint sound of voices. Pulse quickening, she moved stealthily across the sprouting spring grass.

She saw the flash of movement beside her too late. Steely arms grabbed her, ripping the rifle from her hands. She could only gasp before a smooth hand covered her mouth.

"Well, well . . . what have we got heah?" asked the man in a heavy southern drawl. "I reckon we've got us an interloper."

She struggled against him to no avail, trying to scream against his hand.

"Y'all by your lonesome, sugar? Won't Pierre be pleased . . ."

Water. Warm, smelly, choking him.

Creed came awake sputtering. He tried to bat away the stream of water being poured on him, but something held his hands.

"Tres bon . . . 'ee lives."

LaRousse. Ah, yes. It was all coming back. Creed opened his eyes and surveyed his surroundings. There were two others, outlaw types, throwing a rope over the dead hulk of a tree beside the hot spring.

Pierre hauled him up by his arms and the pain returned with a vengeance. "You must be awake for what I 'ave planned, Devereaux."

Creed's breath came heavily. The bastard meant to hang him. Again. He blinked, fighting back the surge of fear. He had nothing to be afraid of, he reminded himself, except for that first shock of pain. He'd done it before. He was ready. Steering him over to Buck, they forced him up into the saddle. He could have fought them, but he didn't. What was the point?

His ribs burned, but his hands, cinched in front of him, had mercifully lost all feeling. He noticed a third man, standing beside the tree looking grim. Downing was his name. He didn't seem to be enjoying this as much as the others.

The one LaRousse called Snake slipped the noose around Creed's neck. He gritted his teeth as the knot was tightened at the back, instead of the side. So, he thought, it would be slow.

"Deed you enjoy murdering Étienne, bounty," LaRousse snarled, "as much as I weel enjoy keeling you?"

"At least as much," he answered. "My only regret is that I won't take you with me, you bastard."

That coyote yip again. The sound tore through Creed's aching head like a dull knife.

"Hey, looky what we got here, Pierre," Snake said, pointing into the wispy darkness.

Creed's heart sank when he saw her, struggling like a snared rabbit in the arms of the card sharp he'd clobbered in the saloon, Erastus Field. He wrenched against the rope, but felt the noose tighten around his neck.

"Creed—" Her golden eyes were desperate, regretful.

"H'llo Devereaux," Field drawled. "I couldn't miss this opportunity to see ya paid back for nearly breakin' my jaw last week. Y' see, cards is only one a mah talents, as Pierre was quick to discovah."

Ignoring Field, Creed turned his haunted gaze on her. "Mariah, dammit! What are you *doing* here?"

"I . . . I found the note. I followed you. I had to."

Meeting his gaze, she tried to tell him not to give up. He closed his eyes and swore.

"Was she alone, Field?" LaRousse demanded.

"Ah didn't see anyone else."

"Where ees 'er 'orse?"

"Back in the fog, I suspect. She was on foot when I caught her creepin' in with her gun." He uncocked the weapon and threw it to the ground.

Mariah flicked a glance into the darkness nearby, but she could see nothing. *Jesse, Wade, where are you?* "Please," she begged LaRousse. "Don't do this."

Casting his own look into the shadows, LaRousse cocked his pistol. " 'Ow does eet feel to know I will 'ave your woman while your neck stretches, Devereaux?"

If looks were lethal, she thought, LaRousse would have been lying in ribbons on the ground. "So help me God, LaRousse, if you hurt her, I'll come back and drag you to hell with me!"

The half-breed laughed demonically. "Let's get on weeth it. I weel enjoy cutting out your 'eart, Devereaux."

Creed looked down at Mariah, his eyes filled with a thousand regrets. He swallowed hard, and the rope around his throat moved. *"Je t'aime,"* he whispered. *"Je t'aime, ma petite."*

Tears sprang to her eyes and tightened her throat. "And I love you."

"A touching scene," Pierre said, and gave Quincy the signal to send Buck off. *"Au revoir, Devereaux."*

"No-ooo!" Mariah screamed at the same moment an explosion severed the rope tying Creed to the tree. Then everything seemed to happen at once. A quick succession of gunshots tore through the air from two directions. LaRousse and his men ducked for cover. When Creed's horse bucked in fear at the sound of the gunfire, she darted for the reins.

"Mariah, get down!" Creed shouted.

She watched in horror as the man beside Buck raised his pistol at Creed's back. In the next second, he jerked backward. Crimson exploded from his chest — arms spread, he fell backward into the dirt.

Mariah could just make out LaRousse's dark form beside a rock fifteen feet away, and the flash of his gun as he returned fire to Pete and Wade. She saw Field lifted off his feet by a gunshot that came from behind her. He staggered forward in the moonlight, then dropped like a stone to the ground. Another one of LaRousse's men tore off on horseback in the dark with a pounding of hoofbeats.

The other man, Snake, headed for the horses, too, but Mahkwi tackled him at a growling run. The man threw his arm up to protect his face, but the wolf latched on viciously, tearing the fabric of his sleeve.

She held tightly to the reins, trying to calm Buck.

"Pardieu," Creed shouted, clutching the saddle horn of the panicked horse, "get the hell out of here, Mariah!"

"I'm not leaving!"

Mariah gave a cry of relief as Jesse emerged from the blackness at a ducking run and snatched the reins from Mariah's hands. "Dammit, I told you to stay put!"

"I—" Another volley of gunfire cut off her words. Jesse reached up to help drag Creed to safety. Creed threw his leg over the back of his saddle, and shouted, "Forget me, get her out of here, Jesse."

But it was too late.

Mariah gave a strangled cry as LaRousse lunged for her out of the darkness. Before she could react, his steely arms were around her and he was dragging her backward through the stench of gunsmoke and fog, the barrel of his gun pressed against her temple.

"I weel keel 'er," LaRousse shouted above the din.

The firing stopped abruptly, the sudden silence deafening. Mariah forgot to breathe. Eyes wide, her gaze was frozen on Creed.

"Move where I can see you!" Pierre screamed, "and drop your guns." There was a frantic note in his voice.

One by one, they did as he asked. At Jesse's command, Mahkwi released the bloody arm of Snake, who scuttled backward weakly. Mahkwi stalked, growling, toward LaRousse and Mariah.

"Call ze devil-wolf off, or she dies now," he warned.

"Mahkwi!" Jesse shouted. "Come."

The wolf snarled and laid her ears flat, then returned to Jesse's side. All the while, LaRousse dragged Mariah backward toward his horse, tied to a stunted pine twenty feet away. Terror clawed at her as she clutched the arm that both choked her and crushed her breast painfully. His body was rock-hard against hers, and damp with sweat.

Creed stepped forward, his hands still bound in front of him. "You coward, LaRousse!" he shouted, tearing the noose from his neck and hurling it aside. "This is between you and me. Leave her out of this."

LaRousse backed up, her body pulled flush up against his. "I'm not ze fool you are, Devereaux. I warn you. Do not come near." Mariah stumbled backward in awkward unison with him. The scent of death filled her nostrils. Her eyes locked with Creed's.

Frantic, Creed tried reasoning. "My father never wronged you, dammit. He was a friend to your mother. She would have taken you if she could have. Your father wouldn't—"

"Inyela, bâtard!" he returned in a confused mixture of Sioux and French. "Do not speak of the dead!"

Creed shook his head, taking a step forward. "She is only dead to you because your father wanted you to believe it so. She's alive and living with the Sioux."

"Saa-aaa!" LaRousse edged backward. "I told you not to move." He gasped. "You theenk zees ees about ze bitch who whelped me? Hah! Eet ees for Étienne, you murdering dog. And for my fozzer, 'oos life you destroyed."

"Then fight me fair. Let her go," Creed rasped. "She means nothing to you."

"Ah, but she does to you. I keel her . . . I keel you,

374

no? I see eet een your eyes."

Creed's breath came in heaving gasps. *Don't. Please, God, don't* . . . "You hurt her, LaRousse, and I'll hunt you down to the ends of the earth. There will be no rock low enough for you to hide."

"You can try . . . you *'ave* tried, Devereaux. And you 'ave failed. You weel always fail, because you are no match for me." Pierre moved the gun away from Mariah for a brief second to grab the reins of the horse behind him. A shot rang out of the darkness, jerking his head backward, erasing everything but ghastly surprise from his expression. Mariah screamed and stumbled forward as his hands fell away. The half-breed pitched backward with a hiss, dead before he struck the ground.

Too relieved to question where the bullet had come from, Creed ran to her as her knees buckled. Looping his arms around her back, he gathered her in the circle of his embrace. She clung to him, trembling, wrapping her arms around his solid strength. She pressed her face against his shirt, inhaling his scent to reassure herself he was alive.

"Oh, Creed . . . Creed . . ."

"It's all right, love. It's all over. You'll be all right now. I'm here," he soothed. As he spoke the words, the truth hit him. *LaRousse was dead. It was finally over.*

Twisting at the ropes still at his wrists, he called, "Jesse, bring your knife and cut these ropes off m —" The rest died on his lips as he caught sight of the man leading his horse slowly through the darkness toward them, his smoking rifle still in his hand.

Mariah felt the sudden tension in Creed's body and she looked up. "Seth —"

Seth's battered expression was inscrutable as he came toward them. His walk was hitched with a limp as if he, too, were in pain. He stopped a few feet away, watching Jesse slice the hemp that locked Creed's arms around Mariah.

"Are you all right?" Seth asked her quietly.

She nodded, fighting back tears. "You came. I . . . I didn't think you would."

"I almost didn't."

But his eyes, she thought, *revealed he would have regretted that.* She watched the muscles in his jaw bunch as his gaze slid to Creed, assessing the damage he'd done to him earlier. The smoldering embers of the anger that had wrought such destruction were still there, brooding just below the surface.

"Thank the Lord you came when you did," Wade said, slapping a hand on Seth's shoulder. Seth nodded but barely acknowledged either him or Jesse. His gaze was fixed on the two people who had turned his life upside down.

Sensing what was to come, Jesse tossed the hemp aside. "I think we'd better start loading up these bodies," he told Wade and the two walked over to join Pete, who was tying Snake's hands behind him.

Seth's eyes strayed to Creed's swollen hand. "It looks broken," he said without a shred of pity.

Creed's mouth curved slightly as he inspected it. "On your jaw," he admitted. Creed nodded toward La-Rousse's body. "That was one hell of a shot."

"Yeah . . . for a blind man." A note of bitterness sounded in his voice.

Creed shook his head, knowing he wasn't talking about the shot. "Seth . . . I—"

"She came to me after you left, you know," Seth said, cutting off the apology he couldn't bear to hear. "For a minute, I actually . . . hoped she'd come to ask for my forgiveness or to offer some kind of reasonable explanation. That it had just been a moment of insanity.

"But she came for you . . . to tell me you were in trouble and to . . . to beg me,"—he snorted—"no, *shame* me into helping you. She was quite brave, considering my state of mind. And quite persuasive."

Mariah stared at the ground, clinging to the strength of Creed's arm.

"You see," Seth continued thickly, "it took a few minutes to realize I'd never inspired that kind of passion in her. Not even close. And I realized she . . . loves you in a way she's never loved me."

Creed opened his mouth as if to object, but grimfaced, Seth stopped him from trying to deny it. "No, it's true. I can see that now. You two actually did me a favor," he added with a growl of angry laughter. "I would have made her miserable and never known why."

Creed's eyes darkened with regret. "It seems inadequate to say I'm sorry for all that's happened, or thank you for saving her life just now. I appear destined to remain in your debt, *mon ami,*" he said, letting his arm slide from Mariah's waist.

"To hell with your debts, Devereaux," Seth snapped, surprising him. "If you're looking for absolution, don't. I'm not ready to give that. Maybe I never will be. But just to set the record straight, not everything in life comes with a price tag—like saving your fool neck *or* hers. But if you must, consider those debts paid. I'll send you your share of the store in full when you let me know where you settle."

Abruptly, Seth stalked to his horse, shoved his rifle into its scabbard, and mounted. Gathering up his reins, his gaze lingered on Mariah for a moment, then slid back to Creed. "You take care of her. If you hurt her, I'll kill you myself."

"Seth—" Mariah called out as he reined to go. He turned back to her. She closed the distance between them, but didn't touch him. "Thank you."

Taking a deep breath, he gave her a curt nod, then kicked his horse back in the direction of town.

As he disappeared into the night, Mariah watched a huge piece of her life vanish and felt an acute sense of loss. Slowly, she turned back to Creed. His beautiful, battered eyes were filled with an emotion she couldn't read. It was different and it terrified her. She wanted to run to him, hold him until he promised never to let her go. But she didn't. He'd said he loved her in a moment of despair, but would he feel the same way without the noose around his neck? Regardless of what Seth thought, she'd never try to force herself on Creed.

Jesse walked up beside Creed, leading Buck. Wade and Pete stood a little apart, holding the leads of the gangs' horses bearing the lifeless bodies of LaRousse, Quincy, and Field. Snake was slumped over his saddle, bleeding, with his hands tied behind his back.

"We'll be heading back to Virginia now," Jesse told Creed, scratching Mahkwi behind the ears. "You comin'?"

Creed shook his head slowly, his eyes on Mariah.

Jesse raised one blond eyebrow. "Mariah? You want me to round up that mare you rustled and bring her back for you?"

"I—"

"She'll ride with me," Creed said, never taking his eyes from her. "We have some talking to do." His look was smoldering, possessive, absolute. It stole her breath away and along with it, any impulse to argue. Her heart leapt with hope.

A twinkle of understanding shone in Jesses's eyes. "Good luck to you both," he said, shaking Creed's good hand. "I've decided to leave in the morning for Ohio to see my folks. So, I guess this is goodbye."

Creed sent him a knowing glance, his eyes warming. "Thanks for everything, Jesse. Keep in touch."

"I will," Jesse replied. Slipping his hat off, he walked over and planted a kiss on Mariah's cheek. "You take care of him, you hear?" he whispered so only she heard it.

She smiled tremulously and squeezed his hands. "If he'll let me. Goodbye, Jesse."

They said their farewells to Wade and Pete and watched them head down the valley to round up the horses they'd left behind. When their dark silhouettes merged with the fog, Creed turned back to her, his ex-

378

pression unreadable.

She held his gaze, unsure of what to do. "Creed, you don't have to say anything . . . I mean, I know what Seth expects us to do, but . . . I understand if—"

"I have a lot of things to say to you, *ma petite,*" he interrupted, those compelling sea green eyes boring into hers. "And none of them has anything to do with Seth." He reached for her hand.

She took it, but didn't dare come any closer until she'd said her piece.

"You should know, I planned on going back to Chicago. I wouldn't have married him . . . even if that kiss had never happened. I couldn't go through with it, knowing how I felt about you."

He stared at her in the dark, his gaze caressing her hair, her eyes, her face. "You couldn't?"

She shook her head. "And I can still go back, if . . ."

"Go back?" he repeated with a look of disbelief. "*Mon Dieu,* Mariah, when I came here tonight, when I thought LaRousse had you, I was out of my mind." He ran a shaky hand over his mouth. "He was right when he said if he'd killed you, he'd have killed me, too. If . . . if anything had happened to you . . . I—"

He drew her to him, pulling her head against his chest. "I love you, *mon coeur,*" he said fiercely. "You're part of me, just as I'm part of you. It took me a long time to accept it, but I've *known* it from the first moment we touched. I was a fool to think I could ever walk away from you. Don't leave me, Mariah."

Joy leapt to her eyes. "I don't want to go. I never wanted to. I went to your room tonight to beg you not to leave. To tell you that I loved you—"

Creed's mouth swooped down on hers, covering the last of her confession. Her lips tasted sweet, like freedom. His heart thudded against his burning ribs as her fingertips skimmed his back, drawing him closer. She was his, *le bon Dieu* . . . she was his.

Their tongues mated—warm, seeking, possessing.

He drew her against him, deepening the kiss, slashing his lips against hers, savoring the feel of her body flush against him, putting guilt and regret behind them. He ignored the pain in his mouth and concentrated on the fullness of his heart.

They kissed again and again under the full moon in the swirling fog, like two people starved, sharing breath back and forth until they had run out of air and were forced to draw apart.

"Say you'll marry me, Mariah," his lips whispered against hers.

She laughed, tears stinging her eyes. "You big idiot. I've been trying to get you to say that for days."

One corner of his battered mouth rose, his breath coming rapidly. "It takes some of us longer than others."

"Of course I'll marry you," she said, throwing her arms around him. He groaned low as she squeezed his ribs. Instinctively, she pulled back. "Oh! Did I hurt you?"

He didn't let her go. Instead, he pulled her closer, grinding his hips against hers to demonstrate the true extent of his discomfort. "Ahh . . ." he groaned again, shuddering at her touch. "If pain was ever pleasure . . ."

She smiled, staring into the dear eyes that looked into her own with such passion. "I love you, Creed Devereaux. I'll love you 'til the day I die."

His eyes sparkled knowingly. "Ah, *bon,* because that will be a very long time, *ma petite.*"

Reaching up, she brushed a kiss along his jawline, loving the shudder her touch invoked. "And what else do you see for us in that crystal ball of yours, my love? What will become of us?"

"Whatever we want, *mon coeur,* whatever we want."

Creed didn't tell her about that little girl with the ebony hair and sea green eyes, or about the other images he glimpsed when her touch traveled through him. Some things were better left to discovery.

A gentle wind swirled and the heavy mist lifted, revealing the clear, moonlit landscape. Creed could see beyond the horizon into his own heart, and for the first time, knew that he didn't stand alone. Sensing there would be a thousand wonderful discoveries in the years ahead, he tightened his arms around the woman he loved.

Creed Devereaux wasn't a man to ignore a feeling.

DISCOVER DEANA JAMES!

CAPTIVE ANGEL   (2524, $4.50/$5.50)
Abandoned, penniless, and suddenly responsible for the biggest tobacco plantation in Colleton County, distraught Caroline Gillard had no time to dissolve into tears. By day the willowy redhead labored to exhaustion beside her slaves . . . but each night left her restless with longing for her wayward husband. She'd make the sea captain regret his betrayal until he begged her to take him back!

MASQUE OF SAPPHIRE   (2885, $4.50/$5.50)
Judith Talbot-Harrow left England with a heavy heart. She was going to America to join a father she despised and a sister she distrusted. She was certainly in no mood to put up with the insulting actions of the arrogant Yankee privateer who boarded her ship, ransacked her things, then "apologized" with an indecent, brazen kiss! She vowed that someday he'd pay dearly for the liberties he had taken and the desires he had awakened.

SPEAK ONLY LOVE   (3439, $4.95/$5.95)
Long ago, the shock of her mother's death had robbed Vivian Marleigh of the power of speech. Now she was being forced to marry a bitter man with brandy on his breath. But she could not say what was in her heart. It was up to the viscount to spark the fires that would melt her icy reserve.

WILD TEXAS HEART   (3205, $4.95/$5.95)
Fan Breckenridge was terrified when the stranger found her near-naked and shivering beneath the Texas stars. Unable to remember who she was or what had happened, all she had in the world was the deed to a patch of land that might yield oil . . . and the fierce loving of this wildcatter who called himself Irons.